Dance with Fireflies

JANE GILL

To granny & mum, with all my love.

CONTENTS

It is better to light a candle than curse the darkness.
Eleanor Roosevelt

ACKNOWLEDGEMENTS

This book would not have been possible without my mother. She has generously shared her anecdotes, memories and a trunk full of fascinating ephemera that my granny had the good sense not to throw away.

I'd like to thank my husband for his continuous support and guidance, without which I would have failed. And I need to thank my son, Alfie, whose passion and appetite for writing is inspirational.

A final thanks to all these lovely people: Charlie Gilbert, Sam Cockerton, Louis Gill and Charles Edwards.

1

VICTORIA DOCK, BOMBAY.

25th March 1939. As Phyllis left the steadiness of the dockside, her stiff new shoes painfully rubbed against both blistered feet that swelled in the heat. She followed Arthur's footsteps up the steep gangplank, until they reached the deck of the vast British troopship bound for Southampton. Baby Maureen now felt heavy in her arms after a long wait. She balanced the wriggling child on her hip for a moment and steadied herself against the hot metal handrail.

The ship was heaving with people. Children clung to their mother's skirts for fear of getting lost in the crowds, as leather suitcases were passed overhead. Arthur handed their boarding papers to a steward dressed in white from head to toe, pristine and fresh, a crisp contrast to the seething mass of moving colour on the dockside below. The steward's hatband bore the name HMT Dorsetshire in neat, gold embroidery. Rows of reassuring lifeboats bearing the ships' name in large, red capital letters lined the decks. The white-hulled ship had been requisitioned to transport troops around the world for the British Army; it smelt of oil, grease and the imminent threat of war. Hitler had already invaded Czechoslovakia and now had his sights firmly set on Danzig.

Phyllis lost sight of Arthur. A wave of anxiety gripped at her dry throat as she tried to call out to him. Then she spotted his broad shoulders beyond a cluster of porters. She weaved through the crowd and reached for his hand; his touch was reassuring as he looked back over his shoulder and gave her one of his half smiles. He puffed on his cigarette, the bitter smoke wafted towards the busy scene below where uniformed troops, wearing solar topees and tropical uniforms, filled the narrow deck. Phyllis thought they looked like thousands of turtles jostling for space on a crowded beach.

A cacophony of noise rose from the dockside; porters shouting, rickshaws pulling up and whistles being sharply blown. Tons of provisions were being loaded into the ship's deep belly by a huge crane that groaned under the strain. Dirty, grey cotton sacks of sea mail post were next to be hauled on board, bound for the motherland. They contained letters spilling over with love, messages of longing, secret affairs and words of lust. Beyond the piles of stacked up cargo, wood smoke hung like an early morning mist as the chai wallahs lit small fires and brewed tea in the cooler shade of the large dockside warehouses. The men drank the sweet milky chai out of clay cups; once thirstily drained, the terracotta containers were tossed away, shattering as they hit the ground. The sharp, red shards lay scattered until the next monsoon rain would turn them back into red, muddy clay. Coolies dressed in turbans and kurtas squatted on their haunches in small groups, eating dhal from dented round metal plates, skilfully scooping the contents up in chapattis. Wiry men in dhotis sold pineapples, mangoes, papayas and limes in vast wicker baskets balanced on their heads. They held machetes and sang out the fruit's names to entice passers-by.

Suddenly the reality of beginning a new life in a country she didn't know seemed like madness to Phyllis. Her head felt light; it was as if she wasn't really there at all but floating above the bustling scene. Phyllis hadn't slept well for weeks, lying awake in the early hours, listening to the sound of the green winged parrots squawking in the Neem trees as dawn broke. She worried that Arthur's family might not like her, understand her or accept her for what she was, an Anglo-Indian. She was not just a daughter of the Raj but one with nutmeg coloured skin and hair as dark as polished teak.

Phyllis looked into Arthur's smiling face. She adored her husband, but doubts about leaving India and the comfort of her family were growing with every lungful of ooplah smelling air that drifted up on the breeze. She desperately wanted to feel the joy that Arthur clearly felt, his eyes shone with excitement and energy, like a teenager who has just tasted his first kiss. He was going back to his family, but she was leaving hers behind, five thousand miles behind.

Her bottom lip quivered uncontrollably as tears trickled down her cheeks, wetting her dry lips.

"I can't do it." She muttered in panic. "I can't do it," she said again, this time a little louder, so that Arthur would hear her.

"Hey, hey, what's all this?" Arthur wrapped her small frame in his arms and kissed her tenderly on the forehead, wiping away her tears with his warm hand that smelt faintly of tobacco. "Remember how much you've always wanted to travel to England and see the landscapes you dream of painting. You'll love it. I know you will. Mums and Peg will make you feel at home." His gentle Irish accent soothed Phyllis's nerves.

"It's just so far away," she said, fiddling with the ties on Maureen's sunhat. "I don't know how to live anywhere else, how to be anywhere other than here."

Phyllis had anticipated this moment ever since marrying Lance Corporal Arthur Dermot Woollett two years before. It was inevitable that The British Army would post him back to England. She'd known all along that she must go with him and couldn't live in her beloved India forever, but she hadn't realised until this very moment, this very second, how hard it would be to leave everything behind.

A few weeks earlier in Benares, Phyllis and her mother, Alice Maude Dover, known to all her friends as Maude, had carefully packed the large trunks for the impending

[handwritten margin notes: "Scene setting; well done" / "too lengthy?" / "hot" / "it's I'd gasped, arrested midsong" / "MW"]

voyage. The women had sat in the living room of Dover House, the family bungalow; its large, central room was furnished with a cane sofa and two matching chairs. Chintz fabric decorated with deep rose pink flowers and lime green foliage covered the cushions. The room's whitewashed walls were adorned with family portraits, Maude's delicate landscape paintings and musty trophies from historical hunting trips. The glassy eyes peeping out from the dusty fur had terrified Phyllis as a child. Jesus agonisingly nailed to a crucifix, looked down over the mahogany piano, its lid wide open from the previous night's singsong. A Bird's Nest fern with its lush green fronds, brightened up the darkest corner of the room that housed the precious gramophone and extensive collection of records. The roof beams remained exposed. Conventional ceilings were avoided; the attic-like space would encourage unwanted houseguests, including snakes and rats. The flapping punka, swished to and fro creating a gentle gush of warm air. Neelam, the wallah, who had one brown and one unusual sapphire coloured eye, sat on the veranda pulling rhythmically on his rope that fed through a hole in the wall. On the other side of the wide veranda, the durzis could be found cross-legged, making a new suit for Wilmot, Phyllis's father. The old durzis squinted at the thread through black-framed glasses that dominated his craggy face. Humming quietly to himself, he pushed his fine needle in and out of the cream linen, the white thread fed between his long, brown toes. His large turban made a useful pincushion.

Phyllis and Maude were in the center of the room,

[handwritten margin notes: "agony arrested" / "agony" / "MW" / "in"]

surrounded by folded clothes, household items and wedding presents. Four large trunks had been carried from the stables earlier in the day and were being aired on the veranda. The two very large trunks were to be packed up and put in the ship's hold and not accessible until England. Two smaller travelling trunks were to be kept in their cabin for the voyage. Selecting the belongings to take to England had been a time-consuming task; luggage space was at a premium. Eventually they settled on the favoured possessions and packed each one with great care; Arthur's wage would not cover such frivolities as replacing things that had been carelessly broken on the voyage.

Dover House's shelves were crammed with books featuring English painters. As long as she could remember, Phyllis had dreamily looked forward to seeing England's landscape and the changing seasons that she loved to study within the books' shiny pages. She admired the paintings by Turner, Constable and Gainsborough, with their hazy spring days, coppiced willows and heavily thatched cottages laden with snow. Phyllis longed to be a good artist and was often found in the shade of the mango tree with her easel and watercolours.

The wedding presents had been the next items to pack. The tray and breadboard from Mr and Mrs Taylor, the glass hand-painted jug and set of six glasses from Miss Sheridan and the electric clock from Phyllis's brother Ernest. A masterful landscape painted by Maude had been wrapped carefully in one of the blankets and placed at the top of one of the large trunks. Phyllis had then looked at her mother and gently closed the lid.

"Goodness only knows where it will all end up. I can't imagine we'll be unpacking any of it for a while." She had sighed.

On arrival in Southampton they would travel to Colchester and bed down at the old lady's house. 'The old lady' was Arthur's affectionate name for his mother, Mrs Elizabeth Woollett. She was a strong-willed Irish woman, who adored her son; he could do no wrong in her eyes. She'd missed him terribly when he joined the army. He had left the family home in Leesfield, at the young age of 17 to get away from a tyrant of a father, a vicar, Frederick Woollett. Frederick would beat Arthur regularly, even though he was a man of the cloth. Elizabeth had left Frederick a few years ago and was living with her daughter. Peg was Arthur's younger sister. There were only two years between them, they were very close and had protected each other when their father was in a blind rage. Arthur despised his father and a few years earlier, on the news of his suicide wrote four simple words in his diary: My father died today.

*

The steward led them down a maze of corridors past dozens of doors until finally arriving at cabin 312. He pushed the door open to reveal a small, dark space with a round porthole at one end, which let in a bright shaft of light, like a pinhole camera.

"Barely bigger than a broom cupboard," whispered Arthur into Phyllis's ear.

Their cabin trunks had been placed in the centre of the space, dwarfing the room. The ceiling fan's dusty blades rotated slowly above them, like the propeller of a plane that would never fly. A pale blue leather sofa occupied one side of the cabin. The steward demonstrated that a large cushioned shelf above the sofa could be pulled down from the wall turning it into a bunk bed. Underneath the compact berth was a storage cupboard full of bedding. A simple wicker cot provided a bed for the baby. Opposite was a dark teak coffee table, its blemished surface hidden under a doily-like tablecloth. Two easy chairs completed the seating area. A ceramic washbasin stood underneath a mirror bolted to the wall. The cabin reminded Phyllis of a room in her old dolls house.

"Is there anything else I can do for you Mr Woollett?" asked the steward looking at the boarding papers to make sure he had the correct name.

"No, that will be all thank you," replied Arthur pressing a few rupees into his discreetly placed hand.

"It's a bit pokey," said Arthur after the steward left.

"Are the cabins always so drab?" replied Phyllis. "I imagined it to be more glamorous somehow."

"It's not usually this dowdy but now The Army have got their hands on it, luxury is not top of the list."

Phyllis wedged open the door with her small suitcase. "Am I allowed to open the porthole?"

"Of course darling, here let me do it," Arthur strode towards the dusty sunlight that beamed into the space that was to be home for the next few weeks.

Phyllis spotted a plan of the deck propped up on the coffee table next to a glass jug filled with water.

She read out the list of facilities to Arthur. "On our deck there are 108 family cabins, a dining hall, lounge area and a nursery. A communal bathroom to be shared between every 10 cabins." Phyllis looked up from the plan and grimaced.

Arthur laughed. "You should try travelling in the troops quarters."

Phyllis continued to read. "There's a smoking room (men only) and a counter selling snacks, soft drinks, notepaper, postcards, pens and soap."

"There's usually a Promenade," said Arthur looking up from the packet of cigarettes he was fiddling with.

"Yes, look, just here, for deck games it says."

"What's this?" asked Arthur, holding up an embossed invitation.

Phyllis's face brightened. "Oh how exciting! We've been invited to a welcome dinner."

The ship was due to set sail at 19.00 hours to catch the out-going tide from Victoria Dock. There was just enough time for Phyllis to unpack the things they needed for their first night on board.

"Just nipping out on deck for a quick smoke. Will you be all right on your own?" asked Arthur, a cigarette already positioned between his lips.

"I'll be up in a minute," replied Phyllis.

She opened the cabin trunks and took out a few things they would need for the evening. She put the toothbrushes in a glass before placing her silk pyjamas on the bed. Phyllis then retrieved her evening dress from the trunk. It had only creased a little on its journey from Benares to Bombay. She hung it up in the tiny wardrobe along with a small muslin bag stuffed with pungent, cloves. She unpacked Arthur's starched white shirt and laid it on the chair.

Phyllis looked at her watch and smiled at Maureen. "It's nearly 7 o'clock, time to go and wave goodbye."

Ernest, her dear elder brother, had promised to wave them off. He lived in Bombay and worked as an engineer but had suffered with a terrible stutter since childhood, which caused him much anxiety. With Maureen safely in her arms, Phyllis left the cabin.

Rope handrails, like thick anaconda bodies, snaked their way along the labyrinth of corridors that led her back outside, where she hoped to find Arthur and get a good view of the crowd forming below on the quayside. The sun was starting to lose its burning heat; the cool sea breeze was a welcome change from the cloying humidity of the hot day. Mustard-yellow smog clung to the taller buildings of the expanding city. Phyllis felt cool, her pretty silk dress flapped gently in the wind, it was soft against her bare legs. She looked down and stroked her small round belly; their next child would be born in England.

Arthur was leaning against a lifeboat, handsome and sturdy, his face relaxed and tanned. The camera Wilmot had given him for his birthday hung from his neck in its brown canvas case. Phyllis studied him for a few minutes before smiling to herself. He sensed her looking and came ambling over.

"There you are, not long now. Oh Phyl, we shall be so happy, I'm sure of it." He gently tickled the baby under her chin and kissed her dark hair whilst pulling his pretty wife closer to him.

"I'm ready," said Phyllis, taking a deep breath.

"Ready for what?" enquired Arthur.

"Ready to leave home," replied Phyllis, smiling up into his handsome face.

The ship's engines, which had been letting out a low grumbling vibration, grew rapidly louder, as a frenzy of activity started up on the dockside. Ropes were being untied and thrown. Plumes of acrid black smoke billowed out from the ship's huge yellow funnel. The gangplank was hauled up onto the side of the ship; they were no longer attached to India. It was time to let go. Phyllis was filled with a bubbling mixture of excitement and panic.

A large crowd: families, friends and sweethearts had gathered to see the ship and its cargo of people off. Hankies were waved and kisses were blown. Just at that moment Ernest came into view. He was dressed smartly as if on his way home from work, with his wife Doreen at his side. He searched the passengers, seeking a glimpse of his favourite sister on the decks.

"Ernest, up here!" Phyllis waved frantically trying to get his attention over the excited voices of the departing passengers and the cheering troops. Ernest caught sight of her and waved his folded newspaper above his head. Phyllis felt an urgent need to hold on to him, she felt like she may never see him again.

"Dear Ernest, goodbye. I'll miss you terribly," she mouthed silently, as her bottom lip trembled.

The ship's foghorn drowned out her voice. It took only minutes before the 'Welcome to India' sign that stood proudly at Victoria Dock faded into the hazy distance. The waving well-wishers were now tiny dots, barely visible. Phyllis realised it was time to wave India goodbye, just for a while anyway. England was to be home now.

2

4000 MILES AWAY

Elizabeth shook out the freshly laundered sheet and let it drift down onto the lumpy horse hair mattress, like a ship's sail catching a gust of wind, before tucking in the sides like a perfectly-wrapped parcel. It was something Peg had taught her after attending her first days' nursing training. She plumped up the eiderdown and her thoughts wandered to Arthur's last sweetheart, dear Elsie.

Elizabeth couldn't help wondering how much easier it would be if her son was coming back from India to marry Elsie, instead of bringing home a semi-native girl. She had never met anyone foreign before. Elizabeth had only given Arthur her blessing for the marriage once she knew more about Phyllis's pedigree. She'd learned from Arthur's letters that Wilmot Dover, Phyllis's father, was a highly respected Anglo-Indian from Benares. He'd earned a first class English degree at Calcutta University and had worked for the Maharajah of Bhinga until the Maharajah's death in 1913. Wilmot had taught all of his children and had gone on to manage the widow's financial affairs. Phyllis's father was a man of high standing within the cantonments where they lived and would often be called upon to settle neighbourhood disputes and quarrels.

Elizabeth tutted as she chased out the cobwebs from under the bed with her dustpan and brush and decided it might be good to have a younger pair of hands to help around the house. She was a bulky woman and struggled to her feet, holding onto the brass bedstead for support. Her old knees were swollen and ached from resting on them too long.

She and Peg rented a small three bedroomed semi-detached house in a quiet Colchester street. They had a front parlour saved for Sunday afternoons and Christmas. A cold, north-facing dining room and a small kitchen were at the back of the house with a pantry off to one side. A scrubbed pine table sat in the middle of the kitchen surrounded by four chairs. In the middle of the table was a wooden pot stand, home to the brown ceramic teapot. Out through the back kitchen door was a small yard where Elizabeth hung her washing and kept her bicycle, not that she rode it much these days, after a collision with a stray dog. A tatty wooden door led to the privy, moss grew on the internal walls like a damp cave, which no amount of scrubbing would remove.

She liked to keep the house clean and tidy. Although Elizabeth found it harder to keep it spotless these days, her rheumatism being more painful than ever after the damp winter. When she had lived in the large vicarage in Oldham with her late husband Frederick, she'd had plenty of help polishing the antique furniture and scrubbing the flagstone floors. She tried hard to forget about her dead husband. It had been difficult to leave him but after a violent row she found herself on her sister-in-law's doorstep in Maidenhead. Lillian had taken her in until she got back on her feet. Elizabeth inherited a small amount of money from her uncle and managed to rent a modest house in Colchester where Peg had started her nursing training. After Frederick's death, his vicar's pension covered Elizabeth's living expenses, if she was frugal. Once Peg had qualified and secured a job as a district nurse she paid her mother a modest weekly rent. Peg also had a car and all her petrol was paid for. No one else in their street had a car, let alone travelled in one. The pride Elizabeth felt when she saw the shiny black vehicle pull up outside their house was immeasurable.

The news reported that Hitler's forces were taking over Europe, spreading slowly like spilt ink on blotting paper. German troops had entered Prague. There was much speculation in the press, at the local church meetings and whist drives. Friends and neighbours chit-chattered of little else. Elizabeth's greatest fear was losing her remaining son. She had already lost her first born. Little Maximilian had only been five years old. He had fallen down the stairs and broken his back. Laid up in bed for a year, he had become very weak and then contracted TB. His limp little body could take no more. Elizabeth had wept for another whole year unable to face the future without him. She had to carry on for the sake of her other two children. Arthur had been four and little Peg only two years old.

After Max's death Frederick's temper had started to reveal itself. His anger had spilled out of every pore, wretched and miserable he took it out on his second son who could never take the place of his angelic first born. He resented Arthur for living whilst Max had been cruelly taken from him. He'd come home from preaching and lock Arthur and Peg in the bedroom they shared, feeding them stale bread and water for days at a time. He'd then slip his narrow leather belt from his dark, wool trousers and thrash the children. His sermons at the local parish church became more and more extreme. Crushed by the vices and sins that he felt surrounded him, he could take no more and lost his faith in God. He gassed himself in his bedroom on 5th August 1931 leaving a will that stated everything was to be left to his daughter Peg but could not be touched for 13 years. He referred to his wife Elizabeth as a murderess, he blamed her for Max's death, after all she had been the only one with him in the house on the day he fell. He wished her to spend the rest of her life in charity. The police found a photograph next to his corpse. It had been torn down the middle, separating himself from his wife and two surviving children.

*

The back door opened, Peg's voice called up the stairs as she made her way into the kitchen.

"Only me Mums!" she shouted.

Elizabeth clambered backwards down the steep stairs, brushing vigorously as she descended, her wide bottom swaying from side to side, in time to the ticking of the large clock in the hall.

"Ah, there you are dear, thought I'd make a start on the spare room for Arthur," she said.

"How long do you think they will be staying?"

"Well, I think Phyllis will have the baby here in Colchester. After that Arthur plans to look for rooms in Catterick, if he's still stationed there. So it will certainly be a few months, maybe longer."

Peg filled the kettle and put it on the stove to boil.

"It's going to be a tight squeeze with all of them. It's not just the baby, but the nappies that need washing and drying every day, the pram, extra food, and a one-year-old. I hope you can cope with the extra burden."

3

THE FIRST SUPPER

The large loud speaker let out a crackling groan, and a young man's voice instructed all passengers to go to their designated deck area for the lifeboat drill. Phyllis and Arthur mingled with their fellow travelling companions. Military people mostly, some travelling alone and others with their wives and children, going home on leave after a six-year stint in India. Government officials and men working for the Indian Civil Service dressed in civvies made up the rest of the passengers on their deck. Arthur was relieved to be travelling as a passenger this time and not in the cramped troop quarters below.

Once the safety drill was over, Phyllis gladly kicked off her uncomfortable shoes in their cabin and gently lay Maureen down in the cot. The rolling motion of the ship lulled the baby into a restful sleep with the sound of the ship's engine softly droning, like a soothing lullaby.

*

Phyllis woke with a start; she had accidently dozed off, too. The 'welcome dinner' was commencing with cocktails in the lounge at 20.00 hours followed by a light supper. Arthur was busy sprucing himself up by the washbasin. He stood in a vest, having discarded his shirt, foamy soapsuds coated his chin. He was busy scraping, in short upward strokes with his blade, carefully working around his moustache, making little scratchy sounds as he did so.

"I didn't mean to have a nap. Have I got enough time to get ready?" asked Phyllis, concerned that she should make a good impression on her first night at dinner. Maude had advised her that when in England she should remember to attend Mass, dress well, eat wisely and to not forget her manners, no matter how others spoke to her. Phyllis had questioned her mother on the last point. "Might people be rude to me?"

"They might be."

"Whatever do you mean?"

"Phyllis darling, you are married to a British man and we are part of The Empire but we are different. Look at the way you are sitting."

Phyllis looked down at her Jodhpur clad legs in the cross-legged position: like a boy.

"Yes, but that's because I've been riding and am now on the floor sorting out my things with you. I wouldn't be like this ordinarily. You are right of course mother. I shall behave impeccably at all times and do my best to be smart, polite and not let the side down."

Maude and her daughter giggled.

"Do you remember that time when Arthur's boss and his wife came to tea and you dropped a boiled egg into his lap?" asked Maude laughing.

"Arthur won't let me forget it," giggled Phyllis.

"And do you recall when you were very young, we went on a days ride with the Maharaja's children and you insisted on riding like a boy and not side saddle?" asked Maude.

"Well, I did manage to hack all the way to Lakhania Dari falls and beat them all, including the men."

"Anyway darling, you know what I mean, just be demure and lady-like when required."

"I promise," replied Phyllis.

*

"Penny for your thoughts?" asked Arthur.

"I was just thinking about mother," smiled Phyllis. "I shall miss her so much." Phyllis slipped out of her creased dress.

Arthur stroked her protruding belly. "Do you think it's a boy or a girl?"

"Most definitely a boy. He will be just like you: handsome, clever and a brilliant dancer."

Arthur took Phyllis by the hand and waltzed her around the small cabin, dodging the trunks, cot, table and chairs as best they could. They crashed laughing onto the sofa, just as the waiter knocked at the door.

"Your drink, sir," called the waiter.

Arthur opened the door, just enough to retrieve his peg of scotch and sign his chit. He didn't want Phyllis to be exposed to the waiter in her silk underwear.

"Crumbs, we need to get our skates on Phyl, we're going to be late," said Arthur, looking at his watch and taking a large gulp from the tumbler.

Phyllis slipped into her simple, pale blue evening dress, the creases only slightly visible. Maude had bought it for her on their last shopping trip, fearing that Phyllis didn't have the right outfits for the voyage and her new life in England.

"You'll probably have to host dinner parties and entertain guests, you'll need to have at least a handful of decent frocks," Maude had instructed her.

She had taught her daughter the skills she'd need in India: painting, tennis, riding, playing the piano, sewing and baking. What she hadn't passed on to her were the skills to run a household. Maude had been shocked to hear that the custom of having even one housemaid had all but died out in England. She had asked Arthur one day who did the chores in his mother's house.

"The old lady," he had replied mischievously.

"Oh, is she the maid?" inquired Maude.

"No, that's what I call my mother. She does it by herself, with a little help from Peg," he laughed.

Maude worried that Phyllis would be ill-equipped to run her own household and decided to give her the treasured hand-written cookery book, given to her by her own mother on the day she married her childhood sweetheart, Wilmot. Within its marbled, cardboard cover, Maude's mother, Emily Eliza had painstakingly written recipes in flowing black ink: Fish on green chillies with aspic jellies, savoury patties and Phyllis's favourite: Pistachio ices. Scattered throughout the book, Maude had added useful household hints and medical treatments, including cures for dysentery, cholera, mosquito bites and tapeworms. Advice on how to rid the house of rats, ants, cockroaches and flies were listed at the back of the book along with useful potions for encouraging hair growth, soften the skin and whiten hands. There was even advice on filtering water and keeping butter cool using a flowerpot.

*

Phyllis looked at her reflection in the cabin's small mirror and felt pleased with her simple outfit. Maude had been right, the blue complimented her skin tone beautifully. They left the cabin and headed down the corridor for the dining salon, delivering Maureen to the nursery on the way, like a little parcel, happily asleep, oblivious to her changing world.

Arthur and Phyllis stepped into the vast room as the pianist played softly in the background. The dining hall had a bar at one end, with a rainbow of different coloured bottles lining the mirrored wall behind. The barmen expertly mixed cocktails and filled chilled glasses with bright, potent concoctions. The room was laid out with large, round tables, eight place settings on each, neatly arranged in perfect symmetry. A waiter carrying a polished silver tray glided over to them offering them a choice of aperitifs. The ship started to pitch slightly as they ventured out into deeper waters.

"Oh crumbs, I'm terribly sorry." A woman in a silky, tight-fitting halter neck dress had steadied herself against Phyllis. She had a neat head of blonde hair made into waves, which framed her pale face. Her young, papery-white cleavage rose and fell as her cochineal lips sucked greedily on her cigarette, leaving a bright red stain at its tip.

"That's quite all right," said Phyllis. "No harm done."

This was not strictly true; sadly the bright red Bloody Mary the woman was sipping had splashed down the front of Phyllis's evening dress.

"Oh golly, please let me help you with that," offered the unnamed woman, dabbing with a napkin, without success, at Phyllis's dress.

"No really," said Phyllis, looking down at her ruined outfit. "It's just an old dress."

This was also not strictly true. Phyllis and Maude had spent all day choosing the silk in Mr Sethi's shop, crammed to the ceiling with delicious fabrics in every conceivable colour and shade. His peacock blue silk would surely be left with a lifelong mark.

"I'll go and change, I'm sure the stain will come out," said Phyllis unsurely.

Arthur looked down at Phyllis's dress. "Good God Phyl, it looks as if you've been shot," he blurted.

The nameless woman laughed at the scene unfolding before her, then her wide horsey smile disappeared behind her sticky red lips. She promptly turned her back and continued to scan the room for someone more interesting to converse with. Phyllis went back to their cabin and changed into her third dress of the day. She found the steward stationed in his Aladdin's cave-like cubbyhole. He was happy to oblige and get the dress laundered, ready for the following evening.

For all their suppers on the voyage, Phyllis and Arthur were allocated a table near the window. Phyllis ventured back into the dining hall to find people starting to take their places. Arthur caught her attention and summoned her over. Name cards had been handwritten and placed at each setting. Phyllis walked clockwise around the table, reading as she went until she got to her own name, Mrs A Woollett. They stood by their table and politely waited for the rest of the guests to join them.

"Oh dear lord," said Phyllis looking down at the floor, "she's heading this way."

"Who?" asked Arthur taking a sip from his drink.

"The woman who spilt her Bloody Mary all down me."

"Don't worry, darling, she won't bite."

"How can you be so sure?" giggled Phyllis.

"Oh, it's the girl I shot," purred the woman, her beautifully coiffured hair shining like a highly polished brass teapot. "I'm Mrs Pearce. Allow me to introduce my husband, Corporal Pearce."

Her husband shook hands firmly with them. "How nice to meet you," he muttered, before sitting down at his assigned seat and tucking the napkin into his tight collar.

After all the introductions and much scraping of chairs on the wooden floor, the table of military men and their wives settled down to eat the first supper of the voyage. Conversations were soon struck up about where they had been stationed, tropical diseases caught, servants endured, the voyage ahead and the pets left behind. Seated to Phyllis's right, Lieutenant Turner, a stout fellow with a booming voice, told everyone who cared to listen how he had travelled from Poona the night before, where he had been stationed and stayed in Bombay overnight.

"A ghastly hotel with cockroaches in the bathroom."

Opposite Phyllis sat chalky-faced Mrs Pearce, who yawned as politely as she could behind her gloved hand. "So Mrs Woollett, how long did you have to live in that hot, filthy country with those smelly little natives?" Her high scratchy voice scurried across the table like a deadly scorpion.

Phyllis's cheeks turned from olive to red as everyone's eyes focussed on her, all the way round the table from Lieutenant Turner to Mrs Jackson, seated to the left of Arthur.

"I suppose I partly am one of those smelly natives," she answered, in the best English accent she could muster.

Arthur almost choked on his drink as he let out a loud laugh. He had never loved Phyllis so much. After the meal was over, the men retired to the bar whilst the women stayed seated, giving them a chance to get to know each other a little better, apart from Mrs Pearce, who had made an early exit feigning a migraine.

Tobacco smoke wafted over from the bar, reminding Phyllis of her father. Wilmot would sit on the veranda of the bungalow each evening having gone through the paperwork on his desk, and then light his pipe. The bearer would hand him a chota peg sundowner, of whisky and soda 'to put the day to bed,' as he would say. The whisky would wet his moustache, which he'd dab with a napkin so it didn't lose its carefully waxed shape. Phyllis felt a stab of longing and said a little prayer to keep him well. He had become less resilient to the unforgiving Indian climate over the last year, particularly in the more humid months. He'd tire easily and come down with fevers more frequently.

Phyllis and Arthur had a stroll along the deck. Arthur went back over the conversation with Mrs Pearce. "Phyl darling, that really was top class," he chuckled.

"Well, I'm glad you found it funny," laughed Phyllis. "It

was so embarrassing I wanted the table to swallow me up."

"Well I think you put her in her place beautifully."

"Oh dear, I hope she doesn't feel too ghastly about it."

"I'm sure she'll get over it," said Arthur, pulling her to him and kissing her soft cheek.

They could hear the distant voices of the troops below, laughing, singing and the faint noise of someone playing the guitar. It was easy to forget that they were travelling on a British troopship, heading back to England, so that Arthur could be redeployed.

"Arthur," sighed Phyllis, into his warm shoulder. "Do you think Britain really will go to war with Germany?"

Arthur lit a cigarette. "I don't know." He held her hand tightly as they looked out to sea. It was as black as charcoal.

*

They woke to the movement of the massive ship slicing through the steep ocean swell. The vessel pitched sharply as Phyllis lay on the bottom bunk feeling nauseous. Arthur and Maureen sat on the floor playing with a little rosewood elephant on wheels that Wilmot had given Maureen the day they had left Benares. As the ship swayed, the little elephant obediently trundled across the floor to the other end of the cabin. Maureen clapped her hands in delight as her favourite toy sped along. Phyllis struggled to get dressed without losing her balance.

"Arthur, I think I need some air, can we go out on deck?" she asked, trying to keep the sickness at bay.

Out on the stormy promenade, the ship's crew were busy tying deckchairs down and stacking tables away. The decks below were devoid of troops.

"Poor chaps, it must be hell down there," commented Phyllis sympathetically, as she peered over the edge of the railing.

"Are you feeling any better darling?" asked Arthur.

"It certainly helps to be out in the fresh air," said Phyllis, holding her hand to her chest as her blouse billowed in the wind.

The loudspeaker sprang into life with a crackle.

"Attention, attention, this is Captain Parker speaking. We are experiencing high seas and are heading for a force nine, this should pass by the morning but I suggest you take care of all your belongings and make safe any breakables. The steward will be checking that all storm covers are closed correctly over the portholes in your cabins. For your own safety, the promenade is now a restricted area until further notice. Dinner this evening will be a cold buffet. Please take extra care when moving around the ship. Thank you for your cooperation."

"We better do as the Captain says," instructed Arthur as he led them back through the heavy door.

They swayed like drunken sailors to the cabin, through the

communal lounge. It was furnished with sofas, chairs, coffee tables and small, green bias topped card tables, some of which were now merrily fox-trotting across the floor by themselves. Playing cards, backgammon and chess that had been neatly stacked on a shelf lay scattered as if ransacked. At the end of the room behind a bamboo partition was the crèche, where a uniformed nursery nurse usually looked after the smaller children. The large painted rocking horse swayed to and fro without the need of a young rider, its coarse, horsehair mane swishing up and down.

A large blackboard hung on the wall near the corridor, listing the coming week's entertainment.

"Oh heavens Arthur look at that, shall we go to the fancy dress party on Wednesday? It could be fun," said Phyllis holding on to her husband for fear of falling over.

Arthur hadn't got that far down the list; he was still contemplating the movie night with Joan Crawford.

"What's that, darling?" he asked.

"Fancy dress," repeated Phyllis, "beginning with C."

"Why not, sounds like a hoot."

Phyllis could be very inventive when it came to costumes, but this would be quite a challenge on a ship with no access to her sewing machine.

"We've got a few days to think about it. At least it should take our minds off this ghastly storm," said Phyllis, lying down on the bunk trying to sway with the boat to contain her seasickness. "I'll never forget the fancy dress parties we used to have in Nainital."

Nainital was a Himalayan hill station. It nestled seven thousand feet high amid snow-capped peaks with the magnificent mountains rising in the distance like giant, marble cathedrals. Phyllis and her sister Muriel would make the long train journey north from the soaring heat of Benares and the plains every summer. Families of the Raj would arrive in droves seeking out its cooler climate, swelling the small towns population and filling its establishments. On 1st April each year Phyllis and Muriel would arrive and stay for six months in the thriving resort that was built up around a beautiful emerald green lake, shaped like a teardrop. The Mall, a popular shopping street, was crammed with British tailors, dressmakers, bakeries, cafes, tearooms and souvenir shops. Phyllis and Muriel ran Barnes', a restaurant on the Mall above Trevillion and Clark, a gents' tailors and breeches maker shop. The restaurant catered for the local gentry, the Anglo-Indian community, British soldiers from the local camp and government officials. The sisters also supplied lunches and cakes for garden, tennis, wedding and birthday parties held on the manicured lawns of the local memsahib's bungalows, which lay dotted about the steep, green hills.

Barnes' restaurant had a wonky teak floor, which was kept highly polished. If the band weren't playing, the gramophone would be kept wound up. White lace curtains that adorned the floor-to-ceiling windows would flap about in the breeze, as if waltzing. Eighteen tables draped with starched cloths clung to the walls of the square room, leaving enough space to dance around its empty centre. There was a small stage to one end, where the band would play. An old, but well tuned piano was positioned to one side. The fully stocked bar filled the other corner of the room, occupied by a barman who mixed the most delicious Martinis. They also hosted tea dances and parties, which had a reputation for being very lively. The restaurant was comfortable and stylish with a certain charm, not least of which were the unmarried Dover sisters; Phyllis and Muriel. They would often work into the early hours then finally clamber upstairs to their small private living quarters and get some sleep. Muriel had strict instructions from Maude to keep an eye on her younger sister Phyllis. Their mother knew what men could be like, particularly young soldiers far from home.

Being four years older than Phyllis, Muriel was very much in control and took responsibility for ordering all the stock they needed, keeping a close eye on the kitchen storeroom. She checked it daily, making a note of every item, no matter how small, in her notebook. If for any reason the stock didn't tally, the staff would be summoned to answer questions, with the threat of a deduction in pay if anything had gone missing. The storeroom housed a large table, its legs stood in little dishes filled with paraffin to keep the black ants from stealing the food. Heavy lidded earthenware pots stored semolina, dried fruit, treacle, gelatine, flour, eggs and sugar. Muriel would hire and sometimes fire the staff. These included cooks, a musolchi, bearers, kitmutgers, a barman, a sweeper, a bheeshi, and a chokidar. Muriel kept the building in good shape too, sometimes arriving weeks before the opening date. Wilmot would travel with her if his work permitted. They would organise the whitewashing of the walls, which had gone mouldy during the damp winter, wash the cane furniture and scrub the grease from the kitchen. Muriel also booked the bands and kept a keen eye on the local competition. The nearby restaurant, Valerio's, was always trying to out-do Barnes' but Muriel was one step ahead and often booked Goddards for the whole season, who were by far the best dance band in the area.

Although Phyllis couldn't so much as grill a cutlet, she was naturally good at baking. She was responsible for making over sixty varieties of cakes including wedding and Christmas cakes, macaroons, chocolate éclairs and jam tarts. Along with her baking duties, Phyllis would help organise the servants, host parties and more often than not end up playing the piano.

Phyllis had met Arthur at a masked ball they'd hosted for the Royal Signals Corps stationed in their summer headquarters at Talital just a few miles down the valley. He'd spent most of the evening dancing and she'd spent most of it making sure the guests were well looked after. Phyllis hadn't seen him staring at her from behind his mask. Arthur approached her at the end of the evening. He'd asked her for a dance even though the band had long since packed up and gone home. He had wound up the gramophone and took her in his strong arms.

"You are the woman I'm going to marry," he'd whispered.

She wasn't sure if she'd heard him correctly, his warm breath still lingered in her ear. His Dublin accent made it hard for her to be sure.

"Pardon me?" she'd said, blushing, thinking she must have misheard this handsome stranger.

"You know what I said," is all he muttered before leaving with a huge smile on his face.

That night a family of black-faced Langur monkeys had called out to each other and as dawn broke Phyllis realised she hadn't slept a wink, going back over and over the previous evening in her mind. She hadn't told Muriel what Arthur had said, not just because Muriel was terribly suspicious when it came to men, generally giving them short thrift, but she wasn't one hundred per cent certain she'd heard him correctly. She hadn't even caught his name.

*

The ship suddenly rolled more violently. Phyllis could hear the porthole getting splashed with sea spray.

"It'll pass, my love, this will be the roughest part of the journey, it won't last long, I promise," said Arthur, looking at her worried face.

She nodded but looked decidedly unconvinced; her complexion had a waxy candle-like hue.

"Oh Arthur, it's unbearable, please make it stop," she pleaded. Phyllis hadn't been on a ship this big before, she'd only sat on the pretty wooden rowing boats in Nainital that took tourists for a row around the lake. The thought of the stormy journey going on much longer was unbearable.

It took two more hideous days of the ship rolling, doors

slamming shut, cups sliding off tables and passengers clinging onto the snaky handrails to rush to the bathrooms to vomit. Passengers with a tougher constitution made their way to the dining hall. Phyllis was unfortunately one of the seasick ones, she felt weak and exhausted as her tired, pregnant body heaved violently into one of the communal toilet bowls.

After two wretched days and nights they woke to find the sky a clear blue and the ship finally stable in a calm sea. Phyllis managed to eat some breakfast for the first time in three days. Her stomach grumbled as she nibbled on her toast and sipped her beef tea.

That night they stood in the cabin getting dressed up for the fancy dress party, relieved that the sea was calm.

"Arthur, stand still, I just need to sort out your bow tie, it's a bit crooked. You look wonderful, now you can look in the mirror." Phyllis adjusted Arthur's tie.

"A dead ringer," laughed Arthur. "I wouldn't have recognised myself."

Charlie Chaplin stood before him. Well, a taller version of him. Phyllis had blacked his moustache and put a bit of kohl under his eyes and borrowed a bowler hat from lost property. He looked quite the part practising his loping walk up and down the cabin.

"And as for you young lady," Arthur eyed up Phyllis. "You are the most ravishing Cleopatra I have ever seen."

Phyllis was in her long blue evening dress; its stain only

known to those who knew of it. A silver sash tied around her waist. She had a bracelet on each wrist and had knotted the corners of her blue silk scarf to each, then wrapped the scarf around her middle so it rested on her bottom. A gold belt made a great headband. With her eyes made up she looked just the ticket.

"Are you sure I look all right? I feel a bit silly. Can you see the stain?" asked Phyllis.

"Stop worrying about the stain, no one will know it's there. You look stunning Phyl, now let's go and join the party," replied Arthur.

All the passengers and crew had made a huge effort to dress up, including Mrs Pearce who made a dramatic entrance as Joan Crawford. Shimmying into the room in a gold, shoulder to ankle sequined gown, she downed one too many champagne cocktails but still won first prize. She stumbled into the arms of Captain Parker as he presented her with a box of chocolates. At the dinner table Mrs Jackson had tutted loudly.

"Did you know, Mrs Pearce went out to India as part of the Fishing Fleet?" she said, leaning in towards Phyllis who was sitting next to her. "Her husband must be at least twenty years older."

"Oh, I had no idea," said Phyllis.

The Fishing Fleet was a crude term used for British girls who travelled to India to find a husband. The richer and more successful they were, the better. Some of the girls were daughters of the Raj who had been sent 'home' to English boarding schools at around the age of five to be educated. Once schooled, they would return to India to be with their families and find a husband. Other members of the Fishing Fleet were often considered too plain, poor or old to ensnare a husband in Britain and travelled to India seeking husbands employed by the British Empire. While almost any single white man would do, hooking a civil servant was everyone's goal. If no husband was found, the virgins travelled home, labelled as 'returned empties.'

Phyllis had come across some of the Fishing Fleet before; they had a reputation for being utterly ruthless in their quest, often attending endless parties, until the right man proposed. The fortunate ones found love sometimes in a matter of days or weeks. Some girls were proposed to on the voyage over from England.

"Oh, and there's Lieutenant Turner, he left his wife and young baby at home in England. He has a terrible reputation, a prolific womaniser. Rumour has it he had at least two Indian mistresses." Mrs Jackson prattled on with various snippets of gossip. Phyllis felt slightly guilty that she knew some of the passengers' secrets.

Out on deck, a few days later Phyllis placed Maureen down on a woolen shawl, under the shade of a lifeboat, then dipped into her grandmother's book, reading up on recipes and household tips that might equip her for England. She wanted to be thought well of by Arthur's mother and worried about failing and being an embarrassment; after all, she'd been surrounded by servants all her life. An ayah looked after her and her siblings when they were younger, a sweeper kept the floors clean of dust, debris and dead insects, a dhobi wallah did all the laundry and the punka wallah kept the house cool, apart from when Maude was pregnant (it was considered dangerous for the unborn child to be in a draught). The scyce would look after their horses and the carriage; they even had a man to empty the four thunder-boxes, which were housed in a small room within the bungalow. A mali would tend to the grounds and they would either send for food to be delivered or get the khansamah, to make a meal in the blackened cookhouse, if they were entertaining guests.

"Ah, there you are, what a blistering afternoon." Arthur sauntered over.

"Look," said Phyllis, pointing triumphantly at the dark shape, like a large upturned boat, on the monotonous hazy-blue horizon. "Land ahoy!"

"Oh good, that'll be Aden coming into view. I'd better start writing my postcard, another couple of hours and we should be dropping anchor."

"We'll probably arrive before the card does."

"I know, but the old lady loves getting them from around the world. She keeps them in a drawer and when she's missing me, she rereads them."

He sat propped up next to Maureen and took out his pen. He wrote to his mother telling her they were all doing well. How there had been a nasty storm that Phyllis had suffered greatly with and that Maureen was a natural sea goer. How the food was jolly good and the fancy dress party had been fun and that they were very much looking forward to seeing her and Peg.

The Port of Aden grew ever closer, as Arthur finished writing his postcard. Phyllis had read how to prepare tamarind syrup, ginger cordial and mosquito repellent. How to stiffen chiffon, get rid of mange in dogs and treat snakebite.

Arthur looked over her shoulder and laughed. "I'm not sure how useful your grandmother's tips will be. There are no poisonous snakes to be found in Essex."

"I thought some of it might come in handy. Do you think we'll hold many dinner parties?" asked Phyllis hopefully, looking up from Emily's handwriting, excited by the thought of a drawing room full of dressed-up guests, a table heaped with platefuls of delicious food and glasses of deep-red claret.

"Oh, I'm not sure the old lady will be too keen, she's not one for socialising these days," replied Arthur.

"I didn't mean when we're staying with your mother, silly. I meant when we have a place of our own."

"Let's get there first shall we? There's plenty of time to think about all that once we've settled in a bit." Arthur smiled at Phyllis and at the thought of his mother opening up the stuffy parlour, pouring glasses of sherry from the dusty decanter and handing out canapés. He'd never seen her host or even attend a drinks, cocktail or dinner party, ever! She wasn't like Maude and Wilmot who seemed to love a constant stream of social functions to attend.

"What are you smiling about?"

"Oh, nothing, just the thought of mother's front parlour full of guests," replied Arthur laughing.

"Why's that so funny?"

"She's not much of a party goer, unlike your parents."

Maureen was asleep in the shade; her little fingers gripped the soft silky label of the shawl. On the deck below, troops cheered each other on. Push-up competitions, three-legged races and tugs of war were being held before the sun drove them back into the shade. A game of cricket was under way, a pair of socks made an improvised ball.

"What do you mean, she's not like my parents?" asked Phyllis tentatively.

"Well," ventured Arthur cautiously. "You must remember she was a vicar's wife for many years so she's never really experienced the sort of social life that your parents enjoy. Since father's death, her and Peg have become very close. They are as thick as thieves sometimes. By the way, you mustn't call my sister Peg. I know that sounds a bit silly but only family are allowed to call her that, you must call her by her proper name; Margaret."

"Oh, I thought I was family?" questioned Phyllis trying to hide her hurt feelings. "Any other strange quirks you haven't told me about?" Her breaking voice threatened to give her away.

"I'm sure they'll all become apparent once you've met them," said Arthur, absently picking the peeling grey paint off the ship's railings.

"Do you think they'll like me?" Phyllis held Arthur's hand and squeezed it gently.

"I'm sure they'll adore you," said Arthur kissing his wife gently on her lips. "Just bear in mind they're not like you. They haven't had the sort of life you have."

"What do you mean?"

"Just don't expect too much."

As the ship dropped anchor just off the shore, about 25 small boats came alongside, jostling for space. The bumboats were like floating shops, piled high with leather belts, beaded necklaces, Aladdin-style slippers with curly toes and little muslin sacks bulging with spices. Passengers emerged from their dark cabins like termites venturing out of their cool mud nests into the Arabian sunshine. They leant over the side of the ship shouting down to the hawkers bobbing about below. Some boats were stacked with fruit. Other boatmen sold delicious freshly-cooked food, tasty Falafel stuffed with chickpeas, beans, onions and garlic, flavoured with coriander and cumin. Dark green vine leaves were filled with allspice, cinnamon, lamb and rice. Bread that looked like large pancakes topped with sesame seeds were balanced in a tall pile. Another boat was stacked with coloured scarves and loose cotton pyjamas flapping gently in the breeze, like colourful prayer flags.

The troops on the deck below were pointing and shouting, baskets were being hauled up by strong arms, deals were made and money lowered. Phyllis found the whole thing utterly thrilling and pointed to a beautiful leather wallet with a camel neatly embossed on the front flap. Arthur waved at the boatman and pointed to the item. The man placed some wallets, a belt and a pair of slippers in a big brown basket then threw up a rope for Arthur to catch. The rope wasn't thrown quite high enough and Arthur struggled to reach it.

"Quick Arthur, next time, grab it," laughed Phyllis excitedly.

The second attempt was a much better throw and Arthur caught it with ease.

"I love this one," beamed Phyllis, picking out the camel wallet. "I'll send it to daddy. What are you going to get Peg, I mean Margaret?"

"I'm not sure what she'd like but I'll get the old lady some spices."

"How about these for your sister?" said Phyllis as she modelled the beautifully crafted leather slippers. Finally agreeing a price with the boatman they put their money in the basket and lowered it down, as if fetching water from a well. All around them people were excitedly examining their goods, sniffing spices and tucking into the delicious delights. Mrs Jackson's husband, Commander Jackson, happily sampled Seera beer, the locally-brewed drink that went down very well with the men on board, while Mrs Jackson sat in the shade on a deck chair, her hands absently feeding cashew nuts one after the other into her mouth, from a bag in her lap, until they were gone. Haggling and purchasing went on all afternoon until the ship was refuelled with coal and restocked with fresh food. As they left the shores of Aden the lights of the harbour's teashops twinkled like an ornate ceiling in a Maharajah's palace.

4

THE QUEEN OF COLOUR

Phyllis dressed quietly, scooping Maureen up in a blanket as she left Arthur sleeping. A small congregation had gathered for an Easter sunrise service out on the dewy deck. As she ventured into the cold morning air, the view took her breath away. The enormous flamingo pink sun hung low in the eastern sky, like a huge lantern, silhouetting the bulbous onion-shaped minarets of the mosques that nestled amongst small settlements along the brown, flat banks. The ship was slowly making its way up the Suez Canal. Farmers out early on their camel carts left trails of chai-coloured dust as they took their crops to market. Fishermen dangled their homemade rods over the side of small jetties that strutted out into the deep water, hoping to catch an early breakfast.

"Good morning, Mrs Woollett," said Father John, the ship's chaplain. "How splendid to see you, and on such a fine morning too."

Phyllis nodded and sat next to Mrs Jackson, who patted the hard bench beside her. The distant call to prayer could be heard from one of the mosques, as Father John started the Mass with a hymn. The little group sang quietly at first, shy of their voices as the scenery drifted slowly past, small sail boats bobbed about in the ship's wake. The Easter prayers and sermon were followed with more singing and then the final hymn, Phyllis's favourite, Victorious. The feeling of fresh possibilities and new beginnings, wrapped around Phyllis like a cashmere shawl. She hugged Maureen to her chest and felt a surge of excitement at what lay ahead.

By lunchtime they had slipped out of the Suez Canal and into the Mediterranean Sea, leaving Asia and Africa behind. The ship's Easter tea party was well under way, mothers' fussed with their children's plates, filling them with toast, buttered eggs and party cake. All the children on board had been invited. They sat at a long table, a life-sized swan made from silver tin foil majestically rose from its centre. Hidden inside were neatly wrapped gifts.

"May I sit with you?" asked a pretty young woman.

"Please, be my guest," replied Phyllis as she helped pull the chair away from the overcrowded table.

"How do you do? I'm Mrs Walker," she said, placing her son in the chair. "We are dreadfully late. I was busy painting and quite lost track of the time. I hope the little hyenas haven't eaten all the food."

Phyllis laughed. "I think there's still a bit left. I'm Mrs Woollett and this is my daughter, Maureen."

"I noticed you at the cocktail party, I've been meaning to introduce myself ever since I saw you covered in a Bloody Mary. I thought you handled it awfully well. I'm quite sure I wouldn't have been so polite."

Phyllis laughed. "Oh, I accidently got my own back later in the evening."

Phyllis relayed the embarrassing conversation about being part native in front of the other dinner guests. Mrs Walker laughed and congratulated Phyllis on her wit.

"What were you doing out in India?" asked Phyllis, intrigued by her new companion.

"Charlie and I, that's my husband, late husband, went to India six years ago, then we had Eddie." Mrs Walker stroked her son's hair and kissed the top of his head. "Sadly, Charlie contracted typhoid, he died, in my arms. That was a year ago, it's taken me this long to finally admit to myself that I must go back to London. It was so hard to leave India. I felt I was leaving Charlie behind."

"Oh, my dear Mrs Walker, I'm so terribly sorry." Phyllis offered her a handkerchief to dab at her tears.

"Thank you, I'm alright now. I'm just not terribly good at talking about it. Enough of the formalities, please call me Kitty."

"Nice to meet you Kitty, I'm Phyllis. Tell me what you like to paint."

They arranged to meet up on deck after breakfast the

following morning. Kitty brought her watercolours and sable brushes in her old artist's box; it was like a pirate's chest full of treasure. It contained little blocks of colours, which dipped in the middle through use; a palette, its gentle inclines stained from previous painting sessions; a couple of soft pencils rattled around at the bottom of the box along with a well-worn putty rubber. Phyllis adored painting and lost herself in Kitty's easy company. Phyllis mixed the paints on the palette: Cobalt Blue with Titanium White for the sea, Prussian Blue with a tiny dab of Indigo for the distant stormy sky and Raw Umber and Venetian Red for the land that now came into view on the horizon. Kitty talked of her family life in London and how she married Charlie, her childhood sweetheart. She spoke of her life with him in India, and the pain of losing him.

The temperature had dropped noticeably and both women wore cardigans and headscarves. Phyllis dipped her large brush into the jam jar of water and soaked the stiff paper. It felt good to be painting again. Maude had taught her how to paint when she was a young girl; they used to go on picnics around the lake in Nainital in the summer months. Phyllis and her mother would set up their easels at the far end of the lake and paint the boat club, a white ramshackle building made of timber. It sat right at the lake's edge and had a balcony that stretched out over the water, little wooden rowing boats moored at its posts. It was a members only club with billiard tables, a bar and a restaurant. They held dances there too. It was funny to think that many years later, Arthur would propose to her on that very balcony.

"There you are," said Arthur, peeking over her shoulder to look at the painting as he kissed the back of his wife's slender neck. "Thought I'd go and keep Jackson company at the bar." Arthur drew on his cigarette as he admired Phyllis's efforts.

"Your dear wife really is a genius," said Kitty. "Not only is she the queen of colour mixing, but she is also a great tonic to me. I was getting a little bored, but now things are looking up a treat."

Phyllis smiled at her new friend and felt she'd known her all her life.

Arthur was happy to see Phyllis so wrapped up in her hobby and her new friend; it certainly helped to pass the time.

That afternoon Arthur and Phyllis played quoits on the sunny deck.

"I can almost feel I'm in a different part of the world. The air has changed somehow, so much fresher," said Phyllis, as she flung the rope ring towards her target. Maureen looked on from Mrs Jackson's large floral lap and squealed when a target was hit.

"Don't throw it too hard," teased Arthur. "It might go skidding off the deck and kill some poor, innocent chap below."

The soldiers could be heard on parade as the Sergeant Major bellowed orders at the tired troops. Arthur thought back to the first voyage he made from England to Bombay nine years before in 1930. The decision to join the army had been an easy one.

He had enlisted in Preston on 11th May 1927, having lied about his age, telling the recruitment officer his profession was gardening. He'd never so much as mowed a lawn. Arthur left the family home; Leesfield Vicarage in Oldham and by 18th June had gained his certificate in Army education at Catterick camp. He was posted to Germany with the Royal Signals to do a wireless course. He loved life in the camp, even though he no longer had his mother to rely on. He learnt how to wash his own clothes, cook and organise himself. He thrived on the independence it gave him. The physical training made him strong. He mastered Morse code with ease and then went on to learn how to lay communication cables and operate a wireless. The basic horse riding skills he'd learnt as a boy whilst growing up in Ireland were harnessed and he became a talented horseman. He took up smoking to become one of the lads and started drinking in the local pub, when leave allowed. Life was good away from his father. He'd become a man.

Arthur's posting to India came through on his 20th birthday. He was ecstatic but his mother had been distraught. He was to spend the next couple of years in Delhi, operating a radio set, then out into the field in Burma. The troopship that took him to India was not unlike HMT Dorsetshire. The mess decks in the cargo space went right down into the deep bowels of the ship, commonly referred to as the 'hell pit'. Row upon row of long tables with benches either side made up each mess housing 28 men. The hammocks stored above the tables by day would be strung up to make the troops sleeping quarters at night. In the morning they were woken with the call, "Rouse up there, lash up and stow." The hammocks had to be lashed up with the blankets inside and stowed above the mess tables so that breakfast could be eaten.

Seasickness had been rife; lots of the lads had never sailed before, including Arthur who found it hard to keep his food down. The smell of vomit clung to their nostrils and no amount of washing of either the men; their clothes or the decks would get rid of the lingering stench. Once the ship got past Gibraltar, conditions became more bearable and as the weather improved further, they could sleep outside, using their blankets for a mattress.

In 1932, two years after his first stint in India and Burma he was posted back to England for a couple of years, stationed at Aldershot. He found he could visit his mother in Colchester more often. He then fell in love with Elsie. She'd visited Colchester to attend a dance, where they met and quickly started dating. They would meet up when he was on leave and go to the local picture house. Arthur would press her up against the apple tree that grew in her front garden, after escorting her home on the last bus. She would let him kiss her if she thought her father wasn't looking. Arthur would smile all the way back to his mother's house, Woodbine in hand. He once cycled 91 miles home from Aldershot to Colchester, just to see her for the weekend. So he had been surprised when she turned down his marriage proposal just before he was posted back to India in 1934. Arthur was to be stationed in Meerut and then on to Talital as a Lance Corporal. He'd felt confused and rejected. Elsie thought she'd play hard to get and wrongly assumed he would be back to propose to her again. She had planned on saying yes. Elsie and Arthur had written love letters every week even after he'd struck up a relationship with Phyllis.

It was at the end of January, in 1935, that Phyllis had suspected something was wrong. They had gone for a picnic at Dorothy's Peak viewpoint, 1,000 feet above Nainital. Sounds of the town had drifted up to the top of the mountain, children played in the streets below and goat's bells tinkled from adjacent hillsides as Arthur had laid down a rug and charmed Phyllis into letting go of her inhibitions and Catholic uptightness. He'd caressed her into submission and she'd given herself willingly. After making love, Phyllis had noticed that he was quiet and not himself at all. She asked him outright whether it was his intention to break off their relationship. Arthur had blurted out that he'd had a girlfriend back home, and that they had been in love. He left out the bit about proposing to Elsie.

Phyllis had given him an ultimatum; she would not see, speak or write to Arthur again until he told Elsie it was over. He wrote Elsie a letter when they returned from their outing. Phyllis watched as he posted it. Arthur had felt terrible, he knew how much pain it would cause Elsie and her father, and come to think of it, his own mother, too. Elizabeth adored Elsie and wanted her for a daughter-in-law. His mother would kill him. A few weeks later Arthur received a letter from his mother telling him that Elsie had suffered a nervous breakdown.

*

"How long till we land in Valletta?" asked Phyllis.

"Two more days," said Arthur as he put his arms around her waist and pulled him to her.

He nuzzled his nose into her warm swan-like neck and then slid his hand gently down onto her bottom, just as Father John appeared. Phyllis recoiled and looked at the floor blushing like a schoolgirl. She still felt like a naughty child. She often wondered if she would ever feel like a grown-up or a slightly silly girl for the rest of her life. Her Catholic upbringing had always filled her with such guilt and utter shame at anything vaguely sexual; the nuns at St Mary's convent, where she had boarded in Nainital from the age of seven to sixteen, had made sure of that. All the girls were instructed to sleep with their arms crossed over their chests at night so there wasn't any wrong doing with their hands and if they died in the night, they would be in the right position to enter heaven. Arthur was constantly telling her to loosen up a bit, they were married now, that it was perfectly natural. She did her best, but the guilt remained.

5

A NIGHT AT THE OPERA

The ship slid gently into The Grand Harbour as the sun rose, lighting up the honey-coloured fortified walls of Valletta.

"It's breathtakingly pretty," said Phyllis. "Like nothing I've ever seen before. Look at the church dome, it's so beautiful."

Huge black cannons pierced the yellow city walls, guarding the Maltese people. Tall houses, blue and green painted shutters not yet open, towered high above the walls. Their residents still happily cocooned in the dark rooms inside. The crew's shouts pierced the silent morning as the ship docked at Barriera wharf. Traders had gathered on the quayside. The men had dark brown skin and wore white shirts with waistcoats and flat white caps. Shutters clanged open as coffee stalls set up for business. Tables and chairs were hastily arranged as steaming hot coffee with almond Figolli cakes were sold to the first customers of the day. Army personnel boarded to check the ship's documentation. The passengers and some of the crew could disembark, as the ship would be docked overnight. The soldiers on the other hand were not so lucky and would have to stay on board.

Arthur thought it would be fun to invite Kitty and Eddie along for a roam around Valletta's narrow streets. He had stopped off here on his last passage to India and knew of a lovely coffee shop in Queen Victoria Square. As Phyllis stepped onto the quayside it felt as though she was still moving, she felt unsteady on her feet and had to hang on to Arthur's arm. They beckoned a carrozzi, its driver glad of the early morning trade. He skillfully turned the horse around, its tail flicking as they trotted up the slope and in through the imposing city walls.

Phyllis looked up at the merchants' houses; enclosed Spanish-style wooden balconies jutted out over the pavements. Big brass doorknockers, verdigris green with years of white polish encrusted in the grooves of the ornate designs, seahorses, dolphins and lions adorned their heavy doors.

They passed the grand frontage of The Royal Opera House, a row of huge columns stood guard outside. Steep streets criss-crossed over each other, some with hundreds of shallow steps stretching up to the pale blue sky. Others were full of washing, flapping dry in the warm sunshine. Large terracotta pots containing spindly olive trees, startling crimson rhododendrons and figs sat welcoming guests at doorways. Thickset women dressed in black were bent down on their hands and knees like an army of black crabs, cleaning the steps outside their houses. They gossiped loudly with their neighbours, arms moving in synchronised scrubbing.

Shops were preparing for the day ahead. Buckets of soapy water were being splashed over the dark pavements. The florist's window was a mass of bright bouquets spilling out onto the road like a pretty summer dress. The fruit and vegetable store-owner stacked his wooden crates from his horse and cart, overflowing with beef tomatoes, courgettes and artichokes.

The carriage jolted to a halt in a beautiful square, lined by a stone arcade to one side. Small shops huddled underneath, selling some of Malta's finest souvenirs. Brightly coloured Mdina glass, intricate silver filigree, so fine Phyllis thought it was lace, and thick hand-knitted shawls from Gozo. To the other side was the imposing bibliotheca, its uniformed armed guard on duty at the large wooden door. Tall plane trees, their bark smooth like slender ladies arms wearing silk evening gloves, reached high over the square. A statue of Queen Victoria sat majestically on a huge throne. A couple of feral cats lay at her feet.

"This way," called Arthur.

He steered them towards the Cafe Cordina, where a curved arch framed the baker's window of sticky delights. The waitress led them to a small table underneath the vaulted ceiling. Her heels clicked on the green and white-tiled floor like castanets as she walked to the counter to place their order.

Maureen chewed eagerly on a honey bun, whilst Eddie did his best to polish off a large meringue, cramming every last crusty pink crumb into his already full mouth.

"It's heavenly to be off the boat for a while," said Kitty.

"I'll go in search of a newspaper and a smoke," said Arthur. "I'll catch up with you in a little while."

Phyllis, Kitty and the children finished their morning coffee and cakes and went for a stroll in the Mediterranean sunshine. The streets were starting to warm up, horses and carts trotted past, porters delivered goods on hand carts. The local Maltese women walked down the streets with their thick black hair flowing down their backs, dark stockinged legs poking out under their knee-length flared skirts. Men dressed in suits gathered in the shade of lemon trees and played backgammon. Phyllis loved it. She could smell onions and garlic frying in dark kitchens hidden behind tatty old shuttered windows that opened out onto the streets.

Phyllis bought a delicate white lace placemat with the eight-point Maltese cross design in its centre and a hand-knitted donkey for the coming baby. The two friends linked arms as they took in all of the wonderful smells, sights and sounds of the waking city. Phyllis wanted to visit the church she had spotted from the ship; its impressive green copper dome dominated the skyline. Kitty looked after the children, whilst Phyllis went in to say a prayer and light a candle. When she reappeared into the daylight from the musty interior, she found Kitty and Arthur sitting on a bench waiting for her. Kitty's eyes lit up when she saw her.

"We need to get you back to the ship, there is work to be done," said Kitty laughing.

"What the devil are you two hatching? You both look very guilty," said Phyllis.

"Never you mind. Just do as you are told, I have a nice surprise for you." Arthur said, his grin flashing from Kitty to Phyllis.

Once back on board the ship, Arthur asked Phyllis to close her eyes. He then placed two opera tickets into the palm of her hand. When she opened them she was overjoyed.

"Carmen, my favourite!"

"Tonight, my darling we shall go to the opera. Kitty will look after Maureen and she has also offered to do your hair and help you get ready," said Arthur, looking rather pleased with himself.

Kitty jumped up and down like an excited child. Phyllis's eyes flooded with tears. She put her arms around Arthur's neck and kissed him full on the lips. Her smile filled her face and tears trickled down her cheeks.

"You lucky girl, Phyllis Woollett," smiled Kitty.

Kitty took Phyllis into her cabin and sat her down on the small stool in front of the mirror. She brushed her friend's hair before neatly rolling small handfuls in damp rags.

"You simply must wear this with your blue dress. You will look absolutely divine," said Kitty as she fastened her diamante necklace around Phyllis's neck.

"You really are a treasure," said Phyllis happily admiring her reflection in the small mirror. She had never had this experience before, not even with her sister Muriel, even though they were so close in age.

"My sister was never one for sharing her things. When I was about thirteen I borrowed one of her dresses without asking. I managed to tear it whilst running home. She completely lost her temper and threw my best pair of shoes down the well! Daddy got wind of it and was absolutely furious; she wasn't allowed to go out for a month, apart from to church. I don't think she ever quite forgave me."

Being an only child, Kitty loved to hear the stories from Phyllis's childhood and thought how dreadful it must be to have an older sister.

Arthur couldn't believe his eyes when Phyllis entered the bar to meet him for an aperitif before they disembarked that evening. Kitty looked very proud of herself as she ushered her into the smoky room, hanging back at the door to see Arthur's delighted expression.

"You look ravishing, " said Arthur as he kissed her gently on the cheek. "You really are quite beautiful."

Mrs Pearce yawned as she sat with her bored husband looking at all the men staring at Phyllis. She flicked some cigarette ash off her dress and looked across at the bar. The barman caught her eye and delivered another flute of champagne to her table, secretly passing her a note as he did so, with the bar chit she needed to sign. Phyllis and Arthur strolled out on deck to see Kitty. The tolling bells from Valletta's churches escaped the city walls, creating a jumble of chimes. Kitty wanted to capture the romantic moment for them and borrowed Arthur's camera. Valletta's skyline made a wonderful backdrop. Kitty only had a couple of treasured pictures of Charlie and wished they had taken more when he was alive.

The theatre was huge, with row upon row of red velvet seats. They took their places on the balcony. Phyllis looked around at the audience now filling up the theatre and caught a glimpse of a turquoise dress in the row along from theirs; she knew instantly it was Mrs Pearce by the loud horsey laugh. Phyllis was shocked though to see the gentleman with her was not her husband, but the barman from the ship. He had his arm around her and was whispering into her ear. Mrs Pearce looked up and saw Phyllis looking at her. Phyllis discreetly looked away and tried hard to put it out of her mind. Arthur had also seen her and nudged Phyllis.

"Crumbs, look who we have for company, not sure Mr Pearce would approve," he whispered, raising his eyebrows in Mrs Pearce's direction.

The curtains went up and Phyllis gasped at the exquisite scenery, a square in Seville with soldiers congregating by the guard's house. The cigarette factory, its yellow stonewalls lit up as if the sun was shining. The orchestra struck up and out swanned Carmen from the factory gates, the gypsy girl swished her black hair and flirted with all the men. She was stunning and sexy, her whole body moved with the music as she twirled around them, teasing them with her pouting red lips. The orchestra played Bizet's rousing music; Phyllis was captivated by Carmen, the soldiers, the dancing, the singing, the set and the music. It was utterly beautiful and by the interval Phyllis felt like she had been in a trance. She left Arthur in the bar and went to use the ladies room.

"Mrs Woollett," she turned round to see Mrs Pearce had followed her in.

"Ah, good evening Mrs Pearce," replied Phyllis, stiffly.

"I trust you won't say anything to my husband about this evening?" said Mrs Pearce. Her tone of voice was more a command than a question.

"What you do and with whom is none of my business Mrs Pearce," replied Phyllis. She left, her heart thumping in her chest. She told Arthur about their conversation when she got back to her seat.

"I've got a good mind to report the barman to his senior Officer," said Arthur, "and her long suffering husband."

"Oh please don't, it'll only make things worse, she already hates me, I'm sure of it," said Phyllis, snuggling into Arthur's shoulder.

The curtains rose and the second act commenced. Phyllis felt her rib cage vibrating with the sheer force of the soprano voice of Carmen, and the tenor voices of Don Jose, the corporal and Escamillo, the bullfighter. The end was always so tragic. Carmen lay on the floor in a pool of blood, a knife through her chest, as her new lover, Escamillo, leaves the bullfighting ring, triumphant from his kill. Jose, realising that, out of sheer jealously, he has killed the woman he loves, sobs violently over her dead body. Phyllis stood up out of the red velvet chair and clapped until her hands stung. Arthur took her by the arm and led her out of the theatre.

"Whatever happens my darling Phyl, never forget this night and how much I adore you and always will," said Arthur lovingly.

Phyllis wanted to walk back to the ship, it was a fine night and although very dark, it felt safe. She held on to the programme tightly as she chatted all the way back about the scenery, the music, the theatre and the audience. And of course, Mrs Pearce and the barman, whatever were they thinking of? Surely they must have thought that someone else from the ship may be at the theatre, too.

Phyllis noticed Mrs Pearce at breakfast the next morning and gave her a cursory nod. Arthur was having none of it though; the barman was nowhere to be seen. Arthur told Phyllis later that he'd had a discreet word with the steward, who had summoned the barman. He was to be stationed in the galley on washing up duty for the rest of the voyage to ensure he wouldn't cause further scandal.

6

SOUTHAMPTON, 17TH APRIL 1939

The ship sounded its loud horn as the powerful tugboats pulled up alongside and guided it into the sheltered dock. Mesmerized by the English landscape she had dreamt of for so long, Phyllis gripped the scarf that wrapped around her head and looked on in amazement as the wind whipped about her, threatening to steal the fine Benares silk away.

"It's so green Arthur, I can't believe how green it is!" she laughed happily, reaching for her husband's cold hand.

The distant landscape was divided into fields edged with low stonewalls. The last of the day's sunshine lit up the small towns nestling in fabric-like creases. A church spire stood upright amongst a muddle of small houses, casting its long spiky shadow like an ancient sundial. Trees huddled together in little clusters, at the edges of the patchwork fields, as black and white cows lazily grazed underneath the peacock blue sky.

"Oh Arthur, I had no idea how beautiful it would be. I can't wait to dock."

"I'm sure you're going to love it," replied Arthur, as he searched for the last cigarette in its soft packet. He felt a sense of unease to be home again. Things were different now. He was a husband and a father, not just a son and brother. He glanced towards Phyllis and his young daughter and told himself they would be fine.

The cabin trunks were packed up and standing, as if to attention, in the doorways of the discarded cabins that had been home for six cramped weeks. Arthur tipped the steward generously, who nodded politely without looking at the warm mix of coins.

They stepped onto the steep gangplank and followed a trail of other passengers that gathered on the dirty dockside. Black oily cranes towered over them, chains clanged and large hooks swayed like giant eagle's talons. Phyllis discovered a one anna coin in the seam of her flimsy coat pocket. She could feel the worn-down letters on its shiny surface as she rubbed it between her fingers. She took it out and threw it as far as she could over the quayside and into the sea, closing her eyes and making a wish as she did so.

"What did you wish for?" Arthur whispered, his warm breath tickling the raised goose bumps on her cold neck.

"If I told you, it wouldn't come true."

She looked up at the enormous grey troopship. A sea of khaki uniforms jostled on the lower decks amidst a throng of excitement, cheers and laughter. Phyllis silently prayed to God, to keep them all safe.

"Phyllis," gushed Kitty. "Oh my dear girl, I thought I'd lost you. Promise you'll write soon. Take care of Arthur and little Maureen. I need to go and find which platform my train leaves from." Kitty gently patted Phyllis's belly. "Let me know when the baby arrives." She hugged her and thrust a piece of crumpled paper into her friend's hand. Phyllis slipped the treasured address into her pocket and gripped onto it for fear of losing it.

"Dear Kitty, I feel like I've known you all my life. Don't forget us."

Arthur and Phyllis had to wait for their luggage to be unloaded. They found an empty table in the drab waiting room café. Mismatched crockery stained with tidemarks, like a dirty sink, filled most of the sticky surface made by a previous customers spillage. Arthur got up to order at the grubby counter.

"Arthur, what are you doing? Surely the bearer will come to us?" Whispered Phyllis looking around nervously for uniformed staff to take their order.

Arthur laughed. "We're not in India anymore." He looked around at the dirty blue walls, were disembarking passengers had scuffed the paint whilst waiting their turn in the long queue.

He ordered a pot of tea with crumpets. Phyllis found the tea to be bitter, hot and tasteless but the crumpets were delicious, and oozed with butter, which dribbled down Arthur's chin. Phyllis retrieved her hankie, that she kept in a ball up the sleeve of her cardigan and wiped away the greasy, yellow dribble. Maureen grizzled; she was tired and cold.

"I'll take her out and get a paper too," suggested Arthur. "I could do with catching up on the news."

"Don't be long," called Phyllis, as he left her sitting alone in the bleak cafe.

Her heart quickened as she watched them go. She looked around the crowded room and felt like a lost child in an unfamiliar place. She scanned the window, eagerly looking for a glimpse of Arthur through the dripping condensation. She felt relieved and foolish as he returned only minutes later. Arthur, oblivious to Phyllis's anxiety, sat down and flicked the broadsheet open. Phyllis read the front-page headlines as Arthur scanned the inside pages. ADOLF HITLER WILL NOT REST TILL HE HAS CITY OF DANZIG IN POLAND. The paper gave off a bitter inky smell as the tips of Arthur's fingers turned shiny and black.

*

The cargo trunks were finally unloaded from the ship's hold. Phyllis held Maureen close to her as they stood in the queue to claim their luggage.

"Lance Corporal Woollett?" questioned a loud voice.

The army car that had been sent to take them to Colchester drew up alongside them. Phyllis pulled her coat more tightly around her, as she felt the cold wind bite at her slim ankles. The luggage was stacked in the back of the vehicle; it didn't look like much now it was piled up in one place.

"What about your hatbox?" asked Arthur.

"I'll keep it on the seat next to me. I don't want to lose it, daddy would never forgive me."

Phyllis placed the circular box containing her precious solar topee on the seat, for fear of it being damaged on the long, bumpy drive. As they left the industrial docklands behind, she was overwhelmed by the amount of white faces that occupied Southampton's busy streets. It seemed strange not to be surrounded by brown faces, Indian faces. Instead, pale faces belonging to long, dark woollen coats took their place. The ladies wore large black hats, polished boots and coats with fur collars.

The pale-faced people were crammed into steamed-up buses, tired after a long day. No bandys, tongas or rickshaws to slow their progress. No beggars on the streets asking for money. No fruit sellers or juice stalls to quench their thirst. No turbans, no saris and absolutely no Indians, just lots of people, white people, hurrying to their homes in their dark suits, dark dresses and woollen stockings. The smell of coal smoke replaced the delicious aroma of wood burning mixed with the cooking smells that made Phyllis's mouth water every evening in India. Kiosks sold stacks of newspapers on street corners. Men huddled around in small groups, sharing talk of Hitler and having a smoke, before heading home to the warmth of their kitchen ranges.

Phyllis marvelled at the tree-lined streets, the large green fields and wide-open parks, as they made their way through the countryside and pretty villages.

The young driver talked non-stop to Arthur about the rumours of war. Hitler had torn up the Munich agreement, which Britain and Germany had signed only six months before. Phyllis was only half listening, their voices merged with the rhythm of the car's engine as she absorbed the new landscape that disappeared past her small window.

She daydreamed of home as sleep tried to claim her tired body. She thought back to one of the last wonderful days spent with her mother. They'd taken the carriage and ventured into Benares with its wonderful array of shops and bazaars to buy items they couldn't get through the mail order service at The Army and Navy store. Phyllis had not only needed new clothes and shoes for the voyage, but also a few well-chosen gifts for Arthur's family in England.

They'd breakfasted early on the veranda; a mild egg curry washed down with a small glass of claret. Then Bipin the scyce had trotted round to the porch from the back of the compound to take the memsahibs on their shopping spree. The small black pony had tossed its head back and forth as it got used to the weight of the carriage. Bipin drove them out into Kennedy Road and down onto The Mall. Both women held their chattas to shade themselves from the February sun. The horse had clip-clopped down the road as Phyllis and Maude chatted happily on the small black leather seat, Maude's arm securely positioned around Phyllis's expanding waist.

The streets had been busy. Rickshaws, their drivers glistening with sweat, hurried businessmen in suits to work. Smartly dressed children in neat uniforms made their way to school laden with armfuls of exercise books. The girls had long shiny plaits that swished from side to side. Bandys delivered their heavy bundles of laundry and supplies to hotels. Nepali porters, their strong muscular dark arms heaved enormous loads on their backs, secured by wide rope straps around their foreheads. Street stalls had already set out their wares and lined both sides of the road. Household goods, toys and clothing dangled from canvas awnings, enticing trade. Women coming back from early morning prayers at Hindu temples with freshly applied orange and red tikka marks smudged on their foreheads. Sacred cows happily scavenged in piles of rubbish as holy men made their way down through the maze of footpaths and roads to the sacred river Ganges.

They'd had a busy morning of shoes, clothes and fabric buying. Mr Sethi had laboriously unravelled most of his shop's fabric stock whilst plying Phyllis and Maude with

Madeira cake and chai. It had been an exhausting experience of haggling before heading to Thatheri bazaar to buy gifts for Phyllis's in-laws. They settled on an engraved brass bon-bon bowl for Peg and a pair of elegant candlesticks for Elizabeth. They'd met Wilmot for afternoon tea at Clarks, their favourite lunch venue in Benares, its large marble lobby felt lavishly cool on their hot bodies that had frazzled in the stifling narrow alleys that harboured the heat. No breeze was allowed to infiltrate the maze-like streets. Wilmot had ordered a bottle of champagne as a surprise for Phyllis who was setting sail the following week.

Phyllis shivered a little as she rubbed her hands together to keep them warm. She smiled at the memory of Wilmot, so proud of his youngest daughter embarking on a new life in England. And now here she was with the light starting to fade as they drove along Colchester's High Street. The shops closing up for the night and its picture house, pubs and hotel filling up with evening customers. The car turned into Maldon Road, driving slowly past the red-bricked houses, looking for the house number. Some of their curtains hadn't been drawn, letting Phyllis steal little glimpses of English life.

"It's on the left," pointed Arthur, "the one with the gate."

Phyllis was disappointed to see the heavy curtains closed, giving no clue as to what lay inside. A low red brick wall boarded the pavement, a privet hedge spilled out over the top, straggly and in need of a trim. The green wooden gate squeaked gently as the wind caught it. The doorstep's brass shone like a new penny in the light of the streetlamp.

A large woman dressed in a plain dress and slippers stood in the doorway. She wiped her hands on the flowery apron tied around her thick waist and rushed down the front path. Phyllis noticed the tight string of pearls around her creased neck. Elizabeth wiped at her tears that wet her already flushed face. Maureen cried at being removed from the warmth of her mother's lap by Elizabeth's unfamiliar hands.

The smell of baking bread and floor polish greeted them at the front door. The hallway felt small and gloomy with steep stairs leading to a dark landing. Elizabeth ushered them into the front parlour, a rare treat indeed, as it wasn't even Sunday. Elizabeth handed Maureen back to Phyllis then removed her pinny.

"We meet at last Phyllis. How was your journey dear?"

"It was mostly fine, thank you and it's so wonderful to meet you at last," replied Phyllis, embarrassed that her cheeks blushed.

Maureen started to cry.

"Oh dear, we have a bit of a cry-baby on our hands. We'll soon see to that, my dears," said Elizabeth.

Phyllis felt she needed to defend Maureen and started to say how she was normally a happy child that it was late and had been a long day, but Elizabeth had already moved to face Arthur.

"My dear boy, come here and give your old mother a kiss. You get more handsome each time you bless me with your company," she kissed him on both cheeks and held his hands in hers.

Arthur hugged his mother tenderly and swallowed hard as his eyes watered.

"It's good to see you Mums."

"Sit down you two, you must be exhausted," said Elizabeth.

Phyllis sat on the small sofa, its hard springs poking into her buttocks. She couldn't take her eyes off the yellow lily of the valley wallpaper, she'd never seen wallpaper before. Indian houses were always whitewashed. The white ants would have devoured the wallpaper in one sitting. She looked around at the lacy antimacassar on the chair arm, the nest of wooden coffee tables and a glass-fronted ornament cabinet, full of china figurines. At last her eyes fell upon something familiar, a piano. She hoped it was tuned. She looked around for a mora to place her feet on but there wasn't one. In India it was essential to keep your feet off the floor, unless you didn't mind mice, rats, cockroaches, spiders and even snakes slithering over them. She placed her legs straight out in front of her instead, raising them a few inches off the floor, at least she could keep an eye on them there.

"Isn't that so Phyllis?" said Elizabeth, in a soft Dublin accent, looking at the awkward way in which Phyllis was sitting.

"I'm sorry, I didn't quite catch that," replied Phyllis, finding her mother-in-law's accent hard to understand.

"Arthur should go outside and smoke, it's not good for my chest," repeated Elizabeth a little louder, as if Phyllis was deaf.

Phyllis noticed Arthur's childlike demeanour in front of his mother as he went to light up in the backyard. She found herself alone with Elizabeth for the first time.

"Well Phyllis, I'm sure we are going to rub along just fine," said Elizabeth smiling.

"Rub along?" questioned Phyllis.

"Oh, it means get along, you know, like each other." Elizabeth added awkwardly.

"Oh, I see, yes I'm sure we will," replied Phyllis, praying to God that the door would open and Arthur would step back through it.

"What's wrong with your feet dear, do they ache?" enquired Elizabeth.

"Oh, no it's just that I didn't want to put them on the floor," replied Phyllis, embarrassed.

"Why ever not?" asked Elizabeth.

"Because," Phyllis looked down at her hands lying in her lap, they looked silly, childish, dark. "Because of the mice, spiders and scorpions," blurted out Phyllis, somehow knowing this was the wrong thing to say.

"You're not in India now you know," chuckled Elizabeth. "We might get the odd mouse in the pantry and spiders in the privy but you'll not be needing a footstool dear, not in my house anyway."

Phyllis sat trying to relax her legs and pondered what a privy might be.

"I have a little gift for the baby. Take your coat off and make yourself at home while I go and fetch it," said Elizabeth.

She went to the back room to fetch the yellow booties she had knitted from some recycled wool. It had originally been one of Frederick's pullovers.

"Now let's get that little one to bed shall we? I'll show you where you'll all be sleeping," said Elizabeth, as she led Phyllis up to the steep staircase to the front bedroom. It was the biggest bedroom in the house. Elizabeth kept it as the spare just in case she ever needed to take in a lodger. It would fetch in a bit more money than the back box room and she wouldn't need to worry about the upheaval of moving all her belongings out of it, if she left it empty. Phyllis was relieved to see a double bed at one end of the room. A small wooden cot sat next to it. Elizabeth had managed to borrow it from one of the neighbours, whose baby had long since grown out of it. A washstand stood in the bay of the window, with a large jug for water and two towels. A bar of fresh soap lay in a small china dish on the white marbled surface.

Phyllis looked up to the ceiling.

"Have we no nets?" she asked, slightly more abruptly than she meant to.

"Nets, what sort of nets?" asked Elizabeth puzzled.

"Mosquito nets," replied Phyllis.

Elizabeth laughed. "You won't be needing those either my dear, this is a civilised country. We don't have your kind of diseases here."

"Oh, I didn't know," said Phyllis.

"You can boil a kettle on the stove in the kitchen for your hot water, then bring it upstairs for a wash, then you can have a bath once a week in the tub downstairs, Fridays would be good as Monday is washday, Wednesday is the day we polish the floors, Thursday is market day and Tuesdays are my turn to do the church charity meetings in the kitchen. Never mind, I won't bother you with the entire house goings on yet, you've only just got in the door." Elizabeth prattled on, leaning her large frame against the creaky iron bedstead.

"Should I also boil the water for drinking? "Asked Phyllis.

"Goodness me, no," laughed Elizabeth. "Our water is perfectly clean."

"And what about the milk?" Asked Phyllis.

"That's clean, too," replied Elizabeth a bit impatiently.

A dark imposing almyra stood upright near the door.

"I've put by a few spare clothes for you dearie in case you didn't have enough warm things, feel free to borrow whatever you see in here." Elizabeth opened its creaky door. Dark brown, black and navy dresses, jumpers and an old wool coat sagged from hangers like upside-down fruit bats on a mango tree. They were ghastly, shapeless and certainly had no style. The aroma of mothballs spilled into the room, its bitter ammonia-like smell clung to her nostrils. Phyllis hoped she would manage without having to delve into the dark cavernous beast that would be watching over them, as they slept.

"I'll go and pop the kettle on dear, come down when you've sorted Maureen out," said Elizabeth.

Phyllis tried to settle Maureen, but she was cold and not used to wearing nightclothes, or having a blanket on her at night. Phyllis then went down to the kitchen to ask Elizabeth where the boff was.

"Boff?" questioned Elizabeth.

"Lavatory, toilet?" explained Phyllis.

Elizabeth opened the back door and pointed to a wooden lean-to at the back of the house. Dangling from a string were neatly torn squares of newspaper. Phyllis hoped she wouldn't be caught short in the middle of the night and vowed to drink nothing after seven o'clock in the evening, just in case. As she went back inside, Maureen was still crying. Phyllis made her way to the bottom of the stairs.

"Now, now, you don't want her thinking she can always have what she wants, leave her be," commanded Elizabeth.

They had already been relegated from the front parlour to the back room. Elizabeth poured the tea and plonked it on the table. Phyllis found it hard to sit and ignore Maureen's cries and looked to Arthur for support, who had now finished his cigarette and was sat reading the paper as he carried on telling his mother about the voyage. He was oblivious to Maureen's cries for attention and Phyllis's pain at having to ignore them.

Phyllis heard a car pull up outside. Heavy footsteps advanced up the side passage to the back door and in stepped Peg; a tall, stocky woman with sharp eyes and a thin mouth, her hair slightly windswept.

"Hello all," she gushed. "Sorry I'm late, you can't hurry a baby if it doesn't want to come out," she added matter of factly. She took Phyllis's hand and gave it a hard squeeze. Phyllis thought she had large hands for a woman.

"Nice to meet you Phyllis, hope your journey wasn't too

arduous?" Before Phyllis could open her mouth, Peg had already made it across the room and into the arms of her elder brother.

"Darling Peg, how are you little sis?" said Arthur, happy at last to have them all together.

Peg shared the story of the dramatic breach berth she had just attended, and then wanted to know all about their voyage. Elizabeth refilled the teapot. Phyllis politely declined the third cup; the images of the outside lavatory still fresh in her mind. Phyllis took Peg up to the front bedroom, to get her first glimpse of the now quiet Maureen.

*

Arthur had two days at home before he was to report to the army base in Catterick. He did his best to make Phyllis feel at home before he left. He put a handful of English coins on the kitchen table and went through them one by one with Phyllis, until she understood her pounds, shillings and pence. They caught the bus into town to practice buying groceries, then pushed Maureen around in her pram in Castle Park, whilst the April rain soaked their clothes. Phyllis loved the dinner-plate-sized lily pads floating on the still water. She felt confident that it wouldn't be long before Arthur would find them some nice cosy rooms they could call their own. At least he wasn't going too far away, just a few hours on a train. Nothing seemed very far away in England to Phyllis, you could get almost anywhere in only a few hours. India felt vast in comparison, it took a couple of days just to get from Benares to Nainital by train, a trip she had done at least twice a year and often alone.

Phyllis wondered how the sale of Barnes' and all its furniture was going. Muriel had announced her engagement to Austin shortly before Phyllis departed for England. Muriel had always been jealous of her younger sister finding a husband first. Once, she suspected the courting couple were up to no good when she caught them on the sofa together, Phyllis with her skirt up around her waist with Arthur's hand disappearing into the folds of silk fabric. She'd called her embarrassed sister a trollop and Arthur a cad. Muriel didn't tell on her but had threatened to many times. Arthur had found his future sister-in-law to be cold and unfriendly after that, always making a point of not giving them any time on their own alone. The date for Muriel and Austin's wedding hadn't yet been decided, but it would certainly be before the end of the year. It wasn't possible to run the restaurant any longer with Phyllis gone and Muriel probably moving away. Wilmot made the decision to close it before the new summer season, leaving him with the task of wrapping up the business, sorting out the accounts and selling it for the best price he could get.

*

Arthur had his long khaki kitbag stuffed with a set of civvies and a few treasured items slung over his shoulder. He promised to write at least twice a week and Phyllis said the same. They held onto each other as they waited for his bus.

"Arthur, I'm frightened. Promise me you'll be back for the birth?" She pleaded, stroking her belly.

"There's nothing to be scared of, the old lady and Peg will help you. I'll get my leave booked as soon as I can, you'll be fine, you always are," said Arthur reassuringly.

Her throat tightened as the bus came into view, this was it, this was goodbye. Tears welled up in her eyes as she let go of his warm, strong body.

She could just see his head of dark brown hair through the bus window as the rain streaked down the fogged up panes, smudging her view of him. She reached into the sleeve of her coat for her hankie. As she looked up again, the bus turned the corner and disappeared down the hill. Her legs felt light, as if they would give way underneath the weight of her pregnant body. She held onto a nearby wall to steady herself and swallowed hard, trying to blink back the flood of tears.

"Now then my little turtledove," said Elizabeth. "Let's have a nice cup of tea before we get on with the chores, that'll keep your mind from dwelling."

Phyllis sat watching her mother-in-law struggle to open the tea caddy, its lid jammed tightly shut.

"Let me help you with that Elizabeth."

"You can call me Mums now, once we've had our tea you can get your pinny on and help prepare supper."

"What's a pinny?"

"Dear lord, I've got a lot to teach you," said Elizabeth, as she tossed her a small yellow apron.

Phyllis looked up at the kitchen clock; supper wasn't for another seven hours. She felt lost, she didn't know what to do, how to be, how to prepare vegetables or how to live in this house that was so very different to everything she had ever known. She disliked its poky little rooms and long dark hallway that connected them all. The cold, the damp kind of cold, that clung to the heavy clothes she now wore. When she first arrived she'd looked over at the cream, ceramic range, a fire was lit in the hearth to the right, and two mysterious doors were to the left. Phyllis hadn't known what these doors were for, she'd thought they were little cupboards, perhaps to store plates, so she had been surprised to see Elizabeth put on a padded glove and take out a golden brown loaf, like Phyllis's smooth pregnant belly, taught and round. The yeasty smell had filled the kitchen and Phyllis had laughed to herself, realising it was an oven. The cookhouse in India was a small building in the compound with a fire pit at one end, near an unglazed window. The walls were black with smoke from years of cooking.

"I've got a little present from India for you, Mums," piped up Phyllis, glad of an excuse to leave the kitchen. She fetched the crumpled parcel from her room and gave it to her. Elizabeth unwrapped the creased Indian newspaper wrapping and expressed her gratitude as best she could. Whatever was she going to do with a pair of ugly candlesticks she had no idea. She put them on the mantelpiece, in pride of place so as not to offend Phyllis. She'd move them into the glass-fronted cabinet later; she couldn't be doing with another trinket to dust. As for the cardamom pods that Arthur had given her, what on earth was she to do with those? She'd never tasted curry but knew she didn't like it. She'd tucked them behind the biscuit tin in the pantry, not hidden exactly but out of sight. She didn't want Phyllis getting any bright ideas about filling the house with the aroma of curry. She'd heard the smell could cling onto curtains for weeks.

Phyllis stood with her hands in a sink of tepid water, wondering how to prepare the strange muddy vegetables that lay gnarled on the wooden draining board. She recognised some of them, muddy potatoes and carrots, but she'd never seen knobbly turnip and swede before. She felt silly as she asked Elizabeth what to do with them. Phyllis wondered what Kitty would say if she could see her now, and inwardly giggled. Elizabeth looked up to the heavens when Phyllis chopped off a bit too much of the potato skin. This girl, pretty as she was, had a thing or two to learn about housekeeping.

Peg came home after her shift and taught Phyllis how to set the fire in the back room. She used the discarded newspapers that were stacked up by the back door. Peg licked her fingers then rolled the paper tightly into slim tubes. Coal was then fetched in a scuttle from the coalbunker in the back yard. The parlour fire was lit every Sunday and the back room was lit everyday at 6.30am from October to April. They were the only heat source in the house and on wet days the clothes were dried in the back room on a big wooden clothes maid that hung heavily from the ceiling. It was quite a job winching it up when the washing was wet, even though it had been through the mangle.

After two weeks Phyllis was exhausted. It was washday, she had done all the household laundry, not just her own but Elizabeth's and Peg's too, including their under garments. Phyllis had been shown how to use the big bristle brush and a slab of carbolic soap that smelt like shoe polish. She sat in the damp back room, on the hard dining chair, that gave no comfort to her throbbing back and sobbed into her sore hands. Itchy chilblains rose up on her slender fingers, as if she'd been stung by an army of red ants. Strands of ebony hair stuck to her steamed-up face. Her knuckles on both hands were red, cracked and bleeding.

Peg tapped her gently on the shoulder, holding crying Maureen in her arms.

"I think someone is teething."

Phyllis sat up and rubbed her aching back. "Oh Peg, I mean Margaret, I must have dozed off."

"Aye, I can see you're finding it a bit tough. How about

on my next day off we take a trip over to Clacton on the train? It's by the sea."

Phyllis appreciated Peg's invitation and gladly accepted. She still found it hard to call her Margaret, but did her best to remember.

Arthur's letters arrived every Monday and Friday with sketchy news of new pals, camp exercises and various mess parties he'd attended. Phyllis wrote of her life with his mother and sister and how she found the housework exhausting. She tried to conceal her true feelings from Arthur so as not to worry him, but confessed that she hadn't realised how hard it would be living without servants. 'The chores seem never ending' she wrote after a long day of laundry and Maureen's teething cries.

One afternoon, when Elizabeth was out shopping and Peg was delivering a baby, Phyllis poked her head around the parlour door and looked longingly at the closed piano. It looked like it had been shut for years, the dust settled around the velvet-rimmed lid. She timidly opened the lid as if it might turn round and bite her. She rested her bare feet gently on the cold brass pedals, which felt exhilarating on the balls of her feet as if she had just stolen a car and was about to drive it away. Phyllis dropped her shoulders, pulled her chin up and started playing gently and quietly, listening out for Elizabeth's arrival at the kitchen door. She got lost in the music and went onto a rousing rendition of Tommy Dorsey's, 'All I remember is you'. By the time she replaced the lid she felt alive. Her face was flushed and her fingers tingled.

"Chee, that's better," she shouted out loud.

She placed the lid down and turned on the wireless to drown out the dull rhythmic tick-tocking of the clock that stood in the hallway. Its dull brass pendulum swaying from side to side, like a wagging finger telling her off.

Elizabeth arrived at the back door and placed the groceries on the table with a loud thud.

"Fill me up a bath, there's a good girl," said Elizabeth slightly short of breath. "I shouldn't be carrying all that shopping with my rheumatism, my knees are killing me."

Phyllis filled up the tin tub from the copper boiler. She could see the laundry billowing outside on the line through the window and suppressed the urge to laugh as her homemade silk knickers flapped happily alongside Elizabeth's enormous bloomers and ugly dress. Phyllis could no longer do the button up on her skirts. She'd reluctantly delved into the almyra and taken out one of Elizabeth's dowdy old dresses. She'd scrubbed and scrubbed it, but the sharp smell of mothballs still clung to the itchy fibres. As she went out to the backyard to check if they were dry, Mrs Brown, the neighbour, gave Phyllis a dismissive nod through the wooden trellis. Phyllis smiled politely as she sniffed at the dress, hoping the smell had left it. She went back into the kitchen to be greeted by the sound of sploshing and the smell of soap coming from the dining room. The wireless had been silenced.

7

THE 10.35 TO CLACTON

In the carriage sat Elizabeth, a wicker hamper at her feet, containing a lunch of tinned ham sandwiches, homemade scones and a clutch of hard-boiled eggs wrapped in a tea towel. Next to her sat Peg, with an overloaded bag, containing a picnic blanket, towel and a flask of tea, peeping through its string-vest-like holes. Phyllis sat beside the window with Maureen on her lap and her topee on her head.

Elizabeth had questioned her choice of headgear on leaving the house.

"Haven't you got a more conventional sunhat, something made of straw perhaps?" Elizabeth had looked in despair at her daughter-in-law on the front step in the ridiculous cork hat.

"This is all I have other than my Chatta."

"What and where is your Chatta?"

"It's an umbrella and it's at the bottom of my trunk with my tennis racket."

"Never mind, we better get a move on or we'll miss the train," concluded Elizabeth, before checking that the front door was locked behind them.

The spitting June rain streaked the train's window with wet droplets. Through the vibrating rivulets, Phyllis could see the estuary at Hythe, then Wivenhoe, its pastel pink and blue merchant houses lining the quayside. The muddy estuary, its tide now low, opened out onto flat marshland. A heron, alarmed by the sudden appearance of the train, dashed out from the long grasses, making Phyllis gasp with delight.

"Phyllis, have you seen these before?" asked Peg.

Phyllis looked over to where Peg was pointing. A huge windmill, its large white triangular sails full of wind, rotated its strong wooden arms. Phyllis had never seen anything like it and thought what a wonderful subject for a painting it would make. She took out her pencil and wrote down the next station name on her watercolour pad: Thorpe Le Soken.

"What are you writing?" asked Elizabeth.

"I thought I'd ask my friend Kitty if she'd like to come and stay before the baby comes. We could get the train and spend the day painting the sailhouse."

"It's called a windmill and I don't think you'll be doing

that dearie, the baby is due soon, you can't just go gadding about the countryside in your condition, you must think of the baby now," retorted Elizabeth, "besides, we have no spare room in the house."

Phyllis thought back to Dover House, the doors of which were always flung open to family, friends and friends of friends. A spare bedroll would be unfurled, a charpoy dragged round from the storeroom, a plate of delicious food prepared. No one was ever turned away. It was just the way it was, friends would travel for days at a time to see you, and they stayed as long as they wanted. Phyllis gazed out of the window feeling gloomy as Constable's landscape sped by: coppiced willows, stubby growth sprouting from their gnarled branches, vast white clouds drifted up in the pale blue sky, small farm buildings with heavy thatched roofs and hay stacks heaped into large domes. Her spirits slowly lifted as she lost herself to the picture-book world outside the carriage.

Phyllis looked down at the basket lying at Elizabeth's feet and felt sad that Arthur wasn't with them. They'd had such exciting picnics when they were courting; hacking up the valley on rented horses from the stables in Barapatthar to Khurpatal, its pretty terraced hillsides stepping down to an emerald green lake. She remembered the valley's waterfall roaring loudly, sending a cooling mist into the crisp mountain air. With the smell of the horses sweat clinging to their jodhpurs, they would spread out a rug under the shade of a tree and flirt outrageously, feeding each other titbits of food from their tiffin tins. Phyllis's heart would quicken and her cheeks flush as Arthur's leg brushed against her own. The clack-clacking call of the black-faced monkeys rudely interrupting them, as they jumped from the lower branches of the trees to snatch whatever they could. Arthur would leap to his feet and shoo them crossly away. Phyllis would laugh at her dear Arthur and those ghastly monkeys, who, given half a chance, would steal everything you owned. Then it would be time to go home and face the cross-examination from Muriel.

"Yes," Phyllis would say. "Of course there were other people with us, don't be ridiculous, no, we didn't go alone. Crikey, anyone would think you were my mother!"

"Clacton on Sea, Clacton on Sea," shouted the ticket inspector as the train jolted to a halt.

Phyllis longed to feel the sand between her toes and the sea on her bare feet. Once away from the sootiness of the station, the seaside's seaweedy smell filled her lungs.

"Ah, sea air at last," laughed Elizabeth. The years seemed to fall from her lined face. For a split second Phyllis caught a glimpse of the carefree young woman Elizabeth had once been. They walked along Marine Parade past the tourist shops, arcades and ice cream kiosks before passing the pavilion where the brass band was tuning up.

The dark shadows from the fast moving clouds raced along the golden sand. Elizabeth sought out a nice spot on the beach, not too far from the public conveniences but not too crowded either. They rented three deckchairs and placed Maureen down on the picnic blanket. Phyllis couldn't wait to take her shoes and stockings off and get Maureen into the sea for a paddle.

"Can't you be a little more discreet?" asked Peg.

Phyllis was balanced on one leg, whilst hitching her dress up over her knees to pull her stockings off. She didn't give a hoot as she marvelled at the silky dry sand spilling in-between her toes. She dodged the little banks of pebbles that gathered in glistening clusters as she walked down the beach to the water's edge. It was grittier than she had expected and cold as her bare feet met the wet sand. She looked across towards the blue-grey horizon and wondered which way India was. She felt as though she was standing on the edge of the world!

"Lunch is ready!" called Peg.

"What have you done with your hat?" asked Elizabeth.

Elizabeth had insisted that Phyllis wear it since she'd brought it; her complexion was quite dark enough.

"I just wanted to feel the wind in my hair," laughed Phyllis, like a child.

"You don't want to get any darker dear, they may think you are one of them," said Elizabeth.

"One of who?"

"An Indian."

"What's wrong with being Indian?"

"Marrying a native, a foreigner. Well, it's just not the done thing, in our country."

"That's ridiculous, your country is our mother country."

Elizabeth sat open mouthed, shocked at Phyllis's retort. A long silence fell between them.

Phyllis was relieved when Elizabeth dozed in the deckchair. The breeze flicked at her thinning hair, which tickled her nose. She batted it away every so often, as if it were a fly. Phyllis picked up her flesh coloured stockings from the flesh coloured sand and tried to shake out the worst of the damp grit. It was even more of an ordeal trying to get her stockings back on, with sand stuck between her toes. Peg held the towel around Phyllis's waist, as Phyllis tried to hoist up the stockings underneath the mothball dress. She lost her balance and her solar topee toppled off her head as she got a fit of the giggles.

Peg finally lost her patience, "for God's sake stand still, people are starting to stare."

Elizabeth's friend had recommended afternoon tea at the Glengariff Hotel. She felt compelled to follow her advice so she could report back on their return. They sat in the garden overlooking the croquet lawn. Phyllis loved the 'thwack' sound, when the wood of the mallet met the wood of the ball. It reminded her of her honeymoon in

Shimla, when she and Arthur played on the lawn after dinner. They had set off to the Cecil Hotel, the day after their wedding in Benares. The wedding party had been held in the bungalow's garden. Her brothers Cyril, Ernest and Maurice had spent the morning carrying rugs outside and laying them on the doob, according to Maude's instructions. A canaut had been strung up to make a shady enclosure. Lloyd Loom chairs and tables were placed according to Maude's roughly drawn plan. The servants laid the tables with the best silver; vases of cream roses stood prettily in the centre of each. The silver cake stand housed one of Phyllis's creations; a beautifully tiered cake covered in cascading iced flowers.

Arthur and Phyllis had arrived through the vast galleried atrium of the Cecil Hotel and sat holding hands on one of the plump sofas. The open fire crackled and spat in the huge fireplace whilst Phyllis admired the grand room with its fine paintings. Phyllis had never felt so complete in her life with her husband sitting beside her, handsome and confident in his dress uniform. Phyllis wore her pale cream silk wedding dress, the delicate silver shoes with a diamante buckle and latticed sides made her feel taller than her height of 5'3". She'd thrown her bouquet of white roses to Muriel, who was worried about being a spin forever.

"Mr and Mrs Woollett, if you'd like to come this way, it would be my pleasure to escort you to your honeymoon suite," the concierge said.

It would take some time to get used to being Mrs Woollett and not Miss Dover. Now they could make love with abandon, no more sneaking about on picnics or snatching ten minutes alone in the restaurant. No more worries about falling pregnant, without a gold band on her finger.

Clacton's pier struck out into the dark sea on the postcard Phyllis had chosen for Arthur. She wrote about their day trip, the sand in her toes, and Maureen's delight at being in the water, the picnic and the sound of croquet that had brought back thoughts of Shimla. She thought it best not to mention his mother's nasty comments and Peg's snappy mood. Phyllis stroked her belly, as she felt a little kick inside her and wondered if Arthur would get leave when the baby arrived.

"Right my dears, I think its time we got a move on, our train goes in half an hour," said Elizabeth, looking more relaxed than Phyllis had ever seen her.

They gathered their things and trudged up through town to the busy station. Phyllis loved the formal gardens that framed the promenade. The Box edging had symmetrical rows of bright orange marigolds with white geranium borders. Delicate blue and white forget-me-nots filled in the gaps, as pretty as a pair of chintz curtains. Phyllis had never seen forget-me-nots before and when Peg told her the name of them, she just had to pick a bunch.

"You can't pick what you want willy nilly," said Elizabeth, embarrassed by her daughter-in-law's behaviour.

"It's only a few flowers. I'm sure nobody will mind."

She thought Arthur might like them too, so she picked a few more when Elizabeth's back was turned.

8

FIREFLIES AND SHOOTING STARS

Phyllis was excused of the heavier household chores due to her increasing size, but was given more of the cooking to do. She tired of the bland food: Irish stew and dumplings; pork chops with cabbage and peas; sausages and mashed potato. Her taste buds craved flavour. She dreamed of chapattis and dhal with lime pickle.

One Thursday afternoon, Elizabeth left Phyllis instructions on how to prepare poached haddock with boiled potatoes and carrots for their supper. Phyllis didn't enjoy cooking, but loved the freedom of having the house to herself. She watched from behind the lace curtains as Elizabeth walked down the pavement towards the bus stop. Once out of sight, Phyllis skipped down the hallway and turned the wireless on. She stood at the draining board, removing the bones from the pale fish and thought about a dish they used to have for breakfast. She went up to her trunk and found Maude's book of recipes. Within its handwritten pages she found what she was looking for, Kedgeree. She rummaged around for her teak spice box she'd bought from the boxwallah the day before she'd departed for England. She put her nose up to it and inhaled deeply. It smelt of everything she adored: cinnamon, cloves, paprika, cumin, turmeric and the sweet aroma of cardamom. She pulled out a yellow stained muslin bag of turmeric before wrapping the box back up in its newspaper. A search at the back of the pantry was rewarded with a small bag of rice. She then boiled two eggs. The large pan of yellow rice was filling the house with smells she knew, comforting and homely.

When Elizabeth arrived home her face hung like a bloodhound's. "What have you done to a perfectly good piece of fish?"

"It's Kedgeree, Mums. I thought you might like a change."

"Whatever gave you that impression?" snapped Elizabeth.

Elizabeth couldn't bring herself to say so, but it actually tasted quite nice, she pushed the yellow rice about the plate and chewed slowly, her mouth slightly open, feigning distaste. She left a little pile of grains at the end of the meal just to demonstrate her dislike of it.

The front bedroom was unbearably hot that night. Phyllis had forgotten to close the curtains and the bright July sunshine had streamed in all day. Even with the sash windows wide open it was airless. Phyllis threw off the covers as she lay on her bed thinking about her siblings. When it got too hot in Benares they would drag their charpoys out onto the veranda and watch for shooting stars through the mosquito nets.

"There, there's one!" one of them would shriek, as a fast-moving effervescent trail streaked across the sky like a splash of white paint flicked onto an artist's dark canvas.

A distant conversation, the waft of a cheroot and gentle music from the gramophone would drift out from the sitting room as Maude and Wilmot played bridge with friends. The occasional thud would make the children jump then giggle as they realised it was only a ripe mango falling from the tree. A warm breeze would rustle the neem tree leaves like an audience clapping its hands. Phyllis's happiest memories were to dance with fireflies. They would magically light up and blink in the dark garden, like little flashing fairy lights. Phyllis and Muriel would prance around the lawn to the sound of the gramophone, pretending to be at a Maharajah's ball. They would poke flowers into each other's hair; the boys would catch the insects and put them in jam jars, then hang them around the veranda to make lanterns. Crickets would chorus noisily as the smell of jasmine scented the humid air.

Phyllis suddenly had a brilliant idea. She dragged her blanket and eiderdown along the landing and down the stairs, being careful not too make too much noise outside Elizabeth's bedroom door. She then crept into the back yard before fetching Maureen and a couple of pillows.

"There we are my little poppet, just like the good old

days," cooed Phyllis to Maureen, settling her down next to her. They lay side by side and Phyllis instinctively smiled up to the star-filled sky. She liked to imagine Wilmot and Maude looking up at the same galaxies, it made her feel closer to them.

"What in the blazes do you think you are up to young lady?" rasped Elizabeth in a squeaky whisper.

Phyllis looked towards the back of the house and saw Elizabeth, her loose grey hair lit up by the moon, as she leant out of the bedroom window in her nightgown, her heavy bosoms resting on the windowsill.

"Get in here at once, anyone would think you crawled out of the gutter."

Phyllis stifled a laugh under the blanket and pretended to be asleep.

"Only dogs and tramps sleep outside in this country," Elizabeth had argued at breakfast the following morning.

"Well, I'm sorry," replied Phyllis. "But where I come from everyone sleeps outside when it's hot, even the Maharajah of Bhinga."

Elizabeth was not amused and huffed and puffed all morning. She banged about loudly as she cleaned out the pantry; washing out a few, almost empty jars of jam that had acquired a hairy layer of mould. Still the jars wouldn't go to waste, she washed them in the sink and left them to drain.

Phyllis received a letter from Arthur after breakfast saying he was to get a few days leave in August, hopefully to coincide with the birth of the baby. Phyllis had a little spring in her step. Elizabeth couldn't blight her day now.

Unless they had to be in the same room, Elizabeth and Phyllis started to avoid each other. Phyllis was always polite and tried to be helpful but Elizabeth's impatience of Phyllis grew daily. Phyllis could see it in the disapproving glances Elizabeth would fire at her. Elizabeth secretly wished Arthur had married Elsie. She was English and understood how things were here. She was straightforward, not eccentric and semi-native. Elsie would have made a good wife, kept a clean house and she knew how to cook a good steak and ale pie.

Elizabeth concentrated on stocking up on foodstuffs just in case Hitler invaded. It took her mind off the difficulties with Phyllis. She got to work pickling eggs, making crab apple jelly, mint jelly, fruit jams and lemon curd. The bubbling sticky sweet liquids hogged the stove, fruit peelings spilt out over the top of the waste bucket that got fed to her friend's chickens. As the pantry filled up with a rainbow of coloured jars, Elizabeth congratulated herself on planning ahead. Phyllis tried to call a truce by making her a Christmas cake but however hard she tried it was never quite good enough for Elizabeth. Phyllis decided to keep the peace and do as she was told, to a point. She kept herself busy with Maureen and wrote letters home to her parents telling them about her new life in England. As usual she left out the less pleasant parts about Elizabeth being a difficult woman to live with. Before sealing the letter she remembered the forget-me-nots that she'd pressed in her watercolour pad and popped them in the envelope, telling her mother about the lovely name and where she'd picked them.

*

It was ten o'clock when Phyllis woke up. She practically fell out of bed, knocking the clock off the bedside table as she did so. It was the day Arthur was due home on leave. She had overslept, no one had woken her and Maureen was gone. She shouted down the landing, "Mums, have you got Maureen?"

She rushed down the stairs to find a note on the kitchen table: 'Didn't want to disturb you, have taken Maureen to meet the train'.

Arthur's train was due to arrive into Colchester in twenty minutes' time. Phyllis was supposed to have had her hair done this morning; to look nice for him, he always liked it when she looked her best. Phyllis dashed back to her bedroom and threw on the mothball dress. She brushed her teeth and dragged a comb through her hair then picked up an apple from the fruit bowl. She slammed the door behind her and waddled as fast as she could to get the bus, it was six stops to Colchester station and would take at least fifteen minutes.

As she reached the steamy railway platform, she could see Arthur in the distance, he held Maureen in one arm, his other linked through Elizabeth's. Phyllis bit her lip and took a deep breath.

"Arthur!" she called, her voice faltering and strained, her throat was tight.

Arthur looked up and saw her; unkempt and dishevelled in the enormous mothball dress. No stockings on her bare legs. He placed Maureen in Peg's arms and sprinted to Phyllis.

He nuzzled his cold nose into her cheek, "Oh Phyllis, my beautiful darling girl I have missed you so much," then added, "Christ, what's that awful smell?"

"It's your mother's ghastly dress," Phyllis whispered, half laughing, half crying. "I can't get the stench of mothballs out of it."

Elizabeth folded her arms across her chest. "Just look at her, she can't even get herself out of bed in the morning, and what a fright she looks too."

Peg drove them back to the house. Arthur and Phyllis sat squashed in the back with Maureen on Arthur's lap. Maureen reached for his moustache and said, "Dadda."

He was thrilled and sang to her all the way home.

"We've had one of those leaflets through the door telling us to get blackout curtains put up over the windows and tape on the glass," sighed Elizabeth over her shoulder to Arthur. "It doesn't seem possible that we might be under attack soon," she added looking up at the beautiful clear sky.

"I hear it's looking more likely than ever. I suggest you get a move on and get organised," replied Arthur.

"Mums has a list as long as her arm of things she wants you to help with," said Peg.

Elizabeth planned to keep Arthur busy now he was home for a few days. She was keen to get chickens in the back yard. If they had their own supply of eggs they wouldn't go hungry.

"After you've built a chicken coop, I'd like you to dig up the flowerbed in the front garden and turn it into a vegetable patch. I've got just enough time to get some spinach, chard, kale and even late potatoes in. Then next spring I can plant beans, tomatoes and maybe a bit of beetroot." Elizabeth dominated the conversation with her plans until they reached Maldon Road, but Phyllis didn't mind, she was just glad to have Arthur's leg rubbing against hers.

Phyllis sat on the back step and watched Arthur work. His strong arms hammering and sawing as he built a chicken run from some scrap wood. She filled Arthur in on all the news from India. Wilmot's sciatica was giving him pain. Barnes' had now been sold, along with all the furniture and crockery.

"Muriel's wedding is causing mother a lot of stress. She

wanted too many guests and a very expensive dress. I think she's planning on inviting the whole of Benares," said Phyllis.

"I pity that poor sod, Austin," said Arthur, laughing.

Phyllis went on to tell him about Kitty's letters, how she was still living in Hampstead with her parents. Eddie had settled at school and she was working in the Richmond theatre to make ends meet.

"I think you're losing your chee chee accent and taking on an Irish twang," teased Arthur.

He put his hammer down and sat next to her.

Phyllis was desperate to tell him how lonely and unhappy she felt. How his mother seemed to find fault in everything she did. But what good would it do? He wouldn't be able to change anything. She didn't want to speak badly of his mother and hurt his feelings.

"Remember when Maureen was born," he said, looking into her eyes and holding her hands. "I was the happiest man in the world." Arthur dropped his gaze and sat staring into his lap. "I miss you sweetheart, and Maureen. I feel like she's growing up so fast, but at least she still knows who I am. When I get back to Catterick I'm going to spend some time looking for a place for you to live, so at least when I get a pass out I can be with you, even if it's just for one night." Arthur placed her small hand in his and gently stroked her fingers. "I know you find it difficult here, but they mean well you know, they just find it hard to adapt to having a new person in the house."

Phyllis felt relieved that Arthur could see her plight, "I'm so glad you understand Arthur. I miss you so much. I miss India. I miss so many things. When this war is over, if it ever comes, we are going back to India aren't we? Maybe Madras, you could apply for the police force again."

"Yes of course we're going back to India. I don't want us to live in England for the rest of our lives, when we could live in India and be treated like Kings. I promise you we shall have servants, a dhobi and a driver, and you won't have to lift a finger," Arthur took her dry, blistered hands in his. "No more housework for these poor, sweet hands of yours," he added, kissing them gently, "I'm sorry."

"What for?"

"For dragging you half way around the world so you can scrub floors on your hands and knees and get bossed about by the old lady."

Phyllis smiled and dried her eyes. "Oh dear Arthur, I do love you. Please don't say anything to her, it will only make it worse once you've gone."

"Talking's not getting the chicken house finished is it?" bellowed Elizabeth from the kitchen window.

Arthur turned his back on his mother and rolled his eyes to the heavens and got back to work, happily chatting in the warm sunshine to Phyllis about his time in Catterick and the specialist communications course he had been on. Some of the chaps he had been stationed with in Meerut had turned up which jollied things along a bit. There was always some function to attend, most of them interminably boring, the odd dance and of course lots of whist drives. Arthur earned most of his drinking and smoking money by winning cash prizes at them. He still hadn't kicked the habit and lit up a Woodbine when he finished fixing the wire onto the cage.

The back gate swung open. "Alright guvner? Where do you want it, in the bunker as usual?" The coalman had on a dirty black apron and hands to match. A bulging, black sack was slung over his left shoulder like a dead body.

"Aye, just tip the whole lot in," instructed Arthur.

Arthur was pleased his mother was getting stocked up on fuel, winter was just a few months away and God only knew what lay ahead. There was talk of rationing if the war started. Elizabeth had lived through it all before in the Great War and knew what to expect. She had been 39 and married to Frederick, he had been a vicar in Stepney at the time. Until 1917 food had been imported from America and Canada but the Germans began submarine warfare on merchant ships and many were sunk. Food prices soared out of reach for all but the richer members of the British population, so rationing had been introduced. Coal was also rationed, depending on the number of rooms in the house. Elizabeth had collected firewood to make the coal go further; taking the pram out with no baby and coming home with an assortment of logs and twigs from the local woods. It had been a grim four years and had left the British feeling vulnerable.

Phyllis had spent a couple of days before Arthur's visit sewing large swathes of heavy black fabric into curtains to fit all seven windows of the house. She had sat at the dining table in the dim back room leaning over her little Wilcox and Gibbs sewing machine until her arms and back throbbed.

"Let's get these wretched curtains up," said Arthur.

He balanced on a dining chair in his mother's bedroom as Phyllis passed him the heavy fabric. Peg busied herself putting tape on the windows. Elizabeth looked after Maureen in the kitchen whilst cooking tea. "I'll make your favourite, Arthur," she shouted up the stairs, "a nice bit of pork with mash and some apple sauce."

Arthur smiled. "You are wonderful, thank you."

He saw Phyllis out of the corner of his eye, "Whatever is the matter old girl, pork and mash isn't so bad is it?"

Phyllis suddenly screamed out in agony as she crumpled to the floor clutching her stomach, her face as white as translucent marble.

"Oh my God," cried Arthur. "Peg quick, help me, it's Phyllis, she's not well."

Peg came rushing into the bedroom. They lifted her onto

Elizabeth's bed. Peg placed her fingers on Phyllis's wrist and checked her pulse. Phyllis clutched at her stomach.

"I think the baby's coming," cried Phyllis, cramping up in pain.

Peg ordered Arthur out of the room. "Go and get my nurse's bag from the car and boil the kettle, grab some towels and get Mums to make some hot sweet tea. Knock before you come back in."

Arthur dashed off to the kitchen, and thanked heaven Peg was a midwife.

"Now then," said Peg in her commanding nurse's voice. "I need you to be brave for me Phyllis."

Phyllis nodded as she gasped for breath, a terrified look on her face. "Is the baby coming?" she gripped tightly onto Peg's arm in panic.

Peg held Phyllis's hand and explained that she needed to examine her. Phyllis shut her eyes and pretended to be someone else, somewhere else, a trick Maude had taught her as a child when she had to visit the tooth doctor and have treatment without an anaesthetic.

"Well done, you're doing really well, everything looks in order," said Peg as she delved between Phyllis's legs. "Your waters have broken. I think if the baby doesn't come in the next couple of hours we'll need to get you into hospital."

Phyllis was frightened; she had never been in an ordinary hospital before. Maureen had been born in the military hospital in Fort William, Calcutta; it had all been very straightforward. Arthur had been at her side throughout the labour but was told to wait outside for the actual birth by a very strict military doctor.

Arthur knocked gently on the door, carrying tea and a kettle of boiled water. Elizabeth trailed behind him, her arms piled with towels and the nurse's bag.

"Is it okay to come in?" he asked anxiously, half expecting to see a bloody, howling baby.

"Come in and bring Phyllis some sweet tea," said Peg.

Peg beckoned Arthur out of the room. "Her waters have broken and the baby seems fine but she isn't dilated and I think we may need to get her to hospital in a while. I can drive you there. There's no reason to panic but she mustn't get an infection."

*

Phyllis lay helpless and scared in the hospital bed. The pain had eased but she'd been instructed to lie down and move as little as possible.

Arthur was allowed to visit; he kissed her on the forehead.

"Whatever is the matter? You look terribly worried. Is it the baby? Is something wrong?" asked Phyllis anxiously.

Arthur sat down on the chair next to the bed.

"No darling it's not the baby. The doctor reassured me that everything would be fine, as long as you take it easy. I have to return to Catterick."

"When?"

"Tonight. I had a telegram earlier saying all leave has been cancelled. Mums will be in to see you later and you don't need to worry about Maureen, she's being well looked after."

"I wished for a boy Arthur, when I threw the coin in the water, a boy who looks just like you," said Phyllis smiling weakly. "Arthur, I can't do this without you."

"You are the strongest person I know Phyllis Woollett. Everything will be all right. I promise."

"Are we going to war? Is this the start?"

"All I've been told is to report to my unit before midnight. I'll write to you when I get back to Catterick. I love you Phyl." He kissed her then turned away from her before she could see his chin tremble and the tears spill from his eyes as he walked as calmly as he could towards the pale green swing door of the ward. Damn the bloody army, he couldn't even stay to be with his wife and see his new baby. His footsteps echoed down the long corridor until he left through the main hospital doors and out into the dazzlingly bright August afternoon. He sat on the hospital steps and lit a cigarette. Shielding his eyes from the sun he looked down the busy street. Rumour of rationing was spreading and people were beginning to stockpile. Arthur took a final long pull on his cigarette and stubbed it out on the step before walking briskly into the town centre. He bought a torch from the hardware shop; it was the last on the shelf. All the batteries had sold out; he hoped Elizabeth had a few put by.

9

EILEEN VALERIE WOOLLETT

"Another girl," grinned Peg.

Phyllis cradled little Eileen in her arms and introduced her to Maureen. "This is your new baby sister, what do you think, beautiful isn't she?"

Maureen screwed up her nose and poked her tongue out.

"Oh dear, sibling rivalry already," laughed Peg.

Peg took Maureen home and left Phyllis to rest. Elizabeth was pleased that all the commotion was over. It had been a worrying time, what with Phyllis in hospital, Maureen to look after and the threat of war ever present. On the wireless there was talk of little else. It could be any day now. Elizabeth sent Arthur a telegram breaking him the news that he was the father to a healthy baby girl. She also sent one to Maude and Wilmot in India.

Just after breakfast the following day, Colchester's first air raid siren sounded. The hospital had a strict drill and all the babies were taken to the shelter in the grounds. This meant separating the babies from their mothers. Phyllis didn't want Eileen to be taken, but matron insisted.

"It's only a practice siren but it must be carried out properly Mrs Woollett," she said easing Eileen, now crying, from Phyllis's arms.

"Where are you taking her?"

It was too late, matron had already bundled her into a large cot on wheels along with all the other new-borns. Working as fast as a kidnapper she had disappeared out through the door and down the corridor. All the mothers were ushered out of their beds and herded down to the hospital basement by the ward nurse. They spent the next hour sitting on the laundry sacks fretting in the dark.

"What if they give us the wrong baby back?" a young mother was asking. "How would we know?" she wailed.

Phyllis wished she could be at home with Maude, the smell of vanilla in her tied up hair and the scent of violets on her soft, warm skin.

The All Clear sounded.

"The mothers can go back now," shouted the ward sister.

She held her clipboard tightly to her chest and ticked off the name of each baby as their mothers reclaimed them. She handed each over, as a baker would distribute freshly baked bread to a queue of eager customers.

It was almost visiting hour. Phyllis was overjoyed at having Eileen back. She sat in bed looking at all the different people stroll in to visit, bringing the smell of the fresh summer afternoon with them. Grandmothers carried shopping bags containing fruit, snacks and fresh nightgowns. New fathers stood with their hands in their pockets, jingling loose change, feeling out of place.

"Phyl, Phyl, there you are, you clever girl." Kitty bounced in behind an enormous bunch of blue cornflowers.

Phyllis's heart skipped a beat. "Kitty, my dear Kitty, how did you know I was here?"

"Arthur sent me a telegram, he told me you were looking a bit lost the last time he saw you and said you could do with a bit of cheering up, so here I am." She planted a big kiss on Phyllis's cheek as she hugged her dear friend. "So this is little Eileen?" she said, picking her up out of the cot. "You are a little poppet aren't you?" Eileen gurgled happily and smiled at Kitty's bright-eyed face.

Kitty plonked herself on the bed. "Now then sweet girl, I have a bag of goodies here for you." Kitty delved into her shopping basket and pulled out a paper bag full of candy coloured macaroons and a dark green mango.

"A mango! I haven't had a mango for months, oh you dear girl, you remembered," said Phyllis, thoroughly surprised and happy that Kitty hadn't forgotten how she'd told her on the voyage it was one of the things she would miss about India.

"I just hope it's survived the journey," replied Kitty, laughing, knowing how much it had pleased Phyllis. "How about we give it a go?" Kitty produced a sharp knife and a tea towel from the bottom of her basket.

"Matron won't approve," said Phyllis laughing.

"Let's draw the curtains around the bed," said Kitty.

Giggling uncontrollably they chopped the delicious fruit into chunks and stuffed it into their mouths, the sticky yellow juice dripped down their chins.

"Phyllis, are you alright?" boomed Elizabeth.

"Oh chee, it's my mother-in-law," mouthed Phyllis silently to Kitty.

"I'm fine Mums, just give me a moment," she said stifling her laugh with her hand over her mouth.

Phyllis and Kitty busily tidied all the evidence away by hiding it under the blanket, just as Elizabeth popped her head around the thin blue curtain.

"Good to see someone's got colour back in their cheeks."

She was always much kinder in other people's company. Phyllis was disappointed to see that Elizabeth hadn't brought Maureen with her.

"She was quite settled with Peg. I didn't want to cause unnecessary upset, so I left her at home."

Elizabeth didn't stay long. She was on her way to church.

"She looks frightening," said Kitty after Elizabeth left.

Phyllis told Kitty about living under the confines of her mother-in-law's roof. Kitty's mouth dropped in horror, as she pictured Phyllis sneakily playing the piano, slipping spices into casseroles as they boiled away on the stove and dragging her bedding outside.

"Why do you put up with it?" asked Kitty. "I'm not sure I would be quite so nice."

"I don't have much choice. Arthur doesn't know the half of it. She's always so much nicer when he's around. I can't exactly return home can I?" replied Phyllis as she stroked Eileen's downy hair.

"Do you wish you'd never come?"

"Not exactly. I wish, well this sounds silly, but I just wish Elizabeth was a bit kinder."

"Maybe she needs to get used to having you and the little ones about. I'm sure things will get better with time." said Kitty kindly.

Kitty spoke of her life in London, how strange it was to be home with her parents again having been independent for such a long time. She hadn't lived at home properly since she was about six years old after being bundled off to boarding school. Her parents had been marvellous though and her father had helped her get a new job as a research assistant at the BBC. Her mother helped to look after Eddie while she was out working. Eddie missed India, as it was all he had known, but had settled down well and liked school.

The dreaded clang of the ward bell rang out, sending visitors to gather their belongings as if a train they had been waiting for had just pulled into the station.

"Kitty, I wish you didn't have to go, it was so good to see you again. Keep writing won't you? And when I'm fit and strong again, I'll come to London and see you."

"Yes, let's meet up and paint or go to the theatre or something wonderful," replied Kitty. "You must meet the family, bring Maureen and Eileen too. Let's hope we're not all bombed to smithereens in the meantime."

*

Phyllis left Colchester maternity hospital on 1st September. She was astounded at how much things had changed in such a short space of time. Heavy sandbags were stacked in doorways. A lorry full of grit tipped its load onto the edge of the road as a row of men stood waiting to shovel it into hessian sacks. The Town Hall had its windows boarded up and some of the cafes and shops had their iron grilles pulled down. Colchester High Street looked like a town under siege. A crocodile of schoolchildren slid their way along the High Street from the railway station to waiting buses.

"Evacuees," piped up Peg. "They say thousands will pass through here from London. We are apparently vulnerable to air attacks due to the engineering factories and the garrison, and," she said nervously, "we're on the flight path to London, of course."

Phyllis studied all the little faces; some were talcum powder white, others radish-red, flushed with excitement. Children as young as five with name labels dangling from their necks and gas masks over their shoulders held small suitcases or parcels. Phyllis looked down at Eileen in her arms and held on to her even more tightly and whispered in her ear. "I'll never let you go."

Phyllis was relieved to get home and shut herself away in the comparative comfort of her bedroom. Maureen slept happily sucking her thumb as Eileen lay in the cot. Arthur still hadn't seen seven-day-old Eileen yet.

"We just need your daddy here, then we'll be all right," Phyllis felt tearful. Every single streetlight was unlit, the blackout had begun. It was horrid being in total darkness, like being trapped alive in a coffin. Phyllis lit the candle that Elizabeth had placed by her bed for emergencies and looked at her girls, fast asleep and perfect.

The next day Elizabeth and Peg showed off their Anderson shelter. It had been installed in the back yard next to the chicken coop. Although it was only the size of a garden shed it almost filled the yard.

"Mr Brown from next door helped bolt all the panels together," said Elizabeth proudly.

Phyllis thought the strange corrugated iron shelter looked like a pigsty. The wavy metal roof looked too thin to save a family from a falling bomb. Phyllis peered inside and thought it rather grim. Elizabeth had put a piece of tarpaulin on the ground then placed the garden bench inside. An old eiderdown had been rolled up for some warmth and placed on the bench. A hurricane lamp sat on a chair. She had put some spare jumpers and blankets in a tea chest along with a battered old Bible. Phyllis hoped that they would never have to use it. It smelt as damp and earthy as the monsoon.

Peg stood at the door with the new gas masks under her arm.

"I picked these up this morning. I think we need to try them on," said Peg.

They smelt bitter, like new rubber tyres but hard with a powdery coating.

Phyllis felt claustrophobic. "Ah, that's awful, I can't wear it, it's too tight," she pulled it off her face.

"You must keep it on for at least half an hour to get used to it," insisted Peg, "that's what it says in the leaflet."

"I'll have another go later, maybe when I go to bed,"

promised Phyllis.

Eileen had a baby's version of the gas mask. It was more like a canvas plumbers' bag with a window. Phyllis didn't put Eileen in it, not wanting to frighten her, even though Peg had insisted.

Three official-looking brown envelopes arrived in the afternoon post along with a letter from Arthur.

"I'll pop the kettle on," said Elizabeth taking her envelope and slitting it open with a butter knife.

"Looks as if our identity cards have arrived," announced Elizabeth, "best fill them out now, just in case."

"What a horrid thought that we may have to be identified by this if we are killed in some ghastly bombing raid," said Peg.

Even the children had been sent their own blue versions. Phyllis felt a little shiver down the back of her spine like a drop of water running down a windowpane.

"Go on then, what does he say?" urged Peg, looking at Arthur's unopened letter in Phyllis's hand.

Phyllis summarised its contents. "He's desperately trying to get leave but was turned down until further notice. He's asked for a photograph of Eileen, and has been looking for rooms in Catterick. He's going to view somewhere later today and he sends his love to all of us." Phyllis looked out of the window towards the pigsty-shelter and smiled at her own reflection in the glass. She would be near him soon.

Peg suggested taking Phyllis to the photographer in the morning; she had a day off and would be able to drive her there. There was talk of petrol rationing but as yet it had not come into force. Phyllis was glad of the offer and wished she and Peg could be friends, but Peg was very matter of fact and functional. Phyllis found it hard to get close to her. She wasn't even allowed to call her Peg.

10

3RD SEPTEMBER 1939

Elizabeth slid the dirty dishes into the sink as Phyllis stood in her choga washing up the breakfast things. There was a friendly tap on the glass in the back door. Elizabeth looked flustered as she caught sight of the visitor through the frosted glazing. Phyllis was closest to the door and opened it with her free hand.

"Hello, is Elizabeth in?" enquired a pretty voice from underneath the floppy cream felt hat, mousy blonde curls sat astride her slender shoulders.

"Yes, of course, come in," replied Phyllis assuming it was one her mother-in-law's church friends.

"Oh hello dear, you're a little early," said Elizabeth.

"Yes, father wants me back by lunchtime to help him with the apples. The orchard floor is covered in them, so I thought I'd get the earlier bus," replied the visitor, as she glanced Phyllis up and down.

"Phyllis, this is Elsie," said Elizabeth. "Arthur's old," she hesitated, "friend."

"Pleased to meet you," said Elsie politely.

Phyllis felt her heart race, as she stood with her hands in the dirty washing up water. Globs of greasy scrambled egg floated on the surface and clung to her wet fingers.

"Oh," said Phyllis. "I wasn't expecting to, um," her voice trailed off, trying to find the right words to say to the jilted ex girlfriend. "I didn't know you were paying us a visit today. Pleased to meet you, Elsie."

Phyllis decided to look her squarely in the eyes and not be intimidated into feeling anything other than pride at being married to Arthur. She wiped her wet hands on the red and white stripy tea towel then thrust out her right hand. Elsie took the warm dark hand into her cold pale one and shook it limply. Elsie sat herself down and took off her jacket and hat. Phyllis noted how at ease she was.

"Pour Elsie a cup of tea, dear." Elizabeth said to Phyllis condescendingly.

Phyllis felt like a common bearer. She made an excuse to leave the room by saying she needed to check on the children. She felt angry with everyone; Arthur, Elizabeth and the waif-like creature who turned up out of the blue, now sat in the kitchen eating a slice of her ginger cake. Phyllis distinctly remembered Arthur describing Elsie as a bit of a country bumpkin, round shouldered, short, small eyes and a nose a bit too large for her face. The woman in the kitchen was tall, well, taller than her anyway, bright eyed, blonde with a turned-up nose which made her look slightly pinched but efficient. Phyllis decided she would go back down to the kitchen and take the children with her.

Then it dawned on Phyllis that Elsie hadn't turned up out of the blue at all. Elizabeth had arranged the visit to coincide with her appointment with the photographer, but Elsie had surprised them all, including Elizabeth, by arriving early. Phyllis felt sure she had done this on purpose to get a good look at her rival. Phyllis wondered whether this was a regular pow-wow.

Phyllis changed into her smartest silk dress. It fell elegantly from the neckline covering her belly that was still raised after giving birth only a week ago. The zip wouldn't do up at the back, so she slipped on a cardigan to cover the gaping fabric and gaily trotted back into the kitchen as if she didn't have a care in the world. She plopped Maureen and Eileen into Elsie's lap.

"This is Maureen and this little one is Eileen," said Phyllis. "I'm just going to see if Vivian can fit me in for a wash and blow dry before our appointment with the photographer."

She left the room with all the dignity she could muster and walked out of the front door holding her head high, a headscarf covering her unwashed hair. She was not going to be humiliated and certainly not by Elizabeth.

Later that morning on their way to the photographer, Phyllis quizzed Peg about Elsie and the frequency of her visits. Peg feigned ignorance on the matter and didn't want to be drawn into giving too much away. Phyllis sensed that it hadn't been the first time Elsie had been round since she'd arrived in Colchester. She felt betrayed, not just by Arthur's description of her, but also by her mother-in-law. Why had she not bothered to mention it? She decided she would confront Elizabeth later.

*

The photographer, Mr Pennington, adjusted his large camera, moving the giraffe-like legs of his tripod here and there. He fiddled with the lens until he was satisfied. There was a choice of backdrops; a Victorian parlour, a library full of books or plain white. Phyllis thought it a shame they couldn't take the pictures outside in a more natural setting. They had always had such fun getting family photographs taken in Benares. They would get the boys to drag the rugs and chairs outside to a nice sunny spot in the garden. It was an event that could last many hours and was always looked forward to. The only downside was that Maude used to make Phyllis and Muriel dress identically in some ghastly cerise velvet dresses with white collars, as if they were twins, which both sisters found utterly annoying.

Phyllis chose the plain white background and laid Eileen on a cream blanket along with the little teddy she had received from the Easter swan on the ship. Once Mr

Pennington had photographed Eileen on her own and felt confident he had captured a sharp image, Phyllis added herself and Maureen to the set, sitting on a wicker chair with both girls on her lap for the final shot.

"Mr Pennington sir, I'm sorry to bother you but I think you need to come and listen to the wireless. The Prime Minister is about to make an important announcement," whispered the photographer's secretary in excitement at her boss and his clients. They rushed into the tiny office to hear the broadcast. Phyllis held her breath as Neville Chamberlain forced out the words: "We are now at war with Germany".

"So, this is it then, we really are going to war. I can't believe it." Peg uncharacteristically reached for Phyllis's hand and squeezed it tightly.

"Oh gosh, I hope Arthur will be safe, what shall we do?" Phyllis held Peg's gaze and felt empty, as though the world would never be the same again.

"We really need to be getting back to Mums," said Peg urgently. "She'll be worried sick."

Mr Pennington promised to develop the pictures right away and get them delivered later. At least Arthur will see a picture of Eileen thought Phyllis, even though he hasn't met her yet. Maybe he never will? Peg could read what Phyllis was thinking.

"Let's get home. Arthur wouldn't want us fretting. We

must keep our wits about us and not panic," said Peg.

Phyllis stared blankly out of the window as they made their way home. People rushed along the streets like rats deserting a sinking ship. They drove past the Post Office, the castle with little boats bobbing up and down on its lake and all the pretty houses full of people, innocent people. Would they still be here tomorrow? It didn't seem possible that all this, all these homes, all these lives and all the places now so familiar could be blown to nothing. They saw an ARP warden handing out leaflets to passers-by; his black metal helmet looked too small and sat uncomfortably on his head. Army lorries full of soldiers trundled past on their way to the coast, followed by trucks loaded up with reels of barbed wire. The newspapers had reported that invasions from the sea were likely. Plans were in place for defences to be built.

The huge searchlights had been placed at each end of the High Street, along with massive anti-aircraft guns that were now manned by soldiers. Wide stripes had appeared around the tree trunks and lampposts that lined the roads to help guide cars on moonless nights. It was hard to get about at night now as there was no light allowed apart from a dimmed torch, which gave off just enough light to see your shoes. Some men had taken to wearing the tails of their shirts tucked out of their trousers so that passing cars could see them. Women even painted the toes of their shoes white. They passed the picture house, its doors now padlocked shut. "What a damn mess" sighed Peg. "I hate those bloody Nazis."

Phyllis was shocked that Peg swore but didn't show it, instead she sat as stiff as an ironing board, staring out of the window, numb with shock that she was living in a country at war. They passed the Co-Op van that continued to deliver groceries, dutifully fulfilling orders placed the previous day.

Elizabeth was standing in the front garden chatting to Mrs Brown, the neighbour, as she waited for them to return home. She held a telegram tightly in her hand. Her taut, lined face relaxed when she saw Peg's car draw up. She hurried them into the kitchen then read out Arthur's telegram. Phyllis noticed it was addressed to her and not Elizabeth.

"I took the liberty of opening it due to the circumstances we find ourselves," said Elizabeth sanctimoniously.

Her crooked smirk gave away the pleasure she felt at having the senior position in the household, like a proper burra-beebee, thought Phyllis. Arthur's telegram suggested that Phyllis and the children needed to leave Colchester. He'd put a deposit down on the rooms he looked at the previous day, but they wouldn't become available until 10th October. He still didn't know when he would get to Colchester to see Eileen.

Elizabeth burst into tears. "It's a terrible day. Frederick would say we are being punished." She looked at Peg who turned away and left the room, her shoulders shuddering up and down as she reached the hallway.

"You see dear," said Elizabeth, looking tearfully at Phyllis. "Today is the anniversary of my dear boy's passing. My late husband always blamed me for Max's death. He said I would rot in hell. Perhaps he was right all along, maybe this is a sign and we will all be bombed in our beds tonight."

Before Phyllis had a chance to answer, Elizabeth stood up out of the chair and snatched up the dustpan and brush. She threw herself into the afternoon chores, sweeping, dusting and polishing. By the evening she was busy in the kitchen washing then boiling a big bowl of blackberries she had foraged the day before, mixing them with sugar to create a dark, blood-like, sticky jam.

Phyllis lay on her bed waiting for the hum of planes or the loud wail of a siren, but none came. She decided she would keep the conversation about Elsie for another day. Elizabeth was clearly too upset for a confrontation and the war had started.

A knock at her bedroom door stirred her aching body.

"These have just arrived for you," said Peg as she tossed a large brown envelope onto Phyllis's bed.

The photographs were beautiful. Phyllis planned to send copies to Arthur and also a set of prints to India. Maude would be delighted and would no doubt get them framed and put on the teapoy.

Phyllis could picture all the old family photographs, some

in intricate silver frames, others in more robust teak; the only wood the termites couldn't destroy. When she was a girl, before she started boarding school, she would lie on her mother's bed on Saturday mornings, looking at them, asking her mother who various people were. She'd pointed at the tall greying man with an elegant beard.

"Who's that?" Phyllis had asked, intrigued.

"That's your great grandfather, Samuel Edward Henderson," Maude replied.

"And who's the man with the brown face?" Phyllis would question innocently.

"That man is Augustine Pereira. Your great grandfather on your father's side, he gave you your beautiful dark complexion and your big brown eyes," said Maude.

He fascinated Phyllis. He looked darker-skinned than the rest of the family.

"And who's that baby on his lap"? Enquired Phyllis, trying hard to place all these people.

"That's Matilda, your grandma," replied Maude.

"Oh, yes, grandma, of course," replied Phyllis.

Phyllis had been severely reprimanded by her parents for saying. 'I hate your ugly black face,' to her grandma when she'd told the ayer that Phyllis should stop playing and have an afternoon nap. Phyllis still felt guilty for saying such a wicked thing even though she had only been about four years old.

"And who's that baby sitting on that lady's lap?" asked Phyllis pointing to another picture.

"That's me on my mother's lap," said Maude.

Phyllis remembered being totally confused as a young girl, until one day Maude drew the family tree in the dust on the path to the well. Phyllis had known from an early age that she wasn't Indian but wasn't completely English either. She sometimes felt like she didn't really belong to any particular country. She'd yearned to go to England as a child, picturing Kings and Queens prancing around in their finery and dancing in their palace gardens. Phyllis longed to visit the scenes from the lids of biscuits tins they bought from Taylors, the English importers: quaint villages and pretty duck ponds with thatched cottages lining the deserted country lanes.

11

FIRST NIGHT IN THE PIGSTY SHELTER

At 3.30am the sharp wailing of the air raid siren pierced every house in Colchester. Phyllis only had to slip on her shoes as she'd slept on top of the bed with all her clothes on in anticipation of being bombed. Her hands shook as she scooped up Maureen.

"Hurry up," barked Peg as she barged into the bedroom and snatched Eileen from her cot. "We have only seven minutes before the planes are on top of us. Don't forget your gas masks."

Phyllis wrapped Maureen in a blanket and dashed down the stairs as quickly as she could manage after Peg and Elizabeth. The sky was clear with no clouds to trap the warmth of the day. Phyllis did a little shudder as she closed the back door behind her, at least with the bright moon they could see where they were going.

The small shelter felt cold as Phyllis lowered herself in through the arched door and down into the damp pit. She closed the metal opening behind her and sat on the bench, hardly daring to breathe. The lumpy eiderdown provided little comfort as they strained to hear for the sound of aircraft above the noise of barking dogs. Eileen hadn't stirred and was still fast asleep in Peg's arms. Maureen had cried when the siren sounded but had settled back down in Phyllis's lap, sucking on her thumb. The thought of sitting here in the depths of winter made Phyllis shiver. She pulled the cuffs of her cardigan over her knuckles.

An hour later the long wailing cry of the All Clear drowned out any other noise, including Elizabeth's heavy breathing. She gave a gasp of relief and suggested they go in and have a cup of cocoa before going back to bed. Neighbours spilled out into the dark street, chatting and grumbling. Elizabeth was exhausted and didn't want to participate. She put a pan of milk on the range whilst Peg went out to see if she could glean any information.

"Put that light out, miss," snapped a man's voice harshly.

It was Mr Thomas, the local warden. The sound of his heavy footsteps grew louder as he hurried along the pavement.

"So sorry, Mr Thomas," said Peg as she shut the front door behind her before joining the neighbours.

The distant sound of shunting trains clanged as the

railway stirred into life. Colchester could breathe again.

Mr and Mrs Brown were in the kitchen when Phyllis came back down the stairs having tucked the children up in bed. It was clear to everyone that they were all terrified, nobody said so, but the mood was one of shock. Even though they had been preparing for a war for months, it was suddenly here and they felt in danger for their lives for the first time. Phyllis sipped her steamy chocolate and wished to God that she were back in India.

"We had the billeting officer knock on our door today," said Mr Brown, talking into his mug, "says we are to get two soldiers living with us within the next couple of days."

"Lucky we've already got a full house," remarked Elizabeth, "although I'm not sure how long for," she continued, looking over towards Phyllis.

The next few days carried on as normal. The milkman still delivered milk from the large churns that balanced on his float, pulled along by the sturdy carthorse. Maureen loved the clip-clop of the horse. Phyllis would take her out along with their milk jug to buy a pint or two for the day. He would scoop his measuring jug into the deep churns and pour the white liquid swiftly into the pale-blue jug that Phyllis held out. He never spilled a drop. He always had plenty of gossip and told Phyllis about the pillboxes that were being erected on the edge of town.

"Ugly, menacing-looking things they are. Over a hundred will be built in total, not sure what good it will do, mind."

He laughed his jovial laugh and carried on his way.

That night Peg decided they needed to implement a bedtime routine to make it easier in case of a raid.

"We'll place an emergency bag by the back door containing candles, a box of matches and a torch."

It became a nightly ritual, which reassured the household that they would be ready. They kept their identity cards and gasmasks on the floor next to their beds.

"I think it would be for the best if Eileen sleeps in my room from now on," added Peg. "It will be quicker to get both children out."

Another air raid started at 6.50am that morning. They decamped to the shelter, grabbing the emergency bag on their way. No traffic could be heard on the roads, no trains, and no planes, just the scraping of potatoes being peeled into a metal pail by Elizabeth. It sat in a puddle of water that had gathered on the waxy tarpaulin. Phyllis had taken a small clutch of old letters to the shelter to help pass the time. Her mother's letters were so beautifully written. The recent ones contained details of Muriel's impending marriage to Austin. Muriel had made her own wedding cake and had huffed and cursed all the way through it, wishing that Phyllis had been there to do it for her. They were going to hold the reception at the bungalow as Phyllis and Arthur had done. Wilmot always put his own little note on the end of each letter. He was looking forward to receiving pictures of baby Eileen and wished them safe in these difficult times. Phyllis pictured Wilmot at his writing desk, sucking on his pipe, as he pondered what to write.

The All Clear sounded at 8.30am. Tired and relieved that no bombs had dropped they went in for breakfast. Phyllis took the children out for a walk and managed to scrounge a bit of stale bread to feed the ducks. Everyone's food waste was now placed in large communal slop barrels. Their nearest one was unfortunately tied to the lamppost by the front gate. The pig farmer emptied it every few days. Mrs Brown was moaning over the fence about her billeted soldiers that had arrived a few days ago.

"I know I get a bit of money for it but all the same, they make a lot of work."

Elizabeth was nodding in agreement, appalled at the idea of strangers in the house.

"Oh my lord, what's that foul smell?"

"Gas!" screamed Mrs Brown. "Get your mask on."

The two women grabbed their masks and scurried to the shelter, skirts flapping and flesh-coloured stockings on show. It was only when Mr Brown came looking for his dinner that they realised the smell was coming from the rotting food in the pig-slop barrel and not the feared gas.

"Oh what buffoons you must think we are Mr Brown," laughed Elizabeth, the gasmask imprint red and raised on her fleshy face.

That evening as they sat in the kitchen after dinner, they could see the powerful beams from the searchlights high up in the sky.

"How about a game of cards?" piped up Elizabeth.

"I'm tired if you don't mind," replied Phyllis. "I think I might have an early night, just in case the siren goes off."

Phyllis climbed into bed with a hot water bottle, more for comfort than warmth. She wrote to Maude and Wilmot, enclosing the photograph of the girls. She sent her fondest wishes to Muriel and Austin and of course all her brothers. She then wrote a long letter to Arthur, trying not to sound desperate. She told him how she longed to be with him, she missed him terribly and felt so lonely at night. She wanted to be held, to be kissed, to be loved. She enclosed the same picture to Arthur and glued the last sprig of little blue and white flowers on the letter and wrote underneath it, 'forget me not, my love'.

*

The boy stood in the rain holding out a telegram, his red bicycle propped up against the front gate.

"Mrs P Woollett?" he enquired, boldly.

"Thank you," said Phyllis taking the telegram from him.

She was still wrapped in her choga. She hadn't managed to get back to sleep after being woken last night, not by a siren but by the soldiers living next door. They'd come home drunk from the pub, crashing into the coalscuttle as they made their way up the side alley. Thoughts of Arthur, her parents and the war had fluttered and scattered around her mind like a pile of dry autumn leaves thrown up into the air by a gust of wind, keeping her awake.

The telegram was from Kitty: 'EDDIE TO BE EVACUATED. WE ARE ARRIVING IN COLCHESTER AT 11.00HRS. PLEASE MEET US AT THE STATION. MUCH LOVE KITTY.'

She packed both girls into the large black pram: top to tail, Maureen propped up and Eileen lying down. She walked into town, pushing the pram as quickly as she could in the fine September rain. She made it to the station with ten minutes to spare and had a cup of tea in the busy platform cafe. She was used to the pounds, shillings and pence that now jingled in her purse. She still liked to keep one rupee in the small coin compartment, just to remind her of home. The platforms swelled to bursting with troops, massive kitbags swung over their shoulders, some arriving, some leaving, some sprinkled with rain, others dry from the trains. Children, lots of them, accompanied by teachers and a few mothers, all followed each other in long snaking queues out of the station to allocated buses, waiting to take them away to their new homes.

"The eleven o'clock train from London Liverpool Street is now arriving at platform two," echoed the female voice from the platform's loudspeaker.

Kitty looked tired and drawn as she helped Eddie and his classmates off the train to join the seething mass on the platform.

The teacher did a headcount as her young pupils left the train. "Twenty two, twenty three, twenty four. Right children, make sure you have all your things then follow me, hold onto the child's coat in front of you, we don't want any of you getting lost now do we? And don't chew your labels," she bellowed as she held up a long broom handle made into a make-shift banner above her head, with the school's name on it.

Phyllis waved at Kitty but couldn't reach her. Kitty beckoned her to follow them as they turned left out of the station and headed towards the temporary bus park. Phyllis eventually caught up with them.

"Oh Phyllis, I'm so glad you could come," said Kitty, hugging her tightly.

Kitty put on a brave face for Eddie. "It's going to be just fine, darling. You'll probably end up on a farm full of animals or maybe a big old house where you can play hide and seek." Kitty held Eddie's little hand firmly as the children queued to board the bus.

The children started to climb the steep steps up into the green double decker. The name Tolleshunt D'Arcy was handwritten on a cardboard sign in its front window.

Kitty held onto Eddie and kissed his soft cheeks. She reluctantly let go of him as the teacher instructed the children to board the bus. Kitty felt as though she couldn't breathe as her chest tightened.

"Goodbye my darling, remember to write soon and tell me all your news. I love you. Daddy would be so proud of you," she shouted as he disappeared in the throng of other small children that funnelled in through the door.

Kitty couldn't find any more words, but she had so much more to say.

"Oh my dear God," said Kitty, almost pleading with Phyllis. "Will I ever see him again?"

Phyllis held her friend as the bus drove tortuously slowly away, billowing out black smoke as it picked up speed. Kitty stood and sobbed, as her boy was taken from her.

"What's it all about, Phyl?" she sobbed. "Why have the two most precious people in my life been taken from me, what's the point?"

"You've done the right thing Kitty, he'll be safer in the country. I'm sure he'll write in the next couple of days, then you'll feel better once you know who he is with. They'll probably place him with a friend. I'm sure it won't be for long."

"Yes Phyl, I know you're right, thank goodness I have you here with me, I couldn't have done it without you."

Kitty hung onto Phyllis's arm as they made their way along the High Street.

"Now, let's get you a nice cup of tea at that tearoom I've told you about," said Phyllis brightly.

They stepped off the busy pavement into Jacklins. The tobacconist smelt damp and woody. The counter had rows of jars filled with flavoured tobacco from around the world. A set of silver scales was placed on the wooden counter. The shelves on the walls behind the old assistant were stacked full of different types of cigars, beautifully carved pipes and packets of cigarettes. It was like a sweet shop for grown-ups thought Phyllis. She loved the smell of rolling tobacco; it reminded her instantly of Wilmot. He would sit on the veranda on a charpoy, normally after a meal, puffing away on his old rosewood pipe. It often went out and he'd have to restoke it, poking at the tobacco with a match as if prodding a bonfire with a stick until he finally managed to suck out a big lungful of smoke and sigh happily.

The tearoom was through the tobacconist shop and up the stairs. Phyllis and Kitty looked out onto the street below. People milled about, soldiers in khaki uniforms were being manoeuvred around in open lorries, like sheep going off to market. Hundreds more evacuees were being led in snaking lines from the station to the waiting buses.

"What do you think will happen, do you think we'll be invaded? What's Arthur doing? Do you know where he'll be sent?" asked Kitty trying to take her mind off Eddie and his sad little face.

They talked quietly; the wireless had briefed them that 'Idle talk costs lives.' Any stranger could be a potential jasoos. The tea arrived along with a plate of teacakes covered with a glass dome to keep them warm. Phyllis tucked into her currant bun. Kitty couldn't eat hers and wrapped it in a napkin to eat on the train home.

"I can't believe what's happening, everything is changing so fast," whispered Phyllis, leaning in closer to Kitty so that no one could overhear their conversation. "I think Arthur wants a bit of the action, it scares me to death."

Kitty stared out of the window, her eyes welling up and the tip of her nose red. "Oh Phyl, I just can't stop thinking about Eddie, he's only six for God's sake, he can barely tie his own shoelaces."

Phyllis held Kitty's hand and squeezed it gently.

"Poor dear Kitty, I really can't imagine how you must be feeling. I can't stand the thought of being parted from the girls, it's bad enough that Peg has decided to take Eileen into her room at night so we can get out of the house quicker in an air raid."

"I wouldn't fall for that one," said Kitty. " She wants her to herself, be careful she doesn't take her off you."

"I am really worried," confessed Phyllis. "I wrote to Arthur about it and he said she was being helpful and kind and not to be so mean."

The siren sounded, piercing the quiet cafe's tranquillity as if someone had dropped a tray full of crockery.

"Bloody hell, are they going to bomb us in broad daylight?" said Kitty.

"To the basement please, as quickly as you can," shouted the manageress.

They grabbed the children and the gasmasks and ran down the stairs. This time Phyllis could hear the dull rumble of planes flying overhead. They sat on sacks of flour and crates containing tinned fruit. Kitty trembled as she thought of Eddie heading for the open countryside.

"He will be all right won't he?"

"Don't go upsetting yourself," said Phyllis. "The planes will be heading somewhere else, they won't drop them on the way, I'm sure."

Kitty cried into her handkerchief. "I've got to get home, I mustn't miss my train."

They waited in silence until the All Clear finally sounded. Phyllis and Kitty hurried to the station so Kitty could catch the 3.10pm to London. They linked arms as they hurried past all the shops; some were boarded up, a few had shutters and sandbags at their doors. The granite-fronted Co-Op had a large sign saying, 'White coats, hats and hatbands on sale here.' These were now selling out fast. Nighttime safety was becoming an issue. Deaths on the roads since the start of the blackout had already been reported. Cars had apparently knocked over unseen pedestrians like skittles in a skittle alley.

Phyllis waved Kitty a tearful goodbye amongst the throng of people on the platform and then headed for home, pushing the large pram past the grocer's. She remembered that Elizabeth had asked her to pick up some spinach on the way home. Phyllis stood in the queue as the greengrocer served his waiting customers. She asked him for 'one spinach,' not knowing what the vegetable looked like or how big it was. He pointed to a box of dark green leaves. "Just the one?" he questioned.

"Oh, silly me, no I'll need a small handful I think," replied an embarrassed Phyllis realising it was saag. There was no one else in the queue behind her so she plucked up the courage to ask him how to prepare it. The old greengrocer was only too pleased to give her advice and told her she'd need a large handful for each person. He even threw in a bag of onions, as they were the last few in the crate.

She stuffed the brown paper bags of vegetables onto the pram's rack, along with the gas masks and walked home. Elizabeth greeted her at the back door with a bucket of dirty nappies and a letter.

"This came for you today, it's from Arthur."

At least she hadn't opened it, thought Phyllis.

"You really need to keep on top of these nappies dear, it's

not hygienic to have them festering in the bucket in the kitchen."

"I'll do it right away," apologised Phyllis.

She handed Elizabeth the bag of vegetables, looking pleased with herself. She was sure Elizabeth liked to test her knowledge of ingredients.

Phyllis savoured the unopened letter in her hand as she sat on her bed, its contents still unknown. She slit the letter open, being careful not to damage its contents. It was good news, Arthur was coming home on 5th October to collect her and the girls and take them back to Catterick. She leapt up from the bed and laughed with joy. Arthur suggested she should get a perm and make herself look pretty for him. She laughed at the image she had in her head of the last time she went to meet him off the train. Large and pregnant in the huge mothball dress, late and dishevelled. She made an appointment with Vivien for the day before his arrival and took her favourite blue striped silk dress out of the smelly almyra and washed it carefully.

"I don't understand it," declared Mrs Brown over the back wall to Phyllis as she was hanging the dress out on the line. "They say Hitler has 70,000 planes ready to bomb us, but where are they? Not that I want them, mind you. I wonder whether it's all nonsense and the war will be over in a few weeks' time."

Phyllis nodded and carried on feeding the nappies

through the mangle. Her gentle hands had toughened up,
her knuckles no longer cracked like they used to.

12

STOLEN THUNDER

Phyllis had slept on her back all night, not daring to move, for fear of ruining her wave perm. The striped dress smelt clean and looked pretty. Her stockings were straight and her hands moisturised. Maureen and Eileen had been bathed the previous night. Phyllis had climbed in afterwards and scrubbed clean every inch of her petite body. She'd picked some bright orange dahlias, the colour of the setting sun, from the last surviving flower bed that ran down the side of the privy and sneaked them up to the bedroom. She hadn't dared to borrow the vase from the parlour. Elizabeth was bound to notice on her weekly dusting rounds and wonder who'd taken it. Instead an old jam jar from the pantry floor would have to do.

The bedroom windows had been opened wide, even though it let in the cold autumn air.

"Oh no, I've forgotten to feed the blasted chickens," she said to Maureen.

Maureen was now one and a half years old and loved the birds that had been delivered unceremoniously in a cardboard box. The milkman had kindly brought them on his cart from the neighbouring farm. Elizabeth was absolutely thrilled with them and vowed not to name them, as she didn't want anyone to get attached to them just in case they needed to eat them in an emergency. Phyllis had secretly done so with Maureen though. The biggest hen was called Hatty because it was big and grey and reminded Phyllis of an elephant. The more delicate hen was named Mrs D after the butcher's thin wife, who liked to natter all day long. Phyllis scattered the chicken food in the pen and checked for any eggs; only one today. The farmer told them that they would get anxious when the sirens sounded at night and not to expect too many eggs until the spring. They'd need time to settle and get through the cold winter.

The pram was packed up and ready at the back door. Phyllis popped the children in and tucked them up snuggly under the woolly blanket. She wrapped herself in her large black coat and being careful not to ruin her hairstyle placed her hat gently over her new curls. Arthur's train was due in an hour, she didn't want to be late and planned on going to the station cafe to have a pot of tea before he arrived to be sure not to be dishevelled. On her walk through the abbey grounds she pictured seeing him in his uniform, the steam sending romantic puffs around their feet; he'd run towards her, lift her off the ground and spin her around.

She had just ordered a pot of tea when she heard a familiar voice.

"Oh goody, have you got enough for two of us?"

"I thought you were working today," said Phyllis forlornly looking up to see Peg striding towards her.

"Oh I swapped my shift so I wouldn't miss Arthur," she replied. "I knew you wouldn't mind. I'm not planning on stealing your thunder. I just wanted to welcome him home."

"Steal my thunder?"

"Oh it doesn't matter, it's just a phrase."

Phyllis's world came crashing down as Peg busily took Eileen out of the pram and tucked her little body into the folds of her cardigan, like an accomplished pickpocket. Phyllis stared, fuming into her teacup and pretended to stir it to prevent herself from crying. By the time she took a sip it had gone cold. She felt so miserable. Maureen had started to whine because her nappy was full and Peg droned on about how to potty train her and how she really should be getting on with it. Peg suddenly jumped out of her chair.

"Oh goody, there he is! I'll go and get him and you stay here with Maureen. I'll bring him over."

Before Phyllis could object, Peg had disappeared down the platform holding Eileen in her arms as if her own. The steam Phyllis had dreamt about now clouded her view and she missed Arthur holding their precious new daughter for the first time.

"There you are my darling, were you hiding from me?" He stood smiling proudly at Eileen in his arms. "You clever old thing Phyl, she's beautiful."

His dark eyes looked watery as he looked at Eileen's beautiful face. Phyllis could barely breathe with the sheer joy of seeing him.

"I have missed you more than you can ever imagine."

He reached out to her and squeezed her to his chest, holding her tightly. "God, I love you."

Phyllis let the tears freely run. He was here, he was safe, he was alive and they were together.

Phyllis felt shy of Arthur as she shared her bed with him for the first time in four months. She climbed under the heavy eiderdown and studied his face. She thought he looked older than when she last saw him, the light of the flickering candle flame picked up the small shiny scar on his forehead. She traced his deep smile lines with her fingertips down to the dimple on his chin. Arthur leant over and blew out the candle. As the darkness wrapped around them the air raid siren whirred into action.

"Blast this bloody war," groaned Arthur.

Phyllis couldn't help but laugh. "What cruel timing it is."

Arthur fumbled around for the torch.

"Perhaps we should stay here and risk it, after all, no

bombs have fallen yet have they?"

There was a loud banging at the bedroom door. "For goodness sake, hurry up and get out. Do you two want to be bombed in your bed?" Elizabeth was furious as she stood, candle in hand on the landing. "Give me Maureen and get a move on."

Phyllis and Arthur grabbed their coats and ran down the stairs and out into the dark back yard. Elizabeth, Maureen, Peg and Eileen were already seated in a line on the bench inside the shelter. Elizabeth was grumpy having been woken up five nights on the trot.

"I'm not sure I can take much more of this," she moaned as she rocked backwards and forwards.

"I've got to be at work in four hours," yawned Peg.

There was a clattering noise by next-door's front gate. The two servicemen stumbled up the pavement and knocked over the pig slop bin, singing 'Roll out the Barrel'. Arthur leapt to his feet and vaulted over the low wall. He gave them what for and threatened to report them if they came home drunk again, disturbing all these good people in their homes, did they have no respect? He got a shovel from the shed and made them clean up the rotting food that had spilt over the pavement and dribbled like vomit into the gutter.

"What's all the bobbery-bob about?" asked Phyllis.

"Bobbery-what?" asked Elizabeth. "What on earth is that

supposed to mean?"

"It means commotion, row," said Phyllis.

"There's been a lot of trouble in the town at night," chipped in Peg. "Lots of them have been warned about their drunken behaviour, urinating in people's gardens and falling over, it's disgusting."

Elizabeth looked worried. "The billeting officer is coming here tomorrow to discuss when we can let them have a room. I've told them you are leaving on 10th October and that I'll need a week to get it ready. I'm not ashamed to admit it but I'm dreading it. Mrs Brown has had nothing but trouble with her two; they're so young, only eighteen I think."

Arthur squeezed his mother's hand. "We're not all bad you know, remember you have me to help you."

"That's all very well but you're not here are you?"

The All Clear siren sounded.

"Oh, thank the lord," said Elizabeth, struggling up out of her seat, "I'll get the kettle on."

"I'm going straight back to bed," said Peg taking Eileen with her.

By the time Phyllis and Arthur got to bed it was three in the morning. They shuffled into each other's arms and drifted to sleep in the warmth of each other's bodies.

13

THE TRAIN TO CATTERICK

The taxi arrived at 10am. It had been a sombre last night in Maldon Road. Elizabeth had made a special roast pork dinner. Phyllis thought it had been like the last supper, waiting for fate to decide their futures. They had talked about when they might meet again.

"Maybe Christmas," suggested Elizabeth hopefully, busying herself with straightening the antimacassars that had a habit of sliding off the arms of the chair.

Arthur took a sip of his whisky, "we'll see."

Phyllis couldn't believe she had only been in England for six months. She perched on the hard sofa and tried to summon up the memory of the bungalow and surround herself with her parents and siblings. She tried to remember what the house smelt like, the slight mildewy scent on the chintz cushions. She struggled to capture the feeling of doob underneath her bare feet.

*

The blue Austin low-loader and its driver waited patiently as Arthur dragged the huge trunks and the pram around to the front of the house.

"Can we get a bicycle on too, do you think?"

"That'll be an extra shilling, but I'm sure we'll manage it," said the burly driver, who proceeded to take off his hat, roll up his sleeves and load the luggage onto the car's drop-down hatch. The pram was strapped on top and Elizabeth's bicycle was tied on the back with thick rope. Elizabeth went to fetch her purse and slipped Arthur a pound to help pay for the taxi. He was always so hard up, she could go without but she didn't want him to.

Mr and Mrs Brown came out when they heard the commotion of the taxi being loaded. They knew how much it would pain Elizabeth to say goodbye to Arthur again. Arthur hugged his mother and fondly told Mrs Brown to look after 'the old lady'.

Elizabeth hugged the children. "Look after them dearie," she whispered into Phyllis's ear.

"I shall do my best," she replied, finding it hard to hide her excitement at leaving.

"Till we meet again then," said Elizabeth politely.

"Oh blast it, I've forgotten my topee," said Phyllis.

"Not sure you'll be needing that silly hat where you're going," replied Elizabeth. "Leave it here, if you like."

Phyllis took a step towards the front door. "No, I'd rather take it with me if you don't mind. Daddy bought it for me. I'd hate to lose it."

"As you wish, we don't have much spare room anyway."

Phyllis dashed upstairs to find it in its box sitting on her bed. She took one last look around the bedroom and felt relieved to be finally leaving Elizabeth's horrid house with its pigsty shelter.

They waved from the car until Elizabeth's silhouette was out of sight. Phyllis felt as if she'd been released from a cage, as free as a bird flying to an unknown place to make a new nest, a nest that would be comfortable and happy.

"You've cheered up a bit," teased Arthur.

"I was trying hard to hide my excitement."

"Well you haven't made a very good job of it, though I must say you've put up with Mums and Peg terribly well. I'm not sure I could live with them."

"Now you tell me!"

"Yes, but could you cope living in a cold Nissen hut with twenty stinking blokes for company?"

"No, I'd rather live with the in-laws. It's a close contest though."

"Seriously Phyl, it's pretty grim bunking up with a load of chaps all the time. I'm so glad you're going to be just down the road. I still think it might have been better if you'd stayed in India though."

"I'm sure things will improve now we have our own place." Phyllis gently squeezed his cold hand.

"God I hope you're right, not that I'll be able to spend that much time with you, but at least you won't be so far away, that's if I don't get posted off somewhere."

Phyllis smiled at him and stroked his face. "At least we won't have your mother breathing down our necks."

Arthur turned his head towards Phyllis and kissed her full on the lips.

A porter stacked their luggage onto a large wooden trolley. The wheels squeaked as he pushed the cumbersome load along the platform and into the luggage room. Phyllis clutched onto her hatbox and convinced Arthur it would be safer in the carriage with them. They would travel to Liverpool Street then a connecting train would take them to Richmond, Yorkshire; she didn't want it to get lost on the way.

The station was full of soldiers arriving to report to Colchester Garrison. Phyllis thought how bizarre it was that she and Arthur were going to Catterick, troops were arriving in Colchester and evacuees were being sent all over the country. Was anyone actually living in their own homes?

Arthur selected their 3rd class carriage. Four of the seats were already occupied by a couple of young men in civvies and a vicar with his daughter. Phyllis placed her handbag on the seat opposite and said good morning as she placed Maureen down. The men shuffled their polished shoes out of her way and nodded hello. Phyllis sat herself down with Eileen on her lap. Arthur went to see which direction the buffet car was. By the time he came back their carriage was full apart from his own empty seat and the one opposite. Arthur always felt a stab of anxiety when he came face to face with a dog-collar, it wasn't that he was against the church, but he'd get flash backs of his father's rage. He could see his shouting face now, screwed up with anger; his red tongue bulging behind bared teeth like a tethered animal fighting for release, spittle firing in all directions. Arthur sat down and positioned himself behind his broadsheet, hoping to keep the starched collar out of sight. As the train chugged out of the station, the last passenger slid the carriage door open and asked Arthur to help her with her suitcase. Arthur put his newspaper down and helped lift the luggage onto the rack. Phyllis glanced around at her new neighbours and wondered who they were and where they were going. She wondered what they thought of her; would they have guessed she was born in India and had only been here a short while? She looked at the girl who had just arrived in the carriage and smiled; she could only be about twenty, she had a nurse's uniform on underneath her coat.

"Muriel's wedding," Phyllis blurted. The whole carriage looked at her.

"Oh, I'm terribly sorry," said Phyllis, blushing. "It's just that you look like my sister Muriel," she nodded towards the nurse, "and she's getting married today, the 10th of October."

Phyllis told the nurse how her sister was marrying a man called Austin in the family home in Benares.

"That's in North East India," Phyllis said with pride.

She thought of Muriel's wedding, out on the lawn; Cyril and Ernest busy rearranging the furniture; Maurice lounging on a charpoy, watching the goings on, sipping cold lemonade; Maude in charge, her long list in hand, ticking off each job with a pencil like a schoolmistress marking homework. Wilmot with his pipe resting in the corner of his mouth, directing all the deliveries that arrived along the driveway, horse-drawn carts loaded with flowers, drinks and food; Champagne glasses, crockery and cutlery borrowed from Clarks hotel arriving in their shiny dark green carriage; the photographer in a rickshaw, its stringy driver dripping with sweat.

The nurse was very young and told Phyllis shyly that she would be working at Great Ormond Street Hospital. She had never been to London before and was really nervous.

The vicar sitting next to her piped up that he came from that part of London and that he and his daughter would happily accompany her to her destination. Once alighted at Liverpool Street, belongings in hand and polite goodbyes passed to their carriage companions, they made their way to platform four.

"Do you always have to make friends with total strangers?" teased Arthur.

"I'm only being friendly and passing the time."

"Well, it's just not the English way."

"What isn't?"

"Letting everyone know all our business."

"Well I like being friendly. Now let's go and get some tea."

Phyllis couldn't believe her eyes when she opened the tearoom door.

"Surprise!" shrieked Kitty, leaping out of her chair.

"Oh my lord, what on earth are you doing here?"

"Once again, your thoughtful husband telegrammed me to tell me you would be here," said Kitty. "I don't know when I'll get the chance to see you again as you will be too far away. Let me introduce you to my father, Alfred."

"It's a real pleasure to meet you my dear, I gather you

have become a very special friend to my daughter," said Alfred.

Phyllis smiled and looked at Kitty. "Yes, she is a very dear friend," said Phyllis.

They sat and ordered tea and toast and caught up on each other's news. "Have you heard from Eddie yet?" enquired Phyllis.

"Gosh, only just, he sent me a postcard saying that he's living in a farmhouse with The Kendalls, they have two children. Apparently they play in the hay barn most of the day and help with the animals; he's loving it. I'm going to try and visit if I can. Mother is knitting him some bed socks because his feet are so cold at night. Mrs Kendall added some reassuring words on the end of the card. She said he had settled in well with her two children and adored milking the cows and collecting the eggs to sell at the gate. Apparently nearly 300 evacuees arrived that day on the buses and there are only 600 people living in the small village. The billeting officers had quite a struggle to find them all homes but somehow they managed it. I imagine there are now children running about all over the place. I just hope Eddie isn't getting into too much mischief." Kitty took a deep breath. "Oh sorry, I'm just so relieved to hear from him."

Phyllis asked for Eddie's address and said she'd write to him, it was always nice to get a letter when you were away from home. She'd loved receiving letters when she was at boarding school, any snippet of family news became infinitely more interesting if you weren't there.

Alfred and Arthur chatted about the impact the war was having on London. "We live just one road away from the heath in Hampstead," said Alfred. "If you ever find yourself at a loose end in London you must visit."

"I would be delighted to, thank you," said Arthur.

"Although the heath isn't what it used to be. Hundreds of lorries arrive every day to take the sand away for the sandbags. Vast swathes of the heath have been dug out. It looks more like the surface of the moon."

"How have the raids been?" asked Arthur.

"Terrible, I can't get used to the siren, it sends my heart pounding every time I hear it. Doris, that's Kitty's mother, has got me sleeping in my clothes. It really is a sight to behold," he laughed.

Phyllis and Kitty talked about Muriel's marriage.

"I can't say I'm overly fond of him to be brutally honest," said Phyllis.

"Why, what's wrong with him?"

"It's hard to put your finger on but he's just a bit sly, bit of a charmer."

"Not to be totally trusted?"

"Exactly."

Phyllis felt sad as she leant out of the train window to say goodbye.

"I shall miss you as always, you must write as soon as you can and tell me all about your new home," smiled Kitty.

"I shall. And I promise I'll write to Eddie soon too."

Kitty reached in her basket just as the train started to move. "I've got you a little house warming present," laughed Kitty.

She tossed something wrapped in newspaper through the window for Phyllis to catch.

"Another mango!" shrieked Phyllis. "You are an angel."

*

It was pitch black by the time the train pulled into Richmond station. The only light came from the glow of the stationmaster's torch and two dim blue lamps that dangled by the blacked-out ticket office.

The carriages and corridors were dimly lit.   Blackout blinds were attached to the windows. Reading had been out of the question; it had been a long, boring journey, and Phyllis was relieved they had arrived. Her legs were numb from sitting on the firm seat, with Eileen asleep across her lap.

"This is our stop," said Arthur as he entered the carriage, bringing a whoosh of colder air with him. He'd stood for much of the journey smoking in the corridor chatting to other soldiers who were also heading for Catterick Camp.

"Richmond, Richmond station," shouted the stationmaster who helped them off the train and pointed them in the direction of the luggage pile now sitting on the platform.

"You wait here with the children. I'll go and collect everything," instructed Arthur.

Phyllis felt the northerly wind swipe at her face and hands. She pulled her hat down over her burning cold ears and took her kid gloves out of her pocket, dropping one as she did so. She looked and looked but couldn't see her brown leather glove lying on the floor. She called the stationmaster over to help find it; it was lying right by her foot. She promised herself that the next time she needed a new pair she would buy white or yellow ones.

"Bloody hell," said Arthur, "I nearly went flying over someone's suitcase. It's treacherous."

The journey in the taxi was frightening. Phyllis couldn't work out how the driver managed to keep the car on the road, his headlights were dimmed so low it was a mystery how they made it at all.

*

Arthur led the way up the dark path and knocked on the door. Phyllis stood behind him with the children. A chink of light and the smell of stew spilled out to greet them as the door opened.

"Come on in me darlins."

Mrs Osmund smiled motheringly at Phyllis as they stood in the narrow hallway, her ample bosom filling the space between them. Phyllis thought Mrs Osmund looked about 50, her hair streaked with grey at the temples. Her face was fresh and plump. Phyllis accidently knocked over a wooden crutch that was leaning against the wall, it clattered to the tiled floor.

"Nivver y'mind it's mi owd feller's," laughed Mrs Osmund. "He'll be along in a jiffy, he's just feeding his lahl bairns."

Phyllis smiled awkwardly, trying her best to follow the conversation. She'd never heard the Yorkshire dialect before and felt embarrassed as she looked to Arthur for translation.

Mrs Osmund led them down the hall into the warm kitchen. There was a range in the corner with a bubbling pot sitting on the top. The lid rattled up and down as the steam escaped.

"Ah thought y' might be famished, help thissen. Mi and the owd feller have had ours, it being late an all."

"Na then." Mr Osmund clomped into the kitchen. Phyllis tried to hide her surprise as she shook hands with the man with one leg. He smiled broadly; some of his teeth were missing and the ones still in his pink gummy mouth were wonky and yellow. He took off his cloth cap and threw it on the overcrowded table.

Mrs Osmund took Maureen by the hand and sat her down on the kitchen table. "Na then ma lass, how' bout a lahl pikelet?"

Phyllis stared wide-eyed, she could never imagine Elizabeth or Peg sitting a child on the same surface that you served your dinner on. Phyllis smiled to herself as Mrs Osmund produced a plateful of hot, buttery crumpets just for Maureen.

Included in the rent of 10 shillings a week was the sole use of the front sitting room and a double bedroom with two single beds and a cot, plus shared use of the kitchen and inside bathroom, which was downstairs just off the kitchen. It had a battered metal tub for bathing and a copper to boil the water. The lino on the floor was scuffed where the door dragged on its faded patterned surface, but it was clean. The lavvy, as Mrs Osmund called it, was in an outhouse near the back door. Next to the kitchen was a glass-roofed lean-to with a pair of once comfy chairs, their stuffing now bursting out of the rotten, brown upholstery as if a bulrush going to seed. On an occasional table lived a striped spider plant and a machete-like mother-in-laws tongue; Mrs Osmund's pride and joy.

Phyllis and Arthur went to bed, full of delicious hotpot. They'd got to know Mr and Mrs Osmund a little better during their first night. Mr Osmund told them how he'd lost his leg. He'd been working as a farm hand when he was a young man and had got tangled up in a combine harvester. He worked in the camp kitchen now, preparing vegetables. He coped with it well, getting the bus from the end of the road and sitting on a stool to do his repetitive work. Mrs Osmund worked as a cleaner in the Walkerville Hotel, but to make ends meet they took in lodgers. Mrs Osmund adored children, but they didn't have any of their own.

"Owd feller's pipes didn't work proper." Mrs Osmund had laughed loudly, spluttering on her dark brown tea.

Phyllis had no idea what she meant but shrieked with embarrassment when Arthur explained it to her later in bed, as the windowpanes rattled behind the blackout curtains.

Phyllis slept heavily, wrapped in Arthur's strong arms, dreaming that she was with her brothers, paddling down the Ganges on a moorpunky. Muriel was stood on the ghats with a mongoose in her arms; they were calling to her. The current took them downstream just as she looked up. "I can't reach you," whispered Phyllis in her sleep. As she stirred and opened her eyes, Arthur lay awake in the half-light studying her face.

"You've been dreaming, sleepyhead."

"I'm worried about Muriel. Will Austin be good to her?"

"I'm quite sure your sister can handle herself perfectly

well, if anything it's Austin who needs to watch out. She won't take any nonsense, I'm quite sure of that."

Phyllis lay staring up at the brown stain that bled into the white ceiling, like spilt tea on a tablecloth. "Did I ever tell you about the mongoose that lived in our compound?"

Arthur shook his head and smiled.

"He lived near the joola. Every day mother would leave out a jug of milk for him on the veranda. He'd sneak up and think he was being really clever by stealing it from under our noses. He was a highly-skilled snake catcher."

"One day my love, we shall have our own mongoose but in the meantime we need to make you feel at home here. How about I go and get some breakfast on the go while you start unpacking?"

Phyllis opened the lid to the trunk that she'd been longing to open since arriving in England. Elizabeth had insisted that Phyllis wouldn't need to open it and scatter her belongings around the place.

"You'll be up and out of here in a jiffy, there's no use unpacking it all now." She'd instructed.

Phyllis's heart skipped as she inhaled a faint whiff of wood smoke mixed with a slight damp smell and Wilmot's favourite pipe tobacco. She pulled away the grey blanket that had kept Maude's painting safe during the journey and held it to her face, taking lungful's of India-tainted air. Maude's Nainital painting balanced on her lap. She traced the brushstrokes with her finger. The copper-green lake, its boathouse nestling at one end with stilted white legs that dipped into the water, like a graceful egret standing in a paddy field, filled Phyllis with joy.

"Mrs Woollett, do you need owt? It's teemin dahn," said Mrs Osmund standing at the door left slightly ajar. She pointed to the rain that lashed against the window. "Ah jus poppin down t'butcher this morn, we could share t'rabbit if tha like?"

"Yes, thank you, perhaps you could show me how to prepare it?" said Phyllis with trepidation.

"Aye lass, will do," nodded Mrs Osmund. "Ay up, tis a grand view," she continued, looking at the painting on Phyllis's lap. "Tha should hang it on parlour wall, make thissen at home flower."

Phyllis followed Mrs Osmund to the parlour.

Suspended from the ceiling was a large cage, housing 40 or so chirruping yellow canaries.

"Don't tha mind em, they're his dickybirds," said Mrs Osmund.

"I'm not sure I like them very much," said Phyllis, unable to hide her feelings. "Could they go and live in the lean-to or outside in the shed or something?"

Mrs Osmund laughed, "T'shed, wait till I tell me owd feller," she laughed and laughed, "t'shed for his bairns."

Mrs Osmund left the room laughing and muttering under her breath, leaving Phyllis to contemplate the cage of birds that tweeted loudly at her presence. She hung the painting over the fireplace and decided she would ask Arthur to have a word with Mr Osmund.

She went back upstairs to delve deeper into the trunk, and placed her hands on the smooth wooden case of her small sewing machine. She cleared a space on a table in the corner of the living room for it. It felt good to have it sitting ready for use again. She thought back to all the things she had created over the years. Her own wedding dress had probably been the hardest, not that the pattern was difficult but the cream Benares silk was expensive, and she was scared of ruining it. Maude suggested the durzis make it for her but Phyllis wanted to do it herself. She wondered what Muriel's dress had been like; no doubt pictures would arrive. Muriel and Austin would be on their honeymoon by now, making their way to Agra.

Phyllis looked at the bobbin loaded with thick black cotton from when she'd made the blackout curtains for Elizabeth. Phyllis felt quite sorry for her now. She would be getting ready for the billeted soldiers. Elizabeth had mentioned the idea of getting a dog, for company and protection; she planned to have it in her bedroom at night so she felt safe. There was also talk of Peg moving in with her friend Susie who lived in a modern flat in the town above the bakery. Elizabeth wasn't happy about it, but Peg desperately wanted her independence.

"Breakfast is served," called Arthur from the kitchen.

He had laid out the cluttered table as best he could with three servings of boiled eggs and toast, with a large pot of strong tea placed in the middle.

"Urgh, that's so strong," choked Phyllis.

"That's how they like it up here," teased Arthur.

She took another sip and felt the tannins coat her teeth.

"We need to work out a simple code. All military post is going to be censored. It will help you know where I am," said Arthur. He popped a piece of toast into his mouth. "Let's use the address on the envelope." He rubbed the bristly whiskers of his moustache between his fingers as he spoke. Phyllis had noticed this new habit, he did it when he was apprehensive or put on the spot.

He took a pencil stub from his jacket pocket and found an old scrap of paper. "If I write 'FOURTH AVENUE' in capital letters, that means I'm still in Catterick. If I write 'Fourth Avenue' in upper and lowercase, that means I've been posted to France. If I write 'fourth avenue' with no capitals, that means I'm going somewhere else in Europe and if I write '4th Avenue' that means I'm on manoeuvres somewhere in Britain."

"Gosh, that's a very clever idea," said Phyllis. She took the scrap of paper from him and slipped it into her purse.

"We need to stock up with food before you head to camp

tomorrow," said Phyllis, looking at the two empty pantry shelves Mrs Osmund had cleared for them. "I'd also like to make a start on the Christmas pudding."

It had been a Dover family tradition to start making the pudding in October, giving the fruity sponge time to mature. As children, Phyllis and her brothers and sisters would take turns to stir the gloopy mixture in the big ceramic bowl with a large wooden spoon. They would toss in the English coins, reusing the same silver sixpences each year. Only when the nutmeg-smelling mixture was safely poured into the pudding basin would Maude allow the children to lick the bowl; its raw sticky coating too tempting, even for fussy Maurice.

*

Phyllis hadn't caught the last few words Arthur had spoken as he'd made his way down the path. The lashing rain on the slate porch roof had stolen them from her. Maureen had clung to her daddy like ivy gripping a drainpipe. Phyllis had to unpeel her tiny fingers from around his neck. As Arthur strode down the road and out of sight, she realised he'd forgotten to talk to Mr Osmund about the canaries.

Before Arthur left they'd discussed the idea of Phyllis doing work to earn some pin money. She took some clean sheets of writing paper from her thinning pad and wrote adverts for her baking services. Once she was happy with her wording, she copied out a few to place in the local shop windows. She did another for her sewing services.

Jane Gill

Phyllis wobbled down the street as she got used to Elizabeth's heavy bicycle. Having placed her adverts in the corner shop and newsagents she cycled past Tindalls, a whitewashed wooden shack that sold everything from potatoes to cider. She then cycled through town to see the army camp. It sprawled over a vast area behind a barbed wire topped fence, like a prison. Placed inside stood row upon row of neat brick houses. Some back to back and some at right angles, these led on to large open spaces where soldiers guarded huge warehouses. Troops were marching up and down a parade ground. Phyllis rested the bicycle against the chain link fence and squinted, trying to see Arthur, but the khaki men were too far away. Tanks were lined up next to a hangar; its doors gaped like a giant's mouth. It looked ugly and out of place on the edge of the Yorkshire Dales.

The sun hung low in the sky; casting a long bicycle-shaped shadow across the road. She headed back towards the Post Office, hoping it was still open. She'd carefully wrapped the wallet from Aden and the Maltese lace in brown paper for Maude and Wilmot. The Christmas parcel would arrive late but then everything did in India, so it didn't really matter. She wished she could be there to see her parents' faces.

Christmas was always such fun in Benares. The whole family would ride excitedly to church in the carriage, before coming back to the bungalow to have a singsong around the piano. Maude would get the mali to chop down a few branches of the Neem tree and plant them in a large terracotta pot; she would then decorate her Kissmiss tree with delicate glass baubles and randomly scatter a few bits of cotton wool to represent snow. She would patiently sit for hours in the living room making paper chains with the children to adorn the bungalow.

The Muslim and Brahmin servants and their children would line up on the veranda, waiting their turn to be wished a Merry Christmas by Maude and Wilmot. Each servant was given a dali containing ribbons, sweets, cakes, flowers and toys. The servants' children would squeal with pleasure as they unwrapped their gifts.

Once the lavish Christmas dinner was eaten, the family would get in the carriage and clip-clop to the Ganges through the gathering crowds to watch the fireworks explode above the holy river. Phyllis could smell it now, the sharp aroma of gunpowder in the air. Children would throw firecrackers at each other, the horse would get jumpy but the scyce was very skilled and kept him trotting along, past The Benares Club and home.

The Benares Club on Kachehari Road was a favourite haunt of the Anglo-Indian men. It was a fine building sitting in the middle of a neat green dhoob lawn with large verandas to each side. Bamboo loungers were dotted about its shade. Rhododendrons and white jasmine grew happily side-by-side around the handsome stone building. Beyond lay the tennis courts and meticulously kept croquet lawn. Rumour had it that the malis would trim parts of the lawn with his scissors and weed with a silver knife and fork. Wilmot would often take the carriage to the club and spend a few happy hours playing billiards. He would drink pegs of whisky whilst playing whist at one of the card tables that lined the club's walls. The enormous oak-panelled billiard room was at the heart of the building. A gallery where men would gather to read the papers, catch up with news from England and share a cigar, looked down onto the massive green baize table. Turbaned bearers were always on hand to take their drinks order. On winter nights, the log fires were beautifully stoked up and in the heat of the summer, the doors would be flung wide open, although the clientele's numbers shrank considerably as the members of the Raj fled to the hills in droves.

As a young girl Phyllis thought of it as an exciting, forbidden, secretive place. She was only allowed in through its heavy teak doors and into its smoky interior once she had turned eighteen, but only into the moorgli-khana and never in the main bar area. The large notice board that greeted them by the door always made fascinating reading. Gramophones, furniture, pianos and even goats were for sale alongside advertisements for piano, tennis, dancing lessons and tutoring for children, including elocution lessons for a perfect English accent.

14

PEARL IRIS PEACOCK

Mrs Osmund came home from work to find pages of damp newspaper draped over the washing line that strung across the lean-to's roof.

"Wha the eck are y'doing flower?"

Phyllis had retrieved some old newspapers from the bundle by the stove and had spread them out on the kitchen table. She'd then painted them with her watercolours; the inky newsprint still visible under the paint's thin surface.

"I'm just making coloured paper for Christmas decorations," said Phyllis cheerfully. "I know it doesn't look much now, but I think they'll be quite pretty once I've finished."

"You's a goodun, allus thinkin o' y' bairns," chuckled Mrs Osmund. Her soft bosoms squashed Phyllis's slight frame as she gave her a hug.

Once dried, Phyllis took out her dressmaking scissors and cut the brittle paper into thin strips. She mixed flour and water to make the creamy, porridge-like glue. It got stuck to her fingers and ended up in her hair as she brushed stray strands from her face. She was so absorbed with cutting and sticking that she didn't hear the knock at the door. A woman stood at the kitchen window, peering in through the dirty panes. Phyllis caught sight of her and nearly jumped with fright.

"Hello, I'm so sorry, I didn't mean to startle you. I did knock on the front door but you were obviously busy," said the woman now standing at the back door, scanning the table covered in old newspaper and glue. She had an ivory complexion with a touch of rose to her soft cheeks. Her smiling eyes shone under bright violet eye shadow. Phyllis looked down at her gluey hands and hurriedly wiped them.

"Are you Mrs Woollett? I'm Mrs Peacock. I'm here about the notice you put in the window in the corner shop. I need a couple of alterations doing on my husband's trousers, he's tall and slim and his flannels are always too large around the waist. I'm totally hopeless when it comes to needlework; in fact I'm more than hopeless, I'm a complete disaster." She finally stopped for breath. "Oh I'm so sorry, I have prattled on rather haven't I?"

*

Phyllis felt nervous as she propped her bicycle up against the freshly painted railings of the imposing stone house.

The front garden was immaculate with clipped box hedging and dormant pruned roses, ready to wake up in the coming spring and shower the garden with colour. Mrs Peacock's young housemaid opened the large front door and showed Phyllis into an elegant drawing room. The open fire roared in the hearth as a Labrador, toasting itself, lay stretched out lazily on a rug. A Christmas tree adorned with baubles and tinsel dominated the large window, blocking out the light.

"The children will be back from school tomorrow." Mrs Peacock appeared through the doorway, a wide smile on her face and a Martini glass in her hand. "I'm so glad you came, I thought I might have put you off with all my chattering. I only have Laddie to talk to when the children are away at school. I get so dreadfully bored."

Laddie's velvety ears pricked up at the sound of his name, he then sighed and laid his head back down on his bear-like paws. Phyllis couldn't take her eyes off the highly polished grand piano at the farthest end of the room. She deftly measured Mr Peacock's old trousers with her dressmaker's tape and wrote down all the details in her notebook. Mrs Peacock noticed a drawing Phyllis had scribbled on one of its pages.

"Do you draw, Mrs Woollett?"

"Not really. I love to paint but haven't done so for a while now. I'm dying to get out into the moors."

Mrs Peacock's face lit up, "Oh that's terrific, I know a

beautiful little place. There's a stone bridge over the river, with heathland, and hills in the distance, it has it all in one vista. How about we go there after Christmas? We could wrap up warm, take a flask of something hot and paint to our heart's content." Mrs Peacock smiled enthusiastically as she put the finishing touches to the already full Christmas tree. "By the way, my name is Pearl, Pearl Iris Peacock. My friends call me Pip."

"I'm Phyllis, my friends call me Phyl."

Phyllis had a few enquiries over the next few days, last minute alterations for party dresses and an order from a lady who hated Christmas cake and required a Victoria sponge. Phyllis happily threw herself into her jobs and also managed to finish making the girls some ragdolls from a remnant of leftover silk.

Arthur's letter arrived on Christmas Eve. It was addressed to '4th Avenue'. Phyllis held her breath as she looked at her notes on the scrap of paper to decipher the code. He was somewhere else in Britain. His letter gave nothing away, only that he was warm and comfortable and wished he could see her and the children at Christmas. Arthur had never really liked Christmas until he'd met Phyllis. His father had always managed to ruin it. Frederick would march the family back from church on Christmas morning with Arthur dressed in his Sunday best, his bottom aching from the hard pew, his fingers and toes numb. Arthur and Peg had to sit quietly until after lunch. The front parlour was cold and austere as they tiptoed around their father's mood, hardly daring to catch his hawk-like eyes. His temper could flare up at the smallest of things. Arthur was always relieved when it was time for his father to return to the church for evensong. The house would be a happier place for a few hours.

A Christmas card had also arrived from Elizabeth. She wanted to visit Catterick to see the children. She was lonely after Peg had gone to live with Susie. Elizabeth didn't like Susie; she was short and quiet with cropped hair and an impish face. The house was empty apart from the new fox terrier, Bridget. Two billeted soldiers now lived with Elizabeth but they were away on manoeuvres for a few weeks. There was talk of an imminent invasion by air and searchlights scoured the night sky for signs of the expected Luftwaffe. Elizabeth was terrified of the Germans breaking in at night; she found it hard to sleep in the house by herself and wedged the front door shut with the ironing board. Mrs Brown had agreed that when the air raid siren sounded they would meet in the shelter so she wouldn't be alone.

Phyllis's heart had skipped a beat at the thought of Elizabeth coming to stay. She'd have to ask her landlady first. Mrs Osmund agreed that Phyllis's mother-in-law could visit for a few days in the New Year. She said the dog could sleep in the kitchen by the range and that Elizabeth could have the lean-to. Phyllis couldn't imagine Elizabeth sleeping with no curtains or heating in the cold lean-to. She'd have to give up her own bedroom and sleep in the front room herself. It would only be for a few days, it's what Arthur would expect of her.

Pip was thrilled with Phyllis's sewing. She paid her a bit extra for doing the job so quickly.

"My husband, Gilbert, will be delighted he doesn't have to walk around with a tight belt on his trousers to stop them falling down. He's in France at the moment at some ghastly army camp. I'm not even sure where. Now you simply must stay for a cup of tea and tell me all about yourself; you're not from around here, of that I am quite sure," said Pip intrigued. Phyllis told Pip about being born and brought up in India.

"The Raj! How exotic! I knew you were something a bit special the moment I clapped eyes on you with glue in your hair. Dear Phyl, I think we are going to become the best of friends," smiled Pip as she gripped Phyllis's hand. "Now how about a nice gin and tonic?" Pip walked over to the drinks cabinet and poured them each a large glass.

Phyllis looked longingly at the piano.

"Do you play? Oh tell me you do, that would simply be the icing on the cake."

"Yes, I used to play a lot," replied Phyllis excitedly, "before, well, before coming to England. I ran a restaurant with my sister."

"A restaurant!" replied Pip. "How terribly exciting, tell me more."

They spoke of India, riding, garden parties and meeting Arthur in Nainital. Pip was enthralled by Phyllis and her experiences in India.

"Anytime you feel like playing the piano, please be my guest, the poor beast just sits there gathering dust when the children are away. Rather like me."

Phyllis laughed as she settled herself down on the plush piano stool. "What would you like me to play?"

"Anything, anything at all." She closed her eyes in anticipation and she wasn't disappointed by Phyllis's playing. "You are wonderful, dear girl. Now I gather the cinema is open again due to the war being phoney and all that gubbins. Lets go to the flicks on Christmas Eve, it will be such fun."

*

Phyllis equipped herself with a torch with greaseproof paper wrapped around its lens. She felt in her pocket for the tin of pepper that Mrs Osmund had given her. "Jus throw it in t' face," she warned.

There was talk of men taking advantage of lone women. Phyllis had never ventured out at night on her own in the blackout and she wasn't really sure it was such a good idea now, she pulled on her long woollen coat and checked herself in the hall mirror for the tenth time. Mr Osmund insisted on accompanying her to the bus stop. Phyllis checked her purse and felt pleased she was earning her own money again.

"In a bit," Mr Osmund called over his shoulder to his wife as he hobbled down the front step.

Phyllis stuck to Mr Osmund's side like glue for fear of falling off a curb or tripping over. She was relieved to reach the main road.

"Tarra then flower, mind ow y' go." Mr Osmund left her at the bus stop and turned back to navigate his way home. Phyllis could hear the light clomp of his wooden leg get quieter as he disappeared into the night. Phyllis was hugely relieved when her bus turned up.

Pip was already standing in the cinema queue when Phyllis finally arrived. The smell of ale and cigarette smoke greeted her as she walked past the troops; most of them were out for the night with the latest local girl on their arm.

Phyllis and Pip settled themselves into the smoky cinema. Pip went to the bar and came back with a couple of whisky and ginger ales just as the Pathe newsreels rolled into action showing Chamberlain heading off to Paris, troops boarding trains and the King and Queen with the two young princesses posing around a perfectly-shaped Christmas tree at Buckingham Palace.

Pip held Phyllis's hand, "down the hatch old girl, here's to our loved ones; Gilbert and Arthur, may they be safe and well. Happy Christmas."

With that she took a large gulp and kicked off her high-heeled shoes, tucking her stockinged feet underneath her bottom. They roared with laughter at 'Goodbye Mr Chips'. It was a cosy film with a feel-good ending. They left the cinema to find a light dusting of snow had covered the ground.

By the time Phyllis arrived home, the children were tucked up in bed. Mrs Osmund was relieved to see her back safely. She grumbled about the blackout as Phyllis made them all cocoa and put the children's presents in the stockings that hung from the mantelpiece. Phyllis took a nibble of the carrot left for Father Christmas and got Mr Osmund to drink the snifter of brandy. As Phyllis lay in bed that night she looked at the sleeping children before turning out the light. What a shame their daddy wasn't going to be with them on Christmas day; it was Eileen's first, too. She shivered as she rolled over; the thin blanket had exposed her shoulder to the cold air. Even her eyeballs felt cold; she hid under the heavy bedclothes and wrapped her arms around the pillow. "I miss you," she whispered.

Mrs Osmund set the fires early so that when Phyllis and the girls came down to open their stockings the rooms would be warm. The pheasant that Mrs Osmund so generously shared was delicious. It was almost as if there was no war on. The King's Christmas speech was broadcast at 3pm. He stuttered his way through the broadcast like a nervous child performing a school play. He spoke awkwardly of hard times ahead, how the British were strong and resilient and how they should all stick together and look after each other. Mrs Osmund smiled lovingly at Phyllis and promised to look after her.

15

8TH JANUARY 1940

Elizabeth squeezed her bulky body out through the train door, dragging her suitcase after her. It fell ungraciously onto the platform with a heavy thud. Her gas mask slung over her shoulder, its canvas strap just long enough to be placed over her head and under one arm, separating her bosoms. Bridget, her newly acquired Fox Terrier was glad to relieve herself against the lamppost that now dripped with dark yellow urine. Elizabeth reprimanded the little wire-haired dog for narrowly missing the suitcase.

Phyllis was sorting out sheets and blankets and tidying her bedroom. Clothes were strewn on the bed. The girl's toys covered the floor. Her trunk sat open, its lid propped against the wall. She still hadn't unpacked all of it. Dust had gathered under the bed. Phyllis felt a sense of dread as she got on her hands and knees and started brushing out the grey fluff that had clung together in big clumps.

"Y' alright in there, flower?" called Mrs Osmund through the bedroom wall just as the taxi pulled up.

"Oh God, I haven't even started on the kitchen yet," yelled Phyllis, almost hysterical with the anticipation of Elizabeth's arrival.

Maureen laughed with delight at her mother's frenzied tidying. Phyllis shoved items into cupboards and tipped things into the trunk. Dirty plates were practically thrown into the sink, splashing soapy water up the wall. It was already midday and Mr Osmund was in the tin tub in the bathroom singing at the top of his voice. Elizabeth would be shocked to find a man in the bath at this time of day.

Mrs Osmund touched Phyllis's shoulder and told her to calm down. "Anyone t'would think t' Queen wa cumin."

"Exactly," laughed Phyllis as she went out to greet the taxi, tidying her messy hair as she opened its door. Elizabeth let Phyllis carry her heavy bag as she led the dog down the path. Mrs Osmund welcomed her into her home and led the way to the kitchen. Elizabeth scanned the cluttered room.

"On Ilkla Moor Baht 'at," sang Mr Osmund, unaware of the 'royal' visitor.

Mrs Osmund laughed and banged on the bathroom door. "Turn it down a bit luvvie, we have a guest."

Phyllis hugged Elizabeth warmly but her mother-in-law visibly winced at her surroundings. Her stiffened lips forced out a grin when she saw the children; a little grubby but well fed and happy. Maureen spied a couple of presents sticking out of Elizabeth's handbag and hoped that one of them was for her. She kissed her granny fondly and made herself comfortable on her wide lap as the grown-ups sat drinking tea and started talking about Hitler again. The British had been sure he was going to invade France on New Year's Eve, although the nation had braced themselves for news, none had come. They'd had the wireless turned on for all six news bulletins throughout the day.

Ration books had been issued a few months before, but today was the first time rationing of bacon, butter and sugar was enforced. Elizabeth had brought her book with her along with her identity card. Mrs Osmund reported that she had seen queues forming outside the butchers on the way to work that morning.

"It looks as though people are panic buying," said Elizabeth. "If we all act like civilised human beings we shall be fine, there is no reason why anyone should starve to death."

Steam rose from the stained teapot's spout. Phyllis had got used to the strong tea but she noticed Elizabeth discreetly wipe the rim of her cracked teacup with her hankie and gasp involuntarily as she tried to swallow the dark brown liquid, as if it were cod liver oil. Mr Osmund then appeared half naked from the bathroom.

"How do?" he nodded, his short towel wrapped around his waist just long enough to cover the top of his stump; steam rising from his semolina coloured shoulders. He clomped his way up the stairs with his crutch.

Phyllis showed Elizabeth the parlour. "This is our sitting room, perhaps you'll be more comfortable in here," said Phyllis, kicking a piece of stray coal under the chair.

"I see you're taking in work," said Elizabeth, eyeing up the sewing machine in the corner of the room. A neat pile of other people's clothes sat next to it with handwritten labels pinned to each item. "What are you now, some kind of dressmaker?"

"I'm just taking in a few sewing jobs. I have Arthur's approval, it'll help make ends meet." Phyllis felt she'd sounded too defensive and decided it would be better to talk of other things.

"Just as long as the girls are being looked after properly," said Elizabeth. She let out a loud groan as she spotted the canaries "Whatever are they doing in here? It can't be healthy, birds carry terrible diseases, ask Peg."

"Why don't we get out for a bit? We could walk to the park with the children, it's a beautiful day."

"If it's all the same to you dear I'd like a little lie down in my room and then we can catch up on all our news later," she looked at Phyllis as if she was a housemaid.

Phyllis led her mother-in-law up the stairs to her bedroom. It looked in some sort of order now and the sheets were clean. Elizabeth smelt the pillow and gave a nod of approval.

"Oh, am I to have Maureen in here with me?"

She'd spotted the second single bed, Snozzles' little furry head was peeking out from the blanket.

"Yes, if that's all right with you. We don't have a lot of space I'm afraid."

Elizabeth smiled properly for the first time since she arrived. "That's just splendid my dear. I'm in need of a little company."

Loud snoring soon emanated from the room. Maureen giggled as she sat on the stairs, waiting for her granny to wake, so she could have her present.

"Come away and leave her alone," hissed Phyllis.

Maureen left her posting and followed her mother into the kitchen. Bridget was curled up on an old blanket that Mrs Osmund produced from the lean-to. Maureen wasn't used to dogs and was cautious of its jumpy behaviour and black gummy mouth, jammed with pointy teeth and long pink tongue.

"Let's take Bridget for a walk shall we? Just to the end of the road and back," said Phyllis.

Maureen was thrilled at the idea and was the first to be ready to go, standing impatiently at the door with her gloves, scarf and coat on. They ventured out into the cold January day, Phyllis held onto Maureen's little gloved hand and wondered what the coming year, 1940, had in store for them.

"Daddy!" shouted Maureen.

"Yes," said Phyllis, "we'll see daddy soon darling."

"Daddy!" said Maureen more forcefully pointing to a soldier walking towards them, a huge box under one arm and a brown package in the other.

Phyllis looked up and caught sight of a tall man in the distance, uniformed and walking with purpose in their direction. As he got closer Phyllis realised it was Arthur, it was Arthur's walk. She wouldn't let herself believe it at first just in case it wasn't him, he hadn't told them he was coming home, but it was him, she could make out his dark moustache.

"Arthur, oh Arthur," Phyllis ran with Maureen.

"Phyllis, darling Phyllis," Arthur placed the large parcels on the pavement and embraced her as if he'd been gone for years. He kissed her cheeks and stroked her hair out of her face.

"Thought I'd surprise you, sweetheart." He plucked Maureen from the pavement and whirled her around in his arms.

"And how's my little poppet?" he asked snuggling his moustache into her neck. It tickled and scratched all at the same time.

"Maureen spotted you first. I didn't dare to think it could be you. I thought you were away?"

"Got back this morning. I've got four days leave, let's pretend its Christmas all over again."

"Where have you been? Or is it a huge secret?"

"I'm not allowed to say, but it's been nowhere exciting."

"Just reassure me that you are eating properly and looking after yourself."

"You're beginning to sound like the old lady," laughed Arthur.

In all the excitement Phyllis forgot to mention that his mother had arrived about an hour ago. Arthur groaned when he realised the dog at the end of the lead was Bridget, his mother's new pet.

"I forgot you'd invited her. I hope she's behaving herself?" he whispered, so Maureen couldn't hear.

"Well, she sort of invited herself. Now you're here everything will be just fine." Phyllis had such a feeling of relief, almost more relieved that Arthur would save her from his mother than the fact that Arthur was home.

"Arthur, is that you?" called Elizabeth, in disbelief.

"Yes Mums, it's me," replied Arthur.

Elizabeth called for him to go and see her, as she was too

exhausted to get out of bed.

Arthur rolled his eyes at Phyllis, "Here we go, I'll just say hello then I'll give you and the girls your Christmas presents."

Arthur ran up the stairs, two at a time before shortly reappearing in the front parlour with his parcels. "I know its a bit late Phyl, but happy Christmas."

Phyllis unwrapped the brown paper, to discover a small black travel gramophone complete with three records. "I don't believe it, where did you get this?"

She was thrilled to be the owner of such a splendid thing. She'd had to leave her precious gramophone in Benares.

"I won it from one of the lads. We had a card game and he'd run out of money."

Phyllis looked happy and sad all at the same time. "Poor chap, he must be feeling a bit glum."

Arthur reassured Phyllis that all was fair when it came to gambling. Even so, Phyllis couldn't help but feel sorry for the unfortunate chap. Arthur placed a large present on Maureen's lap.

"And this one is for you." Maureen's tiny fingers tore at the brown paper to reveal the head of a beautiful doll. Its shiny brown hair fell about her shoulders. As she tore more paper away it revealed a purple velvet jacket with shiny brass buttons and a red tartan kilt around her waist.

"She's all the way from Scotland," said Arthur. "She's a Scotch doll."

From that moment that's what the treasured doll was called; Scotch Doll.

Arthur cradled Eileen and got Maureen to open Eileen's present for her; a fluffy black and white panda. He was almost as big as Eileen and was immediately named Pandy.

That night after supper, Phyllis, Arthur and Elizabeth sat in the front room. Phyllis went to make tea and on her return overheard Elizabeth telling Arthur that she found the house dirty and chaotic, not the sort of house to bring up children. The children looked grubby and Maureen's hair looked like a birds' nest. Elizabeth changed the subject when Phyllis entered the room. "The truth is, I'm scared of living in the house by myself, its hard to get a lodger now I've got the billeted soldiers with me. What if the Germans invade in the middle of the night and knock my door down?"

Arthur tried to reassure his mother that she would be fine; she had good neighbours looking out for her and said perhaps she ought to think about moving back in with Auntie Lillian.

Elizabeth looked at the floor. "No, I think I'll stick it out for the moment," she said. "Phyllis dear, perhaps the children would be better off living with me in Colchester? After all this house is very......" Elizabeth paused to choose her words carefully, "well, very small."

Phyllis looked to Arthur, who in turn picked up the poker and started prodding the glowing coals.

"Thank you for your concern, but we've settled in rather well here and I'm able to see Arthur a little more often. I've also made a friend and have a bit of work. I'm really quite happy," said Phyllis.

"As you wish, but you really must keep on top of things. Maureen looks as though she hasn't had a bath for weeks and there she is with her fingers in her mouth. It's not hygienic."

"Mother, I think Phyllis can manage perfectly well," said Arthur, finally coming to Phyllis's defence.

"Just trying to be helpful," said Elizabeth, feigning offence.

The sitting room door opened. Phyllis had never been so pleased to see Mr Osmund who had a bottle of brandy in his hand. Elizabeth declined but was easily persuaded as Mr Osmund told her a little nip would do her nerves good. Arthur placed the gramophone on the table next to the sewing machine and asked Phyllis for a dance. He waltzed Phyllis around the cramped front parlour. Elizabeth looked on in envy at the love she'd never had with Frederick.

*

An icy draught blew in through the sash windows and up from the gaps in the floorboards, keeping Phyllis and Arthur awake as they lay on the makeshift bed. Eileen's cot had been placed in the corner of the room and she was restless too.

"The old lady means well you know," said Arthur, snuggling up to Phyllis.

"I just feel that she wants to find fault all the time."

"Perhaps you should try and keep things a bit tidier, then she might back off a bit."

Phyllis propped herself up on her elbow and looked at Arthur. "So you think she has a point?"

"Well, the children could do with a bath once a week and Maureen's hair is very knotted."

"Oh that's just marvellous, I have you criticising me as well now, do I?"

"There's no need to get offended. I'm just saying the children might benefit."

Eileen's gentle moaning had turned into a full-blown cry.

"Now you've woken Eileen up," snapped Phyllis, picking her up and placing her in their bed.

Arthur was frustrated; he wanted Phyllis all to himself. He turned over, creating a cold draught between their bodies and pretended to go to sleep.

There had been a heavy frost that night, leaving a thick, opaque layer of hard ice on the inside of the windowpanes. The milk had frozen in the bottles on the front step, pushing out the cardboard seals.

Arthur rolled over to face Phyllis. "I'm sorry, darling. Let's not let that silly disagreement ruin our time together. I've got to be off again in three days and I don't know when I'll see you again."

Phyllis edged her body towards Arthur's. "I'll try to keep on top of things but please don't side with your mother. It's bad enough having her breathing down my neck. I couldn't bear it if you started nagging me as well." replied Phyllis, taking his cold hands and slipping them in between her warm thighs.

"I promise," said Arthur as he kissed her tenderly on the nose, the tip of which was red and cold. "Now let's get you warmed up a bit."

Arthur buried his head under the eiderdown.

"I'm now going to kiss you all over," smiled Arthur, "starting right here." He kissed the tips of her fingers.

*

"What are you so happy about?" asked Elizabeth at the breakfast table.

"Oh nothing, it's just good to be alive," replied Arthur winking at Phyllis. He helped out around the house all day doing the odd jobs that Mr Osmund couldn't manage. Arthur mended a chair leg, laid tarpaulin over the leaky lean-to roof, fixed the lavatory chain and took the children to the park.

Phyllis did her best to tiptoe around Elizabeth. She'd bathed the girls and managed to get a comb through Maureen's knots. She needed to deliver a cocktail dress to a lady across town.

"Just off to deliver the dress," she shouted up to her mother-in-law, "won't be long."

She had also managed to bake a ginger cake that morning. The kitchen had been left in a mess; flour spilt over the pine table and cake tins encrusted with sponge were stacked up in the sink.

Apart from Elizabeth and the children, the house was empty. She walked into the kitchen and surveyed the mess like a crime scene. "Just the kitchen," she said to Bridget. "I'm sure no one will object."

She got started on the paper chains that hung from the ceiling, tearing them down, poking them in through the range's door, as if fuelling the firebox of a steam engine.

Mrs Osmund was surprised when she came home from work to find her kitchen immaculate. The range gleamed, the crusty shelves scrubbed; the lino almost back to its original dark red; and the table cleared of all piles of papers, receipts and leaflets.

"Ah woud nivver had recognised the owd place," said Mrs Osmund, as she bustled in through the back door.

"Well, I had nothing better to do. I hope you don't mind Mrs Osmund," replied Elizabeth.

Mrs Osmund unpacked the contents of her shopping basket onto the newly cleared table. Elizabeth, with a slight frown on her face, quickly snatched up the offending items and placed them in their rightful places on the pantry shelves.

*

His uniform touched the small hairs on Phyllis's bare forearms, sending delicate shivers of delight into her belly. It was Arthur's last night of leave and they'd gone to St Oswald's dance hall. Phyllis had wondered if they'd ever dance again and here they were, foxtrotting. Arthur steered her around the hall like a professional; his hands on her slender waist.

"I love you," whispered Phyllis into his ear.

"I love you, too."

"Would you mind if we sit the next dance out? My feet are killing me," asked Phyllis.

They sauntered back to their drinks table.

"Woollie?" A woman came bounding towards Arthur, an inquisitive smile on her face.

"Oh, Helen, hello," replied Arthur.

"Do you come here often?" she laughed.

Arthur was flustered, Phyllis could tell because he was twiddling his moustache.

"Helen, this is my wife, Phyllis," said Arthur introducing the two women.

"Your wife?" asked Helen puzzled.

"Pleased to meet you," said Phyllis holding out her hand.

"Indeed," said Helen. "Do you have a light, Woollie?"

Arthur took the brass lighter from his top pocket and held the flame to the tip of her cigarette.

"You are an angel. See you around, soldier." Helen then trotted back to the dance floor and picked up with her group of giggling friends.

"Who was that?"

"She's just one of the laundry girls from the camp. We hang out in the mess sometimes."

"Why did she seem so surprised that you are married or do you keep that a secret?" Phyllis's throat was so tight she could barely speak.

"I don't go around discussing my marital status with all and sundry if that's what you mean?"

"I just hope she's not like Mrs Pearce," said Phyllis sharply, not able to disguise her jealousy.

"Who the hell is Mrs Pearce?"

"You know, that ghastly tart on the ship carrying on with the barman."

"Oh her. She's a one off, I'm sure."

"And what about Elsie?"

"What about Elsie?"

"Do you still write to her or is it just your mother that has her in her pocket?"

"That's not fair, Mums is very fond of Elsie. And I'm sorry you had to meet her like that. She's been through a very difficult time. Peg wrote to me and told me what happened. But I have no contact with her. I promise. Please believe me Phyllis when I say you are the only woman for me. I do live in an army camp and there are women there but we only dance and chat and share cigarettes. That's all. No funny business. I promise."

"One more dance for the road and then I'd like to go home."

She was determined to show everyone at the dance hall just who Arthur was married to. She danced like she'd never danced before, energised by adrenalin and jealousy despite her tired feet.

The following morning Arthur packed up his kitbag.

She held on to him tightly. "The thought of you dancing with pretty young girls makes me feel sad." Phyllis felt guilty as the words slipped out of her mouth unguarded.

Arthur fiddled with his moustache. "Now don't be so silly, you know there's no harm in a bit of dancing. Now no more of this nonsense do you promise?"

Phyllis nodded but felt utterly miserable. She wanted to cry and cry; tears spiked at the back of her eyes. She felt like begging him to be faithful but she didn't; she swallowed hard and told him she loved him instead. She didn't want to feel like this, let alone show Arthur she was feeling jealous.

*

A few days later Elizabeth packed, ready for the journey back to Colchester in the morning. She was nervous about going home to an empty house. A German plane on mine-laying operations had been fired upon by anti-aircraft guns above Clacton-on-Sea; it had come crashing down, demolishing fifty houses and killing two people. It had been the first incident of German air activity near Colchester. There had been a few one-off bombings on the Shetland Islands and U-boats had sunk a handful of ships including H.M.S. Courageous, killing six hundred men, but nothing as close to home as Clacton.

Phyllis lay in the sitting room that night, cuddled up with

Eileen for warmth. She comforted herself with the knowledge that Elizabeth was going home tomorrow and she could return to her own bed. The wind howled as the bay window's frame rattled like chattering teeth. She got up and pulled the curtain back to see snow falling. Snowflakes the size of one-penny coins tumbled from the sky. A white blanket of virgin snow covered everything she could see like a freshly iced Christmas cake. She felt a surge of excitement at the thought of something different happening, it changed things, it changed her landscape. But then her heart raced, what if the trains stopped running? Elizabeth would be stranded.

16

THE BIG FREEZE

The snow fell for three days, and was nearly as high as the downstairs windows as it drifted in the bitter, northerly winds. Everything had come to a standstill. All roads were impassable; vehicles were abandoned by the roadsides and stuck in snowdrifts. Nobody could get anywhere other than on foot. The milk, coal, paraffin, groceries and postal deliveries came to an abrupt halt. Most of the shops, if you could reach them, were closed.

The power lines were pulled down by the weight of the snow and the water was frozen in the taps. Even the outside toilet had frozen. Ice had formed on top of the snow, making it treacherously slippery. No telegrams were getting through either.

"What on earth are we going to do, how am I going to get home?" asked Elizabeth, pacing about the sitting room willing the snow to stop.

Phyllis looked at her mother-in-law then looked out at the snow. "I don't think you're going anywhere for a while."

The next few weeks were spent trying to keep warm. They kept all their clothes on, day and night. Phyllis took to wearing a woolly hat in bed.

At night, Phyllis had heard the dull droning engines of the German reconnaissance planes, probably heading for Newcastle, but no bombs were dropped. Invasion seemed unlikely whilst the country was in such blankness; it was as if all maps had been rubbed out, leaving just a faint pencilled outline of the British coastline. Instead of air raid sirens she heard the cracking of iron drain pipes as the expanding ice split them open.

Phyllis volunteered to dig a trench from the back door to the coalbunker.

"What in God's name do you think you look like?" Asked Elizabeth as Phyllis entered the kitchen wearing her jodhpurs and Mr Osmund's large black wellies that rose over her knees.

"They're the only pair of trousers I own," laughed Phyllis. "Send out a search party if I'm not back in half an hour."

Elizabeth sat wringing her painfully cold hands in her lap, groaning every time a blast of cold air escaped into the comparative warmth of the kitchen. After an hour of digging, Phyllis had cleared a narrow path. Mrs Osmund held out the old tin bucket as Phyllis shovelled the glistening fuel into it.

Mr Osmund stoked the range and decided it would be best if they lived in the kitchen to conserve fuel. Phyllis dragged a rug in from the front room and put some cushions on the wooden chairs to make them more comfortable. Mr Osmund put draught excluders made of old newspapers around the bottom of the doors.

"What do we do now?" asked Elizabeth concerned that she may be stuck in the kitchen for the foreseeable future.

"I've got an idea," said Phyllis brightly. "We can play a game called 'My Ship Comes Laden'. You knot a hankie like this," she gestured, "and you throw it at someone as you say 'my ship comes laden with a letter, for example P'. The person who catches it has to name something like pineapples, pickle, peg. You choose any letter you like."

Phyllis took out her hankie and threw it expertly at Elizabeth, shouting out the letter H. It fell to the floor as Elizabeth struggled to catch it. Maureen picked it up and placed it on her grandmother's lap blurting out the word Hitler. They all laughed. Having exhausted the alphabet, they played charades and then whist. By the evening, they lit candles and a paraffin lamp that was stowed away for emergencies. Maureen thought it was all jolly good fun but the adults were starting to suffer from boredom and worry that their situation could get even worse.

"What it we run out of food?" asked Elizabeth.

"I'm sure it won't come to that," replied Phyllis.

"How much coal is in the bunker?"

"Enough for about two weeks if we're careful. You might be warmer in bed, why don't you go on up. I'll bring you a hot water bottle," replied Phyllis.

Five more days of the sub-zero conditions held them captive in the kitchen. Massive icicles hung like glassy fingers from the gutters. Birds stopped singing and perished in the trees, falling to their sad little deaths with a gentle thud into the deep snow. Branches snapped as if they were straw.

Slowly neighbours ventured into the bleak outdoors. People retrieved old prams and handcarts from the piles of possessions stored in garden sheds; anything that could be dragged down the road to the shops to restock the emptying larders. The scene outside reminded Phyllis of a Bruegel painting.

Feigning a headache, Phyllis slipped upstairs to reclaim her bedroom for a couple of hours. She wrapped the eiderdown around her cold body. As she lay on Maureen's bed, she spotted the shoebox stuffed with letters underneath what had become Elizabeth's bed. Phyllis loved to reread these paper treasures. She took one out that had arrived from India a few weeks before Christmas with a picture of Muriel's wedding enclosed. She looked pretty, although she still smiled for photographs with a closed mouth to conceal the crooked eye tooth she was so self-conscious of. Her dress was long and simple, cut on the bias to flatter her figure. She had an orchid bouquet and pale cream shoes. Austin looked dapper in a well-tailored suit, his mother by his side. Also inside the letter was a pressed orchid. Phyllis took it out of the tissue paper and wedged it into the corner of her dressing table mirror.

The letter concluded with a message from Wilmot. He was worried that Gandhi was stirring things up; as leader of The National Congress Party he said he would not support Britain in the war unless India was granted immediate independence. Thousands of freedom fighters had been killed by police gunfire and hundreds of thousands arrested. Wilmot signed off the letter: your loving daddy. She kissed the inky blue words and put the airmail paper to her cheek.

Phyllis then took out a photograph of her and Arthur having a picnic on a hilltop somewhere near Nainital. They'd ridden there with Muriel and a group of friends. Phyllis examined all the details of the photograph. She looked relaxed and smiling, half lying down on a rug with her solar topee covering her dark hair. Next to her and slightly to the front sat Muriel; tucked behind Muriel was Arthur, his legs outstretched, his long socks pulled up to meet his knee-length khaki shorts; a big smile on his face. The rest of their party sat behind them, looking at the camera. Who took the picture? Phyllis couldn't remember, maybe it was one of the bearers who had accompanied them. Phyllis remembered what had happened half an hour before the photograph was taken. It was her birthday and Arthur had slipped her a note on the ride to the picnic spot; he'd wanted to give her a special present. They had slipped away along the ridge and hid amongst the rhododendron bushes. They'd kissed hungrily fearing that Muriel would come looking for them. Arthur had expertly made love to her whilst propped up against the trunk of a tree. Afterwards Arthur picked one of the bright pink flowers and tucked it into the band on Phyllis's hat. She laughed as she looked at the picture with Muriel leant against the picnic basket oblivious to the goings-on.

Phyllis stretched up on tiptoes to retrieve her hat from its box on top of the wardrobe. She blew the thin layer of dust off the lid. The familiar smell of cork took her straight back to India. It was hard to imagine the intensity of the heat in Benares when she was so cold. She put the hat on her head and looked at herself in the mirror. She thought her face had changed, she looked paler and thinner. Her once plump cheeks sagged slightly on her face, her full lips now turned down at the corners. The bags under Phyllis's eyes seemed more permanent.

Elizabeth barged into the room without knocking.

"What are you doing with that thing on your head?"

"Just dreaming," replied Phyllis.

"Day dreaming's no use to anyone. Why don't you go and make yourself useful instead of skulking around up here playing dressing up. Arthur needs his jacket mending, I suggest you get on with it while I have a lie down, my legs are killing me."

Phyllis reluctantly fetched Arthur's tweed jacket from the wardrobe. She'd promised him she would mend the pocket before his next leave.

The sewing machine was in her sitting room where the cold air seemed to cling to the walls. The machine's metal handle made Phyllis's hand numb after only a few turns. She decided to move it into the kitchen; although already overcrowded, she managed to clear a space on the table. As she turned the offending pocket inside out and gathered the frayed material ready for pinning, she felt a small piece of cardboard that had fallen through the lining. Phyllis put her hand in and fished it out. It was a ticket to the Spitfire ball dated 29th November. It was a ticket for two.

*

Mountains of dirty snow now towered on the curbsides as the roads were slowly cleared. Traffic started up again, trains were running and shops reopened. Coal and paraffin were delivered and the power lines restored. Phyllis felt she could throw off her heavy clothes and breathe again as the low sun shone in through the windows, casting criss-cross patterns from the taped glass panes onto the floor, like a carpet of shadows. The melting icicles dripped down the sides of the houses, splashing rhythmically onto the pavements. Phyllis sang along to the slow rhythm.

Elizabeth finally took her seat on the train, glad to leave the chaotic house behind. Out of the taxi's window, on the way to the station, she'd witnessed tanks noisily driving through the usually quiet streets of Catterick. Smoke bellowed from their underbellies, their tracks rattled over the melting snow. The huge convoys were heading for France. Green canvas-covered army trucks sped past, one after the other. Soldiers sang and jeered out of the flapping tarpaulin, happy to be leaving the parade grounds. The trains were packed with troops. Young men dressed in fatigues were jammed into railway stations across Britain; huge rucksacks the size of men strapped to their backs. Sons, husbands and fathers all leaving to defend their country; now under serious threat from Germany. They were summoned away from the love of their families by a simple letter arriving in a manila envelope. Some were taught how to use rifles and bayonets before being sent off as part of the British Expeditionary Force to Europe. Others went into the Navy or Air Force and quickly learnt how to fly a bomber or man a submarine. Elizabeth was filled with dread at the thought of returning to her house on her own. At least she had Bridget. She bent down and stroked the dog curled up by her feet.

On February 3rd, news reached Catterick that a German Heinkel aircraft had been shot down over Whitby, only sixty miles away. It was said to have been seeking out a convoy of British ships in the North Sea. Air raids were becoming more frequent again. Phyllis and the children now had a nightly routine in place. Phyllis slept under the eiderdown with all her clothes on and Maureen would sleep in her siren suit. If a siren sounded, Phyllis would wrap Eileen in a blanket, snatch the gas masks off the hook and run out to the shelter. Each night before Phyllis went to bed she'd check the shelter for puddles and spiders and make sure the lamp had enough paraffin. Then she'd place the dry box of matches on the table.

Mrs Osmund had gone into a screaming panic one day when she saw a black crow land on the shelter's roof. She was convinced that if a crow sat on a dwelling it meant someone would die in it. From that day onwards she would not set foot in the shelter under any circumstances.

Mr Osmund had never bothered. "Ah ain't wekken for nay Nazis," he laughed.

He found it impossible to get out of bed and down the stairs quickly and decided he was better off staying put.

By March, meat was rationed. It was getting harder to prepare a tasty meal from the ingredients they could get hold of. One of Mr Osmund's friends from the camp went hunting with traps and snares in the local woods and would visit on Saturday afternoons with a sack stuffed with his booty, mostly rabbits and a few pigeons, in exchange for a glass of brandy. The animals would be gutted, skinned and plucked by Mr Osmund. Phyllis was relieved she didn't have to do this ghastly job. Mr Osmund would come back into the kitchen from the back garden, his hands covered in blood, feathers stuck to the dark stains on his fingers. His fingernails housed the black, dried-up blood, which would still be there a few days later. The household would tuck into the wild meat with relish; just a small pile of bones would remain on the side of each plate.

Phyllis read in the newspaper that the Germans were desperate to gain air supremacy before their planned land invasion. Air raids were now a nightly occurrence. Steamships, troopships and vessels of all sorts including fishing trawlers were being sunk by mines and torpedoed by German U-boats. The Germans had also seized Norway and Denmark, providing them with bases to launch air raids on the north east of England. Arthur wrote saying he was worried that Catterick was close to Newcastle upon Tyne, Humber and Tynemouth, all major shipbuilding ports. He worried that Phyllis and the children could be in immediate danger and thought it may be better for her to go back to Colchester. Phyllis replied to his letter explaining how happy she was in Catterick and the thought of living with Elizabeth again was too much to contemplate.

*

Arthur's letters continued to arrive once a week, coded as agreed; it was clear he was no longer in Catterick but on manoeuvres somewhere else in the country. Phyllis was relieved he hadn't been sent to France as so many soldiers already had. She searched for clues as to his whereabouts but his tightly scrawled writing gave nothing away. The letters spoke of everyday life, men he was bunked up with, sketchy details of the training he was doing and nights out they had managed to snatch. He enjoyed playing billiards in the mess and gambling on the greyhounds. One of his letters requested that Phyllis must try to draw less from their Post Office account as he had built up a few debts.

Phyllis spent most of her days queuing for food and trying to find new ways to make it go further. She'd fry all the seasonal vegetables in left over dripping and add a pinch of cumin, garam masala and turmeric, turning it into a tasty chiticky served with aloo. Carrot biscuits had become a favourite with Maureen, a recipe Pip had given Phyllis when they last met. Pip and Phyllis saw each other at least twice a week, swapping hand-copied recipes, often supplied by The Ministry of Food. Phyllis played Pip's piano and if the weather was fine, Pip would set up her easels in the garden so they could paint the spring bulbs that burst into life.

Elizabeth's billeted soldiers had been replaced by new ones. She wrote of them fondly, saying they were well-behaved lads and that she felt safer having them in the house at night. Phyllis pictured Elizabeth happy to have someone to mother in Arthur's absence. She secretly hoped this meant there would be no room in the house for herself and the girls. The air raids in Colchester were also getting more frequent and the Anderson shelter's puddle had grown to the size of a small garden pond. Elizabeth wasn't strong enough to bale out all the water so if the soldiers weren't there to help her, she'd wear her wellies, one of which had a hole in.

Phyllis sat down one evening to reply to Arthur's last letter. She took out her writing set, switched on the lamp and rested her legs on a small coffee table that she used as a mora. The habit of not putting her feet on the floor stayed with her. She also still shook her shoes out before placing her feet inside them, just in case a deadly scorpion was lurking. Her writing was getting smaller and smaller with every letter she wrote, just in case she couldn't buy any more paper. She shared her news from India that arrived every few weeks from Maude. Muriel had moved to Karachi as planned with Austin and she was three months pregnant, moaning already about morning sickness and having to give up her career. Phyllis told Arthur how she and Pip had met up for tea in the week and how they'd painted snowdrops whilst wrapped up in their coats. Kitty was delighted to have Eddie home with her again. Phyllis filled him in on all the family news. Eileen was growing fast and guzzling down her food, but always looked pale. Maureen had made a little blonde-haired friend called Jeanie who lived over the road.

Phyllis shifted in her seat as she thought of the jacket she had altered for Arthur a few weeks before. She'd simmered on the edge of jealousy and curiosity, not sure what to do until now. She decided it would be best to get it out in the open, dwelling on it would do no good and she found it hard to ignore. Why should she pretend she hadn't found it? It wasn't like she was snooping through his things. Phyllis decided to glue the ticket onto the letter with a question mark next to it.

She sealed the letter and wound up the gramophone, hoping it would cheer her up, then waltzed around the room, a cushion for a partner. Tears fell, surprising her warm cheeks. She wiped them away with the sleeve of her cardigan and slumped back down into the armchair. Her bottom lip trembled.

"Blast it," she said out loud.

Back in her bedroom, Phyllis slid her writing pad on top of the shoebox. Next to it was an old biscuit tin. After opening its tight lid and looking inside, she felt a sense of reassurance to see the pin money.

*

A few weeks later Phyllis ran down the stairs as the postman fed the post in through the letterbox. Two letters were addressed to Phyllis; one from Arthur now back in Catterick, and a letter from London, Kitty's pretty handwriting now so familiar on the envelope. She made a pot of tea and sat at the kitchen table with both letters staring up at her.

"What's up, flower?" Mrs Osmund's voice sang out as she entered the room, laden with dirty sheets.

Phyllis smiled at her well-meaning landlady and put her head in her hands.

"Oh Mrs Osmund," she said. "I'm so worried about what Arthur's letter will say; he hasn't written for two weeks, not since I implied something quite awful. Do I open Kitty's first and enjoy it before facing Arthur's reply?"

"Ah reckon you know best," said Mrs Osmund as she dragged the washtub from behind the bathroom door and filled it with hot water from the copper, sprinkling soap flakes from a box, ready for the day's washing to begin. She rolled up her sleeves and perched on a small milking stool, humming as she scrubbed, rocking backwards and forwards to the rhythm of her tune. Phyllis poured herself some strong tea and opened Kitty's letter. It was full of news from London. The Thames had frozen over in the big freeze. They had all gone ice-skating and almost forgotten there was a war on as the barrage balloons flew high above the capital's skyline, with the setting sun completing the surreal landscape. Her father was now a firewatcher and spent every other night away from home on the lookout for incendiary bombs. Hampstead tube station had become an air raid shelter, making travelling to work in the morning difficult as people were lying on the platforms from the previous night's raid. Kitty and her mother had taken on an allotment and the digging had blistered her soft hands. Their Jewish neighbours had fled to America, worried about an imminent invasion, leaving their house boarded up. The army were going to commandeer it; soon noisy troops would be arriving and her mother was dreading it.

She put Kitty's letter down on the table and picked up

Arthur's, noticing her hands shake. She carefully slit it open with the kitchen knife. The knock at the back door made Phyllis jump, the knife dropped to the floor with a sharp clatter. Their neighbour, Jeanie's father, stood smiling at the back door.

"Sorry to startle you, Mrs Woollett. Did you hear Eden's broadcast? They want volunteers to join the Home Guard. I was wondering if you had any old tools, pickaxes, forks, crowbars, anything like that in your shed you could donate for weapons?"

Phyllis asked Mrs Osmund, who fetched the old shed key and happily donated an axe and an old rusty pitchfork.

"That'll see them off," she said, cackling as she made her way back to her washing, rubbing the small of her back as she walked.

Phyllis decided to read Arthur's letter up in her room. He was clearly furious, even his handwriting looked cross. Arthur was deeply offended by her insinuation and the tone of her previous letter. "Are you accusing me of infidelity?" he questioned, adding that he felt Phyllis didn't trust him. He had only offered to take one of the WAAFS to the Spitfire ball, as she had just lost her brother in France and she needed jollying up. His letter continued to explain that he didn't normally tell her how bloody awful it was living in barracks and billets all the time, not knowing where he was to be sent next. He described his cold, uncomfortable living conditions, the thin blankets, the tasteless slop they were fed and the basic tin huts. Waking up with the dread of being sent to the front line. He told Phyllis how lucky she was to be warm, well fed and comfortable. He went on to say that he felt she had changed since leaving India. The children were dirty and the house was in chaos. Elizabeth had written to him about the unsatisfactory level of hygiene after she'd got snowed in, reporting that Phyllis acted like a girl, dressing up in silly clothes, dancing to the gramophone and painting with Pip.

Phyllis wiped her tears away, angry with herself for crying. She looked down at her blouse and noticed a dribble of dried egg. Maybe Arthur was right, maybe she had let herself go. She decided to write to her mother; perhaps she could help her; then again Wilmot had been unwell, she didn't want to worry her. Phyllis found herself knocking at Pip's door; having cycled hard all the way, she was quite out of breath. She'd cycled past the police station at the end of Pip's road. A pool of men gathered with axes, old hunting rifles; anything they could find to defend their country from the invading Germans.

"Phyl, whatever is the matter? You look in a terrible state," gasped Pip as she opened the front door.

Phyllis sobbed as she shared the contents of Arthur's letter. "I think he's falling out of love with me, whatever am I going to do?"

Pip pulled Phyllis off the sofa and led her up the stairs to her large bay-windowed bedroom. Next to the pretty dressing table was an enormous cupboard. As Pip opened the door, swathes of fabric fought their way out, pinks, blues, yellow, chiffons, lace and silk; all trying to catch Phyllis's eye.

"Take your pick," said Pip. "You can borrow any of them you like. Next time he has some leave you can stay here, pretend you are in a hotel. I shall go out for the evening and I'm sure Mrs Osmund will look after the children, then you can get the romance back in your life. What do you think?"

Phyllis burst into laughter. "What on earth would I do without you? I shall send him a telegram this afternoon telling him to get a night off as urgently as possible."

Pip poured Phyllis a large sherry and they sat in the drawing room, hatching their plan. Pip said she could get hold of a bit of meat on the black market. She would leave a stew cooking in the oven for them. Phyllis could open the front door in a ball gown; the gramophone would be playing in the background. Phyllis would pour them a drink before leading him up to the bedroom to seduce him.

Phyllis sent Arthur a telegram on the way home but by the time she'd left the Post Office the sherry was starting to wear off and doubts were creeping in. What if he couldn't get leave? What if he was in love with someone else? What if he laughed in her face? But it was too late now; the telegram had been sent. She tried on the deep purple silk gown that she'd chosen from Pip's large collection. She caught sight of herself in the mirror and barely recognised the smiling face looking back at her. She looked grown-up and feminine, like her mother dressed up for one of the Maharaja's banquets. She hemmed the dress the following day and eagerly awaited Arthur's reply. She didn't have to wait long. His telegram arrived a few days later: 'INTRIGUED BY YOUR MESSAGE. WILL TRY AND GET A NIGHT'S PASS NEXT WEEK. TALK OF UNIT MANOEUVRES SOON. WILL DO MY BEST.' The next few days Phyllis kept busy. She made herself a new pair of silk panties, the sort that Arthur adored. She borrowed face cream from Pip and experimented with rag rolling her hair at night to make it curly like Kitty had done on the ship. Mrs Osmund gave her some silk stockings she'd been saving but decided she would probably never wear.

Meanwhile, the Munich agreement that Neville Chamberlain had signed with Hitler had failed. On the 10th of May the Prime Minister resigned. It was now up to Winston Churchill to save Britain from the Nazis. The British Expeditionary Force was being driven out of France and cornered on the beaches of Dunkirk.

17

THE SEDUCTION

"The stew is in the oven and will be ready at 9 o'clock. The whisky is in the decanter on the drinks cabinet and the gramophone is wound up and ready to go." Pip stood smiling at her pretty friend. "You've scrubbed up pretty well, young lady."

Phyllis stood nervously hugging a gin and tonic. Her dark hair fell in delicate waves to her shoulders. Her cheeks glowed from scrubbing them earlier in the bath with a concoction of oatmeal and a tiny bit of her rationed sugar. The silk knickers rubbed tantalisingly against her inner thighs. She wore no shoes but her toenails were painted with Pip's red nail varnish and could just be seen under the opaque silk of Mrs Osmund's stockings.

"When he knocks at the door, I'll leave by the back gate, then I'll come home about midnight and creep into the spare room. You won't even know I'm here."

The friends sat in the drawing room giggling like a couple of schoolgirls.

"What if he doesn't turn up?" Phyllis felt her stomach lurch as she heard footsteps followed by a loud knock at the door. She stood up out of her chair. "Oh my goodness Pip, he's here."

"Stop looking so worried Phyl, he's your husband. You look perfect, now for goodness sake enjoy yourself." Pip put her fur coat on and slipped out the back as Phyllis opened the front door.

"Hello, soldier, looking for a good time?" Arthur nearly fell backwards off the top step as he caught sight of Phyllis; her dress pulled up to reveal her stocking tops.

Arthur was totally speechless as Phyllis poured him a scotch and soda before leading him up the stairs by his tie, to the sound of 'Serenade in Blue'. She lay on the bed and pulled her long purple dress above her thighs revealing her shiny cream silk knickers. The candlelight flickered as her olive thighs peeped out teasingly between the hem of her panties and the top of her black stockings. She knew she was beautiful, she knew at that moment she could win him back as he ripped off his jacket and kissed her. He slid his fingers between her stockings and warm, soft flesh. They made love for hours until finally their bodies lay quietly together.

The smell of stew made Phyllis, feel hungry. She hadn't eaten since breakfast due to nerves; how silly she thought now, being nervous of Arthur. She slipped out of his embrace and wrapped herself in Pip's dressing gown.

"Where do you think you're going? Arthur had woken and lay looking up at her, a large grin on his tired face.

"I need to check on dinner. Are you hungry, darling?" Phyllis felt slightly ridiculous; she was no longer the seductress in a purple ball gown but a semi-naked wife in her friend's bedroom.

"Silly question," laughed Arthur. "I'll come down with you."

They went to the cold kitchen and Phyllis took the bubbling pot out of the oven.

"I'm sorry I doubted you, Arthur."

"You must learn to trust me."

"I'll try harder with the house and the girls. It's just so difficult to keep on top of everything."

"I know, I'm sorry. I was just so angry when I received your letter. I'm training flat out at the moment. The days are long and when I came back to the barracks to find your letter I overreacted."

"Does your mother write to you often about me?"

"You know what she's like, not happy unless she's moaning about something or another. I'll have a word with her about it."

"Okay, but don't go making matters any worse." Phyllis kissed his bare shoulder. "I thought I'd lost you. Not to the war but to another woman."

*

The next morning Phyllis woke to find Arthur's arms still wrapped loosely around her. She looked up the line of his body to his face; his dark eyes were focussed on her. The sound of sobbing was coming from the spare bedroom.

"I think your friend is crying," said Arthur.

"I'd better go and check, I wonder what's wrong?" She knocked gently on the bedroom door and found Pip sitting on the bed with the curtains half drawn, mascara staining her cheeks in dark streaks.

"Oh Phyl, I'm so worried, last night I heard that thousands of boats have been sent to Dunkirk to try and evacuate all the men. There is nowhere to go but the sea. Gilbert will be there now, if he's still alive. I haven't received a letter for three weeks. I don't even know where he is, what will I do if he doesn't come back?" Pip started sobbing again as Phyllis wrapped her arms around her.

"Oh my dearest Pip, you must be so worried. I'll get Arthur to see if he can find out anything."

"How are you dearest Phyl, did your night go well?" asked Pip sweetly.

"I'll tell you later, let's not talk about that now, we need to try and find out what's happened to Gilbert," said Phyllis.

Arthur blushed as he met Pip for the first time over the breakfast table; after all he had made love to Phyllis in her bed only a few hours ago. He left at 10 o'clock promising to find out all he could about Captain Gilbert Peacock. He kissed Phyllis tenderly as they parted.

"Thank you," he whispered as he left.

Pip sat biting her short nails across the table with worry. "How was it Phyl? Were things okay?"

"I don't know. Something was different when we were, you know."

"Making love?"

"It was as if he was making love to someone else."

"It's probably because you haven't been intimate with him for a while."

"I hope you're right Pip, I really do. I want to trust him."

Phyllis listened to the radio broadcast when she arrived home. Fleets of small boats had been braving the choppy Channel to evacuate as many servicemen as possible from the beaches; the numbers of those rescued grew by the hour with each news bulletin. They were not told of the ships that had been sunk and the many lives lost at sea. Phyllis prayed that Gilbert would be safe and that his boat, if he was on one, would make it home.

A few days later, Phyllis was weeding their newly planted

vegetable patch with Mrs Osmund. She felt a trickle of warm liquid spill into her underwear and thought that she may never give Arthur the son he really wanted. They'd talked about it often and planned to call him Hugh. Phyllis thought back to the day she threw her rupee coin into the water at Southampton dock. She'd wished then that she were carrying a boy for Arthur. Phyllis felt the loss of hope deep inside her. If she could just give her husband a boy then everything would be all right.

The Germans were in Boulogne, only 30 miles away from British soil. Elizabeth sent a telegram saying she may be evacuated from Colchester at any moment and had her bags packed. She would write as soon as she knew more. Phyllis worried that Elizabeth would have to come and live in Catterick and pictured her turning up on the doorstep with nowhere else to go, like a refugee.

On 4th June it was reported that over 300,000 men had been rescued from Dunkirk. There was still no sign of Gilbert. Pip had taken to sitting in the bay window waiting for the telegram boy to pull up outside the house.

"Not knowing is almost worse than knowing he's dead," sobbed Pip one day. "The pain of waiting for any news is unbearable; every time I receive a telegram I feel like my heart's stood still in my chest.

Phyllis visited Pip's house every day now, sometimes popping in with the children and sometimes on her own. All the town's signposts had been removed from the roads along with road names and station signs, making

Catterick oddly anonymous.

Phyllis let herself in through the back door that led to Pip's kitchen; she was surprised to see a man with a blackened face dressed in dirty rags sitting at the kitchen table. He crammed a large hunk of bread into his mouth, urgently dipping it into a bowl of hot soup. His right hand was bandaged. Pip stood at the range making tea, she looked up at Phyllis and was almost hysterical as she introduced the man in rags.

"This is my husband Gilbert," she said looking at the filthy man. "He's in a frightful state, but he's alive Phyl. He's alive."

The wounded soldier stood up to shake Phyllis's hand. Phyllis took the dirty-bandaged hand in both of hers and held it gently.

"Welcome home, Gilbert," said Phyllis. "We have all been praying for your safe return."

Maureen hid behind Phyllis's legs, frightened by the tall man who looked like a tramp.

He had a vacant stare in his bloodshot eyes and spoke softly, to no one in particular. "I waded into the cold sea and spent hours waiting in water up to here." He indicated the water line went right up to his chin, looking directly at Phyllis. "The boys were having dogfights above our heads. We had to wait until it was dark before we could board the boats. There were hundreds of them;

fishing boats, even pleasure boats plucking men out of the water. Some of them took the troops straight across the channel to England. Smaller boats ferried them to the large troop ships that couldn't get close enough because of the shallow water." He coughed into his bandaged hand. "There was a boat, but there were about a hundred men in front of me. It filled up quickly as they dragged the freezing cold men on board. There wasn't enough space for me and the next load of lads. We were desperately trying to clamber aboard but we were pushed back." Tears started to stream down his stubbly face. "Suddenly there was an enormous explosion, debris and bodies flew into the sky. The boat I'd missed was blown to pieces." He paused for a moment to swallow. "Within minutes it sank. Some of my friends were on it." He stood up and paced about the kitchen, tears unashamedly streaming down his face. "We waited for ages for another boat to rescue us. I wasn't sure I could hang on that long, my arms and legs were numb and my head throbbed. I felt sick with hunger. I was almost unconscious."

Gilbert had managed to board the next boat risking the dangerous mission; The Royal Daffodil was the River Mersey ferryboat. Its treacherous journeys started from Ramsgate. It made five rescue missions, saving 7,461 service personnel. The last journey was the most dangerous as the swell had whipped up into a storm; waves battered the ferry as it made its journey back to Ramsgate with its precious cargo. Men were crammed like sardines into every available space, above and below deck. The boat was attacked by six German planes from the angry grey skies above. One of their bombs blew a hole below its water line. They all thought they would drown as the water rushed in, but the boat managed to limp back to Ramsgate. Two men were killed. Gilbert's hand was severely damaged as the flying shrapnel split it in two.

"Carried from the jaws of death, that's how Churchill described it. He was right; I was terrified." He put his head in his hands. Phyllis looked at Pip and discreetly mouthed to her that they would go. She picked up the children and left by the back door. It was the first time she had seen for herself the true horror of war. She leant against the sidewall of the house and was violently sick.

18

SUMMER 1940

The Battle of Britain saw Spitfires and Hurricanes intercepting German bombers as the RAF defended Britain's airfields, army bases, shipyards, railway lines, bridges and factories. Hitler was still trying to gain air supremacy but the British were determined not to be beaten. Their aircraft were in the sky day after day, night after night for three months. The humming of the plane's engines was relentless, like a constant swarm of bees. Halifax and Wellington bombers could be heard heading south in the early evenings. The rumble of their loud engines slowly faded as they gained height and disappeared out of view towards the continent. The following morning they could be heard returning from their missions, having dropped all their bombs and used up most of the fuel. Some would only just make it back, tail fins missing and smoke spluttering from the rear. Others would limp back to the airfield and slide on their big metal bellies down the runway. Catterick was attacked in August. The Laing's shipyard and other factories were bombed. As Phyllis came out from the shelter one night she could see the distant sky of Hartlepool red with fire, like a spectacular Indian sunset.

Tea and margarine were now rationed. The brown liquid in her bone china teacup got paler and paler as she topped up the leaves throughout the day with fresh water, until it became flavourless. As summer came, Phyllis fell in love with the garden and experimented with herbs that grew in the overflowing flowerbeds. She sprinkled chives on plain potatoes and steeped mint leaves in water for an alternative to tea. By now the vegetable plot she'd planted with Mrs Osmund in early June was growing into a garden full of edible produce. Even the Anderson shelter was starting to look pretty, bright yellow and red nasturtium climbed steadily up and over the shelter's roof, its delicate veined leaves almost see-through in the summer sunshine as pretty as the finest lace in Valletta.

Arthur had left his camera with Phyllis and asked her to take some decent snaps of their daughters. Phyllis placed the girls on a blanket near the oversized rhubarb leaves but Eileen would get so excited that she'd bob up and down like a hen. All the photographs of Eileen ended up blurred. Maureen would heave the heavy metal watering can down the path to water all the young plants for her mother, with Eileen crawling along behind her. By September they were picking marrows as large as cricket bats. They placed a little wooden trolley outside the front gate to sell any extra produce. They put an old Germolene tin on the table and were always thrilled when they found a few coins jingling at the bottom.

Phyllis adored the long, hot sunny days. She felt at home for the first time since arriving in England and spent most of her time outside. The children had a bucket and spade and would dig the soil pretending it was sand. Maureen loved picking the bright green pea pods; snapping them open to find a neat little row of hard peas. She'd pop them in her mouth pretending they were sweets. Occasionally there would be a glistening, pearly white grub nestled amongst them. Maureen would poke it out with a twig and examine it before helping herself to more.

By early evening they would sit in the garden and admire their day's work. Maureen would get comfortable on Phyllis's lap sucking her thumb, her grubby legs dangling.

"India stories, India stories," Maureen would sing.

Phyllis thought up new stories about India and the granny Maureen was too young to remember. She told her how Maude would sit on one of the cane chairs in the shade of the mango tree, poring over the previous year's seed packets with the mali and boxwallah. His goods would be neatly displayed on a reed mat spread out on the dhoob.

"Like a shop?" asked Maureen.

"Yes, a bit like a mobile shop." Phyllis replied.

"Mother chose deep orange Canna for the veranda, with leaves the size of elephants ears and the sweetest scented sweet peas for the archway that led to the joola."

"Where the mongoose lived?"

"Yes, that's right."

"She would then look at all the other seed packets that lay in the boxwallah's collection and wouldn't be able to resist the purple phlox and pink petunias. She would take tea on the veranda as he neatly put away all his goods and waited to be paid."

"I want to go and see the boxwallah," Maureen would say. "I'd like to buy some seeds."

"One day my love, we shall."

*

Arthur had been in Harrogate but on his return had managed to get a day pass. He brought Lieutenant Thornhill with him; a handsome man, slightly older than Arthur, well spoken and very polite. Phyllis charmed him with her Indian-style stuffed marrow. She hollowed out the pithy insides and stuffed them with saag aloo, then baked them. The afternoon was warm as they spread the picnic blanket out on the tiny lawn that hadn't yet been sacrificed for the vegetable plot. Phyllis thought Arthur seemed pleased with her. The garden was tidy and growing well. The children were clean; even Maureen's hair was washed and tied into pigtails.

Arthur fetched the gramophone from the front room and asked Phyllis for a dance. As they attempted a waltz, Lieutenant Thornhill confessed it had been he who lost the bet; the gramophone had once been his. Phyllis felt awfully guilty but he was rather decent about it and said it was probably much happier in her possession. As Phyllis took the dirty plates into the kitchen, she could hear the men's voices as they chatted and laughed in the early evening sunshine; the lowering sun lit up their trails of cigarette smoke. Maureen had found Arthur's wooden flute in his top pocket and was blowing it like a policeman's whistle. Eileen sat with her hands over her ears and screamed.

The bombers could be heard in the distance as they took off from the airbase. Arthur popped his head around the kitchen door. "That's our cue to go."

Phyllis put her arms around his neck and kissed him gently on the lips.

"I love you. Don't forget me," she whispered.

"Take care of everyone until I get back," he said.

Phyllis watched as the two men left along the front path. She urgently took in every detail of that moment just in case it would be the last time she saw him. She tried to capture the smell of the lavender as he brushed past the swaying stems, their purple flowers waving goodbye. She saw the roof-shaped shadow of the house, threatening to trespass into the neighbour's garden over the road. She examined the detail of his easy walk as he ambled along with his friend, chatting and smoking, along the pavement and out of sight.

A few days after Arthur's visit, Phyllis was sitting in the garden stringing runner beans over a colander. She watched the busy blackbirds picking about for worms and grubs in the soil under the holly bush. They scattered the mud from side to side as they hunted down their dinner. Their oil-like feathers reminded her of the Mynah bird that used to live in the mango tree, it would perch all afternoon chattering loudly and say phrases like; "Maurice is great" and "long live the King." Maurice had taught it a few words whilst lounging on his charpoy with his latest illness. One day the poor bird swallowed a silver christening bracelet that belonged to Phyllis. Maude had to keep the bird in a small box until the necklace emerged. Phyllis was loathe to wear the item afterwards, even though it had been disinfected in a solution of vinegar and baking soda. A few weeks later the Mynah bird disappeared. Phyllis always felt she'd offended the little creature and made a promise to herself that she would wear the bracelet everyday after that. She looked at it on her child-sized wrist and tenderly felt the well-worn cross that dangled from its clasp.

The back gate swung open with a creak. Mr Osmund came hobbling in with alarming news that a German paratrooper was reported to have landed in the Leeds area and that the Germans were gathering on the coasts of Europe ready to invade. Phyllis could see the panic in his eyes. She looked at the children playing in the mud then looked up at the sky and took a deep breath.

"Perhaps we need to equip ourselves, just in case."

Mr Osmund went to the shed and fetched a heavy pickaxe handle, a spade and a garden fork. They agreed that night that they would double-bolt the door at all times and each sleep with a weapon by the bed. Everyone was on tenterhooks; lace curtains twitched when strangers approached and doors quickly closed. The streets that had been filled with children, fell into deathly silence.

19

THE BLITZ

News reports were coming in of the severe bombing of London. Four hundred and thirty people were killed in the East End alone. The raids had started in the afternoon on 24th of August. Londoners ran for their lives as bombs rained down from the cornflower blue sky. It was the start of the Blitz.

Phyllis received a letter from Kitty. Her father Albert had been on fire-watching duty and hadn't returned home. He had been buried in the rubble, as the building he stood on was bombed. Kitty was devastated and her mother was heartbroken. The message at the bottom of her letter continued to fuel Phyllis's anxiety and despair. Arthur was in London and had visited Kitty and her mother for tea. Phyllis had no idea he was in London. It was the most dangerous place in the world to be and Arthur was there. She looked out onto the lavender heads that bobbed about in the breeze and summoned up her memory of Arthur striding away along the path and up the road. She felt sick, her mouth filled with bitter saliva;

what if that was the last time she was ever to see him? What were the last words they'd spoken to each other? She ran upstairs and took out her diary. It had only been a few weeks ago, yet already it was so hard to recall.

After two days of pacing about and trying to keep herself busy she received a telegram. 'DARLING PHYL. ALL FINE. HAD TEA WITH KITTY. DON'T WORRY ABOUT ME. COLCHESTER EVACUATED. MUM AND PEG ABOUT TO MOVE TO SHALDON.' Phyllis kissed the telegram and almost hugged the young telegram boy with relief. She went to find a map to look up Shaldon and discovered the small town sat right on the mouth of the river Teign next to the sea.

Peg wrote a few days later; she'd found a job as a district midwife in Shaldon and a nice little terraced house with a back yard to rent. Peg was looking for suitable rooms for Elizabeth nearby where she would be allowed to take Bridget. Susie, Peg's friend, wouldn't be going with them; she'd turned out to be impossible to live with. Phyllis felt sorry for Susie; she'd never met her but imagined she was probably a decent person. She pictured Peg bossing her about like an old matron in her starched nurse's hat. Phyllis let out a giggle at the thought and wondered if they'd shared more than just a flat.

By the 15th of October Arthur was back in Catterick. Phyllis felt happier knowing he had left London. She'd walk the children up to the camp, and look through the high wire fence, watching all the smart soldiers parading up and down, hoping to catch a glimpse of him.

"There he is!" Maureen would shout hopefully.

"No darling, I don't think that's him."

Maureen loved it when the soldiers saluted to the officer who stood shouting orders at them, his baton placed under his arm. On the walk home she'd salute everyone they passed.

The devastation in London continued. Phyllis prayed for Kitty's safety. Maureen would kneel next to her at night and copy her mother.

"Jesus always answers little girls' prayers," she said to Maureen. "Kitty will be fine. I know it."

Phyllis would finish her prayers with the same ending every night. "Please God, keep Arthur, mother and daddy safe."

She pulled the blackout curtains across the window. The full moon shone in, its reflection catching in the dressing table's mirror. Phyllis gasped. Her grandmother had told her that if you see a full moon in a mirror it brings bad luck. Phyllis hoped it wasn't a bad omen.

A full moon was a bombers' moon. One thousand bombs rained down on London that night. The News Chronicle reported that more than five thousand people were camping in Epping Forest. Phyllis pictured these homeless families living under tarpaulin strung between trees with the winter setting in. Cooking on camp fires like beggars on the streets of Delhi.

Coventry was razed to the ground. The whole nation put on a brave face whilst holding its breath ready for the next bombs to drop and the next death toll to be announced. News came from Arthur that he wouldn't be home for Christmas. He had however been promoted to the rank of officer Lieutenant and enclosed a five shilling note in his letter. He asked Phyllis to buy the girls something special. There really wasn't anything to buy apart from some off-cuts of material. Phyllis busily turned the handle of her sewing machine and made dolls clothes when the children were in bed. Power failures were happening at least twice a week, so she sat in the front room and sewed by candlelight. Her eyes were sore after about an hours sewing and she'd have to stop until the next evening, but she thanked God for her good fortune. Arthur was safe.

20

MAUREEN'S 3RD BIRTHDAY

It was a hard secret to keep. Phyllis had saved up two weeks' rations and had been given two eggs by Pip's neighbour to make a victoria sponge cake with a tinned cherry filling. She'd even managed to scrounge three cake candles from Jeanie's mother.

"Let's go out for a walk, it's a beautiful day." Phyllis put Eileen in the pushchair and Maureen toddled along beside, her woolly hat pulled tight down over her ears.

As they rounded the bend, the bus pulled in. Arthur was sitting waving at them through the window.

"Daddy!" shouted Maureen.

Arthur grabbed his parcel from the seat beside him. Maureen ran to Arthur at full speed and squealed as he lifted her up and threw her high into the air.

"Happy birthday, Snoodles." He hugged Phyllis then Eileen. "How's my favourite girl?"

Phyllis looked up to answer but realised he was talking to Maureen. She felt a tiny stab of jealousy. Perhaps Arthur was right when he called her unreasonably jealous when he'd taken another woman to the Spitfire ball. Phyllis watched them hold hands and chatter away. She felt foolish and selfish and wished she didn't. Back at the house tea was made and Maureen opened the large white box that had been tucked under Arthur's arm. It was another huge doll. Her head was made of china; it had little rosy cheeks on its heart-shaped face.

"Jeanie," smiled Maureen hugging her doll to her chest. "This is my new friend, Jeanie."

Maureen and Jeanie Doll sat next to Arthur on the small cane sofa in the lean-to and watched him stir sugar into his tea; round and round it swirled like a little whirlpool. Maureen was captivated by the brown liquid and thought her daddy was so clever not to spill any over the side of his teacup.

Arthur took out a small package from his jacket pocket. "Happy Christmas, darling, " said Arthur as he handed it to Phyllis. "I hope you like them, thought yours were looking a bit past it." Arthur smiled and got out something for Eileen, too.

Phyllis gasped when she revealed a pair of soft kid gloves.

"Whatever is the matter old girl? You look like you've seen a ghost," quizzed Arthur.

"Oh its nothing. It was very thoughtful of you, thank you," replied Phyllis, placing the gloves on the table.

"I'm glad you like them, they cost half a week's wages," said Arthur. "Why don't you try them on?"

"I'll try them on later, after we've had our cake."

Phyllis sliced the birthday cake into large wedges as Arthur spoke to Maureen about playing billiards in the officer's mess, dances he had attended over Christmas and the friends he had made.

"Who do you dance with if mummy isn't there?" Maureen asked innocently.

"There are lots of ladies that like dancing at the camp. There's a lady called Patricia and her friend Evelyn, but if mummy were there I would dance with her," he said quickly as Phyllis walked back into the room.

His army career was going well and he now rubbed shoulders with Captains and Majors. He was out of the shared barracks and in the Officer's quarters. By the time he was due to leave, Maureen had dozed off, her head on his lap with her thumb in her mouth. Jeanie Doll lay by her side.

"You really need to stop her doing that," frowned Arthur.

"Doing what?" asked Phyllis.

"Sucking her fingers, she'll end up with sticking-out teeth. How's Eileen's potty training coming on? Peg mentioned she should be out of nappies by now."

"Did she?" replied Phyllis.

"I know you probably don't want to, but I think it would be best if you went and lived in Shaldon with Peg. I've seen pictures of the house and it looks really pleasant. The children could play on the beach and Maureen could start going to nursery school. It might be safer than staying here and I think I'm about to be posted off somewhere."

Phyllis had feared this coming; she had said as much to Pip at Christmas. The thought of it filled her with dread. "If you think it's for the best Arthur then of cause I shall. But please don't take sides," replied Phyllis, resigned to the fact that she had no option and must do as he asked.

"It's not about taking sides. It's about staying alive and keeping the children safe."

Arthur could see Phyllis struggle with the thought of living with his sister. "You've just got to try and fit in a bit more. Peg's not so bad."

"What do you mean by fit in, exactly?" asked Phyllis.

"You need to keep on top of things. Like Maureen's hair," he said, stroking the knots at the back of his daughter's head. And the house, you need to keep it clean. I could smell curry today. Peg hates the smell. You just need to do normal things, like sit properly."

Phyllis looked at her crossed legged position.

"You sit like a punka wallah," Arthur twiddled his moustache. "Just try and be a bit more like them."

"I'm not sure I can," said Phyllis. "You married me not Elsie what's-her-name. This is who I am. I don't want to be anyone else."

"There's no need to be so dramatic. I'm only asking you to behave in a civilised manner."

"Have you any idea how hard it is for me? I queue for food most of the day, trying to make something nourishing to feed our children. I have no cook, no dhobi and no bearers. I live in someone else's house with noisy canaries in the front room for company and I just about scrape by on the pittance of an allowance you give me. I bundle the children into the shelter night after night. This bloody country is cold and miserable. I want to go home." She stomped out of the room, her cheeks as flushed as a robins breast, instantly regretting everything she'd said to him as she heard him leave, slamming the door behind him. She ran to the window but he didn't look back, he concentrated on inserting his fingers into his gloves as he strode off purposefully.

Phyllis went back to the lean-to and picked up the new gloves. Her grandmother had given Maude a pair on her

22nd birthday; the very next day her grandmother complained of back pain, then her face swelled; she had a fever and was vomiting. Three months later she was dead, at 43, a victim of Bright's disease. Since then both Phyllis and Maude believed that giving someone a pair of gloves was a sign they were about to part. When Phyllis was a girl, Maude would always give her money so she could buy her own. Phyllis ran upstairs and tucked the gloves away in her chest of drawers and thought perhaps if she never wore them, or looked at them, then everything would be all right.

Phyllis tried to compose a letter to Arthur but found it hard to know what to write, so she wrote what was in her heart. She told him she loved him. She told him she was jealous of other women in his life and never wanted to share him. Her letter continued about how she tried to be a good mother, a good wife but how it was so hard to do it on her own. She decided not to mention the gloves but instead sent a pretty picture of herself and the children. They wore their Sunday best and stood in the garden smiling at the camera. She wrote on the back of the photograph: Love you always Phyllis x. She slipped the photograph in with her letter, licked the bitter glue and pressed down the flap of the envelope. Her life was in Arthur's hands. She couldn't go against his wishes. She had no option but to live with Peg. At least she would be by the sea. Phyllis gave notice to the Osmunds. She would be in Shaldon by the start of the summer.

*

Phyllis visited Pip's house for the last time. They reminisced for hours about when they first met, Phyllis in the kitchen with glue in her hair, the marriage SOS night, as Pip now called it, and the miracle of Gilbert returning home from Dunkirk. They played the piano together and sang at the tops of their voices, slightly tipsy on brandy and revelling in their friendship.

"Remember who you are, Phyl. Don't ever change. Write as soon as you can and when this war is over I shall get on the first train and come and see you."

*

"Tarra, flower!" shouted Mrs Osmund.

Mr Osmund waved his crutch in the air as the taxi pulled away. Jeanie and her mother sat on the curb and waved too. The little girl leant against her pram full of teddies and dolls that Maureen knew so well.

Maureen pressed her face to the window sucking her thumb. "When are we coming back?"

"I'm not sure darling. You can write to Jeanie though."

Phyllis sat with her hatbox on her lap. She felt sad to leave the chaotic house stuffed with clutter. Phyllis had built up a pile of possessions; pictures she'd painted, books bought from jumble sales and jars of yellow piccalilli she had made from the vegetables she'd grown. She gave Mrs Osmund anything worth keeping, and wrapped her paintings in newspaper and string, burning the rest on a bonfire.

Travelling by train was very dangerous. Although the Blitz had ended, daylight raids were common. She saw bombed-out factories, warehouses and torn apart streets on the journey through London. Women carried on about their business as usual, walking past the piles of rubble, to the shops to queue for food, hanging out the laundry and going to work. It looked like a different country, a different century, a different place to the England she had landed in.

It was dusk by the time they pulled into Teignmouth station. Phyllis was relieved that the long journey was over. She collected their luggage, arranging with the porter for it to be delivered by taxi over the bridge that spanned the Teign estuary. Peg had encouraged Phyllis to catch the foot ferry, which left from a silty beach by the dockyard. Arriving in Shaldon this way was far prettier than by road.

Teignmouth's seafront was teeming with soldiers. Large green army tents were pitched on the space where the formal rose gardens once bloomed. They looked as permanent as the grand sandbagged Georgian hotels behind, now used as billets. The smell of cooking wafted from the cookhouse next to the pier; hundreds of soldiers queued in a neat line, waiting for their mess tins to be filled. The beach had 15 feet high barbed wire fencing positioned along its length. Ugly machine gun emplacements protected the estuary. Concrete pillboxes kept lookout along the sea wall, their little slitty eyes watched Phyllis and her hatbox. She wished she'd entrusted it to the taxi driver, she felt conspicuous as wolf whistles and laughing followed her.

Phyllis and the girls waited on the windy beach for the ferry to rescue them. She could see Shaldon's sugar-almond coloured houses just across the water. To the left towered the large tree-topped cliff known as the Ness; the deep red wedge dominated the pastel village below.

An old bearded man steered the ferry, not much bigger than a rowing boat, across the estuary.

"Good evening, memsahib," said the captain as the boat reached the shore. "You must be Mrs Woollett?" His deep dimples formed like rock pools as he smiled.

"Good evening," replied Phyllis, laughing. "How did you know my name?"

"Call it instinct." He donned his hat; a battered old Captain's cap that had seen better days. "We have been expecting your arrival. Captain Chippy at your service. Welcome aboard."

As Shaldon drew nearer, Phyllis could see the small fishing boats on the red sandy beach, lit up by the setting sun, lobster pots and nets piled neatly by. It was one of the prettiest places she had ever seen.

Phyllis had arranged to meet Peg on the beach where the ferry landed, but she was nowhere to be seen. Phyllis had the address of the house written on Peg's last letter. As she felt for it in her pocket, a tall, redheaded woman came striding over.

"Mrs Woollett?" she inquired smiling.

Phyllis looked up to see a happy, freckled face smiling back at her. She was probably older than Phyllis by some twenty years. "Yes, that's me."

The woman thrust her hand into Phyllis's. "Welcome to Shaldon. I'm afraid Miss Woollett has had to go to work, so she asked me to meet you. My name is Mrs Clements."

Phyllis took instantly to this bright, friendly face. "It's so kind of you to meet me. I was a little worried when I couldn't see Peg, I mean Margaret, I mean Miss Woollett," stumbled Phyllis.

"Here, let me help you with the children," she said, gently taking Eileen from her. "It's not far," said Mrs Clements, pointing to a narrow lane.

"Are you a good friend of Peg's? I mean Miss Woollett," asked Phyllis.

Mrs Clements laughed nervously. "Well, not exactly. My husband and I have an allotment and we sell the vegetables from a cart. Miss Woollett was called out this afternoon to an emergency and I just happened to be on her doorstep. She was worried she wouldn't be back in time for your arrival so I offered to meet you."

"How kind of you. I'm sure I wouldn't have known what to do if you hadn't been standing there."

The small white terraced house was nestled in Dagmar Street, just one road back from the beach. Phyllis was enthralled with the pretty thatched cottages that were dotted around the village and marvelled at its quaintness.

Peg had left a plate of thin jam sandwiches for their supper, the edges of which had dried out and curled.

"I'll leave you to settle in. Miss Woollett said she should be home first thing in the morning. Will you be alright?" asked Mrs Clements.

"Yes, perfectly thank you, you have been so kind."

As Phyllis lay in the unfamiliar bedroom that night, she mulled over the last few hours. Mrs Clements had been so friendly. She'd said that if Phyllis wanted to help with the allotment she would give her some produce in exchange.

The caw-caw laugh of the gulls outside her window woke her from her deep sleep. She thought she was still in Catterick until she glimpsed the ceiling and realised the comfortingly familiar stain had vanished. She couldn't wait to get the girls up to explore the beach; she wanted to dip their tiny toes into the rippling water. She wanted the sea air to fill her lungs, but their beds lay crumpled and empty. She stood at the top of the landing, the sound of muffled voices rose from downstairs. Peg sat in the kitchen, feeding toast to Eileen, who was sitting on her lap. Maureen was in a highchair at the table. It was a neat little scene. It made Phyllis feel uneasy, not that she didn't like things to be neat; she just knew she wouldn't be able to keep it that way.

Phyllis took a deep breath and tried to remember Arthur's advice to be normal, to be more like them. She entered the kitchen with a big smile on her face. "Good morning Peg, I mean Margaret, so nice to see you again." kissing her on the cheek.

"Morning Phyllis, did you sleep well?"

"Yes, I think it must be the sea air. I've always wanted to live by the sea. When I was a girl I used to make watery puddles in the dirt with a pail of water from the well. I'd dip my doll's feet into the murky water and my brother Cyril would moor up his wooden sailing boat to take them on a voyage. Always to England," laughed Phyllis. "I can't wait to get the girls down to the beach."

"First things first," replied Peg. "Let's get your trunk upstairs and your bicycle in the shed."

"Yes of course, how silly of me. I forgot, there's always something to be done."

By lunchtime Phyllis finally got out of Peg's grasp, she practically prised Eileen from her. It was a beautiful July day. They sat next to one of the fishing boats, the mast of which jangled and tinkled like glass bangles on a wrist, reminding Phyllis of her old ayher. They watched as the ferry went mesmerizingly to and fro, ferrying women with shopping bags and mothers with children. The only men in Phyllis's view were Chippy, who had already waved at her, and a man with a slight limp, beach combing.

The clang of metal against metal echoed across the water like a dinner gong calling diners to be seated. Its rhythm was relentless but not unpleasant as the Morgan Giles shipyard worked around the clock to build torpedo boats for the Navy. Phyllis watched Maureen digging holes, the red sand staining the soles of her soft bare feet. She looked so happy, her little hands working quickly as the hole grew deeper.

"Good afternoon my dear, you must be Mrs Woollett?" the man with the limp had walked up the beach clutching an armful of driftwood.

Phyllis looked up shyly. "Yes, indeed I am."

The man tipped his Panama hat. "I knew it was you by your magnificent hat, you don't see many in this part of the world. I'm Mr Clements, I believe you met my wife last night."

"How nice to meet you. Yes, your wife was most helpful and kind," replied Phyllis. She noticed he was a little breathless. "Would you like to share my rug?"

He tipped his hat again and sat himself next to her.

"I'm not as young as I used to be," he smiled as he dabbed his shiny forehead with his handkerchief as if blotting wet ink on a page.

Mr Clements knew all the boats in the harbour and named each one in turn. He told Phyllis who owned them and what each fisherman caught. Some were mackerel catchers, others trawled further out to sea for cod. Some of the boats including Lady Cable had been commandeered for the Dunkirk evacuation over a year before; a few hadn't made it back. Others had rescued hundreds of men.

Fishing was becoming a risky profession, as trawlers were open to attack from German bombers. Mr Clements shared his worry of the enemy being only across the channel. He was part of the Home Guard and had been issued with a rifle.

"We'll be getting the same barbed wire as Teignmouth soon," he said, "not sure if we'll be allowed on the beach much longer."

He warned her of the 'hit and run' raids the past few months. "The German aircraft fly low over the sea. Then before you know it they are right on top of you. They're aiming for the shipyard and the bridge, but the gunners fire at civilians too. Always think ahead, where to run to if you hear a siren or a plane, drop everything, grab the children and get to safety. Be very careful not to be too exposed, hide under a lobster pot if you have to."

"Phyllis!" Elizabeth stood waving on the edge of the beach, Bridget at her feet and a letter in her hand. "There you are my dear. I came to find you at the house but Peg said you were so impatient to get to the beach that you'd already left. Good morning Mr Clements, I trust you are well?"

"All the better for bumping into your daughter-in-law."

Phyllis stood up and dutifully kissed her mother-in-law, the smell of stale mothballs lingered. "Hello Mums, you're looking very well, the sea air must suit you," said Phyllis.

"Thank you dear. It occurred to me this morning that we haven't met since the Christmas I got snowed in at your house in Catterick, a year and a half ago. How was your journey?"

"It was very busy but we managed to get a seat. It's just so wonderful to be by the sea."

"Don't go getting your hopes up. Peg runs a tight ship."

"A tight ship?"

"Well organised, ship shape."

Elizabeth was pleased to see the children again and praised Maureen on her sandcastle and Eileen on her milky complexion.

"You have grown," she remarked, looking at the children before turning to Phyllis. "Have they no shoes?"

Mr Clements offered her his place on the rug and politely

made his excuses to leave.

"You two obviously have a lot of catching up to do and I have beans to pick. You are most welcome at the allotment," he said turning to Phyllis. "It's just up the road, behind the searchlight."

Elizabeth gave him a cursory nod and then handed Phyllis a letter from Arthur. "He's going away."

Phyllis took the letter and read it quickly. He was going to embark at the end of July. Phyllis felt at once light-headed. The moment she'd been dreading for the last two years was here."Where, where do you think he'll be sent?" Phyllis looked anxiously at Elizabeth.

"I don't know anymore than you dear. We'll have to be patient. He probably doesn't know himself yet." Elizabeth took her letter back from Phyllis and stowed it safely in her handbag.

As Phyllis walked the children home from the beach, her thoughts turned back to the last time she saw her husband. It wasn't the day the lavender waved goodbye but the day they'd had a row about the state of the children and her inability to be normal. She wished to God she could turn back the clock, she wished they hadn't argued. How had it come to this? Did Arthur still love her? Had he ever truly loved her or was she just an exotic trinket that no longer fitted?

When she got home she found a freshly penned daily rota

pinned to the back of the kitchen door:

HOW TO LOOK AFTER THE CHILDREN

7.30am. Rise and shine. Pot children and dress self while they are enthroned.

7.40am. Dress and wash children.

8am. Downstairs, children in front room playing while you prepare breakfast.

8.30am. Breakfast.

9am. Wash up and tidy sitting room and leave children to play, then tidy bedrooms.

10.30am. Get ready and go shopping.

11.30am. Prepare dinner, if possible leave to cook while you take kiddies for a walk, first giving them a drink of milk and let them sleep.

1pm. Dinner etc.

2.30pm. Out for walk.

5pm. Tea and playtime.

6.15pm. Drink, wash, bed.

7pm. Washing and ironing, mending etc.

PHYLLIS'S WEEKLY JOBS

Sunday - bath self and kiddies.

Monday - washday.

Tuesday - sweep/wash floors.

Wednesday - ironing.

Thursday - clean windows/front step/lavatory.

Friday - clean out fires/range.

Phyllis wanted to rip the paper from the drawing pins holding it in place and tear it into tiny pieces, but Arthur would be furious if he discovered that his wife and sister had fallen out on the first day of her arrival, particularly after their last chat.

*

As the warm summer months came to an end, a sea mail letter arrived from Arthur. It had a red crayon line scrawled over the envelope and was marked 'Censored'. He told Phyllis that he had embarked from Gourock in Scotland at the end of July but could not divulge his whereabouts or destination. Phyllis sat on her bed with her old school atlas and tried to work out where he could be, his letter had taken months to reach her, it must be a long voyage, possibly to the Middle East or Asia.

There was an urgent knock on the bedroom door. "Phyllis, the girls have got high temperatures and Eileen has a rash on her tummy and says she feels sick. I think they have chicken pox." Peg looked alarmed as they both examined the girls for further symptoms. Phyllis discovered itchy spots behind Maureen's ear.

"I can't have chicken pox in the house, I'm in contact with pregnant women everyday. We'll have to get them to the hospital," said Peg.

"What, the girls?" gasped Phyllis.

"Of course the girls, who did you think I meant, the pregnant women?" Peg was fretting and pacing around the stuffy room. "This is all I need," she added, her starched white collar not quite concealing her scarlet stress rash that crept up her neck. A car was sent for and the girls were carted off to Teignmouth hospital.

Phyllis spent that night alone in the house. She realised, as she lay awake that it was the first night in her whole life that she had spent alone, not another soul breathed under the house's slate roof. At midnight the air raid siren bellowed out its ghastly shrill and Phyllis's heart lurched. Her instinct was to run to the children. Instead she hid in the cage-like Morrison shelter in the front room. She rested her head on the old biscuit tin that Peg had insisted she put all her important papers; the passports, birth and marriage certificates and Post Office book. She lay there terrified that the hospital would be hit and was relieved when next-door's cockerel crowed the neighbourhood awake as dawn finally broke.

Peg had instructed Phyllis not to see the girls for at least five days until their watery blisters had crusted over and they were no longer contagious. The hospital said it would get word to Peg when the time came. Phyllis was alone with her worry. She wrote letters to make sense of it all; one to Pip, one to Kitty, one to Arthur and one to her mother. She told her mother how lonely and miserable she felt without the children and Arthur, unable to be of any comfort to any of them. She reminded her mother of the time she and Muriel had chicken pox and how the ayah had made a bed out of neem leaves for them to sleep on. Maude had laughed at the idea but their chickenpox symptoms were certainly not as lasting as their school friend's symptoms had been.

Phyllis decided to visit Mrs Clements. "You must stop worrying, you need to be strong for them, they'll need feeding up when they get home. If you help me weed today, you can take a box of vegetables home with you."

The cart was an old door balanced on a set of pram wheels. Mr Clements had nailed on discarded orange crates in rows to place the produce in. They would stock it up in the morning then trundle it slowly, due to Mr Clements emphysema, down Marine Parade and along the narrow back streets, selling the newly-harvested vegetables that his wife had picked that morning. Mrs Clements would ring a little hand bell to let people know they were approaching, front doors would open and headscarfed women would spill out onto the street forming an orderly, chattering line. Broad beans, beetroot, spinach, leeks and the last of the tomatoes were stacked in colourful piles, like a market stall.

Elizabeth had invited Phyllis to tea. She rented a room around the corner in Fore Street next door to the hairdressers. She frowned when she realised Phyllis had been digging in the allotment, having spotted grime under her fingernails. Elizabeth thought the Clements to be common, selling their produce on the streets like gypsies.

"Mrs Clements is not a close friend of Peg's you know. She mingles with the likes of Peg's old cleaner Mrs Wilson. She was a terrible cleaner. Peg got rid of her because you were coming to live here."

Phyllis was stunned. Did Peg expect her to do all the household chores? Is that why she'd invited her to Shaldon? When Phyllis got home she was so furious she ripped the job list off the kitchen door and scored a thick pencil line through half of her allocated chores. She was not here to be someone's coolie. She pinned the list back on the door, she then went to the beach knowing full well that Peg would be fuming to find the windows hadn't been cleaned and the lavatory hadn't been scrubbed. She would be outraged to see her precious list defaced.

As the sun went down Phyllis decided it was time to face the music and wander home, carrying her shoes, with sand between her toes; her feet as bare as the day she was born. Peg's car was parked near the house. Phyllis felt slightly sick at the confrontation she knew she'd started. When Phyllis put her key in the lock it wouldn't turn. She felt foolish having to bang on the door to be let in. Peg made her wait a few minutes before getting herself out of the kitchen chair and opening the door.

"Where have you been?" she scowled like a cross parent, looking down at Phyllis's dirty feet.

"I went for a lovely stroll along the beach." She said dumping her sandy shoes in the porch, the red grains scattering like frightened mice all over the clean tiles.

"How dare you come here thinking you can do whatever you damn well please, waltzing around in that stupid hat, making friends with all and sundry and going barefoot like a native. Just you wait till Arthur hears about your antics. You're not part of the bloody Raj now you know!"

"I have not come here to be your slave, Margaret. Or should I call you Peg like all your other family members? I am your sister-in-law, not your coolie. I will do half the chores but I absolutely refuse to be treated like a maid, an unpaid one at that. I am now going to get my children." Phyllis put on her hat, gloves and shoes and ran to catch the ferry to Teignmouth.

Maureen was reluctant to go home, having made a new friend and Eileen had picked up a bad cough. Phyllis hugged the girls and cried with relief that they were all together again. It was 7 o'clock when they got back to the house. Peg was ironing by candlelight; the power had been cut. Elizabeth was sitting in the kitchen in semi-darkness, the candlelight lit up the spittle on her lips.

"What's this all about?" she thrust the list at Phyllis.

"This is between Peg and I."

"Since when did you call her Peg?"

"Since the day we became equals."

21

BLOOD RED RIBBON

Phyllis wrote to Arthur every week and even though she didn't know where he was, letters could be sent to his regiment and would find their way to him eventually. She wrote of the awful argument she'd had with Peg, and of Eileen's cough, which seemed to be getting worse with the damp sea air. Phyllis thought it would be better for everyone if they returned to India. After all, Arthur wasn't even in England anymore.

By the end of October Phyllis received an Aerograph from Arthur. He'd travelled on the HMT Strathallen to Basra. Arthur didn't give much away other than he was well and the food was bearable. He couldn't disclose his movements due to the heavy censoring of his mail, any slight giveaway as to his location were either cut out or scored through with thick black pen.

His journey to the Middle East had taken the long way round, past the Cape of Good Hope, up the Mozambique Channel and into the Indian Ocean. The Suez Canal was too dangerous for troopships to pass through. The ship had stopped off in Cape Town for a few days and the troops had 'partied' with the local women and drank the local beer. It was very hot and they had changed into their tropical uniforms. Destroyers and a Sunderland flying boat had escorted the ship for part of the journey. They'd crossed the equator on August the 24th. Schools of porpoises swam alongside the ship. They arrived in Bombay on 20th of September then transferred to the Lancashire, an old trooper that had been used in the Great War. They were allowed to disembark two days later, through 'The Gateway to India'. By the 25th it was time for Arthur's regiment to leave for Basra. They arrived on the 1st of October in a sandstorm and camped out in the hot desert.

Phyllis sat on her bed and reread Arthur's words. The tone of his writing was quite matter of fact. He urged Phyllis to take Eileen back to the hospital to get her chest x-rayed if she still had her cough. He told her it would be impossible for them to travel back to India now. The journey to Basra had been dangerous; his ship was nearly torpedoed, there was no way she could leave England, not until the war was over, it was unlikely the War Office would grant her permission. She confided in Mrs Clements about how alone she felt. She told her how Elizabeth popped in every day at 7pm to check that everything was as it should be, she normally found fault with something. She also told Mrs Clements that it was clear from Arthur's letters that her in-laws were reporting back to him. Phyllis felt spied on.

*

It was 7th of December 1941. Peg and Phyllis sat in the draughty front room knitting socks for Arthur. They listened to the evening broadcast and learnt that the Japanese had attacked the US fleet in Pearl Harbour. The Americans were now entering the war as Allies of the British. Peg met Phyllis's eyes for the first time since their argument and allowed herself a small smile. With the force of the Yanks behind them the war would surely be brought to a quick end and everything could get back to normal. The next day the Japanese had invaded Malaya and by the 15th, Burma, and the Far East. Phyllis worried for Arthur, she wasn't sure if he was still in Basra or not. She knew he was working in the Signals section, which meant he could be anywhere. The click-clacking of knitting needles threatened to drown out the broadcaster's voice as she listened for any clue as to where Arthur might be stationed.

She waited every day for the post to arrive and finally, on the 19th of December, she received her third letter in over four months of him leaving England. He was still in Basra; it was hot and dusty and a challenging place to work. Rations were good though and he shared a tent with a decent chap. Whisky and cigarettes were in ample supply. They got time off but there was nowhere to go so they played cricket and football in the hot sand. It was so hot it could burn the skin off the bottom of their feet.

Arthur's socks were finally finished, a little wonky around the heel but wearable. Phyllis packed them up with the girl's homemade Christmas cards. Shaldon's Post Office was closed on Mondays so she travelled to Teignmouth. She also needed to buy material, ribbon and provisions for the coming week.

"Hello memsahib, no hat today?" cackled Chippy's voice over the sound of the boats' noisy engine.

"Not today. I've packed it away for the winter."

They chugged out into the shallow water.

"Shit! Excuse my language. Shall I turn her back or keep going?" asked a panicking Chippy.

Two Messerschmitts had appeared on the horizon.

"Hurry, they're coming straight at us," yelled Phyllis.

As the planes were upon them, Phyllis could see the pilot; he wore large goggles over his face. A hose fed oxygen into a black mask covering his nose and mouth. He looked like part of the machine he was flying. She could see the force he used to steer the grey plane down towards them as he pushed down hard on his joystick. The plane swooped fiercely on the little ferry like a bird of prey chasing a mouse.

"Take cover!" yelled Chippy.

Phyllis remembered what Mr Clements had said. She shoved the children onto the wet floor of the boat and threw herself on top of them, lying as flat as she could. Bullets fired down as Chippy twisted the handle of the throttle. The engine screeched loudly under the strain, sending plumes of purple smoke out behind them. The front of the boat reared up into the air, sending Phyllis and the children sliding down towards Chippy's feet. Chippy skillfully weaved in and out of the larger boats that were anchored in the estuary.

"Stay down!" he yelled. "The bastards are coming back."

He just managed to get the boat into the coal yard quay, tucking in under its large roof. The bullets ricocheted off the corrugated tin. Phyllis sat up and pulled the screaming children off the floor. Chippy had a small wound. A bullet had bounced off the roof, grazing his arm. They sat in shock as the over-heated engine spluttered to a halt and the sound of the planes grew quieter.

"I think they've gone," gasped Phyllis.

"I think I've blown the engine," said Chippy.

"I think you are a hero," said Phyllis, crying and laughing all at the same time. She looked at his wound; he winced as she pulled back the bloodied wool of his jumper, it was bleeding, not badly but it needed bandaging. She walked with him to the First Aid tent on Teignmouth's seafront.

"I'll have a brandy, then I'll be as right as rain," said Chippy feeling like a war hero.

Phyllis made her way to the Post Office even though she wanted to head straight home. She knew Peg would criticise her if she didn't post Arthur's much-needed socks. The larder was nearly empty too; they had nothing for tea. The queues for meat and margarine were smaller than usual; the German planes had sent people scurrying home.

"What if they come back, mummy?" whined Maureen.

"We don't need to worry about them," replied Phyllis in what she hoped sounded like a reassuring tone. "They've gone now."

Two days later Peg drove the children up the hill behind Shaldon to look for holly and mistletoe in the hedges and fields. They'd parked the car in a gateway and foraged around an old orchard. A small flock of sheep grazed happily in the lush grass. Peg and Maureen climbed a tree to retrieve their prize as little Eileen sat at the bottom of the large trunk. They picked armfuls of mistletoe covered in milky berries, the powdery leaves staining their arms green. As they walked back along the narrow lane to the car, Peg spotted a German plane coming straight for them; as it started to dive down she dropped her armfuls of greenery and pushed the girls into a muddy drainage ditch before jumping on top of them with such force that Maureen screamed with pain. Bullets once again rained down on them. Peg was certain they would all be killed.

The plane turned and came back to look for them. She'd managed to take off her mac and hid all three of them underneath it. They lay still not daring to breath. After a few minutes of firing the plane gave up and went on its way. Peg uncovered the girls; amazingly, everyone was unharmed. The field was covered with dead sheep; bloodstained woolly bodies lay slaughtered all around. Peg noticed Maureen's white ribbon was missing from her plait and told her to go back into the field and find it. Maureen was petrified of the dead animals but she obeyed her auntie and found the ribbon lying on the grass splattered with warm sheep's blood.

22

DUMPOKE AND PISHPASH

With Peg away at work, Phyllis was able to take over the kitchen and prepare the dumpoke for their Christmas dinner, leaving it to bake in the oven whilst they went to morning Mass. She used the last of the spices she'd been saving. Her small packets now lay empty; every last gram used up. She hoped Maude would send some in her next parcel. The sweet, pungent aromas reminded her of the spice wallah towing his bicycle trailer up and down the drives of the cantonment, honking the horn and shouting his arrival. The khansamah would beckon him to the cookhouse and the animated haggling would begin. After much shaking of heads and sucking of teeth, a deal would be struck. The deep-scented powders, seeds and bark would be poured from hessian sacks onto the brass scales that hung from the bicycle's handlebars, before being expertly tipped into cones made from newspaper. As well as a small duck for the dumpoke, Phyllis had managed to get a scrap of oxtail from Mr Orsman, the butcher, which she put in the pishpash along with the rice.

"What's that ghastly smell?" inquired Elizabeth, looking for evidence of dirty pots and pans as she made her daily rounds. "Why on earth are there saucers full of liquid under the table legs?"

"It keeps the ants off the food."

"What ants?"

"Exactly, anyway Happy Christmas. Would you like a glass of sherry?"

"Yes please, dear. Now, where are the children? I have some presents for them."

"They've just popped over to see the Clements. They had some little gifts for them."

"They've gone on their own?"

"It's only 5 minutes away."

"But it will be getting dark soon. What if we have a raid or worse still, are invaded? I'm not happy, not happy at all," she said, shuffling herself into the armchair in front of the fire with Bridget settling herself as near to the heat as possible.

"I told them to be back by 4.30. It will be fine."

"I don't agree. I think you should fetch them. They have already been shot at twice in the past few weeks."

The front door rattled and in clomped Maureen, gripping

Eileen's hand; sweets stuffed into her grubby mouth.

"There you see, they are fine."

The children settled in front of the fire and unwrapped the gifts from Elizabeth.

"I had a card from Mr and Mrs Brown in Colchester. They say the Americans have arrived in town, some are as black as tar." Elizabeth lowered her voice to a whisper and pulled her cardigan tightly around her ample bosom as if the black GIs could hear her. "I wouldn't want one of those billeted in my house, you never know what bad habits they have, of course they have separate social clubs. The blacks go to St Bartolphs and the whites to St Nicholas."

Phyllis was used to her in-law's racist views and had seen plenty of it in India too with exclusive clubs for whites only. Most of the Raj treated the Indians like children. No wonder resentment was building, particularly amongst the intellectuals. Gandhi was calling for all the British to leave. Wilmot had expressed his concern in his last letter to her and had urged her to hang on in England for as long as she could. Elizabeth put her feet up on the Morrison shelter. She moaned that her legs were swollen due to all the queuing.

"Peg has got her hands on the inheritance from her father," said Elizabeth boldly, the sherry having loosened her tongue. "She's thinking of moving to Herefordshire."

This was news to Phyllis who had assumed that Peg would settle in Shaldon, at least for a while.

"She's asked Arthur if she can take Eileen with her, feed her up a bit, sort out that cough of hers."

"Whatever are you talking about?" quizzed Phyllis standing up out of her chair. "Her chest has been looked at and x-rayed; there is nothing wrong with her, she'll just grow out of it, that's what the doctor said." Phyllis picked Eileen up off the floor and wiped the edges of her mouth with her hankie.

"Oh, I think we all know she'd be better off with Peg; they get on so well, it'll do her the world of good," replied Elizabeth, talking into her schooner.

"Do who the world of good, Eileen or Peg? If she wants to play at being mummy why doesn't she go and have her own children?" Phyllis had now raised her voice and was pacing the room. She slammed her glass down on the mantelpiece, more abruptly than she'd meant to, its delicate base snapped off the stem. Eileen started to cry.

"You shouldn't be so ungrateful, Peg would look after her as if she were her own," said Elizabeth.

"But she's not hers. She's mine. I will not allow it."

Phyllis barely slept, having worried all night about how to tackle Peg. She decided the best line of attack was to try to talk some sense into her. No one in their right mind would take a child away from its mother. She knocked on

Peg's bedroom door and entered without permission.

"What do you think you're doing? " groaned Peg.

"Peg, sorry to barge in on you like this but I gather you plan to take Eileen to Herefordshire. It really wouldn't be in her best interests. I'm going to have to put my foot down. I will not allow it," said Phyllis looking into the dark space where she could just make out Peg's slumbering outline.

"In her best interests? You are the one who lets the children run around the neighbourhood on their own with no shoes. You can't cook a decent plate of food and little Eileen is suffering from rickets and a bad chest. They'll turn into a couple of guttersnipes if someone doesn't step in and do something."

"I will not let you take Eileen from me."

"We'll see about that. It's too late anyway. Arthur thinks it's a good idea." She passed Phyllis an envelope.

Arthur had given his consent that Eileen should live with Peg to enable her to get the best start in life. The chest x-ray may have not found anything wrong, but according to Peg's previous letter to him, the doctor had suspected Eileen had the early stages of rickets.

"I'm not agreeing to this. Why don't you have your own babies, or is it that you're so frigid you can't?"

"Just what exactly are you implying?"

It was Boxing Day. The Post Office was closed; Phyllis had to wait until the following day to send Arthur her urgent plea. She thought carefully about how to word it: 'PLEASE RETHINK YOUR DECISION REGARDING EILEEN. THIS WILL NOT BENEFIT HER. IT WOULD BREAK MY HEART. PLEASE DON'T DO THIS. ALL MY LOVE PHYLLIS.'

Phyllis didn't hear from Arthur until the end of February. He had left Basra for Baghdad from where he'd been evacuated to a hospital in Karachi. He had not received her telegram and therefore made no mention of it. He was suffering from terrifying nightmares, waking up screaming in the middle of the night, his whole body rigid with paralysis. He fell asleep whilst on duty and his legs would give way beneath him. He was now laid up in bed having blood tests. "Ward sister Hilda Taylor is looking after me terribly well," he wrote. They think I have narcolepsy, nothing serious, runs in the family apparently. His spirits seemed uplifted and he wrote how he was happy to be in a clean bed with half-decent food surrounded by pretty English nurses. Phyllis was relieved he was safe but it didn't help her situation back in England. Peg was still determined to take Eileen and openly discussed it with the child in front of Phyllis.

"When we live in Herefordshire we can eat raspberries everyday for tea, you can have your own bedroom and I'll buy you a brand new tricycle." Phyllis overheard her saying one morning.

Apart from a few shillings rattling around in the tin, Phyllis's savings had been spent. She had just enough money saved up for her trip to London. She planned to visit Kitty and ask her advice about Eileen. It was also a good excuse to explore the capital. Phyllis had longed to go and see the sights: Buckingham Palace, Big Ben and St Pauls Cathedral, all of which had miraculously survived the Blitz. Many buildings were still in ruins but the streets had been cleared, buses were running and the Underground was functioning during the day.

Arthur was furious when he heard Phyllis's plans via the letters he received from Elizabeth. He strongly advised her against going to London. He'd been there during the Blitz and felt it was a very unsafe place to be, particularly with the children. He also insisted that Peg should take Eileen to Herefordshire. It would do Phyllis good to have a break and have only Maureen to care for.

Phyllis showed Mrs Clements Arthur's letter.

"I just don't know what to think," said Phyllis as she filled the heavy kettle and put it on the range. "I don't want Eileen to go. I might never get her back. I'm also worried about taking on the house by myself. I don't have enough money and I've never had to do it before. I wouldn't know what to do."

Mrs Clements smiled. "One thing at a time. I can help you sort out how to budget and run the house."

"I need to make some money but no one is ordering cakes

like they used to, what with the rationing."

"How about PG's?

"PG's?"

"Paying guests. I hear they pay well and Shaldon is a beautiful place to come for a holiday. Why don't you ask your friend Kitty to help you find some holidaymakers from London?"

"But the house," said Phyllis looking around her kitchen. "I can't seem to keep on top of it. We had so many servants in India. I used to think what a pain they were to manage as I watched my mother struggle, trying to make sure they were doing things correctly." Phyllis laughed. "I'd give anything now just to have even one servant. My mother would fuss when things weren't done correctly. I remember her fuming once as she caught one of the kitchen staff using his unwashed toes as a toast rack."

Mrs Clements roared with laughter. "That's really quite disgusting!" she dabbed at her eyes as the tears rolled down her cheeks.

"Dear Mrs Woollett, I think it's time you called me Jessie."

"And I think it's time you called me Phyllis."

"Dear Phyllis, you are not alone. I will help you."

23

BLACK TALCUM POWDER

The smudged-charcoal clouds chased the packed train all the way to London. The heavens opened just as it pulled into Paddington. Phyllis didn't own an umbrella, she'd brought her chatta from India but it sat unused at the bottom of the trunk alongside her tennis racket.

Kitty stood on the platform, eagerly hunting the alighting passengers until she spotted Phyllis and Maureen in the crowd. Phyllis had decided to leave Eileen in Shaldon, as she wasn't happy when walking too far and would constantly ask to be carried.

"Phyl! Maureen! How wonderful to see you," said Kitty as she flung her arms enthusiastically around them. "It's been so long."

"Can you believe it's been two and a half years?" replied Phyllis hugging her friend.

"You haven't changed a jot," replied Kitty. "But as for you young lady, what a grown up girl you are. You must be ready to start school?" Kitty picked up Maureen and kissed her on the cheeks.

"I'm four years and one month exactly."

"Well in that case I've just missed your birthday, so I'm going to buy you a very special treat."

Maureen was thrilled and held Kitty's outstretched hand as they descended the steps towards the Underground, the floor of which was covered with puddles created by dripping umbrellas and wet rain coats. The wind whooshed from the tunnel's black mouth, bringing with it a gust of stale air as the rattling train pulled slowly into the station. As it weaved its way to Hyde Park Corner, Phyllis thought she was going to be sick. She was relieved when the train came to a grinding halt and as they left the station, she took a deep lungful of city air, and tasted the damp earthy brick dust in her mouth. Red mountains made from bricks were piled high on each side of the cleared streets. Some houses still stood, with all but one or two walls remaining, their wallpaper on show, like a pair of undignified ladies bloomers. Iron fireplaces clung to the walls where no one was left to keep warm and no rooms to heat, just empty spaces remained hanging in mid air.

"Are you alright dear Phyl? You look a little pale. I barely notice how awful it is anymore," said Kitty looking at the devastated city around her.

"Where are all the people, the people who lived here?"

"Some have travelled out of the city and are camped out in woods, others have moved away to stay with relatives but thousands have been killed."

"Perhaps Arthur was right, perhaps we shouldn't have come?"

They passed fine Georgian buildings and walked under the Wellington Arch into Constitution Hill. As they walked up the wide road, lined by plane trees that sheltered them from the April rain, Phyllis felt a lump in her throat. "I'm so sorry to hear about your father Kitty, it must have been awful for you and your mother."

"I just can't believe he's gone. No one sits in his chair in the drawing room, just in case we hear his key turn in the front door." Kitty searched for her hankie. "I miss him so much Phyl; after I lost Charlie it was so awful but I knew I still had my father; now he's gone, too."

Maureen pointed to Buckingham Palace as it came into view, the Royal Standard flapping high above its roof, like a colourful sari hanging out to dry. She tugged at Phyllis's arm to hurry her up. The palace was much larger than Phyllis had imagined. She bought Maureen a small paper flag on a stick and another to send home. They peered through the gaps in the cold, black railings.

"If the flag is flying it means the King is home," Kitty said excitedly to Maureen.

"I hope we see him," said Maureen as she poked her arm through the railings and waved her little flag.

Phyllis walked over to the policeman on gate duty. "Will we see the King?" She asked.

"If you wait here madam, you may see something," he replied.

Only moments later the gates opened and out slid a sleek black car, purring like a panther. King George VI sat in the back, waving his cupped hand. Phyllis was sure he smiled at them. Not only was he the King of England but also the Emperor of India.

"I can't wait to tell Daddy," said Phyllis excitedly, like a child. "My father was involved with the Royal Durbar in 1911 when the King was proclaimed Emperor. All the Maharajahs had been invited to attend the ceremony but the poor Maharajah that daddy worked for felt rebuffed at being allocated such a terrible seat, so he delegated the task of sorting it out to daddy."

"Did he manage it?" asked Kitty.

"Yes, the Maharajah was delighted."

"How amazing. I must have been here a hundred times and I've never clapped eyes on him before, and you manage it on your first visit!" said Kitty looking at Maureen who continued to wave her flag with extra vigour at the shiny car as it disappeared down the wide Mall and out of sight.

They chatted about it all the way to the Lyons Corner House, a lively restaurant that Kitty thought Phyllis might like; it reminded her of Cafe Cordona in Valletta. She'd suggested hopping back on the Underground but Phyllis decided it would be nicer to walk to Marble Arch in spite of the rain.

The waiter took their damp coats and seated them near the five-piece band. Maureen was captivated by the musicians on the small, raised stage, unable to take her eyes off the double bass that she thought looked like a giant violin. Phyllis tucked her little paper flag into the side pocket of her handbag and decided to write to Wilmot as soon as she got home to tell him her news. She needed to write to Arthur, too. She hadn't heard from him since his letter from the hospital bed in Karachi. She had no idea if he was still there or if he had received any of her letters.

"How is Eileen doing?" asked Kitty across the small table.

"Peg is determined to take her away. Elizabeth is on Peg's side and so, it seems, is Arthur," sighed Phyllis.

She told Kitty she felt outnumbered and was on the brink of giving in. Phyllis stroked Maureen's hair and gently pulled her thumb out of her mouth. "Arthur hates her sucking her thumb, says her top lip is starting to curl upwards."

"Is everything okay between you and Arthur?" Kitty looked concerned as she took hold of Phyllis's hand. She noticed how her wedding ring slid up and down her thin finger, threatening to slide over her bony knuckle.

"No, not really," she looked over at Maureen. "Perhaps we can talk later."

They travelled on the Underground to Hampstead. Phyllis shut her eyes the whole way and prayed silently that they would make it out alive. They walked past the pockmarked heath, its quarried surface bordered by neat rows of allotments that were dug on the flatter heathland. Women in overalls worked on the plots, digging in mounds of steaming manure. Kitty pointed out her allotment. She had taken on the whole plot since her father had been killed.

Once home, the two friends sat alone in the drawing room. Phyllis had been careful to avoid Albert's old chair; his cushion still moulded to the shape of his back. Maureen had been put to bed, complaining of a tummy ache, having eaten two sticky toffee puddings.

"Now then, tell me all about it, what's been going on?" asked Kitty.

"I don't know where to start," said Phyllis. "Arthur's mother is constantly watching me. She and Peg are bullying me into giving up Eileen. They think I'm a pretty hopeless case, not good enough for Arthur."

Kitty listened as Phyllis told her how she felt.

"Arthur is slipping away from me."

Kitty poured another drink and stoked the fire.

"I know Peg and Elizabeth write to Arthur detailing my many faults," said Phyllis. "He refers to them in his letters, not that I've had one since he was lying in his sick bed in Karachi over two months ago." She told her about Pip's idea of the marriage SOS night. Kitty finally laughed as she imagined Phyllis going to all that effort to woo her own husband. Then Kitty felt sad as she thought of the day they had spent in Valletta.

Phyllis travelled back to Shaldon happy to have seen Kitty and London. Although London was devastated, it was still a city, still a working, living and breathing city. Her problems seemed minor compared to the people who slept in the windy stations night after night with few or no belongings. On the train home she made the enormous decision to let Eileen go, just for a few months, just to cure her chesty cough and build her strength up. It would stop Peg and Elizabeth from nagging at her. Peg could feed her up and spoil her and then she would get her daughter back. As long as Eileen was happy and well, that's all that really mattered. They'd have a special tea party, a proper send off. She'd go and visit in a few weeks. She told herself it would be fine. Kitty had agreed to help Phyllis find some Paying Guests. She could keep herself busy and earn a little money until Eileen's return.

While Phyllis and Maureen had been in London a bomb had fallen on Shaldon. According to Chippy it had bounced and skidded all the way down Fore Street, landing unexploded on The Green. It narrowly missed Dr Clare's daughter who had been playing on her bike with her friends in the afternoon sunshine. Bomb disposal personnel from the Royal Engineers had cordoned off the area and defused it. Everyone in the vicinity had been evacuated to the school for safety. Phyllis rushed back to the house hoping to find news of Eileen. A note was waiting for her. It was written on the back of an old Co-Op price list, propped up against the teapot. She gasped as she read the pencilled handwriting. Peg had decided to travel to Herefordshire to see the place she was planning on renting. If she liked it they would probably stay and send for a few things. They wouldn't need much as it was already furnished. Peg had packed a few of Eileen's clothes and would telegraph once they knew their plans.

The 500lb bomb had impacted hard on the adjacent street, causing large bomb-shaped footprints along the tarmacked road. The vibrations had shaken the foundations of the house and soot had been sprinkled like black talcum powder from each chimney into every room. A thick layer covered every surface. Phyllis dashed up the sooty stairs to Eileen's bedroom. Pandy lay discarded on the pillow. The chest of draws was flung open, most of its contents missing. It looked as though the house had been burgled. Most of Eileen's little homemade clothes had gone. Phyllis sat down on the bed and cradled Pandy in her arms. How was Eileen going to sleep at night without him? She always fell asleep rubbing his silky black ear on her nose.

"Eileen, Eileen." Phyllis hugged Pandy and rocked gently on the bed.

She slept with Pandy and Maureen that night; all three of them wrapped up in a large eiderdown in the sooty house. Black tears streaked Phyllis's cheeks.

"Thank God I still have you, my sweet little one." She stroked Maureen's hair until they fell asleep.

*

On the 6th of April news came through that HMS Dorsetshire and HMS Cornwall had been bombed and sunk within minutes of each other in the Indian Ocean, west of Ceylon, by the Japanese Navy. Phyllis felt sick at the thought of all those young men, hundreds of them, perishing at sea. The lucky ones had clung to rafts, managing to survive all night in the cold waters. She couldn't sleep, fearing that Arthur was amongst them.

Elizabeth popped in on her usual evening rounds, wanting to share her worries with Phyllis. "I'm so worried about my dear boy," she said fretfully. "What if he was on one of those ships?"

Phyllis couldn't look Elizabeth in the eye. She hated her for letting Peg snatch Eileen without saying goodbye.

"I don't know. I don't know anything anymore." Phyllis tucked a stray strand of hair from her face and tucked it neatly behind her ear.

"Only time will tell," concluded Elizabeth as she struggled to get back on her feet and out of the kitchen chair.

"Have you had word from Peg yet?" asked Phyllis. "She said she'd write, it's been nearly a week and I haven't heard from her. I thought I would by now."

"Oh yes, I meant to say, a letter arrived yesterday. Peg said they were bedding in nicely. I think Eileen took a few days to settle. I'm sure you'll hear in due course," smiled Elizabeth.

"I want to send Pandy to Eileen. I don't think she'll sleep without him," said Phyllis, feeling she needed an excuse to contact her own daughter.

"Oh, I wouldn't bother to go to all that effort. I think Peg has bought her a new one."

"It's no effort," replied Phyllis a little sharply. "It's what I want to do."

"As you wish," said Elizabeth.

A whole week went by before a scruffily written letter arrived from Arthur saying he had been posted to Rawalpindi in northern India. He was having a few weeks leave in Srinagar before taking up his new post. He'd decided to rent a houseboat. His tone was jolly and upbeat. He had been promoted to acting Captain and had temporary membership at the Srinagar Club, which was most accommodating. "I confess I am not alone", he wrote, "but am accompanied by the ward sister from

Karachi hospital." By coincidence she had been granted the same leave. He assumed, quite wrongly, that Phyllis wouldn't mind.

Phyllis stared at the letter as she leant against the mantelpiece, still warm from the dying fire. She was furious. She'd been fretting all week, picturing his body lying at the bottom of the ocean, his lungs full of salty water, yet here he was lounging about on a houseboat on Dal Lake and frequenting a swanky club with another woman. She pictured them making love in the wood-panelled bedroom with a view to the peaceful lake through its carved doorway; the breeze gently wafting in, cooling their sweaty, entwined bodies within the cotton sheets. She pictured Kashmiri servants in their white uniforms serving them cinnamon, cardamom and saffron tea with honey and plates of delicious spicy food. They would pretend to be married. Phyllis wondered if the ward sister carried a fake wedding ring in her pocket for such occasions.

She screwed the letter up and threw it into the fire. The edge of the paper flared up, producing a dancing, crimson flame, like an exotic flamenco dancer. In seconds it had turned to a grey, powdery ash. She wished instantly she hadn't burnt it; for the life of her she couldn't recall the woman's name. For some reason it seemed important to her now.

The next few days kept Phyllis busy; she wrote to the War Office asking for a passage back to India, then she wrote to Peg to set a deadline for Eileen's return. She enrolled Maureen at Mrs Anderson's kindergarten school just down the road, thinking it would help Maureen prepare for primary school if they were still in England when the new term started in September. It would also free up time for Phyllis to make a living by taking in the Paying Guests that Kitty was helping to find.

By the end of April it became clear that Peg had no intention of returning Eileen. She even suggested she leave Eileen behind in England when Phyllis eventually returned to India. Peg had also been looking at boarding schools for Eileen and had found Croft Castle Catholic School to be most suitable. Arthur's subsequent letters from Rawalpindi supported Peg's ideas. He also wrote that if anything should happen to him, then it would be up to Phyllis to decide the best course of action, but for now she was to do as he said.

Kitty had found a nice family who wanted to stay in Shaldon for the first week in May, just a week away. Phyllis looked around at the untidy living room; every surface was piled with books, newspapers and toys. The floor needed a thorough scrub; even the whitewashed walls needed a wash down after the bomb had fallen. Sooty cobwebs clung to the picture rail like black mourning lace. She dropped Maureen at Mrs Anderson's for her first morning at kindergarten then rolled her sleeves up, got down on her hands and knees and scrubbed every floor, every surface and laundered all the bedding. She played the wireless, singing along to keep herself going. What would her mother and father think if they could see her now? They'd pictured her being a lady, maybe with a maid to help with the dishes, dhobi, cleaning and cooking. They'd imagined her having afternoon tea on the lawn with other young mothers, playing a game of croquet or horse riding through the woods in the afternoon sunshine. Phyllis tutted out loud and laughed at how naive they had been. She looked out at the ugly grey sky through the grubby lace curtains and decided they needed to go in the tub, too.

Jessie arrived to help clear Peg's bedroom and make it into the guest room. They put Peg's clutter in the small wooden shed that doubled up as a coal store in the back yard. In the past few days the rain had been as relentless as the devastating Blitz on the city of Bath. Phyllis hoped the shed wouldn't leak and ruin any of Peg's things.

Phyllis felt very proud of herself as they sat drinking tea in the tidy kitchen. She put her aching feet up on the opposite chair and laughed.

"I think we deserve a nice cup of tea," smiled Jessie, black coal dust smudged on her freckled cheeks.

"I never thought I'd become a landlady," said Phyllis, giggling with exhaustion as she rubbed the coal mark off Jessie's face with the edge of a damp tea towel.

Jessie had become very fond of Phyllis. She loved the way she shut all the windows and doors at dusk for two hours, an old habit of keeping the mosquitos out at night; how she made chapattis instead of sandwiches and called breakfast chota hazri. She loved spotting her on the beach in her solar topee, her skin slightly darker than everyone else's, blissfully ignorant of how exotic she was.

*

Phyllis felt nervous as she went to answer the knock at the door. She could see the neat little family of four through the frosted glass panels, like a watery family portrait.

"Take a deep breath," she told her reflection as she checked her hair in the mirror and practised her smile, a landlady smile, not over friendly and not too formal.

Elizabeth had instructed her the night before on the etiquette involved in running a respectable guesthouse. "It's a business," she'd said. "Just remember you are doing it to make money, not friends."

Phyllis opened the door to find Mr and Mrs White with identical twin daughters and identical leather suitcases at their feet.

"Good Day Mrs Woollett. Mr White." He shook Phyllis's hand and with the other tipped his trilby to reveal a smooth baldhead. Maureen, who was sitting at the bottom of the stairs, praying to God that at least one of the children would be a boy, thought it looked like a large egg. She was utterly disappointed to see not just one but two neat girls and worse still, dressed exactly the same. She longed to have someone to climb trees and make catapults with. They didn't look as though they were going to be getting their frilly frocks dirty.

Mr White wore round tortoiseshell glasses. A neatly trimmed moustache, tinged with nicotine yellow, covered his top lip.

"Pleased to meet you," smiled Phyllis.

"This is my wife," said Mr White. She nodded politely under her dark crimson felt hat, a neat feather tucked into one side. She wore matching kid gloves and a string of white pearls around her neck; her holiday clothes.

"And these are my daughters, Bonny and Ruby. Say hello, girls."

"How do you do?" they said in unison.

"Pleased to meet you all. Please come in, I'll show you to your room," said Phyllis, relieved to meet her first guests who seemed very well mannered.

"You must be twins," said Phyllis to Bonny and Ruby as she looked at their identical woollen coats and matching pink gingham frocks. Their hair was tidy and pulled high into bunches, secured with bright pink bows. They giggled and nodded as they excitedly made their way up the stairs behind Phyllis, who carried both suitcases. She led them into the bedroom hoping that their expectations weren't too high. The room she and Jessie had carefully prepared was clean but simple.

"I'll cook your evening meals for 6 o'clock if that's suitable?" asked Phyllis.

"That'll do nicely dear," said Mrs White. "Let me give you our ration books. Have you had much bother here?"

Phyllis told her about the raids and the few bombs that had fallen in the vicinity.

"We have an Anderson shelter in the front room and a sturdy kitchen table. Please feel free to squeeze in too if you hear the siren."

The family approved of the neatly made-up room and promptly went off to explore the village, with their gasmasks slung over their shoulders. Phyllis dropped Maureen off at Mrs Anderson's and headed for Teignmouth to buy ingredients for the next few suppers. The June sunshine warmed her cheeks as Chippy asked how she was finding her new career.

"Well, I must say they seem awfully nice. I'm not sure what to feed them though. Do you think it would be acceptable to feed them chapatti, kedgeree and dahl?" asked Phyllis laughing, a little nervously.

"If your cooking is fit for a Maharajah then I'm sure it's fit for them."

"Yes, but I only cooked cakes for him not dinners."

"Stop fretting and cook what you like to eat. I'm sure they'll love it too," replied Chippy, as he gently banked the boat onto the small beach.

She reached for her purse. "Put your money away, memsahib. You know I won't take it," said Chippy.

"You really are too kind, Chippy. Bless you."

Since the day they were shot at Chippy had refused to take any fares from Phyllis, calling her his lucky memsahib. Instead of payment she would send Maureen to the beach with leftover scrambled egg-filled chapattis from breakfast, which he would devour as if he hadn't eaten for a week.

Teignmouth was full of soldiers, some marching on parade, others queuing for food and a few playing football on the wide promenade. They were bored of being cooped up in their billets. Some had seen action, bandaged wounds on show; others were fresh-faced, trained and ready for dispatch. Phyllis bought flour, rice, a few scraps of lamb for her pishpash and some haddock. She popped in to see Jessie on the way home, who gave her a bag of unsold vegetables for her chiticky.

Elizabeth agreed she wouldn't visit at teatime as it might be inconvenient but would pop in at lunchtime instead, just to make sure everything was as it should be. Her lips curled in horror as Phyllis told her of her planned menus. "They won't like that Indian food. They are paying you a decent price for decent food. I don't know where you get these silly ideas from."

The White family eagerly ate up every morsel that Phyllis put in front of them, marvelling at flavours they'd never tasted before. Mr White wiped his plate clean each night with a hunk of bread. Phyllis was delighted when she found a shilling tip left for her on the bedside table with a sincere note of thanks for their comfortable stay and her imaginative food. Mrs White had even requested Phyllis's 'yellow rice' recipe. Maureen had enjoyed their company too, particularly Ruby who had turned out to be a dab hand at catching fish and crabs. They'd made little rods out of sticks and string then attached slimy earthworms to hooks Chippy had made for them out of old barbed wire.

Phyllis enjoyed having Paying Guests. She loved the company of other people and began to look forward to answering the door to different families and couples, wondering what the next batch would be like. She got used to tidying the house and planning the meals. Some were quiet like Mr and Mrs Taylor the newly-weds, who barely said a word and blushed every morning at breakfast, they could have barely been eighteen.

"What's that noise?' Maureen asked in the middle of the night as the bed in the next room creaked.

"Must be the wind rattling the windows," Phyllis would say, lying awake and thinking of Arthur; willing his body to be next to hers, warm and strong.

Another PG, Mr Cotton, was the first customer as the doors opened at The Clifford Arms, propping up the bar and playing cards with the locals. He was also the last out.

He'd come back stinking of beer and cigarettes whilst his mouse-like wife sat watching the fishing boats go to and fro. Meanwhile the tin under Phyllis's bed was filling up handsomely and she felt happy that with her earnings and Arthur's allowance, she could afford to pay the rent.

With the month of June came many more bombing raids. A few bombs landed on Teignmouth but it was Plymouth that bore the brunt. Crowds stood on the beach one night and watched in horror as the sky glowed a hot, burning, red to the west. Britain had done its fair share of bombing too, taking just 90 minutes to drop 1000 bombs on Cologne. The heavily populated city had been obliterated; like a city made of matchsticks. Phyllis felt her heart quicken; she pictured the innocent German families and thought they couldn't all be fascists supporting Hitler. She thought of all the mothers, like her, husbands away at war, left at home to look after the children and keep the homes intact for when they returned, if they returned. She felt sure Germany would retaliate with similar actions. They took extra care with the blackout curtains that night and slept in the Anderson shelter.

As Phyllis and Maureen lay in the shelter listening for the rumble of planes, she took out the photograph of Eileen that Peg had finally sent her. Eileen stood next to a brand new tricycle, her face slightly blurry from her head bobbing. She wore a woollen kilt and patterned jumper. The timbered cottage stood in the centre of a well-kept garden. Phyllis had studied the picture a hundred times over. "I'll be coming for you soon I promise. Daddy will see that this isn't right, he'll make it all better darling, he'll tell auntie Peg to send you home, I promise he will." Phyllis kissed the photograph and held it to her chest.

"Do you miss Eileen?" asked Maureen.

"Yes my darling, and daddy," said Phyllis tearily.

"My daddy or your daddy?"

"Both, I miss them both so very much."

"I miss daddy too," said Maureen snuggling up to Phyllis. "I wish he would come home soon then I can have a baby brother."

Maureen longed so much for a brother she thought she would die. It would be so much more fun than playing with Eileen, who might as well have moved to the moon.

As they lay on the hard floor, Phyllis thought about asking Peg if they could all stay with her until the bombing eased; but the thought of living under the same roof filled her with dread. She couldn't bring herself to ask. Besides, her savings tin was starting to fill up again.

Instead she wrote to Peg, telling her she was going to visit Eileen for a few days around her third birthday at the end of August. Peg wasn't overjoyed when she opened Phyllis's letter. It would ruin all her birthday plans for Eileen. They had been living in Wigmore for almost five months and had built up a collection of neighbourhood friends. She hadn't been honest about the details of their sudden residency and had told a few of the local mothers about Phyllis's neglect of Eileen and how she had rickets. According to Peg, the girl's mother had done nothing to remedy it, leaving her no other choice than to take the girl away and look after her properly. According to Peg, Phyllis took no interest in Eileen and no longer wanted her; she was in effect an orphan.

*

Phyllis and Maureen arrived on the early train into Leominster station. Peg approached them from the platform as if meeting strangers. Eileen clung to Peg's dark skirt and looked wide-eyed at her mother.

"Eileen, my dear Eileen." Phyllis ran to her daughter and picked her up to hug her.

"Careful you don't crease her dress," said Peg sourly, "it's fresh on this morning."

Phyllis took no notice and kissed Eileen all over her pudgy cheeks. She looked a picture of health in her brand new clothes. Her hair shone and her eyes were as bright as gemstones. Maureen looked down at her scuffed shoes and hid them behind the suitcase. She was scruffy next to her clean sister and felt awkward as they travelled in the back of Peg's car to the house. Maureen was to share Eileen's bedroom for the two days they were staying. It was a large attic room with wide, wonky, floorboards and a sloping ceiling. Maureen couldn't believe her eyes as Eileen proudly showed off all her new clothes. She had a separate drawer for everything; one for socks, all paired up in a drawer on their own; one for ribbons and another full of pretty jumpers. Maureen took off her dirty socks with holes in and tried on a scrumptious new red pair. They felt soft against her grubby feet; it was like dipping them into fine, warm sand. She then took out a cream-coloured jumper with blue swallows flying across its front. It was a tight but it felt so nice that she decided to keep it on, thinking it might please auntie Peg who hadn't smiled since they'd arrived.

"What on earth do you think you are up to young lady?" asked Peg almost hysterical on the landing outside the open bedroom door. "Did I give you permission to try on those clothes?"

Maureen burst into tears as Peg practically ripped them from her little body, pulling the jumper off her head so quickly it hurt her chin.

"The first thing you need my dear girl is a hot bath. Wait in here until I call you down."

Maureen sat on Eileen's bed feeling sad, not daring to move in case she received another telling off. Eileen put her arm round her older sister to comfort her. They could hear Peg and their mother arguing; something about how filthy Maureen was and how dare she help herself to things like a common thief. Phyllis was dispatched into the garden to dig potatoes for their tea.

Maureen was summoned to the cold kitchen where a

large tin bath had been placed half full with steaming water. Maureen couldn't remember the last time she'd had a bath. She was supposed to have one every Sunday after Phyllis, but the water was normally cold by the time her mother got out, and the ritual would be forgotten or put off till the following week. Peg insisted she get in before the water went cold but Maureen didn't want to get undressed in front of her.

"For goodness sake child, just get on with it. I haven't got all day." Peg snapped impatiently.

Maureen placed her clothes in a heap on the floor and dipped her toe into the scolding water; she thought she'd be boiled alive like a crab in a cooking pot and quickly took it out again. Peg was putting up with no nonsense. She picked up Maureen's naked body and placed her in it as if placing a sheep in a sheep dip. Her little body went bright red. Peg then scrubbed her with a rough flannel and carbolic soap. Maureen's lower lip quivered uncontrollably but she was determined not to cry, gritting her teeth until it was time to get out. She lay in Eileen's bed that night and vowed never to come to the nasty house ever again.

Peg had organised a small party for Eileen's birthday. She'd been tempted to cancel it when Phyllis had announced her imminent arrival on the same day. Peg didn't want her new friends and neighbours finding out the truth about Eileen. But Eileen had caused such a fuss about the party being cancelled that Peg decided to risk it and go ahead. A few of the neighbours turned up with other young children. They played hide and seek in the large garden. The neighbours ignored Phyllis as best they could; she was after all the wicked mother who had abandoned her child, leaving poor Peg to bring up her niece by herself.

Phyllis tried again to persuade Peg to let her take Eileen with them as they waited for the return train home. Peg's answer was plain and simple: "No". Arthur had sanctioned it and that was that. The decision had been made regardless of what Phyllis or Eileen wanted. Eileen clung to her mother not wanting to be left behind, she screamed and kicked and cried as Peg pulled her away.

"Look what you've done, she was perfectly settled before you came stirring things up," hissed Peg.

Peg took Eileen away before the train arrived. "There's no point in us all standing around. I'll write and let you know when she starts school."

Eileen yelled for her mummy as she was dragged down the platform and into the car. Phyllis stood open-mouthed, tears streaming down her face with Maureen and their suitcase as the car drove away.

A letter from India was waiting for her on her return to Shaldon. It was from Maude saying how much she missed Phyllis. She sent news of the family; Ernest and Doreen were still trying for a child of their own. Cyril had been promoted to department head at the university but still had no wife in tow. Maurice was poorly again. Muriel hadn't taken well to motherhood even though baby Eric was a dear little thing. Muriel was now back working for the Indian Navy and dear Wilmot was suffering from bouts of fever and lethargy. Maude hoped it was just the heat but he was looking thinner these days and she worried he might have malaria. He still managed to visit the club at least once a week to play billiards and discuss politics, despite his condition. Maude was still keenly riding and playing tennis. She enclosed the coriander seeds that Phyllis had requested, but wasn't sure they would grow in the cold British climate, along with some fennel seeds to try. Maude suggested putting them on a sunny windowsill indoors to get them germinating, like the chilli seeds she had sent some months before, which had now turned into a beautiful bush full of little green shiny pods; their hot fiery contents adding much needed flavour to Phyllis's growing repertoire of dishes. Phyllis pictured her mother just as she was when she'd last seen her over three years ago; her hair in a wispy bun, some strands clinging to her face on that hot April morning. The heat was at its worst then and beads of sweat had gathered on her powdered top lip.

Phyllis put down the letter and picked up the framed sepia photograph on the mantelpiece of her parents on their wedding day. Wilmot was so young and handsome standing behind Maude, who sat upright and elegant with her large white lace collar draped over her shoulders. She picked the letter back up and read Wilmot's note at the bottom of the page, his handwriting getting smaller and smaller as he ran out of space. Gandhi and members of the Congress party had been arrested and imprisoned. India was becoming unstable and he worried about the future. The Raj was collapsing and Anglo-Indians were talking of leaving. Muriel even voiced the possibility of going to England once the war was over. Cyril thought Australia could be an option for him and his career. The thought of her siblings leaving India had never occurred to her before. She felt disconcerted at the thought of them scattered around the globe. She worried there would be no one to go back to when the time came. Phyllis hadn't heard from Arthur since the Rawalpindi letter. As she lay in bed that night, the candle's flaming light danced, ghost-like on the walls. She wrote in her diary: "Am I married, widowed or divorced?" She worried about not setting eyes on India or indeed Arthur again.

*

The sirens sounded just as the bombs started to fall. Phyllis grabbed Maureen and ran down the stairs two at a time, crawling into the Anderson shelter as she heard the ack ack of the anti-aircraft guns. Beams of white light darted around the black night as the searchlights tried to keep track of the enemy planes. Then one fell, spiralling out of control before plummeting into the sea.

Jessie called round in the morning to make sure they were unharmed after the raid. She found Phyllis constructing a telegram to Arthur.

"I want to know if anything has happened between him

and the nurse and what he intends to do about getting Eileen back," she said desperately. "I just want to go home. I need to be in India. Do you think I'll be able to get Eileen back? I can't leave her here, not with Peg." She sobbed louder at the thought of leaving without Eileen.

Jessie could sense panic in Phyllis's voice as she held her and tried to calm her down. "I'm sure Arthur will come to his senses."

"But what if he gets killed or leaves me? What if he abandons me?"

"Phyl, he's not going to leave you. I'm sure he has every intention of coming home and getting you all back to India, but at the moment he's stuck on the other side of the world. He hasn't seen you in a long time. You just have to keep praying that everything will be all right. Now why don't you post your telegram, then we could go and fetch the chickens that you wanted from the farm."

They used an old crate from the shed and balanced it on the bicycle handlebars. The chickens flapped and clucked as the bicycle negotiated the potholed lanes. Maureen took to them instantly and named them Cosy and Bundle and after her favourite cartoon puppy and a kitten that featured in Phyllis's daily newspaper. She spent the afternoon drawing pictures of them for Arthur. Phyllis promised to send the best one in the next letter to him.

Phyllis received a letter from Arthur towards the end of September. He was in Madras having passed a medical, and was about to be shipped to Ceylon. He swore on his life that nothing of any importance had happened between him and Hilda; they had found companionship in difficult circumstances and it meant nothing to him. Hilly, as he then referred to her, was on her way back to England to get married anyway. He confessed to feeling lonely and adrift in their marriage. He urged her to keep up appearances; her main priority must be to look after Maureen properly. He also stipulated that under no circumstances was Maureen to be sent to a state school when the time came. He praised Peg on the care she lavished on Eileen, and urged Phyllis to feel grateful that Peg was giving her such a good home.

Phyllis tutted as she read the nurse's name again: Hilly, Hilda. She had no time to dwell; more guests were arriving in the morning, beds needed making and floors needed cleaning. She folded the letter and tucked it behind a picture on the mantelpiece.

She dreamt of Wilmot that night. He appeared in the kitchen as she was putting bed sheets through the mangle. "There you are my darling Phyl, it's time to come home now." He scooped her up as if she weighed no more than a feather and carried her all the way back to Benares. She woke when a hand stroked her forehead.

"Mummy, you were saying 'daddy' in your sleep." Maureen stood beside her, her forehead slightly frowning.

"Oh take no notice of me. I was just dreaming about going home."

"Was I with you? I don't want you to leave me behind and I don't want to go and live with auntie Peg either."

"Don't worry, I'm not going to leave you or Eileen behind. Now we have a new family coming to stay today; you can help by collecting the eggs."

*

She drew back the heavy blackout curtains that shrouded the draughty windows and looked around her shabby bedroom.

"What happened to that girl I used to know? What happened to me?" she asked the stranger in the mirror.

As she ironed the sheets for the guest bed she thought of Eileen in Herefordshire, surrounded by new things, things Phyllis didn't know about, new dolls, teddies, books and clothes. She tried to summon up Arthur's handsome face but found it hard these days without looking at a photograph. Where was he? Somewhere in Ceylon, maybe in an army camp, asleep in a tent or perhaps in decent quarters, now he was a Major. Phyllis wondered what Major's wives did. Did they live like this? On their own somewhere, hidden away behind a peeling front door, thousands of miles from their husband's, thousands of miles from home.

24

MISSION INDULGENCE

Phyllis sat on the bed and opened her pocket diary to the 18th of October 1942. How extravagant it seemed now that such a thing would be printed in gold. She took out her pencil and wrote in capital letters across the top: 'MISSION INDULGENCE.' She underlined it, pressing the stub down hard. Underneath her deliciously selfish headline she began to write her list, starting with 'PIANO.' Only yesterday she'd noticed a second-hand one advertised in the Post Office window. It would give her something happy to pursue until she could return to India. She then wrote: 'DANCING LESSONS.' These were held every Thursday evening in the village hall, just across the road from her front door. She'd seen the flushed women emptying out of the hall, like children spilling out of school at home time. The last words on her list were 'SPANISH CLASSES WITH JESSIE.' Jessie had to been trying to persuade Phyllis for months to join her at the weekly conversational classes. Phyllis felt shy of chatting to strangers in a language she didn't feel confident with.

"That's the whole point of it," Jessie had teased. "You speak it so you get better at it. Please come with me. I know you'll enjoy it."

Phyllis was thrilled to get the piano for £5. Jessie and Mr Clements, who she now called David, agreed to help her push it home, around the village green, along the length of Fore Street, passing Elizabeth's house until reaching Dagmar Street.

"It's got wheels," said David. "I'm sure it won't be that hard to push."

They started off quite well, with a few words of encouragement along the way. Mr Denner, the shopkeeper, leant a hand to get it up the slight incline. The bomb imprints proved tricky; the road surface dipped and the wheels got stuck in the tarmac ruts. Mr Denner shoved his shoulder up against the piano and pushed hard until it got back onto a more level surface.

Elizabeth heard the commotion and was horrified when she looked out of her bedroom window to discover the carry-on. Phyllis was making a spectacle of herself as usual, heaving and pushing the large piano with all her might whilst laughing uncontrollably. People were stopping and staring; some helping, some laughing and pointing. By the time they got the piano to Dagmar Street they had five burly chaps on hand and one less wheel.

The helpers manoeuvred it over the step and into Phyllis's front room. The previous owner's fingers had become too arthritic to play; it had sat gathering dust for some years and was in need of tuning. Phyllis unpacked her sheet music that was stowed in her trunk and sent a message to the local piano tuner in Teignmouth, asking him for an appointment as soon as possible. Elizabeth arrived for her daily visit and scolded Phyllis for the spectacle she'd created; reminding her she was a Major's wife, not a member of a travelling circus.

"You are an embarrassment to me. I have a certain standing in the community now you know. I don't know what you see in the Clements."

"And you embarrass me with your ridiculous snobbery."

"Just look at the state of your net curtains. They have black finger marks all over them and a rip at the top, have you no pride at all?"

The following day, the landlady, Mrs Lesley, knocked on the door to collect the rent. She always came on the last Friday of every month. Phyllis had the money ready in an envelope. Mrs Lesley was a kind woman. She always had time for a chat and a quick brew. She shared her local news generously but not in a gossipy way like Elizabeth.

"My eldest, that's Betty, well she's getting married in November. I've saved all my rations to make the wedding cake. I was wondering if you would help me make it. I gather you used to bake cakes for the Maharajahs back in India."

"I would be delighted," said Phyllis, flattered.

They arranged to meet again on the 5th of November. Mrs Lesley would bring the ingredients to Phyllis's kitchen and they would make the cake together.

*

The piano tuner arrived with his hammer and mutes. He fiddled around for hours tightening and loosening strings until he was happy with the sound. Just as he was tuning the last key there was a loud bang on the front door. Phyllis assumed the neighbours were fed up with the tuneless din and was about to apologise, but instead found a couple of men in dirty overalls standing next to a cart full of tangled iron railings.

"We've come to get your railings, missy," said the one with the flat cap.

Phyllis looked down the street. All the railings to the left were gone; like a mouth with no teeth, hers were next in line. The other workman was already attacking the railings with his large hacksaw, its teeth screeched like a hyena as they sawed through the metal struts.

"They'll go to good use," he said looking up at the sky. "They'll be made into Spitfires. That should sort those Nazis out." He grunted as he got on with his heavy work, hammering down the leftover shards of splintered metal with a large lump hammer. Glistening sweat trickled down his face into the grimy creases of his neck.

A week later Mrs Lesley returned carrying a heavy basket of ingredients. Despite Elizabeth's attempts to brand Phyllis useless and dirty, Mrs Lesley found Phyllis kind and rather good company. She thought Elizabeth was jealous of her daughter-in-law's interesting looks, straight white teeth and the ability to have fun and of course, more importantly, to have the love of Arthur.

They chatted as they worked, mixing the fat with the sugar before combining the eggs to make a shiny, gloopy mixture. Mrs Lesley was intrigued by Phyllis's life in India and was full of admiration at the thought of Phyllis running a restaurant in the Himalayan foothills. Mrs Lesley confessed to having never left Devon. They added the flour and dried fruit: dates, figs and sultanas. Phyllis's secret ingredient to keep the cake moist was grated carrot; it was also an easy ingredient to get hold of. They popped the two greased round tins into the hot oven and set about cleaning up, ready to make the marzipan icing.

"Would you like to lick the spoon?" asked Phyllis, laughing. "I'll lick the bowl."

They giggled as Phyllis rubbed her finger around the residue in the bowl and Mrs Lesley licked the sticky spoon like a lollipop.

There was a knock at the back door; Elizabeth breezed in as if she lived there.

"Oh, I didn't know you were here Mrs Lesley," muttered Elizabeth. "What are you two up to?" She looked in surprise at the two women laughing like children, raw cake mixture round their mouths.

"Phyllis kindly agreed to bake Betty's wedding cake for me," replied Mrs Lesley, happy to give Phyllis a much-needed boost in her mother-in-laws' eyes.

Elizabeth felt cheated not knowing this juicy morsel of information.

"Secretive little cow," muttered Elizabeth under her breath as she let herself out again having sipped her tea as quickly as she could, convinced that Phyllis must be earning money that Arthur wouldn't hear about. The two-tiered wedding cake was a great success and Mrs Lesley went out of her way to recommend Phyllis to her circle of friends and beyond. Her baking would help Phyllis to make ends meet in the leaner winter months.

25

THE TWIG TREE

Peg had finally agreed to let Eileen visit Shaldon for Christmas. She worried that all the hard work of getting Eileen healthy and settled would be ruined by Phyllis and her lack of discipline with the children. Elizabeth's recent letter to Peg confirmed that Phyllis was a complete failure when it came to bringing up the children. According to Elizabeth, Maureen had turned into a hooligan. Her nails were black with grime, just like the coalman's and her language was just as filthy. She was allowed to roam freely about the streets like a stray dog, playing with Mary, the shoe repairer's child. Only the other day Elizabeth had to tell Maureen off for wearing her best Sunday coat to play tennis. Maureen and Mary had strung a long piece of rope across the road to use as a net, tying each end to opposite gateposts.

Whilst Maureen had become a tomboy, climbing trees, playing in the street and crawling under the barbed wire to look at the anti-aircraft guns for a dare, Eileen had become spoilt. On Christmas Eve, her first evening home, she climbed onto the mantelpiece in the bedroom and hurled herself off it, pretending to parachute out of a plane. The more Phyllis told her off, the more Maureen and Eileen screamed with laughter. Maureen copied Eileen, but jumped even higher so she could bash the dusty lampshade before landing on the mattress.

"Maureen!" shouted Elizabeth as she climbed the stairs on her nightly visit. "What on earth do you think you are doing?"

"I'm only doing what Eileen did," said Maureen, flushed with excitement but feeling bad for telling on her sister.

Eileen denied any wrongdoing and Elizabeth again pointed the finger of blame at Maureen.

"They're just excited because it's Christmas Eve, they'll settle down in a minute," said Phyllis, trying to defend the girls' behaviour.

"It's time you learnt how to discipline your children Phyllis, I really can't imagine what Arthur would make of it."

Elizabeth wrote to Arthur, telling him how Maureen was out of control, she was also developing 'thick Indian lips' as she continued to suck at her fingers.

Once Elizabeth had left and the girls were settled in bed, Phyllis hung her treasured indian glass baubles carefully on the ends of the prickly fir tree branches she'd collected from the top of the Ness. She wrapped her little

Christmas gifts in scraps of fabric, collected over the course of the year. She hid them in the twig tree that filled the room with the smell of pine forest.

Elizabeth returned on Christmas day after Phyllis and the girls had been to morning Mass.

"My legs are playing me up again today," said Elizabeth grimly.

Her large body thumped down heavily in the chair, like a large sack of coal.

Phyllis poured Elizabeth a small glass of sherry. "Happy Christmas," said Phyllis cheerfully, adding "Chin, chin" as they clinked glasses.

"Oh, it's too sweet, even for me," grumbled Elizabeth.

Phyllis retreated to the kitchen and thanked god her mother-in-law wasn't staying for dinner.

Arthur had sent a picture of himself holding a fluffy Alsatian puppy to Maureen. On the back he'd scrawled: 'Happy Christmas Snoodles. When we are together again we shall have a beautiful puppy, just like this one. Love you more than ever, Daddy.' Maureen went round the rest of the day telling anyone in earshot that her daddy had got her a puppy for Christmas. She kept the treasured photograph in her pocket being careful not to crease it when digging holes on the beach with Mary. When Phyllis had read the short message she felt a little spark of hope that prodded at her breaking heart. 'When we are together again.' Words, not even written to her, but filling her with renewed hope that everything was going to be all right.

Phyllis had also received a present. It was the size of a shoebox and had arrived from India in early December. Wilmot had written clear instructions for it not to be opened until the 25th. Phyllis always obeyed her father and hadn't dreamt of even having a little peak. Somehow she thought he would know if she did. Inside was a dusky pink silk nightie, wrapped in tissue paper, made by the durzis. She stroked the smooth material against her cheek. She marvelled at the neat rows of hand-sewn stitches, like little train tracks. The durzis had been coming to the bungalow and making the family's clothes for as long as she could remember. He must have been at least 70 years old and had the most appalling eyesight. Phyllis and her brothers had hidden his glasses once whilst playing a game of dare. She'd tried them on to make Cyril laugh but hadn't been able to see a thing through the thick lenses.

She wrapped the nightie back up in tissue paper and decided to save it for her next night with Arthur. He would love the feel of the silk on her body as he slowly slipped the nightdress up her legs to her delicate thighs. Also inside the package had been a present for each of the girls; for Maureen a pretty necklace of brightly-coloured glass beads and for Eileen a set of hand-carved farm animals.

Phyllis's least favourite present was from Elizabeth, a dish mop from the Co-Op. Phyllis had seen them for sale in a large bin marked: Bargain, two for 1/- Phyllis wondered who the other lucky recipient was.

"Thought it might come in handy," said Elizabeth as she passed over her gift. "Anyway I must be getting back home. Mrs Alden will be wondering where I've got to."

Mrs Alden was a wealthy widow who Elizabeth lodged with. She had spared Elizabeth the discomfort of having to eat Christmas dinner with Phyllis by inviting Elizabeth to dine with her in the downstairs parlour. Mrs Alden's face was always aghast at the stories Elizabeth told about Phyllis. She took great pity on Elizabeth for having such an undignified daughter-in-law.

With the candles lit and the blackout curtains drawn. Phyllis opened the piano lid and placed her carol music on the stand in preparation for her next guests; Jessie and David. They ate leftover chicken wrapped in chapattis with pickled onions and raita. Jessie tried to copy Phyllis's ease at eating with her hands but gave up when a pickled onion dropped to the floor and rolled under the sofa. David got down on all fours and pretended to be an elephant as the girls took it in turns to ride him around the small room. They all sang along as Phyllis played Christmas songs.

As they got up to leave, Jessie hugged Phyllis. "If anything should ever happen to you and Arthur. David and I would be here for the girls."

"That means more than you can ever know. Thank you dearest Jessie and God bless you."

"We really have had the most splendid evening, thank you," said David as he kissed Phyllis's hand.

*

Peg had driven from Herefordshire to collect Eileen, along with a few items stored in the shed. Phyllis noticed she still left a few boxes behind; poking out of one of them was the brass bon-bon dish she had given Peg from India. Peg was glad to get Eileen away from Phyllis's house. She later told her mother she could have wept at the sight of Eileen's dirty hair, it couldn't have been washed for the whole two weeks. Eileen was scrubbed from head to toe the moment they got home and deloused just in case, even though it was ten in the evening and Eileen craved sleep. Peg didn't want her dirty body contaminating the clean sheets.

Eileen missed her mother who had spent hours playing games with her, lying on the floor indulging her fantasy world; pretending to be a farmer, lining up all her wooden animals and putting them in make-belief fields marked out with string. She'd read her new annual to her from cover to cover in the candle's dim light. The little pool of oily wax had dripped down the candlestick and onto the mantelpiece. The smooth globules grew as if alive. Eileen stared mesmerized. Her mother had stroked her hair and kissed her goodnight, tucking Pandy in with her. Auntie Peg wouldn't let her sleep with teddies, she said they were full of dust that would aggravate her chest. Eileen would wait till she heard Peg clomp down the uncarpeted stairs, then creep over to the sideboard and snatch the first teddy she could find. Her stowaway would be concealed under the heavy blankets till morning.

*

February brought news from Benares. Doctor Madley confirmed Maude's suspicions; Wilmot had malaria. Maude told Phyllis not to worry; there were all sorts of new drugs known to be very effective. Phyllis felt further away from home than ever before; she still hadn't heard any more from the War Office. The chances of getting a passage to India were unlikely. She looked down the narrow hall towards the dhobi pile that needed her attention and wished she'd never come to England. She vowed to go to church the next day and light a candle for Wilmot. She was going to light one for Arthur too but she was so cross with him, having received such a horrible letter the previous day.

In his latest communication Arthur had written that his mother was embarrassed to be seen with Phyllis and the children and wouldn't accompany them in public until she dressed them accordingly. He questioned what she was doing with the children, and showed concern for them. He blamed Phyllis for the fact that Maureen still sucked her thumb.

Phyllis wrote an abrupt reply to Arthur. She told him how much she adored the children and would give her life for them. She added that she fed them properly and spent all her spare money on their clothes. She was always trying to make ends meet by taking in sewing work, cake making and Paying Guests. She pointed out that surely Paying Guests wouldn't recommend her to their friends if the house were as awful as Elizabeth made out. She begged him to agree to let Eileen come home. Phyllis finished the letter by telling Arthur how she felt that his mother and sister were slowly poisoning him against her, drip-feeding lies and exaggerating things. She wrote saying how much she loved him, how the thought of losing him tore her apart, how her heart ached to see him. 'Please don't believe everything Mums and Peg tell you.' She wrote.

Phyllis took Maureen to the beach. She was horrified to see barbed wire being installed along the whole stretch of red sand. It dominated the pretty view, cutting them off from the opposite sandy headland of Teignmouth. The soldiers worked fast, banging the heavy posts into the soft ground, unravelling foot after foot of barbed wire. A thin stretch of sand behind the fence was left accessible but paddling was no longer allowed. A large notice read: BATHING AND THE LAUNCH OF UNAUTHORISED BOATS IS FORBIDDEN. Chippy's ferry had also been moved further up the estuary. Maureen was very disappointed at not being able to paddle about in the shallows anymore. She sulked on the walk home, scuffing the toes of her shoes on the pavement, rubbing off the dull red colour to reveal the original brown leather.

A letter had arrived in the second post; its handwritten address written in violet ink gave away the identity of the sender. Kitty wrote how the Luftwaffe had renewed their attacks on London. The raids were frequent and terrifying. Kitty's home still stood but many more had been razed to the ground. She also had some wonderful news and hoped it would cheer Phyllis up; she'd enclosed a photograph as if to prove her good fortune. She had fallen in love. He was an American GI billeted in the Jewish house next door. Phyllis turned the photograph over; he was tall, handsome and as black as molasses. Phyllis thought they looked really happy, the way they stood, his arm gently around her waist. Kitty was proudly looking up into his warm eyes. Phyllis smiled and propped it up on the mantelpiece, how lucky Kitty was to find love again. Walter came from New Jersey and when the war was over he was going to marry Kitty and take her and Eddie there. America, the land of plenty, even their army had better equipment, better planes, ships and rations than Britain.

Elizabeth turned up, puffing and breathless at teatime. She'd dashed back from Newton Abbot before nightfall, to share her news with Phyllis.

"Madame Mystique asked if anyone in the room had a loved one with a scar on their face, maybe somewhere on their head. Well of course I gasped."

Madame Mystique had caught her first séance victim of the evening.

"She asked if he had dark hair." Elizabeth shuffled in her chair. "I replied yes. Then she said, 'I think this person is far away from you.' She then said that he's in danger, but is brave and that many depend on him," Elizabeth took a sip of her luke-warm tea.

Madame Mystique's chair had squeaked feebly under her weight. Elizabeth had been sitting in a circle with four other desperate women, all of their sons and some of their husbands away at war. They'd held hands and rested them on the round table; a lamp with a red light bulb had cast a gloomy shadow over their middle-aged faces. Elizabeth's hands had been sweaty and tense.

"She said he is safe for now. But he must be warned; he is in danger. We're to tell him not to trust a dark stranger, he means him ill." Said Elizabeth almost in a whisper.

Phyllis frowned at Elizabeth's predictions. "Do you believe her?"

"Of course I do, she has revealed many things; she told my neighbour, Mrs Crawley, that someone close to her would keel over before the end of the week and three days later her dog died."

Phyllis stifled a laugh by pretending to cough.

Elizabeth spied the new photograph on the mantelpiece. "Who's that?"

"That," replied Phyllis. "Is Kitty and her fiancé, Walter."

"But her husband isn't long dead, he'll be turning in his grave," replied Elizabeth curtly, "and he's, he's," she looked around hoping no one would hear her say the word, "black."

Phyllis got rid of her mother-in-law as fast as she could.

"Would you like to read Maureen a story before bedtime while I make her some hot milk? Then I need to get on with some sewing."

Elizabeth took Maureen up the stairs. Phyllis picked up the photograph and smiled. Then she thought back to her own superstitions. The yellow kid gloves were still packed in her chest of drawers upstairs. Perhaps she was being silly. She should wear them after all. She fetched them and placed them on the side table in the hall.

By the time Elizabeth returned downstairs, Phyllis had made her weekly facemask out of whisked egg whites, oats and a pinch of sugar.

"You gave me the fright of my life, what on earth are you doing with that stuff all over your face?" asked a jumpy Elizabeth.

"It keeps my skin looking young. I don't want to be a wrinkled up old prune when Arthur gets home."

"What a waste of a good egg," frowned Elizabeth as she left via the front door. Phyllis stood in the porch and mischievously waved her goodbye down the street, knowing full well it would embarrass her beyond belief if anyone saw.

Phyllis kissed Maureen goodnight. Since she'd found out that Wilmot was ill, they'd got into the habit of blowing a kiss to him every night with their prayers. They'd got out an atlas and worked out the direction of Benares.

"Blow long and hard to make sure it reaches him."

26

A SILVER SWAN

Arthur's next letter arrived with news that he was living in a dense jungle in Ceylon. He shared his mud hut with white ants, mosquitos and rats. The air was heavy with humidity. Leeches fell off the trees and latched onto any exposed flesh, sucking thirstily until they became large sagging bags of blood. Arthur spoke of palm trees laden with coconuts, the noisy fruit bats that squealed and shrieked at dusk and the chorus of frogs that kept sleep away. He went on to mention how they had been to an RAF concert in Colombo a few weeks before arriving at the jungle camp and how he'd been struck by the beauty of the Sinhalese women. Arthur sent his love to the children and praised Maureen on her handwriting and drawings. He insisted that Peg should hang onto Eileen; her health had clearly improved by being in her care. Phyllis put this recent letter with her other growing pile of correspondence. She'd moved them from a shoebox to an old suitcase, still stowed under the bed. She caught sight of her tired reflection in the dressing table mirror and made herself a nercha out loud.

"I promise you Arthur, I will not give in. I'm not going to stop loving you. That's a promise I made on my wedding day. I shall be true to you till the day I die. I just pray you will do the same," she sobbed.

Eileen's much-anticipated Easter visit hadn't come soon enough for Phyllis. She'd sat up for hours the night before, making a foil swan. She'd come across a sketch she'd made of the one on the ship and decided to copy it. She couldn't waste too much tin foil so sculpted the basic shape from newspapers then covered it tightly in foil. It was much smaller than the ship's swan but still very pretty. Phyllis put little presents of sweets and ribbons in the hollow of its crinkled body.

Phyllis, Maureen and Eileen got into the double bed on their first morning back together to eat a breakfast of chapattis stuffed with scrambled eggs and chives. Phyllis put the silver swan on the bed. Maureen and Eileen shrieked with delight as they unwrapped their gifts. A familiar knock on the front door stalled their excited unwrapping. Phyllis looked at the bedside clock; it was gone midday. Maureen peered underneath the net curtains and saw the top of a large black hat.

"Granny!" yelled Maureen.

Phyllis had quite forgotten that Elizabeth was coming round for Easter lunch. Elizabeth had been to church and was ready for a large plate of food. The three of them scrambled to action as their wide eyes met, giggling with terror. Elizabeth would go mad if she thought they were still in bed at this time of day and eating chota hazri in it too. Maureen leant out of the bedroom window.

"Coming granny, we are making you a surprise."

"Well don't take too long dear, my legs are killing me," replied Elizabeth. "Why is the door locked, have you not been to Mass?"

She propped herself up against the garden wall and sighed. Meanwhile upstairs, clothes were thrown on, hair was scraped back into bunches and dirty plates were hidden in the wardrobe. They were all at the bottom of the stairs with Phyllis opening the front door two minutes later. Eileen had been nominated to hold the Easter swan. She presented it to her granny with a big smile.

"Happy Easter, granny," the girls sang.

"Well, that is a nice surprise," said Elizabeth, looking at the crumpled silver neck of the swan. "How charming."

Phyllis rushed to the kitchen and lit the range. The kettle would take an age to boil so she dragged out the emergency primus stove instead. Elizabeth liked a traditional roast dinner at Easter; she had had one every year and this was not the year to break the habit. Phyllis had ordered a chicken from the butchers but wasn't sure how to cook a whole one. Jessie had come to the rescue the night before and removed its giblets and chopped its neck and feet off. Dinner was finally served at 2.30pm, an hour and a half late. Phyllis was pleased with her efforts but Elizabeth moaned all afternoon how her body would be all out of tune. It would take her days to get over it.

Having waved off her mother-in-law, Phyllis was unaware that Elizabeth intended to inform Arthur in her next letter that she thought Phyllis utterly lazy. Elizabeth was shocked that anyone in their right mind would serve dinner up on cold plates one and a half hours late with hair barely brushed and no stockings on; bare feet in fact!

*

On the 13th of May 1943, Phyllis listened to the news broadcast and learnt that the Germans and Italians had surrendered in North Africa. Arthur was still in Ceylon, learning Urdu and training the Ceylon army. He sent regular letters, at least two a month. The weather had been intolerably hot leading up to the monsoon. When the rain finally came it started with large, heavy drops. They hammered on the hard baked red mud, leaving big dark splashes. They came faster and faster until the whole camp swam in a watery orange pool. Troops dug trenches to drain off the warm red rain. Arthur tried to plug the leaks in his hut's roof with large banana leaves. The cloying mud stuck to his boots, weighing him down as if they were made of brick.

As a child, Phyllis would sit looking at the dry, brown lawn, longing for the monsoon downpours. She could smell the sweet, earthy scent of the rain before it fell.

Every child in the neighbourhood would come out from the shady houses and dance along the roads and pavements that turned into shallow fast-flowing rivers. Fractious parents stopped frowning and sang with joy at the sight of the fat raindrops. The servant's children joined Phyllis and her siblings as they chased around the garden. Rain would fall like a waterfall from the roof of the bungalow. Leaks would spring up in every room. The sweeper had to grab old pails and pans and place them under the worst of the leaks. Maude would inspect them every half an hour or so and get them emptied out into the already-flooded garden. Once the rain stopped, the air would feel cleaner. Children would head to the nearby flat-roofed houses with their brightly-coloured kites, ground glass pasted onto their strings.

*

Elizabeth received a letter from Arthur and wasn't quite sure what to do with her newfound knowledge. Arthur was unhappy. His rank of Major had been reverted to Captain; he was 'surplus to establishment'. He was immensely cross, having put in all the training and passing his Urdu exams that had eluded him for so many months. He went on to confess that he had been unfaithful to Phyllis and felt utterly rotten about it, but the women in Colombo were beautiful and he'd found them hard to resist. He felt bad for what he had done but thought that his marriage was slipping away from him. He hadn't seen Phyllis for many years. Phyllis no longer seemed like his wife, but someone he knew long ago, in a past life. He urged Elizabeth that under no circumstances was she to talk to Phyllis about it. It was a secret for the moment, until he could bring himself to tell her. Elizabeth felt glee run through her veins; then a sharp stab of guilt, just a little one. Elizabeth concluded that Phyllis had brought it on herself. How many times had she warned her to sort it out, clean up her act? No, Elizabeth consoled herself, Phyllis only had herself to blame for what was to come. Elizabeth called in on Phyllis as usual. She found it hard to look Phyllis in the eye. Phyllis sensed something was wrong.

"Have you heard from Arthur?" she asked Elizabeth. "You seem a bit jumpy."

"Yes, yes I have."

"No dark stranger has emerged from the shadows then?"

"Thankfully no. There's not much to report, except that he's furious about being reverted to Captain. I'm not sure what it means, maybe he will be posted on somewhere." Elizabeth looked glum and sat looking at her hands. Phyllis assumed it was because Arthur was being demoted and she would no longer be a Major's mother.

"I must get on, I have more guests arriving in the morning." said Phyllis, glad to find an excuse to get rid of Elizabeth.

By the middle of the summer Phyllis had taken in family after family, all glad to get away from big cities, which were still being heavily targeted. In retaliation, Hamburg had been carpet-bombed by the Allies and practically obliterated in the process. Queues for food were getting longer as most foodstuffs were now rationed: rice, dried fruit, tinned tomatoes, biscuits and sausages had all been added to the long list, as well as soap, coal, gas, electricity and even clothes.

The savings tin was full again, but goods had become expensive and there really was nothing much to buy in the shops. Clothes were altered and realtered, their seams picked apart again and again to be fashioned into new garments. Old wellies were mended with discarded car tyres, if you weren't lucky enough to have one of those then cardboard would have to do, replacing the soggy mush after every heavy shower. Arthur reduced Phyllis's allowance. He said he was in debt to the tune of £64 due to his wages being reduced to a Captain's. The truth was he'd got wind that Phyllis was doing rather well as a landlady and that she was squirreling it away for a rainy day and Arthur was spending all his money, and more, on whisky in the officer's mess tent, Woodbines and frequent visits to Colombo where he happily spent his last rupees on good-looking Sinhalese women.

*

Both girls started school in September, but not together. Eileen was sent to Croft Castle, just as Peg had wanted. The imposing gothic building stood at the end of a long drive, its leaded windows gave no clues as to what lay inside. Dormitories full of young Catholic girls replaced suits of armour and large oil paintings that had once adorned its gloomy rooms. Peg kitted Eileen out in the smart uniform and took her to the front entrance guarded by a stone dragon to one side. She handed Eileen and her school trunk over to the headmistress in the oak-panelled hallway then drove away, leaving Eileen weeping into her new white handkerchief. She was four years and one month old, the youngest pupil to board full time. Phyllis was furious with Peg for sending Eileen off to boarding school so young. Peg insisted it would do her good and backed it up by pointing out Maureen's bad behaviour, besides Peg had work to do and relying on childcare was proving difficult with her shift patterns.

Back in Teignmouth, Maureen had started at The Convent of Notre Dame School. She was five and a half. She boarded four nights a week, coming home every Friday afternoon and going back to school on Monday mornings. She settled in quickly and adored the company of the other girls, particularly the attention of the older pupils, who loved to comb her long, dark hair. Maureen looked very smart in her navy blue frock; two white pearl buttons at the neck and white cuffs at the wrists. Only her scuffed knees gave any clue to her tomboy behaviour.

27

THE BOMBSHELL

Arthur's letter reached Phyllis one Friday in October; she was packing a lunch to eat with Maureen on the weekly Friday collection from school. They often sat on the sea wall to eat their picnic tea if the wind wasn't too cold. Phyllis slit open the pale blue envelope with the sharp kitchen knife she'd been slicing the cucumber with. It's green juice stained the absorbent edges of the paper. She glanced at the kitchen clock and realised she would be late for Maureen so she stowed the letter in her pocket, grabbed the tiffin box full of samosas and chunks of cucumber and ran for the ferry.

"Good morning memsahib, and how are we today?" asked Chippy, a big wide smile on his weathered face.

"Very well thanks, Chippy."

"Any news on that husband of yours?"

"As a matter of fact I've just received a letter."

She took the slightly crumpled, cucumber-stained letter from her pocket and started to read.

"Is everything alright? You've turned the colour of putty," added Chippy.

She felt like sharing the ghastly contents of Arthur's letter but instead pretended she was fine. The words on the almost transparent pages were as icy as the sea's easterly wind. Arthur wrote of his frequent trips to Colombo and hinted for the first time that their marriage was over and perhaps Phyllis should file for a divorce. He would confess adultery and it would all be over very quickly.

When Phyllis reached the other side of the estuary she needed to sit somewhere, anywhere, and gather her thoughts. She sat herself down on a sandy lobster pot and re-read the letter. She whispered, pleading at the letter as if Arthur could hear her, "I will not share you. I cannot share you. I need you Arthur. Please don't do this to me, to us."

She sat in a daze looking back over the narrow, rippling, stretch of water to Shaldon. Chippy's ferry had already reached the other side and had picked up the next batch of passengers. They alighted just a little way along the beach from Phyllis. She could just make out Elizabeth and Bridget amongst the small batch of passengers. Phyllis gathered herself, the tiffin box, and the letter and ran up the beach towards Elizabeth, tears streaked her face, dried bits of seaweed stuck to her coat.

"What tales have you been telling Arthur?"

"I don't know what you mean dear."

"Oh, I think you do. Take a look at this." She thrust Arthur's letter, its thin pages flapping in her mother-in-law's face.

The other passengers looked around at the disturbance and hurriedly walked away; it was none of their business.

"Well, you've brought it all upon yourself."

"You already know don't you? He's asked for a divorce!"

"He wrote last month. He's not happy with you anymore."

"But he's not been with me! Why did you feel you had to judge me, stick your nose in, and report back to him every time I didn't live up to your ridiculous standards? You've ruined everything!"

"No, you have ruined everything!" snapped Elizabeth, pointing her straight-gloved finger in Phyllis's face.

By the time Phyllis reached the school lobby she was half an hour late. Maureen stood eagerly waiting, her coat already buttoned and her shoes laced up. Her face lit up when she spotted her mother running up the drive. They held hands as they made their way down to the sea wall. They normally loved sitting together looking out to sea, spotting distant fishing boats, seagulls circling like vultures for any scraps with the waves hurling themselves at the sea wall. Phyllis and Maureen would squeal with delight if their woolly stockinged legs were splashed with the freezing cold water. But today Phyllis was quiet and Maureen had picked up on her sombre mood.

"Are you missing daddy?"

Phyllis put her arms around Maureen and held her. "Yes sweetheart, very much," she replied. "Let's write him a nice long letter and tell him how much we love him."

They found a little tucked-away cafe. Phyllis got out her small writing pad. Maureen used Phyllis's pencil and drew a picture of the family: Mummy, Daddy, Maureen, Eileen and a baby.

"Who's the little baby?" asked Phyllis.

"That's my baby brother."

"But you haven't got a baby brother."

"I know, but I pray every night that one day I will. You said God will always answer my prayers and I have been very good and prayed everyday."

"Have you remembered to blow a kiss to grandpa when you say your prayers?" asked Phyllis, trying to divert the conversation.

"Of course I have, every night."

Phyllis kissed Maureen's head; her hair smelt clean, she

looked happy and beautiful. Phyllis wanted to grab her hand, fetch Eileen, get on a boat and disappear towards the rising sun to India, to the love of her parents.

*

For five consecutive nights the air raid siren wailed Phyllis awake at midnight. She decided after the second night, to sleep in the Morrison shelter. She found it hard to sleep in the cramped cage and wondered if anyone would notice if she was dead anyway. Arthur didn't love her anymore and Peg had stolen Eileen. She lay there listening to the bombers rumbling low in the night sky, like prowling predators sniffing out their prey as they headed menacingly up the River Teign towards Newton Abbot. As she lay in the pitch black, she felt trapped, like the yellow-feathered birds in Catterick. She prayed with all her being that Eileen and Maureen would be safe; that Arthur would see sense and that her father's malaria would be cured.

Phyllis had written to Maude, no longer able to protect her from the truth. 'Arthur wants to leave me' she wrote, 'he has been unfaithful and no longer loves me.' She went on to blame Elizabeth for meddling and spying on her, reporting back to her son of her every move. Phyllis cried herself to sleep clutching her favourite wedding photograph wishing more than anything that she could reverse time and start their marriage all over again. She knew things had not been perfect between them, how could they be? They hadn't seen each other for years.

Phyllis composed a letter in her head to Arthur, as she lay awake waiting for the bombs to kill her, alone in a cage, far away from home.

The next morning she wrote down what she could remember. She questioned Arthur as to what had gone wrong. The last time they had seen each other in Catterick he had loved her, hadn't he? What about the night at Pip's house when she gave herself to him; was that not proof that she would do anything for him? She wrote how she'd spent the previous afternoon with Maureen, her sweet innocent mind longing for a brother. She folded up Maureen's family drawing and sealed the letter ready for posting.

*

When Arthur's reply finally came, the postmark was stamped Bombay. Phyllis opened the letter with nervous anticipation; she noticed that her hands were trembling. The date at the top of the letter was January 14th 1944, their seventh wedding anniversary. Hoping for some news that he had changed his mind, she scanned the letter for any hint of an apology, regret or a change of heart. But there were none. He wrote that he had six weeks leave before being posted to Burma. He was exhausted and had decided to stay with Ernest and Doreen. They were wonderful, very welcoming and let him decamp to their spare room. He loved Bombay, swapping the camp bed for a divan and the damp jungle for a vibrant city. What he didn't tell her was how he also enjoyed swapping the company of sweaty soldiers for fine-looking women at society parties. Doreen came from a large Anglo-Indian Bombay family; there were balls and parties to attend almost every night. At least half a dozen embossed invitations were stacked on the marble mantelpiece each week. Phyllis slumped down on the kitchen chair.

"What about me?" she cried out loud. "What have I done to deserve this?"

She decided to write to Ernest and Doreen to get their view. At least they were with Arthur, they could talk him round, tell him how much she loved him, how the girls needed their father, how he couldn't just abandon her in England. She decided to send a telegram, it would be quicker. The sea mail would take six weeks or more by which time it would be too late; Arthur would be in Burma. The Post Office was busy, a queue stretched out of the door and down the road. It was a cold day, Valentine's Day. Women stood chattering about husbands, sons and boyfriends far away. Telegrams were hurriedly scribbled on scraps of paper then transferred to the official telegram form at the counter. Its private contents were then handed over to Mrs Bolitho, the postmistress. She absent-mindedly licked her lips in anticipation, as she saw Phyllis Woollett join the queue. Mrs Bolitho had made friends with Elizabeth and knew all about her disappointing daughter-in-law. Phyllis didn't want Mrs Bolitho knowing her business and decided to take the boat over to Teignmouth's Post Office instead; she needed to take Maureen some new shoes anyway.

*

Chippy helped Phyllis back on to the boat, her errands complete. He told her there had been a major scare; someone thought they'd spotted a U-boat just off the shore. The RAF and Navy had been scrambled. A Spitfire had swooped overhead and a patrol boat launched from the quayside. Armed soldiers had clung to the speeding vessel as it sped out over the breaking waves. The U-boat turned out to be a stack of wooden crates tied together with rope.

"Probably dropped by a fishing boat by accident," quipped Chippy.

"Better safe than sorry I suppose," said Phyllis, absently.

"Is everything all right memsahib?"

"Oh, I'm just a little tired, Chippy. Too many nights in the shelter I'm afraid."

"I expect you'd like to be heading back to India?"

"If I could I'd be on the next available boat, but it doesn't look as if I'll be able to return for some time yet, not until the war is over I suppose."

Phyllis thanked Chippy for the ride and strolled to the Clements house to find Jessie peeling potatoes. Phyllis told her about the Post Office queue and the ghastly Mrs Bolitho.

"Oh, she's the most frightful woman," agreed Jessie. "She knows everyone's business and isn't terribly discreet."

David came in from the kitchen. "There we are girls, a nice pot of tea."

"I'm glad you're here. I came to ask you about Burma, I know very little about it. Arthur is being posted there. I'm so worried he'll find himself on the frontline for the first time and against the Japs. Are they really as ruthless as people say they are?"

"Well I know the Japanese took Rangoon a couple of years ago. The British are now leading the South East Asian Command under General Slim. We're fighting alongside Indians, Gurkhas and Africans. It's a very hostile place to be posted, I'm afraid."

Phyllis's bottom lip turned downwards; it always did when she was about to cry. "I'm sorry, crying is the only thing I seem to be any good at these days."

"Poor dear Phyl," said Jessie, "you must stay strong for the girls, how are the dear little things?

"Eileen has settled down at school. She's learnt to write her name, she sends me little drawings and Peg sends me the odd photograph and school report." Phyllis sighed. "She's so young, I miss her so much."

"And how's Maureen?"

"Oh, she's very happy, she gets spoilt rotten by all the

older girls. She seems so much older than Eileen and she's only away four nights a week." She let out a little laugh. "Poor sister Catherine had to tell her off the other day for eating toilet paper. She's got it into her head that if she eats it she will stutter like uncle Ernest. She wanted to find out if it was true or not. The worrying thing is she does already have a small stutter."

"I'm quite sure she'll grow out of it," reassured Jessie.

Jessie finished preparing the potatoes. "We're having vegetable pie. Would you like to stay for dinner?"

Phyllis could see they only really had enough for two. She lied by saying she already had something prepared and waiting at home.

"I'd better be getting back," said Phyllis as she took the dirty cups through to the kitchen.

"Oh, take one of these with you, we have a bit of glut at the moment". Jessie plucked up a bright orange pumpkin from a crate in the pantry.

"You'll have to tell me how to prepare it. I don't even know what it is!" said Phyllis.

Jessie laughed as they walked toward the front gate. "I'll call in on you tomorrow and show you how to cook it. But in the meantime go and do some painting or play the piano, take your mind off Arthur and his wretched mother." She kissed Phyllis fondly on the cheek and waved her goodbye.

Even though Phyllis and Elizabeth had exchanged terrible words that day on the beach, Elizabeth still insisted on calling round at the usual time.

"You are still my daughter-in-law." She told Phyllis. "The girls are my granddaughters. Even if you think it's my fault, you'll just have to get on with it."

The next day Phyllis sat on the beach, her easel's wooden feet pushed firmly into the soft sand; paints and a jam jar of seawater placed at her feet. She was pleased with her painting, the choppy estuary in the foreground, washing up to the red sand beyond with the tatty fisherman's huts clustered at the top of the beach. Small wooden boats dragged up in front of them; seagulls perching on empty lobster pots, enticed by the stale smell of fish. In the centre of the picture was Chippy and his ferry. He wore a bright red jumper and his worn-out Captain's hat.

*

By April, Phyllis received news that Arthur was to leave Bombay for Burma. He wrote that Doreen and Ernest had been very kind to him whilst in Bombay. Doreen had given him a silver hip flask as a parting gift and allowed him to leave his spare kit in their apartment.

There was no mention of Phyllis's telegram to Ernest. Maybe it hadn't arrived. Maybe Ernest had been too embarrassed to speak to Arthur about its contents. Then again maybe he had, but Arthur would surely be angry. She could picture Ernest, his gentle voice stammering out the words in her telegram. Arthur would have been cross, shocked even, to be confronted about his infidelity by his brother-in-law and ashamed that he was planning to abandon Phyllis and his children. Perhaps Ernest would write soon and tell her what had happened.

She had heard from her other brother Cyril. He was worried about Wilmot. He had visited Benares for a few weeks whilst on annual leave and had been shocked by his frail appearance. Wilmot was considerably thinner, his once healthy dark skin, now dry and creased like discarded newspaper. His dark brown eyes were sunken and distant. Cyril had cried when he left to go back to Allahabad. Maude had put on a brave face and told Cyril that his father was responding well to the drugs that were stuffed into the bathroom cabinet. But Cyril could see that his once-strong father was deteriorating quickly. Cyril urged Phyllis to get back to India as soon as she could. 'I think our beloved father is dying,' he wrote.

Phyllis knew her father was ill, but hadn't realised how seriously. She felt she was in the wrong place; her father needed her. She needed him. The War Office was still insisting that until further notice no exit permits would be granted. So instead Phyllis sent letters, lots of them, telling him how much she loved him. She enclosed photographs of her and Maureen sitting on Shaldon beach with Bridget. Happy pictures of their life in England, not the real one, not the one where she sits alone at night reading Arthur's letters, watching his love for her die. Not the life where she tosses and turns all night under the heavy blankets in the icebox house, unable to get warm as the coal bucket is empty. And not the one where her mother-in-law walks in unannounced and criticises her. She wrote instead of how she sits at her bedroom window blowing kisses to the rising sun, sending him her love everyday. He writes back, his writing more scrawled and scruffy than before. He tells her how much he misses her; her energy and love of life; her spirit of adventure; her resourcefulness. He confides that he loves her more than the others, he always had. He signed his letter 'your loving daddy'. His PS was political as usual; Gandhi had been released from prison, he needed surgery on his hand, the Raj didn't want him dying on them whilst locked up in their care.

28

MAY DAY FAIR, SHALDON, 1944

The two-tiered cake was magnificent; snowdrops and bluebells made from icing sugar delicately adorned each perfectly smooth layer. The head of the May Day committee, Mrs Greenslade, had asked Phyllis if she would be kind enough to make the cake; all the ingredients would be donated by the church's congregation. Phyllis had been flattered to be asked and had based the design on one she'd made for the Maharajah of Binga's birthday. Five hundred guests, including Maude and Wilmot, had been invited to a lavish party in the Oudh palace grounds to celebrate.

The May Day fair was to be held on The Village Green. Phyllis plaited Maureen's hair then pinned up her own, rolling sections into little sausage shapes before securing them around her head like a crown.

"You need some flowers for your crown made of hair," said Maureen, running off to find some. She returned with a bunch of daisies and buttercups.

"Now you look like an Indian Princess."

Phyllis laughed. She slipped on her kid gloves, once tight around her fingers but now stretched with wear. They left the house; Phyllis carrying the cake and Maureen holding the silver stand that had once been the throne to the Maharajah's birthday cake.

They followed the procession of the May Queen, who sat proudly on a bale of hay that balanced on the milkman's daffodil-festooned horse-drawn cart. The May Queen was surrounded by girls all waving and smiling at their proud mothers who lined the narrow, winding street. Phyllis delivered her cake to the refreshment stand on a trestle table decked with faded bunting.

"Phyllis, that's really beautiful. You clever girl." Jessie came striding over holding her hat as the sea breeze made the grey felt brim flap about her face.

A length of ribbon was ceremoniously cut and the old mayor declared the celebrations officially open. They sat and had tea whilst watching the maypole dancing; the ribbons twisted and turned, creating a beautiful rainbow of colours down the length of the tall pole. The small brass band played and the children, mostly locals and a handful of evacuees joined in the running races. The egg and spoon race was the most popular as they got to eat the hard-boiled eggs at the finish line. Maureen loved it, she was good at running and entered each race with gusto, returning every so often to Phyllis with muddy knees and another prize.

Phyllis chatted and mingled with women from the village who clustered around in small groups. The London Inn was doing a good trade; men including Mr Sheerman were sitting on the pub wall laughing and joking, downing a welcome pint.

"How's that piano of yours, Mrs Woollett? Did you ever find the missing wheel?"

"It's wonderful, thank you. By chance, Maureen found it in the gutter."

Lots of people complimented Phyllis on her wonderful cake. Even Elizabeth who was sitting on a church hall chair had to admit it was a good effort.

"Do you have to mingle with the likes of the road sweeper? Honestly Phyllis, I give up, I really do."

Phyllis was about to tell Elizabeth not to be such a snob but her raffle ticket number was called out. A selection of random prizes were displayed on a table: a jar of homemade jam, a bar of soap, a hat pin, a dish mop (identical to the one Elizabeth had given her for Christmas) and a box of white cotton handkerchiefs with a tartan border. Phyllis chose the hankies and decided to send them to Wilmot.

Then the rain came, gently at first.

"It's just a small shower," people muttered to each other hopefully. "It will blow over."

But it didn't blow over and the little groups began to disperse, back to their dry homes under the darkening skies. The tombola prizes were hurriedly packed into boxes, trestle tables were dismantled and their legs folded quickly away.

Phyllis helped Elizabeth home. Arthur would never forgive her if she'd left her stranded in the rain. Phyllis and Maureen then ran, holding hands as they shrieked with laughter through the downpour to get home.

Once dried off, Phyllis wrapped herself in her choga and wrote to Wilmot, telling him about the day they'd had. She described the way Maureen enjoyed all the races and won lots of them, beating many of the boys; how her raffle ticket had been called and she'd been embarrassed, her hair dotted with wilting flowers, walking to the front of the clapping crowd to choose a prize. She wrapped up the handkerchiefs and decided to take her letter and the gift for Wilmot to the Post Office in Teignmouth in the morning.

The sun went down over the wet rooftops that gleamed like dung beetle's wings.

"Only me." Elizabeth hobbled into the hallway as she let herself in through the back door, shaking the rain off her umbrella behind her.

"I'll put the kettle on," announced Phyllis. She had hoped Elizabeth wouldn't call this evening after all they had seen each other only a few hours ago.

"Oh, are you ready for bed? It's only 7 o'clock," asked Elizabeth, looking at her attire.

"No I was just so wet through, I needed to change."

"Into a dressing gown?"

"I'll get Maureen off to bed. She's got school in the morning, she'll be shattered after all that running," said Phyllis as she led Maureen up the stairs.

"Don't mind me. I'll just have my tea, then I'll be off."

There was a loud banging at the front door just as Phyllis had got to the last line of the book she was reading to Maureen. Phyllis thought it would be Mrs Greenslade with the cake stand; she'd promised to return it once the fair had finished.

"Just coming," sang Phyllis, skipping down the stairs. She saw through the glass panel that it wasn't Mrs Greenslade. It was a telegram boy; his dark peaked cap instantly gave him away. Phyllis's heart did a little skip. She opened the door and took the small manila envelope. It was different from the usual telegrams. It had the word PRIORITY written in red on a blue band vertically down the left hand side. Phyllis knew this one contained bad news. Her breath shortened and her heart quickened. The boy stood upright in the porch in his blue uniform, he knew it was bad news too and respectfully looked down at his shoes as Phyllis tore it open. As she read the pencilled handwriting she crumpled like an injured sparrow to the floor.

"No!" She cried out. "No!" She clutched onto the doorframe for balance.

"Sorry Madam, do you want to send a reply?" asked the embarrassed telegram boy, sad that he'd brought bad news.

Phyllis couldn't answer and just shook her head.

"Whatever is the matter?" shouted Elizabeth from the kitchen. She hurried down the hall as best she could and helped Phyllis up and into the front room.

"Is it news of your father?" she asked, urgently searching Phyllis's stricken face for some clue. "Is it Wilmot?"

"No, it's not daddy," she whispered. "It's Arthur."

"What do you mean its Arthur?"

"He's dead."

Elizabeth took the telegram from her clenched hands. Phyllis must be mistaken, she needed to read it for herself; 'DEEPLY REGRET TO INFORM YOU THAT A REPORT DATED 27TH APRIL 1944 RECEIVED FROM INDIA THAT CAPTAIN ADW WOOLLETT ROYAL CORPS OF SIGNALS HAS BEEN KILLED IN ACTION IN BURMA. THE ARMY COUNCIL OFFER YOU THEIR SINCERE SYMPATHY. UNDERSECRETARY OF STATE FOR WAR.'

Elizabeth slumped into the chair and howled into a cushion. Phyllis put her arms around her mother-in-law and wept into her shoulder.

"How am I going to tell Maureen?" asked Phyllis.

"Do it now, don't put it off till the morning, she will know something is wrong. You must do it now."

Phyllis left Elizabeth cradling the cushion and walked slowly up the stairs. It didn't seem real. Only moments before she had been trotting down them wondering how to get rid of Elizabeth, and now Arthur was dead. Maureen was still awake; she'd heard the commotion.

"Who was that at the door, mummy?"

Phyllis sat down on her bed and pulled Maureen to her, looking into her questioning eyes.

"I'm so sorry, Maureen. It was one of the angels from heaven. Because your daddy is so brave and special, God has decided to take him up to heaven to be with him."

"What do you mean?" asked Maureen, her brow furrowing. "You mean he's, d-d-d-dead?"

"Yes, my darling," replied Phyllis.

"You are a liar!" screamed Maureen "You p-p-p-promised that if I prayed every night that God would listen to my prayers." Maureen grabbed the blanket and pulled it over her face and started howling for Jeanie Doll.

Phyllis carried her kicking and screaming into her bedroom and tucked her up in the big double bed.

"I'll be back in a minute. I'll find Jeanie Doll and come straight back, I promise."

"I don't b-b-b-believe you!"

Phyllis went down the stairs hoping that at any moment she would wake up out of this nightmare. But the stairs under her feet were solid and the telegram was still lying on the table. Elizabeth had made Maureen a mug of milky cocoa.

"How has she taken it?" asked Elizabeth.

"She's distraught."

"I'll take this up to her if you like," said Elizabeth, holding the steaming mug in one hand and Jeanie in the other. Phyllis nodded and sat down. She picked up the telegram again and reread it. It didn't say when Arthur had been killed or how. There was so little information. She was now a widow.

Eventually Elizabeth left to go home. The two women hugged; something they hadn't done for a long time. Maureen had cried herself to sleep sucking her fingers. Phyllis tucked herself in next to her little body unable to settle. Every time she shut her eyes she pictured Arthur's bloodied body lying alone in a jungle.

Elizabeth visited early the next morning.

Phyllis slipped on her coat. "I need some air."

"Take as long as you need dear. We'll be okay here for a bit, won't we Maureen?" But Maureen was so sad she couldn't speak.

Phyllis could see Chippy heading towards Shaldon as she walked along the narrow stretch of beach. He unloaded his only passenger and wandered over for a chat. He could tell that Phyllis had been crying; her eyes were red and puffy.

"Whatever is the matter with my memsahib today, not bad news I hope?"

"It's Arthur, my husband. He's been," she couldn't say the ugly word, once she did it really would be true. She forced it out; "killed." There, she'd said it, it was true. Phyllis burst into tears. Poor old Chippy wasn't good at this sort of thing; he patted her on the shoulder in way of consolation.

"Oh dear, dear," he sighed. "This bloody war has claimed another life." He took a flask of brandy from his inside pocket. "Have a little nip of this."

Phyllis took the flask and gulped its fiery contents, which contrasted with the cold of its mouthpiece.

She needed to be alone and decided to walk up to the Ness. It was peaceful on top of the sloping cliff. She would be able to gather her thoughts that were spinning faster and faster like a whirling dervish in her tired head.

The view from the windy headland stretched down over the estuary's mouth to Teignmouth and beyond to Dawlish. It was beautiful. The early morning sun lit up Teignmouth's large houses that stood near the water's edge. Soldiers were milling about like an army of khaki ants. Phyllis leant against the iron railings that stopped sightseers from plunging two hundred feet to the sea. She looked towards the English Channel; the deep blue waters turned black, as the sea got deeper. It swelled and moved like a living beast that was just stirring from a long night's sleep. She stood and stared. She recalled standing on the ship's deck with Arthur on the voyage to England. They had looked out into the dark night, into the dark sea, wondering if the war would actually happen. Now it had killed him. She remembered his arms placed firmly around her pregnant waist. Her thoughts turned to Eileen and how she could tell her that her daddy was dead. Hours passed as she studied all the people along the beachfront in Teignmouth, going about their daily business. She felt like screaming at them, telling them that her husband has just been killed; how can they carry on as if nothing has happened?

Phyllis hadn't noticed how cold she had become; the sun had started to dip in the milky blue sky. Her hands were numb; she'd forgotten to put her gloves on.

"The gloves!" she gasped. "I should never have worn those blasted gloves."

"Are you alright dear?" a woman's voice asked gently

from behind.

Phyllis turned to see one of the ladies from the May Day party with a scruffy little mongrel at her feet.

"Sorry," said Phyllis. "I didn't see you there."

"Come and sit down a minute, you look a little weary," the woman steered Phyllis away from the cliff edge to a bench under the oak trees. "You're Mrs Woollett, aren't you? The lady from India?"

She introduced herself as Miss Smith, the retired headmistress at the primary school in Shaldon.

Phyllis told her what had happened; the telegram, the shock of reading it, Maureen's anger, Eileen being away; the wretched gloves Arthur had given her and how her father was dying and she needed to get home.

"To India?"

"Yes, to India."

"Why don't you walk back home with me, we'll get you warmed up a bit."

Miss Smith linked her arm through Phyllis's as they made their way back down the Ness. Her little cream cottage bordered the village green. It was charming. Its glossy blue door opened straight into a bright sitting room. A small row of clean wellington boots lined the skirting board, their owners at school. Miss Smith saw Phyllis looking at them in wonder.

"I have some evacuee children from Bristol staying with me, two girls and a boy. Their street was bombed out a few weeks ago, they have settled in very well considering."

Family pictures adorned the mantelpiece. A small fire was already lit; it just needed a little prod with the brass poker to get the flames flaring up. Miss Smith took off her mac and went into the tiny kitchen, leaving Phyllis to warm her hands in front of the fire. They had tea and talked some more. Miss Smith suggested that Phyllis should send her family a telegram. They would need to know about Arthur's death and would in return be able to offer Phyllis words of comfort. Phyllis thanked Miss Smith for her kindness and made the short walk home.

Elizabeth was beside herself with worry. "Where on earth have you been? You've been gone for hours." Her eyes were red and bloodshot.

"I'm so sorry. I lost track of time." I've just come to get some money, I need to send Ernest a telegram."

"Yes, of course, you must. You should send one to Peg too. She'll need to know."

"She'll need to tell Eileen. Do you think Eileen will be alright, hearing the news from Peg rather than me?" asked Phyllis.

"Of course she will, dear. Peg's a nurse, she'll know just what to say."

Phyllis went to the Post Office, feeling a little faint from lack of sleep and food as she dictated the telegram to Mrs Bolitho: 'DEAREST ERNEST. WE RECEIVED THE SAD NEWS YESTERDAY THAT ARTHUR WAS KILLED IN ACTION IN BURMA. PLEASE TELL MOTHER AND DADDY. MY HEART IS BROKEN. YOUR LOVING SISTER PHYLLIS.' She sent another one to Peg, asking her to break the news to Eileen as gently as she could. Mrs Bolitho expressed her sincerest condolences.

Phyllis went into the church and lit a candle for Arthur. By the time she got home it was dark; Elizabeth had put Maureen to bed, she grumbled that all she could find to eat in the house was a stale loaf and two eggs. Elizabeth let herself out as Phyllis went up the stairs and kissed Maureen goodnight.

"Goodnight angel." She kissed her on the forehead.

"Will daddy be in h-h-h-h-heaven?" asked Maureen, her small voice speaking for the first time that day.

"Yes. He'll be with his daddy and his little brother Max; they will be sitting on a cloud looking down on us now. Daddy will be so proud of his big grown up girl. You can stay at home with me this week. I'll tell the school tomorrow, now try and get some sleep."

Maureen was happy to have a week at home with her mother but her overwhelming worry was that she would never get the brother she had been hoping for. This made her very sad as she sat on the toilet nibbling toilet paper the next morning.

*

"She was right," said Elizabeth a few days later.

"Who?"

"Madame Mystique; she said a dark stranger meant him ill, it must have been the Jap that killed him." Elizabeth looked at Phyllis. "At least my beloved son will be at peace now, he will suffer no more."

Phyllis thought of her own superstitions and went to find the yellow kid gloves, the last thing Arthur had given her. She couldn't risk any more goodbyes; bringing them into the front room, she threw them on the fire.

"What on earth are you doing?" asked Elizabeth.

"Something I should have done a long time ago."

Sympathy cards; their deathly white lilies and silver calligraphy, started to drop onto the worn-out coir mat. Phyllis hated the morbid cards and didn't want to display them. Maude sent an airgraph immediately on hearing the news. 'My heart aches for you,' she wrote. Maude thought it would be best to keep the news from Wilmot; it would be too much for him. She told Phyllis how much she missed and loved her. Ernest sent a telegram sending his deepest sympathies.

Peg's letter came a few days later; she had sat Eileen down underneath the apple tree, its baby-pink blossom just bursting from of its green buds. She told Eileen that her daddy died peacefully in Burma, a land far away and that he was a brave soldier and she must always be very proud to be his daughter. They lit a candle under the tree for him. Eileen was upset that the man in the picture by her bedside she called daddy was dead. She tried to summon up a memory of him but none came.

Mrs Lesley, the Clements, Kitty, Pip, the Osmunds and the Browns all sent cards expressing their deepest sympathies. Then a brown envelope with the words 'ON HER MAJESTY'S SERVICE' fell on the mat with the afternoon post. Inside revealed another envelope, but this one was cream with the royal crest printed on the reverse. Mrs P.M. Wollett was typed on the front, her name misspelt. Inside was a sheet of Buckingham Palace notepaper. A typed message read: 'The Queen and I offer you our heartfelt sympathy in your great sorrow. We pray that your country's gratitude for a life so nobly given in its service may bring you some measure of consolation. Signed George R.I.' Phyllis thought about the time she'd seen the King coming out of Buckingham Palace and her excitement as he'd waved at them through his steamed-up window. Little did she know that two years later he would be signing a consolation letter for her.

Two weeks later Phyllis was shocked to find another letter had arrived this time from Burma. Arthur's handwriting clearly addressed the envelope. A small surge of hope filled Phyllis's tired body. Maybe someone had got it wrong; maybe he was alive after all. She opened the blue envelope carefully, her hands shaking uncontrollably. It was dated the 19th of April 1944, just three days before he died. He wrote that he was living in a bamboo hut. He'd adopted an Alsatian called Rickie. The dog had already chewed up three photographs. Phyllis lay the short letter on the table; the last thing he wrote to her, still no kisses for her, just love to the children. She'd thought just for a few seconds that he wasn't dead, that it might have been a case of mistaken identity. Her hands were still shaking when she folded the letter and put it on the mantelpiece. She caught sight of herself in the mirror. Her eyes had dark circles under them.

"Pull yourself together, Phyllis Woollett," she said to her own reflection. "He didn't even love you anymore. He said so, remember? But I still love you Arthur, with all my aching heart I love you."

"Who are you talking to, mummy?" Maureen had come downstairs without Phyllis hearing her.

"Oh, just talking some sense into my silly old head, nothing for you to worry about darling, let's go and have a walk to the beach shall we?"

They grabbed the little basket that lived by the door with a bucket and spade, and a rug, and headed to the little red beach. Phyllis looked back towards the letter and blew it a kiss.

"Goodbye Arthur. I will always love you."

What the letter hadn't said was how he'd been herded like cattle on an over-crowded troop train across India, from the comfort of Bombay, east to a bustling transit camp in Chittagong. He'd then travelled south by army truck to the foot of the Ngakedauk Pass (known as the Okeydokey pass to the troops) it was an arduous eight hour hike over dangerous terrain to complete his seventeen day journey from Bombay to his camp at Htinshabyin in the state of Arakan, Burma. The men marched for up to 20 miles a day, sleeping in foxholes. Troops were being evacuated with dysentery and malaria. Arthur passed the scene of the Battle of the Admin Box, where only a month before the Japanese had used machetes to slaughter enemy medical staff and patients. Corpses lay rotting in the clearing. It was the most harrowing sight he'd seen since becoming a soldier and it shocked him greatly. The Japanese were all around, hidden in dugout trenches and the surrounding hills. Every so often gunfire would start up as snipers took aim. Arthur realised he could be dead in an instant.

He was in camp for only four days after joining his regiment, the 71 Brigade Signals Section, who were charged with recovering and laying cables. Arthur, a Signals Officer, had gone out on a recce about one mile south of HQ with two other men: Neville Benke and Khadam Hussein. They'd set off at 11.00hrs dressed in jungle-green battledress, tin hats and boots. The sky was clear and the sun beat down relentlessly. They'd arranged a lift on one of the Bren gun carriers, which would be taking supplies to the forward company. They made up a small supply convoy, travelling over scrubby land that had once been paddy fields. Bushes and stunted trees dotted the landscape, which could be harbouring the enemy. They reached Htinshabyin in half an hour and waited for the promised RAF air strike to provide cover. It didn't happen; instead a spotter plane appeared in the sky. Supplies from the first Bren gun carrier were unloaded and delivered on foot to the platoon. The spotter plane then vanished over the hills and out of sight. The Japanese saw their chance to attack. The whistle of the mortar bomb gave no time to take cover. Arthur was hit in the chest, causing wounds that he would die from a few hours later. Neville's leg was broken and Khadam lay severely wounded. The men lay bleeding for maybe an hour or two, barely able to speak. Arthur's breathing was laboured. He asked Neville to write to Phyllis before drawing his last breath. Khadam had ceased calling out having been hit by further mortar attacks; he later died of his wounds, too. At around 2pm an English voice called out from the tall grass. A patrol had found them. Sadly it was too late for Arthur and Khadam. Neville, the only survivor, was stretchered out on top of a Bren gun carrier and then transferred to a field hospital in Chittagong. The dead were recovered and taken to the camp morgue.

29

GETTING READY TO LEAVE

Maureen was sleeping through the night again and had gone back to school on the advice of Sister Catherine. This allowed Phyllis to attend to the pile of letters that demanded her attention, some of which warranted a reply and some of which could be put to one side.

A long letter of condolence had arrived from Doreen and Ernest, detailing the last time they had seen Arthur and how much he talked about the girls, particularly Maureen, who was the apple of his eye. Maude had written to say she regretted to share this at such a difficult time but Wilmot was suffering from anaemia and an enlarged spleen as well as the malaria. He could no longer work and had taken to lying on his charpoy most days. Maurice was not working either, leaving only Cyril and Ernest to pay the rent on the bungalow and the servant's wages. Maude had given up playing tennis to look after Wilmot, and bridge parties were a thing of the past.

Phyllis received frequent requests from people looking for lodgings by the sea who had heard how homely other people's stays had been with her. But Phyllis was too busy selling the furniture and getting ready to leave England. She'd sent a plea to the War Office asking for a voyage on compassionate grounds; she was a war widow.

Phyllis looked up when she heard another letter dropping through the letterbox. The smudged postmark read 'Chittagong, India.' On opening it, she was amazed to find it was a letter from Neville Benke, the soldier who had been with Arthur when he died. At last she would have answers to the questions she had been asking since Arthur's death. Neville wrote how Arthur had been brave, right up to the end. Assuming they were about to be finished off by the Japs, they reminisced about their families. Arthur told Neville he would give anything to see Phyllis and the girls again. He showed Neville a picture he carried with him in the top pocket of his shirt; a faded dry forget-me-not flower taped to the back. The photograph was of Phyllis smiling on Shaldon beach with Maureen and Eileen in their knitted swimming costumes. Arthur asked Neville to write to Phyllis if he didn't make it to tell her that he was sorry, that he had not been good enough for her, that he didn't deserve her love. There was no address on the letter, no way of thanking this wonderful man; the man who had heard Arthur's last words.

Phyllis started to sell her possessions. Toys, side tables, the pram and the bicycle were the first to go. She would need money for the voyage and something to live on when they got there. Elizabeth was fraught with worry as she saw Phyllis's house emptying.

"He's only just dead, can't you wait till the dust is settled?"

"I have nothing here anymore."

Elizabeth was anxious about losing Maureen and Eileen. She grabbed hold of Phyllis's hand. "You still have Peg and me dear," cried Elizabeth.

"I've already made up my mind. I'm going on the first passage I can get."

Phyllis also wanted Eileen back and wrote to Peg weekly but her sister-in-law insisted that Eileen was doing well and needed to stay at Croft Castle for some stability. Phyllis reluctantly agreed that Eileen could stay until the Christmas holidays. If they were lucky enough to get a passage to India before, she would send for her earlier.

When Elizabeth returned home, she sat at the small desk in her bedroom and wrote a letter to Peg. She reported that Phyllis's house was more of a disgrace than ever, every drawer had been emptied out, their contents picked through. She told Peg that it broke her heart to think of those two little girls having to go to Phyllis's native land; to live amongst people they barely knew, with the risk of tropical disease and illness. She told Peg that Phyllis had even stopped ironing her clothes as she had sold the ironing board. She concluded the letter with thoughts about Arthur: At least he won't have to put up with Phyllis's filthy ways anymore, she was glad he was dead. She leant back in her chair and looked at the last words she had written. A smile adorned her face; yes, he was at peace now, no more suffering for her beloved son.

Elizabeth hadn't meant to reveal her feelings to Phyllis but when she visited her a few days later she was appalled to discover the chickens out of their cage and roaming freely around the house.

"What in God's name is going on?" screamed Elizabeth.

"Oh, I let them out of their coop for a little exercise but the back door was open and I was so busy sorting things upstairs that I didn't notice," laughed Phyllis.

"Well don't just stand there woman, do something about it," shouted Elizabeth, as she slipped on a fresh dropping, landing heavily on her ample buttocks.

The two women herded the clucking chickens back into the yard and into their cage.

"I'm glad he's dead, at least he won't have to put up with you anymore," said Elizabeth sharply.

"I beg your pardon?"

"You heard me," replied Elizabeth as she slammed the door behind her, rubbing her backside as she limped back home like a lame mule.

30

OPERATION OVERLORD

Chippy spoke of large ships anchoring just off the coast all night. He'd stood in his boat hut with his binoculars trained on the sea, as if he were a sailor in a crow's nest. The wireless that morning reported that a large-scale operation had taken place. At the newsstand, the Daily Herald's bold headline read ALLIED TANK ADVANCE OF SIX MILES AFTER BREAKTHROUGH - *Enemy counter attacks are beaten back!* The mood in the town was positive; surely this was a sign that the Germans were spreading themselves too thinly. A large photograph of hundreds of troops, tin hats on, landing on the beaches in ships and landing craft was pictured on the front page. A detailed map finished the article, showing where the ships and paratroopers had landed and how much ground had been won as our troops pushed back the enemy line.

The Allies led by General Eisenhower invaded Normandy by air, land and sea. It was the largest amphibious invasion in history. Over 5,000 ships were involved in the operation, landing on the code-named beaches of Utah, Omaha, Juno and Sword. The shore was a seething mass of landing craft depositing 160,000 British, American and Canadian troops on its beaches. The sky was black with paratroopers; 13,000 of them dropped to the ground. They had taken the Germans by surprise. The weather had been terrible at the beginning of June and Rommel had taken leave to celebrate his wife's birthday, vast numbers of German troops were ordered to stand down. The invasion had been planned for the 5th of June but the sea had been too rough. British ships and boats had to hold back, some sheltering in inlets and harbours on the south coast of England. The French resistance had been coordinated by the BBC to broadcast its French service from London. They were tasked with sabotaging railway lines, ambushing roads, telephone exchanges and electrical substations. Coded messages in French were broadcast throughout the day: Les carrottes sont cuites (The carrots are cooked) and Les des sont jetes (The dice have been thrown).

All five beachheads were taken. The Germans didn't have enough manpower to fight the Russians to their East and the British, Americans, Canadians and French to the West.

Phyllis became ever hopeful that the war was coming to an end and her passage would be granted, but once again it was turned down. Civilians were not a priority; it was still too dangerous to transport them. She was told to apply again in a few month's time. She was devastated by the news as Wilmot's condition was rapidly deteriorating. Elizabeth meanwhile, was relieved that Phyllis couldn't leave. It meant she could hang on to memories of Arthur through Maureen who had his eyes; she was a pretty little thing even if she did have her mother's lips and had started to stutter.

On the 18th of July, news came that the Japanese had withdrawn from Burma. Phyllis felt proud that Arthur had played his part but also sad that only three months after his death it was all over there. If only he'd kept himself safe, he would still be alive and on his way back to Bombay.

Phyllis's possessions continued to disappear at an alarming rate; a large aluminium-preserving pan one day, a pile of dusty books from the shelf the next. Elizabeth gasped as she saw Phyllis sell the bathtub to the farmer for a drinking trough for his cows. "Why are you packing up when you haven't got a passage? Where are you going to wash?" she'd asked Phyllis.

"I need to be ready and I'll wash in the sink."

The savings tin burst with pound notes from her sales. It felt good to be throwing off the possessions that tied her to England. She opened the lid of her large lead-lined trunk; her silk chatta still stowed at the bottom, having never been used in all the time she'd been in England, its delicate silver handle now tarnished. She unclipped the clasp that kept the silk wrapped around the handle. It opened out as if a new flower coming to life. It formed a bell shape that revealed pretty hand-embroidered turquoise butterflies sitting on sprigs of yellow honeysuckle. It was one of the prettiest things Phyllis owned. She decided to give it to Jessie as a leaving present. Phyllis emptied the heavy trunk and dragged it down the steep stairs and into the near-empty living room. She looked towards the fireplace, where her latest painting was propped on the mantelpiece. It was the view to Teignmouth with Chippy in his red jumper. She picked up the painting and wrapped it in newspaper.

The sun felt warm on her back as she sauntered to the beach in her topee with the newspaper parcel under one arm and the chatta in the other. She decided to air it, before giving it to Jessie.

"I've come to give you this gift," announced Phyllis as she handed the parcel to Chippy. "You have been so kind to me, let alone saving our lives that day. I shall never forget you and your lovely ferry."

"Are you finally off then?" enquired Chippy, taking the painting wrapped in newspaper.

"Well I'm not going just yet, but as soon as I can get a passage, I'll be gone," said Phyllis.

He took her hand and theatrically kissed the back of it. "It has been an honour and a delight knowing you, memsahib," he took the painting from its newspaper wrapping and stood admiring the beautiful watercolour.

Phyllis left the beach and walked to Jessie's allotment. The streets were busier than usual. More evacuees had arrived earlier in the week. The children pointed at Phyllis's topee and chatta; they had never seen anyone like her before. Jessie was scraping out the weeds that had tucked themselves in between the beetroot and carrots.

"My dearest Phyllis, what a lovely surprise, how are you?" asked Jessie, standing up and shielding her eyes from the glaring sun.

"I'd very much like you to have this. I'm keeping busy by getting rid of things, just in case I get a passage and don't have much warning." Phyllis handed over her chatta to Jessie who was overwhelmed with its beauty.

"It's made from Benares silk. Mother gave it to me on my eighteenth birthday. It would make me happy to think that I have left a little part of me here." Phyllis suddenly burst into tears.

Jessie wrapped her arm around her friend's shoulders and held her tightly.

"I miss him so much. I had a letter the other day from the officer with Arthur when he died. I think he may still have loved me; there might have been a chance for us."

Jessie carried on hugging Phyllis as she poured out her grief for the first time since Arthur had died.

"Let it all out my love," Jessie soothed.

Phyllis told Jessie about Elizabeth's evil remark.

"What a nasty woman she is; glad that her own son is dead. I can barely believe anyone could be so cruel. It's no surprise you want to leave."

Jessie offered to help Phyllis sell her things and lend her anything she needed in the meantime.

"I have an idea!" Jessie blurted excitedly. "We can advertise all your things on the vegetable cart."

She fetched some scraps of paper and the pair spent the next hour writing a list of items for sale, with a price for each; a rocking horse, dolls house, dolls pram, mangle, set of blankets, kettle, a set of lace antimacassars, a brass bon-bon bowl, a small primus stove, children's wellington boots and an indian dhuri. David stuck the list to the side of his cart with a drawing pin the next day and by the end of that week Phyllis had received many buyers at her door. She worried about selling Scotch Doll; after all it was Maureen's second favourite doll after Jeanie. Phyllis hoped Maureen would be too excited at the thought of going to India to notice she'd been sold. Phyllis didn't mention it on her daughter's next weekend home from school and fortunately Maureen didn't notice the empty shelf where Scotch Doll normally sat.

"We'll be seeing grandma, grandpa and all your uncles, aunties and cousin Eric, just as soon as we get permission to travel," said Phyllis as she tucked Maureen up in bed.

"Tell me about the m-m-m-mango tree again."

"You'll love it. We used to throw sticks at the fruit to knock them to the ground. Once Cyril accidently hit a sleeping rat snake that was coiled up in one of its higher branches. I've never run so fast in all my life!"

Phyllis spoke of all the servants they had, each one with a different job.

"There's even a servant to keep you cool."

"Does that mean you won't have to do the d-d-d-d-dhobi anymore?"

"That's right," smiled Phyllis. "I'll no longer need to get down on my hands and knees and scrub the floor, either. Instead I'm going to spend my time teaching you how to ride a horse and play tennis."

Maureen asked about the heat, the monsoon rain, the cockroaches, snakes and lizards. It all sounded so exotic. She clapped her hands in excitement.

"How l-l-l-long will it take to get there?"

"About six weeks."

"Will Eileen come too?"

"Of course she will. Don't worry, I'm not going to leave either of you here."

"Will we ever come b-b-b-back to England?"

"Probably not, my darling."

Maureen went to sleep thinking of lions and cheetahs, mangos and bananas. Phyllis looked around the near-empty house, excited that all she needed was a piece of paper with permission to travel and to get Eileen back. She sat on her trunk reading the newspaper, willing the war to end so she could get off this island and sail home. The headline brought encouraging news; PARIS LIBERATED.

*

Two more months went by. The October nights were drawing in and the blackout curtailed most evening activity as the clocks had changed. The autumn air smelt damp and mossy as the low winter sun lost its warmth bringing with it Phyllis's growing anxiety that Wilmot would not see the year out. She'd received a telegram from Cyril. It said Wilmot's condition was becoming critical; 'He could slip away from us any day'. Phyllis was distraught. To make matters worse, Elizabeth let it slip that Eileen needed her tonsils removing and had been in hospital for the past week. Phyllis couldn't believe she hadn't been informed and wrote to Peg demanding an explanation. Phyllis left the house to catch the last post in the foulest of moods, muttering under her breath what a ghastly creature Peg was.

"Hello, Mrs Woollett." Miss Smith was waving to her from across the road. "How are you, dear?"

"Oh, Miss Smith, I didn't see you there. I didn't want to miss the last post."

"Have you got time to have a cup of tea with me?"

Phyllis and Miss Smith walked past the post box to her house on the green.

"How have things been?"

Phyllis told her all about the plans to secure a passage home as soon as possible, but the War Office wouldn't let her travel. She went on to tell her how Eileen's tonsils had been removed without Phyllis's knowledge. Miss Smith sat back in her seat listening and nodding.

"Good lord, you mean she hadn't even told you? I suggest you get her back with you just as soon as you can; it sounds to me as though she regards Eileen as her own". Miss Smith was perched on the edge of her seat, stirring the sugar vigorously into her strong tea, just like Arthur used to. It swirled around the bone china teacup threatening to spill over the sides. Miss Smith suggested that Phyllis should write to the War Office again enclosing a copy of the letter from Cyril. Troopships were still travelling east; there must be a way of boarding one. The Germans were now so weak that even Hitler's officers had plotted to kill him.

There was a loud knock at the front door; not waiting for it to be answered, three noisy children spilled into the front room taking off their shoes and chatting excitedly about the walk home from school. One of the boys had found a spent bullet case on the beach; it would go on the trophy shelf back home in Bristol along with his prized shrapnel. Phyllis finished her tea before returning to her cold, empty house. It reminded her of a desolate and uninviting waiting room. She lit a small fire with the last of the coal; her month's rations already used up. Phyllis put on one of Arthur's old wool jumpers; it's elbows thin and worn. She pulled it closely to her small body and wrapped her arms around herself, sitting cross-legged on the bare floorboards next to the pathetic single flame. The power had been cut once again, the third night in a row. She lit the storm lamp and copied out Cyril's letter, word for word in the flickering light. The next morning she posted the urgent plea to the War Office, begging them to let her travel home. She also sent a telegram to Peg telling her she was coming to visit for the Christmas school play at the end of November, and had plans to stay at the nearby convent. She would be taking Eileen home with her and would need all her things ready in a suitcase.

Phyllis went out into the dusky evening and slipped under the barbed wire to access the beach to gather driftwood. Most of it had already been picked up, but a few small worn-down sticks, the bark stripped away revealing the shiny grain, lay like jewels on the out-of-bounds sand. She stashed them in an empty sand bag.

31

SILENT NIGHT

Jessie offered to accompany Phyllis to Croft Castle to see Eileen's carol concert and help bring her home. The local convent had replied to Phyllis's request for a room by return of post saying it would be most suitable to have them to stay. They could have two small rooms with a simple breakfast. Peg wrote to Phyllis that if she was going to spoil everything by going to the school concert and taking Eileen away, then she wanted nothing more to do with Phyllis or the child ever again. She would not be attending the concert and did not want to see Phyllis. She would leave a case of Eileen's belongings at the school for her to collect and under no circumstances was she to visit the house. She went on to say how painful she found having Eileen so cruelly taken from her.

*

The narrow pews were packed with excited siblings and parents, mostly mothers. Phyllis was relieved that she couldn't see Peg's broad shouldered outline as she entered the pretty 13th century church that nestled on the edge of the school grounds. Eileen stood next to the ivy-decked alter, draped in a sheet to resemble an angel. She was only five years old, but tall for her age. Phyllis waved her carol sheet excitedly, hoping to catch her eye. Eileen blushed, embarrassed by her mother's attention. After the carol concert each child held a candle in a jam jar and sang Silent Night as they walked down the aisle. Phyllis and Eileen's eyes met for a split second. Phyllis realised how much she had missed her daughter and how wonderful it would be to get her home. Jessie took out her hankie and wiped her moist eyes, she held Phyllis's cold hand as they followed the children out of the church and into the grand oak-panelled entrance hall of Croft Castle.

The children were given watery, hot cocoa with biscuits as the parents mingled in chattering clusters. One of the mothers recognised Phyllis from Eileen's birthday party.

"Mrs Woollett, isn't it? I gather you are going to take Eileen home this time?" Her little finger was angled out to one side as she sipped from her teacup. Her tweed suit hugged her slightly bulging figure. She was just Peg's type, thought Phyllis.

"I never wanted her to come here in the first place. Peg snatched her from me," said Phyllis, looking directly at the woman.

Phyllis didn't care who she offended or if she gave Peg a bad name, in fact she was rather enjoying herself. Jessie stifled a giggle into her tea.

"But Peg told me you didn't want your daughter, almost abandoned her. Neglected, that's how she described Eileen. She said she'd had to rescue her."

Phyllis laughed, almost a little too loudly for the occasion, "I'm afraid it really couldn't be further from the truth. Is that why I was shunned at the birthday party?"

"Yes. It looks like your sister-in-law has spun quite a yarn. Please accept my apologies." Without waiting for a reply she turned on her heels and hurried off to find her daughter.

Eileen came sliding along the polished parquet floor in her ballet shoes, nearly knocking Phyllis over.

"Sweetheart, you were wonderful."

"Where's auntie Peg?" asked Eileen, her little worried face searching the small huddle of parents. "I couldn't see her in the church either."

"I'm afraid she wasn't feeling very well. She said to say sorry she couldn't make it, but sends you all her love. Let's gather your things from the dormitory and say goodbye to your friends, then we'll go to the convent and catch the train home tomorrow."

"What about auntie Peg? She'll be cross if I don't say goodbye."

"Don't worry about that for the moment, my darling," said Phyllis, wanting to change the subject. "I have a

Christmas surprise to tell you."

Eileen liked surprises. Peg was always bringing her new gifts; a blue teddy, a dolls pram and bright ribbons. She wondered what it could be.

After a peaceful night in the convent's cell-like room, they had breakfast and set out on the train journey home. Eileen quite forgot about Peg as she looked forward to her surprise.

"Can I have it now mummy?" she asked, as the train chugged through the Herefordshire countryside into Gloucestershire, passing its pretty honey-coloured Cotswold stone villages.

"Have what darling?" said Phyllis absently, quite forgotten that she'd promised Eileen anything.

"My surprise, silly."

"Oh, that," said Phyllis looking at Jessie for reassurance. "The big surprise isn't really a thing, it's more of an adventure. Grandma and grandpa Dover would very much like to meet you, so I thought it would be nice to get on a big ship and sail across the sea to India and stay with them for a while." Phyllis felt pleased with her explanation.

"What about auntie Peg and school?"

"We can write to them and send them photographs. You'll love India. I remember when I was your age I used to ride the pony around the compound, climb the neem tree and once Cyril and I chased a cobra out of the house. Cyril got his cricket bat and whacked it over the head, poor thing. The ice cream wallah would cycle up the drive and make us the most delicious ginger ice cream I have ever eaten, and the sugar cane seller would stand on the other side of our gate pressing the long dark canes through a huge grinder, like our mangle."

Eileen sat studying her mother's animated face; her cheeks flushed with excitement. India sounded far away and not like England at all.

"Can I take Pandy with me?"

Phyllis smiled at Eileen's innocent face. "Well, we certainly won't be leaving him behind. I don't think he'd be very happy, would he?"

"Does that mean I don't have to have a hot bath every night before bedtime?"

Phyllis put her arms around Eileen and held her. "Not if you don't want to."

Phyllis was aware they hadn't yet spoken about Arthur. It had been seven months since his death. Phyllis decided to leave it for now and talk about it when they got back to Shaldon. She'd get the photograph album out when all three of them were together. They could look at pictures of the family, the wedding, the bungalow and Arthur.

By the time the train pulled into Teignmouth station the

temperature had dropped to below zero. Phyllis and Jessie huddled out onto the platform, carrying Eileen and her luggage. David was there to meet them. He'd also prepared a fire in Phyllis's empty house. Its welcome glow of flickering flames lit up the stark living room. They drank hot tea and talked about Christmas; it was only three weeks away. Phyllis said they may be on their way by then and didn't want to go to any trouble. Jessie and David decided that if Phyllis and the girls were still in England they would bring over some food and a few games for the children. Phyllis agreed that David would come round the night before and slaughter one of the chickens, not something Phyllis relished but it would make a special last Christmas feast. David agreed to have the other chicken; he'd put it in the allotment. They'd dismantle the coop that he made for Phyllis and wheel it over. All Phyllis needed to get rid of now was the piano. Miss Smith was coming over in the morning to take a look, thinking her evacuee children might like it.

*

Miss Smith hadn't visited Phyllis's house before and was surprised by its emptiness.

"You really are ready to leave at the drop of a hat aren't you?" she said, looking at the bare walls, floor and near-empty sitting room.

The only two things left in the front room were the piano and the Morrison shelter.

"Any day now hopefully," replied Phyllis. "The War Office keeps promising me that I'm a priority case since I sent them a copy of Cyril's letter; because it is a repatriation they will pay our fare too, but I fear it will be too late."

She showed Miss Smith her latest letter from Maude. 'Your father is so unwell, I don't think he can hang on for you much longer, he knows you are doing everything you can to get home. He knows how much you love him.'

"We must telegraph the War Office at once with another urgent plea. Leave it to me. I shall do it on my way home. In the meantime let me take a closer look at the piano," said Miss Smith.

She pressed each key gently then rolled up her sleeves as she balanced on the rim of the Morrison shelter. She played a rousing rendition of 'It's a long way to Tipperary'. Phyllis joined in the singing as Miss Smith sang at the top of her soprano voice.

They didn't hear Elizabeth let herself in.

"What time do you call this?" she enquired sharply, not bothering to hold her tongue even in company anymore. "Surely you have more important things to do than lark about like a couple of silly girls. Really Miss Smith, I thought you knew better. Eileen needs dressing and the pots need doing, it's a good job I'm here." With that she bustled off down the hall like an overstuffed turkey and started boiling water for the washing up.

Miss Smith looked at Phyllis, her mouth wide open. "Oh dear. Have we done something to upset her?"

Phyllis smiled at dear Miss Smith, who must have been at least 10 years Elizabeth's senior. Her neat grey hair scraped back elegantly in a bun, her glasses sliding gently down her nose as she happily banged on the black and white ivory keys, turning the music sheet over every few minutes. Having come to the end of the tune she said she'd happily pay £5 for the piano. Before Miss Smith left for home, they composed a telegram to the War Office stating that without brave men like Captain Woollett, the war in Burma may still be going on. The requests of the widows and children left behind should be dealt with as urgently and compassionately as possible.

*

The chicken's neck had been rung and a couple of Arthur's old brown socks dangled from the mantelpiece like large tobacco leaves hanging out to dry. Phyllis had warned the girls that Father Christmas was only bringing one present each this year, not because they hadn't been good, but because they wouldn't have room in their luggage. She reassured them that Father Christmas would deliver a couple of presents under grandma and grandpa's tree too as she tucked them up in the remaining bed.

Phyllis decided it was the right time to show her daughters the photograph album. She squeezed between them and opened the book's mottled cover. Thin tracing paper separated each page of small black and white photographs. The girls sleepily adjusted their bodies to face the matt black pages.

"This is daddy and me on our wedding day," said Phyllis, pointing to a photograph of her and Arthur. He was standing in his dress uniform with his shoulders back and his chin slightly cocked towards her. His hair was combed back from his high forehead and he looked rather serious. Phyllis stood with her arm linked through his. She wore a simple white dress, nipped in at her slender waist. She clutched a bouquet of pale cream roses that matched the crown of flowers on her headpiece.

"You look beautiful, mummy," said Maureen as she studied the picture of her parents.

"What was daddy like?" asked Eileen.

"Well, he was very handsome, as you can see, and brave. He is very proud of you both," said Phyllis unable to hold back the tears. "He loves you very much."

"Is he in heaven now?" asked Eileen.

"Yes darling, he's there, looking down and keeping us safe."

She turned the page. There was a picture of her brothers and Muriel, standing in front of a large bungalow, surrounded by trees; a horse and carriage parked to one side. A boy lay on a charpoy in the shadows, probably Maurice. Phyllis pointed at each face in turn, naming her siblings and revealing their ages and characteristics. The next picture was of Maude in her Sunday best. Trays of cakes were set out on the table. Bearers dressed in white stood discreetly to one side. The next picture was of Wilmot and a young Phyllis, probably about five years old; she was sitting on her father's lap fiddling with his waxed moustache. They were smiling at each other, not at the camera; it was natural, unlike the other very posed pictures. Phyllis looked at Maureen and Eileen to find them both fast asleep; she climbed out of bed, tucking them in as she left.

"Goodnight my little darlings. Soon, my loves, everything will be alright." She tiptoed down the hall and placed a present for each of them in the empty socks.

*

"Happy Christmas," chorused Jessie and David. They'd pushed their cart laden with festive items up to the porch. Phyllis couldn't believe her eyes. David had chopped down a small fir tree and had placed it in a bucket of sand. Jessie had adorned it with homemade decorations made from flotsam and jetsam salvaged from the beach. Old bits of string threaded through limpet shells dangled from its spiky branches. Bits of gnarled driftwood made into an angel topped the tree, gull's feathers stuck to its sides for wings. A small pail of coal sat at one end of the cart. David put it in the front room next to the piano as Jessie unloaded vegetables, a bottle of dark crimson sloe gin and a present each for the girls.

After dinner they said a toast.

"To absent friends." Phyllis whispered quietly as she looked towards the mantelpiece for the wedding photograph of her and Arthur. It wasn't there, but packed neatly within the pages of a book and stowed in the trunk they were using as a table. The Clement's nephew, Robert, had been shot dead on the fields of Arnhem; he was seventeen and Jessie's sister's only child.

"To Arthur and Robert," said David as he raised his glass of purple gin to the air.

"To Arthur and Robert," repeated Jessie and Phyllis.

By five o'clock Chippy and his grandson Frankie had arrived with a pork pie and a tin of peaches.

"It's all I could muster up," confessed Chippy as he stood on the doorstep in his Captain's cap.

Then came Miss Smith with her three evacuees. Maureen was thrilled to finally have a boy to play with, an older one too. She showed him her new peashooter that David had made. The children drifted off into the kitchen, poking the range fire with a stick and burning the old chicken bones. They fired dried peas across the room, seeing who could hit the teapot. By the end of the evening it was Phyllis's turn to play the piano, she found the music to 'We'll Meet Again'. The grown-ups were in the front room, singing along to the sound of the piano. Elizabeth hadn't planned to call on Christmas Day, choosing to visit on Boxing Day instead, she didn't want to be seen mingling with the waifs and strays of Shaldon.

32

PERMISSION TO TRAVEL

Phyllis decided to send Eileen to school with Maureen. Sister Catherine cobbled together a suitable uniform from lost property, knowing that she would only be attending for a short while.

"I thought we were going to India. I hate school!" Eileen shouted on her first day.

"You have to go to school until we get permission to travel. I'll come and get you for the weekend. Maureen will be with you."

"I don't have to stay all term without you?"

"Of course not, it's not like Croft Castle. I'll be back in four days. I promise."

A letter arrived whilst Phyllis had been in Teignmouth; a government department address was printed in the top-left corner. She thought it was probably something to do with her war widow's pension or the settlement of

Arthur's estate.

"Yes, oh yes, finally!" she danced around the house singing with abandon. "We are going home!"

The letter informed her that the War Office had given her and her two daughters permission to travel to India on the next available troopship from Liverpool. She would be responsible for arranging the relevant documentation. A family passport would be required and Eileen's birth certificate, along with her marriage certificate. In the interests of national security, a date could not be given, but a telegram would be sent in due course, giving approximately two days advance warning.

"Two days! Is that all?" asked Jessie after Phyllis shared her good news.

"Am I doing the right thing?" she asked Jessie. "What if everything has changed in India?"

"Stop fretting, you've been dreaming of this day for a long time," said Jessie. "You can always come back."

"Yes, you're right. I can always come back."

"I need to go up to the Ness, to think about Arthur, to think about everything."

"Would you like some company?"

"No thank you. I need to be alone."

The Ness was exposed, the trees that bravely grew on the

top, grappled with the strong inshore winds, their large trunks slanted inland. Phyllis walked over to the iron railings and looked beyond the rusting struts to the craggy Devonshire coastline, its undulating headlands hiding little sandy coves and clear blue inlets. Fishing boats bobbed about on the inky swell as the hammering sound of the boat yard banged rhythmically on, audible even up here. She could see Chippy's little ferry going to and fro across the estuary, as it had done for so many years. It was almost a year since Arthur's death; she recalled the day she found out as if it were yesterday; the memory still so painfully near the surface, not yet tucked away and out of sight. She dreamt about Arthur every night and still prayed for him before she went to sleep. Phyllis could hear a train leaving Teignmouth station, chugging along the line to Dawlish as it picked up speed. She wished she were on it with the children and her large trunk, heading for Liverpool. "Please wait for us daddy, we'll be with you soon," she said out loud.

Elizabeth was upset with Phyllis's news.

"What do you mean, any day now?" she questioned. "I haven't had a chance to say goodbye to the children, and what about Peg?"

"You can come to the station and wave us off."

Elizabeth shrugged. "If my legs can make it."

"As for Peg," said Phyllis. "She had her chance to come to the school concert but rebuffed Eileen if you remember? Eileen was very upset. Peg has told me she wants nothing more to do with her. I'm not sure there's much more to be done."

Phyllis spent the next few days packing the last of her things. She breezed around the house and found herself smiling again for the first time since Arthur died. Miss Smith came for the piano with two burly men from the coal yard to help push it all the way to her house. David dismantled the chicken coop, taking the one remaining bird with him. The house was empty, apart from one pan, one kettle, one set of bedding, and the basic furniture that came with the house. Phyllis's trunk was now full to bursting in the front room; the label read 'Woollett, Bombay, India.' The words thrilled her every time she brushed past it. She swept and scrubbed and polished the house until it gleamed, ready for its next tenants. Phyllis sent a telegram to Sister Catherine at the school, asking her assistance in getting the girls' belongings ready.

33

6TH JANUARY 1945.

A telegram arrived mid-morning. Phyllis assumed it would be from Ernest wanting to know what date her ship would be arriving. The pencilled words swam about on the paper as she tried to hold it still. It was from Ernest but it wasn't about her arrival.

By the time Elizabeth visited that evening, the house had fallen into darkness, but the blackout curtains were not drawn over the windows. Elizabeth thought Phyllis must be out but when she tried the door, it was unlocked.

"Only me, are you in?" called Elizabeth. As she flicked on the light, she gasped in horror.

Phyllis was lying on the floor at the bottom of the stairs, wearing her solar topee.

Elizabeth felt Phyllis's pulse. "Oh, thank the lord," she whispered. She went next door to get help. "Send for Doctor Clare at once," she ordered.

One of the neighbour's children was dispatched to fetch the doctor. The boy glimpsed Phyllis's limp body though the open door. He ran to Doctor Clare's house and banged the knocker loudly.

"Come quickly. I think the Indian lady is dead!"

Doctor Clare came running, still chewing his wife's chicken pie and brushing crumbs from his beard. Phyllis was now propped up against the trunk sipping from a glass of water.

"Thank you doctor," said Elizabeth. "I think she must have fainted. At first I thought she was dead."

"Daddy," whispered Phyllis. "It's daddy who's dead."

"Oh my dear girl," cried out Elizabeth.

"I didn't make it in time. I didn't say goodbye," spluttered Phyllis.

Rumours spread through the village that the Indian lady was dead. Jessie came rushing in through the front door. Her face was as pale as milk. "Phyllis, my dear girl, thank God you are alive." She took over from Elizabeth and hugged her like a daughter. Between the three of them they carried Phyllis up the stairs and into the bedroom. One thin sheet and a threadbare brown blanket covered the bed.

"Mrs Woollett, why have you no things in your house?" asked the doctor, worried for the children's well-being, having once treated Eileen for rickets.

"I'm due to leave for India any day now. I've sold all my belongings and packed up everything. I was trying to get back in time to say goodbye to daddy, but it's too late. He died yesterday." Her voice trailed off into a series of heavy sobs.

Doctor Clare gave Phyllis a sedative to help her sleep. Jessie said she would stay with her overnight and keep an eye on her. Elizabeth hobbled home and cried herself to sleep in her own bedroom. She cried for the dead, for the living and for herself.

Days went by in a blur for Phyllis. Jessie, Miss Smith and Elizabeth took it in turns to look after her, bustling about in the kitchen, boiling vegetable soup and baking soda bread. After a week in bed, Phyllis was at last strong enough to make it down the stairs, her hip and arm still badly bruised from the fall.

"The doctor said if you hadn't been wearing your silly hat; his words, not mine, it could have been a lot worse," said Jessie.

Phyllis managed a smile. "I can't even remember going up stairs, let alone falling down them."

January turned into February but still no date of passage had arrived. Phyllis didn't feel the urgency to get home that she'd felt when Wilmot was alive, but the emptiness of not only the house but also her heart was getting her down. She prayed she would be told soon.

*

Back in India, Maude grieved for Wilmot; her husband of half a century. He had been a good man; faithful, honest, kind and a wonderful father to their five children. He'd worked hard all his life to provide for them, but now he was gone. Apart from a handful of shares that Maude had inherited from her mother, she had no savings left; she'd spent all their money on doctors and medicine. She worried constantly about the future and how she was going to manage without him. She couldn't afford to pay all the servants; only having enough money to keep on the didwan, one churprassis, the khansamah and the messalgie. Muriel had insisted she go and live with her and Austin in Karachi but Maude was too grief stricken to think beyond getting through each day. The stress of moving out of the family home was too much to contemplate. Instead, Maude stepped into her black mourning dress and sat on the veranda, sitting so still and silent that the mongoose would come within inches to claim his morning milk.

Phyllis couldn't bear the thought of her mother worrying about money. She sent her a Postal Order for £30. She bumped into Jessie on her way home. "I've been looking for you. I've organised a little surprise," said Jessie, leading Phyllis by the arm. She guided her along the road and down to the narrow strip of beach. Jessie had placed her small garden table on the sand next to the barbed wire fencing. She'd hauled two chairs along the street from the allotment and placed them either side. Jessie's best bone china teapot, cups and saucers were arranged neatly on the flapping white tablecloth.

"Thought you could do with cheering up a bit."

"You are the dearest friend Jessie."

Jessie poured them a cup of tea and placed two hard-boiled eggs and toast soldiers on each plate.

"Elizabeth was at your house, she said to give you this if I found you. I think she thought it might be important," said Jessie, passing over a slightly crumpled envelope from her coat pocket.

"The 16th of February." Phyllis looked at Jessie. "It's my date of travel from the War Office."

"That's the day after tomorrow!"

Phyllis didn't know whether to laugh or cry. She hugged Jessie, not feeling the pain of her bruises as her friend squeezed her gently.

"So this is it, you're finally going."

"I will never forget you, or the kindness you and David have shown me from the moment we met."

"We'll miss you and your hat, dearest Phyllis," laughed Jessie, hugging her again.

"It's the middle of winter and you're sitting on the beach. What in God's name are you two up to?" asked Chippy looking bemused.

"I have my travel date Chippy," replied Phyllis. "I leave in the morning."

"Well in that case, we should celebrate," laughed Chippy. He produced his little silver flask and downed its contents.

"What time will madam be requiring the ferry?"

Phyllis thought it through for a moment with Jessie. "I'll need to get the 10.30 train. I've got to pick the girls up from school and arrange a taxi to get the luggage to the station." Suddenly Phyllis felt flustered, it was such short notice after all the months of waiting.

Jessie took over. "Chippy, could you book Phyllis a taxi for the luggage?" she asked.

"Consider it done," he replied, pretending to salute.

"I'll make you up a packed lunch for your journey," said Jessie. "All you need to do is to book a hotel for tomorrow night. What time do you sail?"

"Crumbs, I have no idea." Phyllis looked at the letter again. "It says; Board at midday. Sail at 16.00hrs. Disembark from Princes Landing Stage. Liverpool. HMS Stratheden." Her face lit up. "I can't wait to tell the girls".

"What about you know who?" asked Jessie.

"Gosh, I'd quite forgotten about her."

*

"Tomorrow!" exclaimed Elizabeth. "But that's so soon!"

"I know, but now Jessie is helping me organise everything it will be fine. I just need to book a hotel in Liverpool and hand over my keys to Mrs Lesley."

"The Adelphi," said Elizabeth. "That's the hotel everyone stays at when waiting for the large ships. Comes at a price though I would think."

Phyllis still had money in her savings tin as well as her Post Office account. Since Arthur died, her war widows pension was paid monthly and was considerably more than the dwindling allowance Arthur used to send. "I'll send a telegram to see if I can book a room."

That night Phyllis lay alone in the house. She'd spent so long concentrating on getting to India that she hadn't realised how much she was going to miss Devon and her friends. She'd even miss Elizabeth in a strange way. Little did she know that on hearing Phyllis's news, Elizabeth had written to Peg confirming Phyllis's imminent departure, explaining her concern at Phyllis travelling as a Captain's widow. 'She'll not know how to conduct herself with dignity and decorum. Her clothes are scruffy and her hair is always untidy. I dread to think what a spectacle she will make of herself.'

34

THE LONG JOURNEY HOME

Phyllis dressed quickly, the sparseness of her bedroom not making her linger. She gathered up the last possessions lying on the dressing table. The taxi pulled up at 9am as arranged. Within minutes the driver strapped her large trunk onto the taxi's luggage rack.

"Going far madam?" he asked curiously.

"India," replied Phyllis. She could barely believe it herself as she spoke the words out loud. "My daughters and I are sailing home tomorrow."

A lump developed in her throat. Arthur should be with them and Wilmot should be waiting at the bungalow's green gates in Benares. But the two men she loved more than any others in the world were not here. Arthur would not be escorting her on the long voyage and Wilmot would not be welcoming her home.

"Phew, India, that must be a month away by sea?" he asked, fascinated.

"About three weeks. Torpedoes permitting," joked Phyllis, thankful to have her mind diverted by this roughly-shaven man who didn't know of the heartbreak that swelled inside her.

"Would you like me to take you to the station as well madam?"

"No, thank you. I'm going to take the ferry for the last time. I promised Chippy I'd say goodbye." Phyllis held her discoloured cream hatbox.

"Would you like me to take your hat for you?"

"No, thank you," she said, "this always stays with me. If you could just drop off the trunks in the luggage room at the station," she said, handing him the fare. "I'll catch up with them shortly."

"Good luck on the voyage. I hope the sea stays calm."

The taxi left a trail of blue fumes as it disappeared down Dagmar Street and out of sight by the thatched cottage Maureen called 'the hairy house'.

Phyllis locked the door of the terraced house and looked up at its scruffy frontage. The taped windows needed a new coat of paint, it looked incomplete with the wounds of the railing stumps brutally hammered flat into the concrete. She hoped that one day they would reinstate the glossy black rods and make the house whole again. The battered front door reminded her of the ghastly afternoon when the telegram boy had stood so innocently bringing her news of not just Arthur's death but eight months later, Wilmot's too. Phyllis walked slowly to the beach, soaking up the pretty view and thought how much her mother would love it, with its sugared almond coloured houses. It all seemed so ordinary to Phyllis now, with its narrow lanes and beautiful river beach, its pointy church spires and sea air.

Chippy sat waiting on his boat, which bobbed gently up and down. He wore his red polo neck jumper pulled loosely up to his white bearded chin; protecting him from the cold winter morning. He sucked on his pipe as he chatted to Jessie and David. The smoke spiralled above his head; there was barely a breeze. She could hear the sound of the dockyard, its early shift of workers already hammering an out-of-key tune.

Jessie and Phyllis cried as they hugged goodbye.

"Promise you will write the moment you get there and tell us all your news, we want to know that you and the girls are safe," she said, holding Phyllis tightly, not wanting to let go.

"I promise," vowed Phyllis.

Jessie handed Phyllis a parcel full of delicious treats for the journey. David stepped forward and gently hugged Phyllis too. "We will miss you so much dear. Take care of the children and promise to send pictures," he said, holding both Phyllis's and Jessie's hands.

"Thank you David for everything, you are both such dear friends. I really don't know how I would have managed without you." Phyllis turned to go; she could no longer hold onto her tears, her bottom lip trembled uncontrollably. Chippy took her hand and helped her into the boat.

He tipped his Captain's cap. "I think it would be only right and proper if you wore your hat too, memsahib."

"Why, most certainly Chippy," laughed Phyllis, placing the topee on her head.

At that moment Miss Smith came rushing down the beach.

"Phyllis! I ran all the way. I thought I was going to miss you!" She ran into the sea, quite forgetting she had her shoes on, handing Phyllis a small gift wrapped in brown paper. "Just a little something for the voyage," she said breathlessly. "Take care dear and don't forget to write."

"I promise I will. Thanks for everything."

Phyllis sat on the damp wooden seat. The sun had risen and lit up the little copper-red beach. Her small group of friends huddled together and waved her goodbye, blowing kisses and smiling at Phyllis and Chippy in their incongruous headgear.

"You've got a nice group of friends there, memsahib."

"Yes," said Phyllis, tears rolling down her face. "I have. I only wish Arthur had known them all too. And of course you Chippy. I'll never forget the day you saved our lives. I appreciate your friendship and kindness enormously. You are a splendid man and I hope that this ghastly war ends once and for all and we may all live in peace".

"Here, here," said Chippy, taking a sip from his flask.

"One for the road?"

"One for the road. Chin, chin." Phyllis took a small sip of the sharp whisky, trying not to wince as it burnt her throat.

She laughed as she left the boat and waved goodbye, knowing that this time tomorrow she would be getting on an enormous troopship and heading home.

The girls were ready and stood waiting at the convent door, smartly dressed in matching tartan wool dresses. They wore ribbons in their hair: a small suitcase each by their feet. They said goodbye to Sister Catherine who stood on the top step, her brown habit reaching the floor. Her over-sized silver cross hung from a long chain and dazzled them as it caught the morning sun. The girl's friends lined the steps to the driveway, waving and hugging them both goodbye. Phyllis, Maureen and Eileen walked to the station, stopping to send a telegram to The Adelphi Hotel to reserve a room.

Phyllis checked with the stationmaster that the trunks had arrived and had been safely loaded into the train's luggage compartment.

"It's all sorted, madam," he said, pointing to the locomotive waiting at the platform.

Phyllis bought a paper from the newsstand and read that Dresden had been heavily bombed the night before. A large photograph showed the once-busy city in ruins. Hollow facades rose amongst piles of rubble, like ghostly faces with gaping holes for eyes and mouths. It looked like the war was finally coming to an end. As she looked up from her paper, she caught sight of Elizabeth waiting in the teashop with Bridget loyally curled up under her chair. Elizabeth looked old and lonely. It struck Phyllis that once she left Shaldon, her mother-in-law would only have her church friends left for support. Peg was still in Herefordshire. Elizabeth's legs swelled under the weight of her body and her lungs rasped as she made her way down the busy platform to say goodbye. Maureen and Eileen dutifully kissed their tearful granny goodbye. Bridget jumped up excitedly as they stroked her wiry brown coat.

"Now remember your manners," Elizabeth reminded Maureen, "and stop sucking your thumb; you're not a baby anymore."

"And as for you young lady," she said to Eileen, "remember to write to your old granny. I want to hear all about India."

Elizabeth wiped her eyes with her hankie as the girls climbed the steps into the carriage.

"Look after them, dear. Make Arthur proud."

"I will. Don't worry about them. Everything will be fine. Take care of yourself."

The two women gingerly embraced as the guard's whistle blew. Phyllis climbed the steps and leant out of the window with the girls. They waved until their granny and Bridget, her little tail wagging, were two tiny black dots on the distant platform.

Jessie's parcel contained spam sandwiches wrapped in greaseproof paper, hard-boiled eggs with funny faces drawn on the shell with pencil. Apple pie and a little present wrapped beautifully in tissue for each of them. Eileen opened hers first it was a tiny teddy wearing a red waistcoat. Maureen was now the besotted owner of a little furry rabbit with long soft ears; it fitted perfectly into the palm of her hand. Phyllis opened her present; it was a guidebook of south Devon walks. She knew Jessie had treasured its worn-out pages and felt touched that she'd wanted her to have it.

*

The Adelphi Hotel was only a short drive from the station. As they got to the junction at Ranelagh Street they could see Lewis's department store; its blackened shell was all that remained of the magnificent shop. It had taken a direct hit in the Liverpool blitz of 1941. Now only piles of rubble could be seen through its large window frames where high couture used to be admired and coveted. On the opposite side of the street, in stark contrast to the gutted shop, stood the very grand white marble Adelphi. It had miraculously come through the bombings unscathed apart from some shattered windows. The grand entrance teemed with transient visitors. Taxis pulled up outside, horse-drawn carriages dropped guests at the revolving, front doors. Uniformed doormen came out to greet the new arrivals, efficiently taking their luggage and giving instructions. Phyllis and the girls looked up at the seven-storey building in awe.

The Adelphi's interior was like stepping into a lavish ocean liner. Chandeliers were suspended from the high ceilings, like expensive earrings. A charming receptionist assured Phyllis that her telegram had been received and a reservation for her and the children made. As they left the grand lobby to enter the lift, they could hear American and Canadian accents, some checking in and some checking out for the long transatlantic voyage west. Phyllis thought of Kitty. She'd mentioned in her last letter that as soon as Walter was back from Manila they'd be heading to America to marry.

Large iron radiators pumped out heat into their enormous bedroom. The girls flung off their hats and coats and jumped up and down excitedly on one of the big brass beds. Phyllis turned on the shower and laughed as hot water came gushing down monsoon-like, she slipped quickly out of her travelling clothes and stood under the hot rain.

That night they ate in the grand banqueting hall. Phyllis selected a table in the corner, next to huge floor-to-ceiling windows that were concealed by massive swathes of blackout fabric.

"Will your husband be joining you tonight?" the waiter had asked as he seated them.

"Not tonight," Phyllis replied.

The girls watched other guests dining at the surrounding tables and giggled with delight. Well-dressed women clad in floaty chiffon sat nibbling at morsels of food balanced on the end of their forks. After dinner, the diners sat smoking; their cigarette holders were as long as Phyllis's arm. Maureen was mesmerised. Phyllis had to keep nudging the girls to remind them not to stare.

"But they are l-l-l-l-looking at us too mummy," Maureen replied sulkily.

It was true, the threesome that huddled together in the corner looked out of place. Phyllis was wearing her favourite silk dress with a slim belt and her flat shoes with slightly scuffed toes. Her hair was rolled up in her usual sausage style, crowning her head. The girls sat in their matching tartan dresses, wide-eyed as they ordered dessert from a large trolley full of creamy, sticky delights.

They ended their evening with a drink in the Sefton

Suite, a bar replicating the first-class smoking lounge on the Titanic. Phyllis ordered a gin sling for herself and lemonade with ice for the girls. They sat on the bar stools sipping from cocktail glasses. The girls had never had ice before and happily crunched the cubes. They helped themselves to handfuls of peanuts laid out in silver bowls on the mahogany bar. The barman winked, and then refilled his little dishes. They were having the time of their lives.

35

PRINCES LANDING STAGE, FEBRUARY 1945

The huge bulk of the SS Stratheden towered over Phyllis and the girls as they made their way onto the pontoon-style landing stage. The ship had already been loaded with provisions, troops and cargo, including Phyllis's trunk. The handful of passengers were the last to board as the troopship groaned like an old man, its large ropes tugging against the dockside. Maureen led them up the gangplank, excited at boarding the massive ship. At the summit stood the ship's steward. Phyllis smiled nervously and handed him their boarding card.

"Cabin 400. Follow me please, madam."

He led them up three levels of metal staircases. Now a Captain's widow, Phyllis was entitled to better quarters than the ones they'd travelled to England in. Before the ship had been requisitioned for the war, C deck had been the first-class quarters, accommodating over 500 passengers. The once grand interior was now faded by war; the paintwork was peeling and the upholstery worn. It reminded Phyllis of a stately home in decline. The deck below theirs, known originally as 'tourist class,' had been stripped out to house the troops. Row upon row of hammocks filled up the cavernous space. It no longer resembled a cruise liner. On their way to the cabin, they passed a small swimming pool at the ship's stern, but much to the disappointment of the girls it was being used to store army apparel; gun parts, tins of grease and machinery. It was covered with large oilskins and roped off with a notice: ARMY PERSONEL ONLY. NO SMOKING.

Their berth had a double bed for Phyllis and bunks for the girls. From the top bunk they could peek out of the porthole. Next to Phyllis's bed stood a dressing table with a small stool, two armchairs and a sink. A thin rug covered the floor.

"Oh thank goodness," said Phyllis, "we're port side, which means that once we get to the Suez Canal we won't suffer with the heat. Now why don't you two choose which bunk you are going to sleep in?"

Maureen being the eldest had already claimed the top bunk, so Eileen tucked her teddy under one of the blankets on the bottom bunk to mark her territory.

"I left him behind!" blurted out Maureen.

"Who, darling?" asked Phyllis.

"Rabbit," sobbed Maureen.

"Oh sweetheart, it must be back at the hotel. I'll write to them and ask to send it on if they find it."

"Can't we go back and get him? I left him on the b-b-b-b-bed," pleaded Maureen.

No amount of persuasion would make Phyllis go back. Maureen cried her little heart out knowing she would never see rabbit and his long ears again.

"Mrs Woollett," the steward knocked on the cabin door and entered. "If there is anything you need, I'm stationed across the corridor in the steward's office. I'm here to make sure your journey is as safe and comfortable as possible." He smiled and pointed out the twelve bathrooms positioned in the centre of the deck to be shared between the cabins. "Only three are in operation so you'll need to fill out a booking form to secure a bathroom slot. There are 22 other passengers travelling with us on this deck so it shouldn't be too much of a problem. A short briefing will be held after dinner in the lounge at 20.00hrs, where you shall be told more about the journey, including meal times and safety procedures." He passed her two pieces of paper. "This is the proposed route. And this is the layout of the ship. You'll find most of the facilities out of use. A lot of the decks are restricted access only. You'll learn more at the briefing later. In the meantime you are free to explore all unrestricted areas."

Phyllis took the notes from the steward, excited to see

their route. It was considered relatively safe for ships to travel through the Suez Canal again since the end of 1943. Their route would be almost exactly the same as the one they made in 1939 albeit in reverse: Liverpool, Gibraltar, Algiers, Marseilles, Malta, Port Said, Aden and finally Bombay.

Phyllis and the girls left the cabin to explore. A promenade deck stretched along both the port and starboard sides of the ship with a larger space at the bow in peacetime it would have housed the nursery and children's play area. It was now used as a gun emplacement and ammunition hold, guarded and manned by a team of six soldiers who stood underneath the gun's large grey barrel.

The next deck up still had many of the P&O cruise liner's original features. A low-ceilinged library and reading room, its shelves almost empty, only a few unwanted books remained. The dusty smell reminded Phyllis of Wilmot's study. Phyllis adored his large atlas that stood cover to cover with books on algebra and ancient history. He'd sit in his little room located off the central living area and work by the light of a bright kerosene lamp. Moths flirted dangerously close about the flames as he copied down notes and planned lessons. Phyllis loved to watch him. She studied his serious expression as the punka flapped gently above his head, wafting sheets of paper around his crowded desk. Individual sheets would occasionally be picked up by a gust of warm air and fall to the floor like a defeated paper kite. Wilmot's writing hand would dart from left to right across the page, scribbling lists, diagrams and charts as his other turned pages of various textbooks. Phyllis would sit quietly, entranced by her father whilst her brothers chased cockroaches around the room with any implement they could find, a badminton racket, a book or one of Maude's newspapers. A loud cheer would fill the room when a cockroach was unlucky enough to be squashed, it's red body splattered on the wall like a large betel juice stain. Maude would eventually gather Phyllis up and carry her to her mosquito net shrouded bed. Phyllis felt safe and happy in her white cocoon.

Phyllis and the girls left the library and moved further along the ship's corridor to discover a large dancing area, its dull floor, once highly polished, had chairs stacked and strapped to the panelled walls around its perimeter. It certainly hadn't seen any dancing since it had been carrying troops.

"I remember dancing with your daddy on the voyage over as if it was yesterday," Phyllis said to the girls.

"Teach us how to dance mummy," they sang in chorus.

"I haven't danced for ages. I'm probably a bit rusty."

"Please mummy, please," the girls begged.

Phyllis relented and took off her shoes. "Alright, Eileen you can go first and Maureen you can be the band on the little stage over there." Phyllis pointed to a small platform as she placed Eileen's feet on top of her own.

"One, two, three, two, two, three." They pranced around the wide-open space, with Maureen drumming out a rhythm on the back of a chair. Eileen was having a fit of the giggles and Phyllis was humming a tune with her eyes half closed, just as other passengers were being shown along the corridor to their cabin.

"And this is the disused dance floor," the steward said, appearing from the darkness to show a Major and his wife the way to their cabin.

"Well, it was disused," said the steward, stifling a smile as the Major in full uniform coughed politely. His stringy wife stared at Phyllis and the two children; her narrow-lipped mouth gaped open in utter bewilderment.

"Really!" is all she could think of to say.

The steward led the couple away as Phyllis, Maureen and Eileen collapsed in fits of stifled laughter.

It had just gone four o'clock by the time the ship was unshackled from Liverpool dock. Phyllis and the girls stood waving from the empty promenade deck as the tugboat pulled them into the grey River Mersey. They waved goodbye to strangers wrapped in heavy winter coats, and to England; the only country Eileen had ever known.

"Goodbye r-r-r-r-rabbit!" shouted Maureen. She waved miserably in the direction of the hotel, hoping he would be returned. Eileen laughed as her pigtails danced in the wind. Phyllis put her arms around both of them and wept with joy at finally being on their way. England became a hazy grey shape on the horizon as the low cloud clung to the sea and the ship picked up speed. The deck became drizzly and cold. Phyllis took the girls inside to wait for the welcome sound of the dinner bell.

The square dining room was sparsely populated with only a handful of diners. Across from Phyllis sat a grey-haired man in his late fifties, his head buried in a large broadsheet. Phyllis was relieved to see it wasn't going to be a formal voyage of dressing up, cocktail parties and dancing; she hadn't got the clothes, husband or indeed the inclination for it. Once Phyllis and the girls finished their dinner of watercress soup, lamb cutlets and sponge pudding, the man made eye contact and ambled over.

"Doctor Liptrot, chief medical officer." He stood awkwardly waiting to shake Phyllis's hand.

"Mrs Woollett," replied Phyllis. His handshake was firm; he squeezed a little too hard.

"And these two young ladies must be your daughters?"

The girls were giggling uncontrollably at this man's ridiculous name, cupping their hands over their mouths to stifle their laughter.

The other passengers had drifted in the direction of the lounge to wait for the voyage briefing.

Doctor Liptrot insisted on ordering a scotch on the rocks. "Purely medicinal, you understand." He winked at Phyllis and escorted her and the girls to join the other passengers.

Phyllis counted about thirty people in the room. A short wiry man in a navy uniform entered, voices hushed as he took his place in front of a large mirrored wall.

"Good evening ladies and gentlemen. I'm Chief Petty Officer Crow. I won't bore you all for too long but I'd just like to say a few words." Not used to addressing passengers, he cleared his throat nervously. "Firstly, welcome aboard the SS Stratheden. As you know, this is an armed troop ship and not a luxury cruise liner." He stopped to give a small smile. "Therefore, there are a few rules you will need to adhere to. Blackout must be observed until further notice. Meals are to be served in one sitting at the set times. The children will be permitted to dine in the adult's dining room." He gave a small nod in Phyllis's direction; Maureen and Eileen being the only children on the ship. "The troops will be on training exercises throughout the journey, rehearsing 'action stations' and carrying out firing practice. You will be notified via the tannoy system of any outside areas of the ship that will become out of bounds during these drills". He looked up from his notes. "Finally, I'd like to remind you all that we are still at war and could come under enemy attack. In the unlikely event of this happening, the crew will give you instructions. You will be relieved to hear that you will no longer need to carry your gas masks around with you. Any questions?"

Doctor Liptrot stood up. "Will we be stopping off en route anywhere?"

"I'm afraid I can't disclose that information at this time but I will let you know in due course."

"Will there be any entertainment on board?" asked the narrow-lipped Major's wife.

"Not as such," replied Chief Petty Officer Crow. "We have a small selection of films on board which will be shown three times a week in the lounge, there are a few card tables for the bridge players amongst you. The piano still exists in the bar area, which incidentally has a relatively decent stock of spirits and we have a few deck games for when we arrive in hotter climes."

"Is there a laundry service?" piped up a woman's high voice from the other side of the room.

"I'm afraid not, but there is a communal washing line on D deck, starboard side, if you wish to use it."

Doctor Liptrot looked confidingly at Phyllis. "This is going to be a tedious trip unless you can play the piano old girl."

He'd intended to whisper this confidential view but had spoken more loudly than he had thought; most of the surrounding passengers were in earshot and looked at the doctor in amusement.

Phyllis thought how much Elizabeth would have hated

Doctor Liptrot, even though he was a doctor. Phyllis decided he would make an entertaining companion on the long voyage.

"As a matter of fact I can," she replied.

At lunch the following day, Phyllis and the girls bumped into the Major's wife.

"Your husband has been looking for you," she said. "He's in the library."

It hadn't occurred to Phyllis that people would think she and Doctor Liptrot were a couple; an odd couple, but a couple nonetheless.

"Oh, but you must be mistaken, Mrs?" Phyllis paused, as she did not know this woman's name.

"Mrs Onion," she pronounced it O-nyon.

"My husband, Captain Woollett, was killed in action in Burma nearly a year ago, it can't possibly have been him," replied Phyllis.

"Oh my goodness. I thought the man sitting next to you last night was your husband."

"Well you were mistaken, good day to you Mrs Onion," said Phyllis. She wished Kitty or Pip were here to have some fun with. Never mind, she would have to settle for the doctor.

Like the rhythmic movement of the ship surging through

the swell of the Atlantic, Phyllis and the girls slipped into their own routine. Up at 7am for breakfast, lunch at 12.30pm, afternoon tea at 4pm and dinner at 8pm. The girls loved playing tiggy, tiggy touchwood on the deck after lunch, wrapped in their woolly jumpers. The doctor was sometimes persuaded to join in their games, he turned out to be quite a good sport. Phyllis spent her time writing letters to friends in England and to her mother in India; telling them of the voyage so far, how they had passed Gibraltar and were on their way to Malta. She lay in her bed that night listening to the hum of the ship, hoping they would get through the Mediterranean safely. Only yesterday Phyllis had felt the ship shudder as it dropped a depth charge. The officer in charge wouldn't confirm if it was just for practice or a real threat of an enemy submarine lurking in the deep, ocean beneath them. Phyllis checked the lifejackets were on hand just in case. The girls spent most of their time outside if the weather permitted. They borrowed wool from Phyllis's knitting bag and dangled it over the railings to the troops below. The joy of getting a response from the men was rewarded with squeals of delight as they reeled up the red wool to find old cigarette butts tied to the end. Wool fishing became a favourite past time and kept the girls amused for hours while the doctor sat with Phyllis on the promenade telling her stories of tropical diseases he'd treated in India.

"Smallpox, cholera, dysentery, malaria, typhoid, hepatitis, dhobi rash, as an army doctor, I've seen it all, Mrs Woollett. Ghastly business. That's not the only trouble India has. Gandhi is determined to knock the British Raj off its perch with his Quit India Campaign. Government posts are being given to Indians now instead of exclusively to the British. Mark my words, this is the beginning of the end of The Empire."

Phyllis knew Gandhi's independence campaign was gaining momentum from her mother's letters. Maude had voiced her concerns that the only country she had ever known might want to chuck her out. 'Where on earth would I go?' she wrote. 'I don't belong anywhere else, my parents were born here and their parents before them.' Phyllis wrote back telling her mother not to worry; they would face it together now she was on her way home. Phyllis had doubts, just little ones, that she was doing the right thing; perhaps Maude should have come to England instead? Her other worry was Eileen. Would she be strong enough to cope with the heat and the diseases the doctor spoke of? She recalled how Maude used to record her and her siblings temperatures in a notebook when they had fevers. Maude would battle with wet towels and ice blocks until the mercury went back down.

Phyllis put her worries to one side as her thoughts turned to Maureen's seventh birthday. She had a word with the steward who said they could make a modest cake for the occasion. Phyllis had bought her a present; A Book of Naughty Children by Enid Blyton. Maureen adored its front cover depicting children running around wildly chasing geese in their pretty frocks and brightly coloured shorts. On hearing it was Maureen's birthday, the doctor gave her a little travelling sewing kit he kept with him. It's blue leather pouch stored five small quantities of different-coloured thread, two needles and ten pins stuck into a piece of padded cream velvet. The cake was served at afternoon tea. It turned out to be a jolly affair. Even Mrs Onion joined in singing Happy Birthday whilst Phyllis played the piano.

After the tea party, the wool fishing continued. Eileen was astonished when she pulled up her strand of wool to find a small ornamental cow made of glass on the end. She was thrilled with her good fortune, but when she was told it was meant for Maureen, the birthday girl, she would not give it up. Maureen was beside herself with misery. No rabbit and now no cow.

"I caught it," is all she kept saying until Maureen gave up and buried herself in her new book, hiding in a lifeboat, giving Phyllis the fright of her life.

The following day Phyllis booked a bathroom slot. Firing practice was scheduled: instructions were posted under each cabin door, requesting passengers to stay inside. Phyllis locked the girls in the cabin; it was the only way she could be certain they wouldn't escape. Having lounged in the bathtub for half an hour she returned to find the cabin empty. She searched under the beds, in the small wardrobe and under the dressing table; the girls were nowhere to be seen. She then noticed the porthole was open. She raced out of the cabin with her hair still wrapped in her towel turban and ran on deck, frantically calling their names. Phyllis was furious to find them happily sitting on the ship's railings, legs dangling over the edge as two soldiers held onto them, laughing and pointing as the guns fired out to sea at a target of old crates. The soldiers missed their own children and were only too happy to have Maureen and Eileen's company. Phyllis politely thanked the soldiers for taking care of the girls before marching them back inside. Mrs Onion heard the commotion outside her cabin and poked her head round the door.

"Going native already, Mrs Woollett?" she asked, setting eyes upon the toweling turban.

*

They woke to see land from the porthole. Phyllis barely recognised the coastline of Malta. Some of Valletta's old buildings still stood, but much of the pretty cumin-coloured skyline was turned into piles of rubble, its thick city walls punctured with gaping holes. Home to Britain's most important Mediterranean naval base, its proximity to Sicily and the Italians made it an easy target.

During 1942 more bombs fell here than in London with Malta encountering 154 days and nights of continuous bombing compared to 57 in London. Fourteen supply ships had been sent to help feed and refuel the Maltese as their supplies would only last another ten days. Nine out of the fourteen ships had been sunk in Operation Pedestal, most of which lay at the bottom of the harbour.

Phyllis and the girls stood on deck as they docked only yards away from where Phyllis and Arthur had moored. The sunken ships from Operation Pedestal lay deep beneath them.

"Shocking isn't it?" said Doctor Liptrot as he joined them on the sunny deck.

"I came here with Arthur, my husband, in 1939. It was the last time I think I was truly happy. We went to the Royal Opera House and watched Carmen. I still have the programme. But now it's all gone, the Opera House, Arthur and daddy."

"You must look to the future now. You have your whole life ahead of you, two beautiful daughters and a mother who's waiting for you."

"Yes, thank God I have them."

"I've heard that Queen Victoria's statue still stands, surrounded by rubble, she always was a tough old bird."

Phyllis managed a laugh. "At least we'll be taking on fresh supplies. I'm getting so bored with tinned spam and potatoes," said Phyllis.

Maureen and Eileen stared over the ship's railings in amazement as crates of food were hauled on board. Boxes overflowing with large green melons, the size of footballs, were winched onto the deck below. Wooden crates piled with golden peaches and apricots alongside slippery silver fish stored in buckets of ice, were stacked on the quayside.

That night Phyllis wrote to Kitty, explaining her shock at seeing Valletta and how she was relieved at not being allowed to disembark. The thought of retracing their happy steps through the broken city walls was too painful. She hoped Kitty would receive the letter. Phyllis pictured Kitty, Eddie and Walter boarding an ocean liner from the same docks in Liverpool to start their new life in America.

Two days later the ship made its way past Port Said and the sandy banks of the Suez Canal. Half way through the canal at the Great Bitter Lake, where the straight edges are interrupted by a large spoon-shaped curve, they passed two troopships making their way home. The troops whooped and cheered at each other, waving and wishing each other luck.

"Say hello to good old Blighty," they shouted.

The platoon's band set up at the bow of the ship next to the disused swimming pool and played God Save the King. The mood on board was one of excitement as the sun warmed the troops' anaemic white flesh. The food was becoming tasty and plentiful. Phyllis felt a sense of excitement that night as they sailed past Egypt; its villages and dwellings lit up in the dark like precious jewels. She could see fishermen's fires burning brightly near the water's edge; the smell of spices and grilled fish made her mouth water.

"Nearly home," said Phyllis as she closed her eyes and thanked God for the safe passage.

As they spilled into the Red Sea the next day, Eileen was bewildered to find it was still blue and not red.

"But Maureen said it was red," she complained, "but it's still boring old blue," she sulked. "Blue, blue, blue."

"Why don't you write to auntie Peg and tell her all about it." Phyllis suggested brightly.

"No, she doesn't like me anymore. I don't want to write to her."

"Now you know that's not true. She just misses you, that's all. You must write some letters soon, we'll be in Aden tomorrow where the post will be taken off the ship," said Phyllis gently.

"I'll write to daddy," said Eileen.

"Oh," said Phyllis, "but daddy's in heaven, I'm not sure they get post there."

"I'd like to write to him anyway," said Eileen.

Phyllis gave her a notepad and pencil. "Then you must write and tell him how you are."

Phyllis's heart broke at the sight of Eileen's little face, her tongue peeping out of her mouth as she concentrated on holding her pencil tightly, writing to her dead daddy.

Phyllis told Doctor Liptrot about it after dinner when the girls were on deck stargazing.

"At least she's not bottling it up," he said. "I'm no psychologist but it's good that she feels she can have some contact with her father. I certainly wouldn't discourage it."

Phyllis read Eileen's letter that night before pretending to post it in the ship's post-box. Eileen told her daddy they had been eating melons and watching the big guns being fired. She had the bottom bunk and her Pandy was in the big trunk at the bottom of the boat.

36

BUMBOATS AND BANANAS

The craggy volcano craters loomed behind the port of Aden as the temperature soared. Maureen and Eileen were ecstatic as the small bumboats approached the ship when they dropped anchor off Steamer Point.

"What are those funny yellow things?" Eileen asked.

"Bananas!" shouted Maureen. "Please mummy can we have s-s-s-s-some, please."

Phyllis waved to the man on the banana boat and haggled for a small bunch. Eileen and Maureen ate them eagerly, having mastered the art of peeling the tasty fruit. They watched with amazement as small Arab boys dived into the sea, as confident as cormorants, to catch coins that the troops threw in for them. The soldiers had swapped their heavy woollen fatigues and trench coats for lightweight tropical uniforms made up of knee-length white shorts and short-sleeved shirts. The busy scene on the sand-coloured dock thrilled Maureen and Eileen. Men were dressed in long tunics, their dark Arab faces barely visible behind lengths of fabric wrapped around their heads. They steered camel carts laden with the ship's provisions.

Doctor Liptrot was like a walking encyclopaedia and happily answered all the girl's questions about the things they excitedly pointed to.

"The tunics are called dishdashas," said the doctor, "and the head gear is a keffiyeh. It's the Arabic version of a sunhat," he said tapping Maureen's head. "And you see the big mountain behind the port?" the girls nodded, "Well, that's an old volcano, the port is in the crater."

Lots of little brightly coloured boats pulled up alongside, selling similar goods to the ones Phyllis had seen on the voyage over. Phyllis bought the girls a small leather purse each and a pair of leather slippers for her mother. They feasted on roasted cashew nuts dipped in chilli powder. Doctor Liptrot treated himself to a couple of bottles of beer and a fat cigar. The troops were having a fantastic time; the frenzy of haggling went on for hours. The girls continued wool fishing late into the afternoon as 100 tons of coal was brought alongside on a coal lighter. Bamboo ladders were propped against the side of the Stratheden. Shore labour was used to haul each heavy bag up the steep rungs. By the end of the four hours it took to manoeuvre all the coal from one boat to the other, the labourers were black and shiny and dripping with sweat.

As the light faded, the ship set sail to the sound of the troops singing. The girls were sleepily tucked up in their bunks, the cabin cool again after the sweltering day. The sound of the troops singing drifted in through the open porthole as Phyllis went to the lounge to meet the doctor.

"You have a spring in your step, Mrs Woollett," he observed as she took a seat beside him.

"Only five days to go," she smiled, "I've been looking forward to this for a long time."

"What will you do when you arrive?"

"I've arranged to stay with my brother Ernest and his wife for a week in Bombay, then we'll get the train to Benares and stay in the family bungalow with my mother."

"Will you work?"

"I don't know what's going to happen. Muriel, my sister, is keen for us to live with her in Karachi. Her son Eric needs looking after whilst she's working. The only trouble is she's such a bossy boots, I'm not sure I want to." said Phyllis.

"You must do what's right for you. You'll get more of a feel for it once you're there, I'm sure."

"What a wise old owl you are, Doctor Liptrot."

"Less of the old, young lady," he teased. "Now how about a bit of music?"

Phyllis walked over to the piano; there were only a few other passengers in the lounge. She looked through the little box of sheet music and found Vera Lynn's The White Cliffs of Dover. Phyllis opened the varnished lid and settled herself on the stool. She played gently at first, not wanting to disturb the quiet rhythm of the ship as it headed peacefully into the Arabian Sea.

By the time Phyllis reached the chorus, other passengers had come out of their cabins to see who was playing the piano so well. By the end of the song, most of the passengers on C Deck had gathered around the tatty old piano with the petite Mrs Woollett playing wartime tunes. Everyone applauded and joined in with the next tune, some with tears in their eyes as they remembered loved ones lost or family and friends left behind. Phyllis looked up from the keys to see the odd collection of people, like flotsam and jetsam washed up on a beach, linking arms and swaying with nostalgia.

"More!" yelled Doctor Liptrot when the music came to an end.

Phyllis played a few more songs, livelier ones that got a few couples dancing, including Major Onion and his wife. Phyllis finally exhausted her repertoire and handed over the playing to someone else. She laughed when Doctor Liptrot whispered, a little too loudly, "It's enough to bring tears to your eyes," pointing to Major Onion and his wife.

The next few days got hotter and hotter. Phyllis loved the heat but hated the movement of the ship and felt queasy as they pitched and rolled about in the open sea.

"At least I haven't got morning sickness this time," said Phyllis, as Doctor Liptrot gave her some essence of ginger he'd always found useful when treating seasickness.

It worked a treat and Phyllis soon found herself back on the warm deck with the girls watching the wildlife. They shrieked with delight as the flying fish hurled themselves from the dark blue water, rising a few feet above the surface and flapping their tails, their wing-like fins propelling them like ungainly birds.

Phyllis started playing the piano every evening as the passengers gathered after dinner looking forward to some entertainment to pass the time. They all talked of the food they would eat after years of rationing, the dinner parties they would attend and the balls they would dress up for. They would buy the finest silks in the bazaars and make pretty dresses. Clothes rationing had taken a considerable toll on the ladie's wardrobes. The dress Phyllis wore was at least six years old and really needed replacing; the delicate fabric was scalded yellow around the collar where she'd used a hot iron to flatten it. Phyllis thought dreamily of going to her favourite shop and buying the finest cloth she could afford to make dresses for the girls and herself.

37

MONDAY 12TH MARCH 1945

It rose from the sea like a large humpback whale. Phyllis woke the girls and ran out on deck in her choga. The air smelt different; no longer of the salty fishiness of the sea but of smoky, damp land. She could almost taste it as she gulped in deep breaths.

"Can you smell it?" Phyllis asked the girls.

"No," they both replied sleepily, not sure what their mother was talking about.

Doctor Liptrot came to see the sighting of the land. "Ahh, the unmistakable smell of India. Nothing quite like it."

Phyllis smiled at the girls, "See, Doctor Liptrot can smell it too, so it must be true."

The land grew bigger and bigger. Phyllis could barely contain her excitement at breakfast and rushed down her poached egg and toast, before hurrying back out on deck. The troops cheered as the land became so close they could make out the Victorian architecture along the coast road. The smell of ooplah fires wafted out to the ship bringing with it the smell of spices. As the ship jostled for space on the dockside next to the Gateway to India, hordes of hawkers, beggars, rickshaw drivers and tongas pulled by oxen and large black buffalo came surging along the quayside, ready for trade.

Young shoeshine boys jostled for business, targeting unsuspecting customers on the dockside like sharks circling their prey. They hauled little wooden boxes on their backs hoping for a passing sahib to give them the nod. You could hear their young voices sing "Shoe shine, shoe shine, only ten anna."

Scrawny Rajastani women wearing shabby lehengas, the mirror work on their blouses catching the sun, balanced listless babies on their meagre hips. With one thin brown arm outstretched they begged the crowd for baksheesh. The Military Police threatened them with large wooden batons. The beggars slipped away and hid amongst the jostling hawkers until reemerging moments later.

Eileen's eyes grew bigger and bigger in amazement and fear as she witnessed a cow wandering around on its own, eating piles of rotting rubbish next to a man with a deformed face, just an open hole where his nose should have been. She held Phyllis's hand, gripping it tightly.

"I don't like it."

"Now sweetheart, there's no need to be frightened. Once

we get through the crowds things will calm down a bit, you'll soon get used to it."

It was hot, dusty, smelly and loud and Phyllis loved it. Her smile beamed across her face. Her eyes gleamed with the thrill of taking in the wonderful chaos and mayhem that unfolded before them.

"There you are old girl, you look positively radiant and the colour has flushed back to your cheeks." The doctor stood with two glasses of champagne in his hands. "Welcome home, Mrs Woollett."

"Thank you Doctor Liptrot, you have been a very fine companion on what could have been a long and lonely journey."

"Ditto," he said simply, downing his champagne. "To India!" he said.

"To India!" replied Phyllis.

The passengers were allowed to disembark before the troops, who had to wait their turn on the crowded decks. They cheered as Phyllis and the girls walked down the gangplank. Maureen and Eileen beamed back at the large ship that had been their playground for the past few weeks and waved to their wool-fishing friends. The luggage trunks were loaded onto a covered tonga pulled by oxen. Phyllis slipped into a few words of Hindi, negotiating a good price to get them to Byculla, a residential district in Bombay where Ernest and Doreen rented the top floor of a large villa. Phyllis looked around, hoping to see Ernest. He'd written to say he would be waiting for them if he could get time off work. Instead a grubby man in a dhoti carrying a shallow round basket under his arm caught Phyllis's eye. He sidled up to Maureen from the shadows and laughed; his bright red betel nut stained mouth startled Maureen. He took the lid off his basket and thrust it in her face. Maureen screamed as the cobra's head popped out like a jack-in-a-box.

Phyllis shooed the man away and told the girls to climb onto the tonga. They were relieved to mount the cart and be in relative safety, under cover and away from all the mysterious, dark, intruding eyes. Hawkers selling fruit, glass bangles and chai all jostled for Phyllis's attention, grabbing at her sleeves and shouting their price.

"Don't worry, my darlings," Phyllis shouted to the girls, "you'll soon get used to it."

Phyllis was smiling and happy. She gave the driver the address of the apartment and off they went with a large jolt. Phyllis's topee toppled off her head and landed on the dirty road before being run over by the tonga's large back wheel.

"My hat!" screamed Phyllis. "My hat, stop!"

She climbed down to discover it smashed to pieces, it's cork insides splayed on the pot-holed road like a dead albino rat. "Blast it!"

"Phy-Phy-Phy-Phyllis!" A man's voice shouted from a rickshaw speeding down the road towards them.

Phyllis looked up to see Ernest waving frantically from the back of the rickshaw.

"Ernest!" Phyllis's world stood still as she soaked up the sight of her eldest brother. The traffic tooted and rumbled past her as she stood with her broken hat at her feet. She suddenly realised how lonely she'd been all these years away from home.

Ernest thrust some rupees into his rickshaw driver's hand and expertly darted across the busy road towards her. She stood up straight, forgetting the squashed topee.

"Dear Phyl, sorry I'm l- l- l-late," stuttered Ernest, his boyish face slightly older than when Phyllis had last seen him, gold-rimmed glasses now resting on his nose.

"It's so good to see you," said Phyllis. "You look very distinguished with your new glasses," she added laughing.

"Welcome home little s-s-s-sis." He wrapped his arms around Phyllis. "So much has happened while you've been away." His tall body shuddered against her as he tried not to cry.

"How's mother?" asked Phyllis gently wiping his tears.

"S-S-S-She's lost without father, it's been hard for her."

They held onto each other for a few minutes, taking each

other in. Phyllis buried her head in her brother's shirt that smelt of the washing soap that the dhobi always used.

"We've all missed you. P-P-P-Phyl. I'm so sorry about Arthur, it must have been s-s-s-s-simply ghastly for you."

"It hasn't been easy, but we have got through it and made it home. I can't quite believe we are here."

"The g-g-g-g-irls, where are they?" asked Ernest, looking into the tonga. "T-t-t-there you are, hiding from your uncle Ernest. What beautiful young ladies I see before me. Is this r-r-r-r-really Maureen, the little baby I said goodbye to?" He picked up Maureen and squeezed her tightly. "A-a-a-a-and this must be little Eileen?" He plucked Eileen up in his other strong brown arm and kissed her gently on the cheek. "Pleased to meet you."

The girls instantly fell in love with their tall, tanned uncle Ernest. He had a happy face like their mother's. His dark glossy hair was parted to one side. He wore a crisp white shirt tucked into neat tailored trousers with a back leather belt around his slim waist.

They squeezed into the back of the tonga and headed to the apartment, only a short distance away along bumpy roads. The girls pointed excitedly at every new sight, feeling safer now they had uncle Ernest with them. Mangoes were heaped in piles by the side of the road and Hindu temples, with their bright carvings, towered gaudily above them into the deep blue sky. Whole families: parents with multiple children sped by on motorbikes, balanced like circus acts. Men grinding sugar cane stood on street corners. A boy with a pole, balanced on his shoulders, dangled cages full of squawking birds as he ambled along the pavement past beggars, mostly children, their skinny brown bodies dressed in rags.

"It seems so much louder and busier than I remember it," shouted Phyllis over the noise of the car horns, bicycle bells, clopping hooves, shouting hawkers and tooting motorbikes. "There seem to be more people, more traffic and more beggars," continued Phyllis.

"It's only b-b-b-because you're not used to it," replied Ernest.

The smell of deep-fried pokoras, samosas, piles of chapattis and large mounds of rice, enormous metal pans bubbling over with chat and curry all added to the rich flavour of Bombay. Phyllis felt her dark heavy cloak of loneliness slip off her shoulders and fall to the floor, like a snake shedding its dry, dull old skin, and smiled contentedly at Ernest who gently squeezed her hand.

The apartment was at the top of a once elegant, whitewashed colonial villa, its rendered facade now in need of a fresh coat of paint. Doreen and Kay were waiting for them as they climbed the stone steps to the front door.

"My dearest Phyl," said Doreen as she came down the steps, her arms wide open. "It's so good to see you again after all this time. Come on in and sit yourselves down, you must all be exhausted."

Maureen, Eileen and Kay made friends instantly even though Kay now 16, considered herself an adult. The dollies she had grown out of soon covered the wooden floor. The grown-ups sat in the drawing room, an electric fan whirred slowly above their heads; the long blades created a gentle breeze in the humid heat.

"We recently exchanged the punka wallah for the fan, its not as efficient but a darn sight cheaper," said Doreen.

"I can't bear th-th-the noise of the wretched thing, give me a punka w-w-w-wallah any day." piped up Ernest

They spoke for hours after a light lunch of grilled pomfrets with mint and coriander chutney and a large bowl of rice. Phyllis updated them on the circumstances in which Arthur was killed, having learnt more about it from Neville's letter. They talked of Wilmot and how Maude was coping with living without the man she had relied on all her married life.

"S-s-s-s-shes finding it hard to cope w-w-w-w-without him" stuttered Ernest. She'll be very glad to have you home." Ernest put his arm around Phyllis "We are all g-g-g-glad to have you home."

Phyllis asked after Maurice. He was still living in the bungalow with Maude.

"I think it's a double-edged sword," said Doreen. "On one hand he needs looking after but on the other he is company for Maude."

"I hear Muriel is k-k-k-k-keen to get you all to Karachi to look after Eric?" asked Ernest.

"I know. Mother is just as anxious about it as I am. If we can, I think we should stay in the bungalow, at least for a while anyway." said Phyllis.

"The problem is she's s-s-s-s-spent most of their savings on m-m-medication for father, I don't think there's any money left."

They then went on to speak about Cyril, who was still working hard in Quetta and feeling the ever-present threat of the Quit India Campaign snapping at his heels; lesser-qualified Indian professors were being promoted over him to become department heads.

Phyllis and the girls slept in the spare room.

"Now don't forget to shake your shoes out in the morning," advised Phyllis. "You never know where a scorpion might be lurking. And make sure you use the boiled water from the jug."

They shared a single bed in the spare room. It was draped with a large mosquito net strung from the ceiling. This was the room where Arthur stayed on his last leave before travelling to Burma. Just as Phyllis was about to open the almyra to put their clothes away, Doreen appeared.

"Oh, don't put your clothes in there dearest, it's full of

junk, there won't be room. I'll bring you a chair to pop them on."

Hot and tired and unable to sleep, Phyllis lay wide-awake listening to the sound of the cicadas and barking dogs; she missed the movement of the ship. It felt so stuffy being cooped up in a hot room without the sea breeze coming in through the porthole. She got up and tiptoed to the almyra, something about Doreen's manner earlier had made Phyllis curious. Doreen had been jumpy.

Phyllis opened the large mirrored door and found it almost empty. A dark blue army dress uniform was hanging from the rail. It was Arthur's; he'd worn it when they'd got married. Above the rail was a shelf with a shoebox on it. Phyllis's heart was pounding so fast she could hear it in her ears and was sure it would wake the girls, but they were blissfully unaware that their mother was poking about. Phyllis checked the pockets of Arthur's jacket, just an old chit for a round of drinks at a bar in Ceylon. His penny whistle was in his top pocket. The last time she'd heard him play was when Lieutenant Thornhill visited the house in Catterick and they'd danced in the garden. Dear Lieutenant Thornhill, he was dead now too.

Phyllis slipped the heavy jacket off the wooden hanger and hugged it to her chest. It smelt like him, his slightly perfumed pomade and his cigarettes that he never could give up. She danced quietly around the dark room with it, the tears fell again for the second time that day as she realised how much she missed him. She put the jacket on the chair and took down the shoebox. She opened the lid to discover tidy bundles of letters tied with string. The first batch were from Phyllis, under those were pictures of her and the girls on Shaldon beach. Phyllis smiled, glad that he'd kept them. Next were a few letters from Peg and Elizabeth. Curiosity got the better of her and she slipped the letter from the secrecy of the envelope. The letter from Elizabeth to Arthur started with mundane information, the weather, how many raids they had endured that week, and the local Shaldon gossip. But Elizabeth didn't stop at the niceties, she filled Arthur in on Phyllis and her 'slutty ways' too, how she had turned a perfectly good house into a pigsty, how the girls were dirty and unruly especially Maureen. Phyllis was a disgrace and she wanted to wash her hands of her, if it wasn't for the children she would have done a long time ago and advised Arthur to do the same.

Phyllis, her hands shaking, stuffed the letter back in the box. She felt ashamed at reading words not meant for her but also felt utter rage at Elizabeth. It confirmed what Phyllis had thought all along. Elizabeth had poisoned Arthur against her; if it hadn't been for Elizabeth, Arthur would still love her, she was sure of it. How could he have been so stupid?

Underneath Elizabeth's letters was a bundle from London with lilac handwriting she didn't recognise. At the very bottom of the box, hidden under a layer of tissue paper, were letters and notes with no postmarks, hand delivered.

38

MY DEAREST WOOLLIE

Phyllis felt she was prying into parts of Arthur's life that she had no right to go. The letters were not addressed to her. They were for Arthur's eyes only. She felt she was stealing something from him, betraying him in some way. But now she'd found them she couldn't ignore them, she needed to know who they were from and what they contained, there was no going back. Her hands trembled even more as she read the first lines. They were addressed to 'My dearest Woollie'. She turned the small pale blue pages over to see who they were from. They were signed: 'I will love you always, Hilly x'. The nurse he holidayed with in Kashmir, Hilda Taylor; she was the one going off to be married, the one Arthur said meant nothing to him.

Phyllis found comfort from the cold wall on her slender back as she leant against it. She read the passionately written letters, filled with tormented love and soul-searching heartache. Phyllis wept quietly. He had loved this woman, he'd loved her very much but she was already engaged to someone else and would not renege on her promise. She wrote of her father's disappointment if she were to run away with Arthur as he'd urged her to do. She wrote of her pain at having to end their love affair and declared that she would love him always. Phyllis put the letter down and looked out of the window. Through the mosquito mesh she could see Bombay coming to life, it was getting light. Small groups of families huddled together on the pavement lying on little more than sheets of cardboard as a bed; an old pile of rags used as a pillow, an old tin can to drink out of and a small stack of wood to cook on. She picked the letter from the floor and returned it to the box.

Resting next to the box was a photograph album. She took a deep breath before opening its thick pages. Photographs were neatly stuck in by their corners; four to a page. They were black and white photographs but had been carefully coloured in by Arthur with watercolour paints. She studied Arthur's face as he sat next to Hilda on the houseboat. He looked happy. He was in love with this woman, Phyllis could tell. It was how he used to look at Phyllis before he became impatient with her; before his bloody mother and interfering sister poked their noses in where they weren't wanted. Phyllis thumped the page in anger, not at Hilda or Arthur but angry with those two evil women back in England who ruined everything. Maureen stirred as she heard her mother then turned over and went back to sleep, happily sucking her thumb.

The photographs continued, page after page of Hilda or Arthur or both of them, posing for the camera, sitting on the pretty houseboat being waited on by bearers. Hilda looked trim and neat, little dark-rimmed glasses balanced on her delicate nose. She wore pretty clothes and sported beautifully waved hair, very lady-like, very tidy. Phyllis caught a glimpse of herself in the almyra's large mirror; her long hair slightly greasy from the journey and the heat of the day, hung down unbrushed over her skinny shoulders. She put the photograph album back where she found it and took out the last of the letters at the bottom of the shoebox; the hand delivered ones.

39

WHO THE HELL IS B?

"What are your plans today?" was as far as Doreen got before she caught sight of Phyllis's accusing face. "Ah, you found them."

"Why didn't you tell me?" asked Phyllis. "I want to know everything, you owe me that at least."

"Let's pack the children off with Ernest. He can take them to get ices, then I will tell you everything," replied Doreen anxiously.

The children were excited to get out of the hot apartment and away from the whirring drone of the ceiling fans. Ernest was relieved to take the three children out and leave Doreen to break the news to his dear sister. The apartment door was pulled shut. Phyllis could hear the girls chatter in excitement as they jumped down the front steps with Uncle Ernest. Doreen suggested they sit on the balcony to catch a breeze. The humidity was rising and would get worse before the start of the monsoon in June.

"Who the hell is B?"

"Phyllis, I've wanted to tell you but it's been extremely difficult being stuck in the middle. I told Arthur he should tell you himself."

"Tell me what, exactly? That he was insanely in love with this person called B that he planned to divorce me when the war was over and live with her here in Bombay? What the hell was I supposed to do, just conveniently disappear? And what about the children, his children?" Phyllis got up out of her chair and leant over the balcony's railings. "I want to know how long it's been going on, who she is and where he met her. Everything." Phyllis looked her sister-in-law directly in the eyes. "Just promise you won't lie to me."

Doreen poured them tea. "Phyl, I'm so sorry, I never meant for you to be hurt like this. I'm very fond of you. You know I am. Arthur stayed here just before Christmas; he had about ten weeks leave before heading to Burma. He was exhausted, tired of living in terrible conditions, sharing huts in remote jungles in Ceylon. He did love you Phyl, he really did but he hadn't seen you for four years. He felt he didn't know you anymore. He got news from his family that you had let yourself go, that you didn't look after the girls properly. He was looking for some normality within the chaos of the war; friends of his died, he even had to shoot his own dog before he left camp. Arthur had changed Phyl." Doreen took a sip of the amber tea then dabbed at the corners of her mouth with a napkin. "The war changed him as it has changed so many men. He needed the easy company of women. He was on the rebound from Hilda, you know about her?"

"Yes," confirmed Phyllis with a nod. "I had suspected there was more to it than friendship, but now I know for sure, he was in love with her."

"She went back to England and married her Captain as planned. He just needed some fun. I took him to parties with Kay and me. He danced, he drank and he forgot his problems. I don't think he meant to fall in love with B," said Doreen.

"Who is she, where did he meet her?" asked Phyllis.

"Phyl are you sure you want to put yourself through all of this? He's gone now, does it matter anymore?"

"Yes," retorted Phyllis. "He's still my husband and the girl's father. Please tell me everything. I need to know."

"We went to a New Year's Eve party at the Old Taj Hotel. It was a very exclusive do. Lots of dignitaries and Bombay's high society were on the guest list. The women were beautiful, in amazing dresses, dripping with jewels. The banquet was lavish, no expense spared. We decided to let our hair down and celebrate the New Year in style. We drank champagne and danced until the early hours. You know what Arthur was like, he danced with many women that night, but by the end of the evening he'd struck up a friendship with B. She was the younger sister of Leo, an old flame of mine. I'm so sorry Phyl, I didn't know they would fall for each other." Doreen placed her hand gently on her sister-in-law's, but Phyllis pulled away. "They kept sloping off to the kala juggah. The relationship was secret at first, but Arthur confessed to Ernest that things were getting pretty serious between them. He said B wanted him to divorce you and marry her. She was starting to get jealous and possessive and insisted that he should stop writing to you and that he should give up his children and forget you. I think Arthur soon realised that she was trying to control him. He seemed almost relieved to be boarding the train to Chittagong. Phyl, he knew he'd let you down." Doreen put her arm around Phyllis's shoulder. "I'm so sorry, really I am."

"Did you try and stop them. Did you try and talk some sense into Arthur?"

"Ernest tried, but Arthur wouldn't listen. As you know, your dear brother isn't exactly forceful; he found the whole business most awkward. He even wrote to your mother about it, asking what he should do." said Doreen.

"Mother never told me," said Phyllis. "She hinted he was having a good time, but didn't mention anyone specifically. He wrote to me asking for a divorce. I still thought there might be some hope, that he'd come back from the war and we would put it all behind us, move back to India and have a decent life, together."

"Phyl, I'm sorry. I didn't want to tell you this but I think she was carrying his child."

The apartment door flung open. Ernest and the girls came trailing in with ices and balloons from the street vendors and tales of what they had seen. Eileen talked about the pootly nautch in the maidan. Maureen came running out onto the balcony with Jeanie Doll in her hand; her hair had been cut off, making the doll ugly and boy like.

"What in heaven's name have you done to Jeanie's hair?' asked Phyllis.

"Kay said it would grow back, so I cut it o-o-o-o-off," cried Maureen, realising now that this wouldn't be possible.

"Oh darling, daddy bought you Jeanie."

"But daddy's d-d-d-d-dead and he had a girlfriend. He used to go out dancing with her every n-n-n-n-night," said Maureen crossly.

"Who told you that?" asked Phyllis.

"Kay," replied Maureen sulkily.

"Well don't believe everything Kay tells you," said Phyllis. "Jeanie's hair won't grow back and daddy did not have a girlfriend."

Maureen ran from the balcony crying.

"I'm so s-s-s-sorry Phyl, if there had been anything I

could have d-d-d-done I would have. I tried speaking to Arthur after I got your telegram but he wouldn't l-l-l-listen. He was convinced his mother's t-t-t-t-tales were true. I'm s-s-s-sorry," said Ernest.

"I know you would have done your best, he's broken my heart and now it's too late to sort it all out. He was the only man I ever loved." Phyllis held onto her brother tightly. "I shall not love again."

"How long will you be s-s-s-staying?" he asked gently.

"I think it's time I went home. Could you send a messenger to get my ticket? I'll leave in the morning."

"Of course. Mother is desperate to see you. I'll send M-M-M-Meeta right away."

The chuprassis was dispatched to the station to book the travel arrangements. Later that day Phyllis held her tickets for the overnight train to Benares. She looked at them and smiled. It was a long journey but she couldn't wait to get on the Muzaffarpur Express, away from Bombay, away from Arthur's last happy moments, away from B.

40

DOVER HOUSE

The mango tree looked taller and the old bungalow seemed scruffier than she remembered. The grass-like doob was brown and parched. The sticking-out tree that she and her friends used to meet under still stuck out near the bend in the road.

"When the monsoon rain comes it will be as green as peas," Phyllis said to the children pointing to the badminton court.

The chaukidar unlocked the bright green iron gates and welcomed them into the dusty compound with a 'namaste' and a nod of the head.

"Welcome to home, Mrs Woollett. Your mother is waiting happily for you," he said in faltering English.

As the tonga drew nearer to the bungalow, Phyllis could see a woman sitting in the shade under the cover of the veranda, sipping tea, a large sunhat on her head.

"Stop the horse please," Phyllis instructed the driver. "This is it, this is Dover House."

Phyllis and the girls climbed down from the cart.

"Phyllis darling, is that you?" shouted Maude from the cool shadow.

"Yes mother, it's me. I'm home!"

Maude ran towards her daughter still holding her teacup, the contents spilling down the front of her black dress.

"Oh, my darling, darling child." said Maude, tears streaming down her lined face.

"Mother, oh mother," cried Phyllis as she flung herself into Maude's bosom. "I have missed you so much."

They clung onto each other, crying and laughing; the pain of missing each other bubbling to the surface and at last able to come out.

"I never thought this day would come. Thank God you are safe," whispered Maude gently.

Phyllis thought she would smile forever as she looked at the mongoose's jug still placed on the table; the badminton net still strung up on the lawn and the old punka wallah still pulling the string tied around his big toe.

Maude bent down to look into Maureen's eyes. "My dear sweet Maureen, what a pleasure it is to see you again.

Grandpa would have been very proud of you, what a beautiful young lady you have become."

Maureen was in awe as her elegant grandma took her by both hands and pulled her closer, kissing her gently on the top of her head.

"And this little poppet is Eileen," said Phyllis, proudly introducing Eileen to her grandma for the first time.

Music drifted out of Maurice's room from the gramophone and onto the veranda along with a very handsome, slightly scruffy young man.

"Phyl!" Maurice ran the length of the veranda, buttoning up his shirt and plucking Phyllis off her feet as if she were a child. He kissed her glowing cheeks and span her round and round before collapsing onto the charpoy that tripped him over.

"Maurice, you haven't changed a bit, let me take a good look at you. Your hair is a little longer and your moustache a little thicker," she teased, plucking at the hair on his upper lip.

Maureen and Eileen stood dumbfounded by this striking young man, so familiar and happy with their mother.

"Girls, come here and meet your dear uncle Maurice."

Phyllis showed the girls around their new home. Its high ceilings felt spacious as they ran from room to room looking at all the unusual objects. The tiger's head still hung from the wall, making Eileen cry. They sat all afternoon in the cool shade of the veranda under the punka as it rocked gently to and fro. They drank lime and soda, now a favourite with the girls. Maurice and Maude wanted to hear all about England and the voyage. Phyllis had to guard what she really thought about her in-laws, not wanting to upset the girls. Maurice showed the girls the gardens, the mango tree, the Mynah birds and the joola as Maude and Phyllis gossiped and laughed on the shady veranda like long-lost friends.

Since Wilmot died, barely two months before, Maude had given up her daily routine. She used to wake at five, have tea and toast, and then go for a drive in the carriage or an early morning ride, maybe a game of tennis. At seven she'd have a light fish curry washed down with a glass of claret before the daily household inspection: checking the storeroom with the cook, weighing out that day's food and keeping records of the supplies in a little notebook. Eggs and flour had a habit of going missing, you couldn't be too careful. She'd check that the sweeper had swept all the rooms and the thunder-boxes had been emptied. Maude would read on the veranda under the punka till lunch, take callers from noon till two then retire to bed till sundown. Perhaps a little visit to the club to read the papers, play bridge and have a gossip, then home to bed before starting the same thing all over again the following day. The last memsahibs of the crumbling Raj still clung onto the life they had carved out for themselves. Most days chits would be sent via a churprassis inviting friends to functions: dinner parties, tennis matches, polo games and bridge tournaments. But since burying Wilmot in January, Maude would nap for most of the day and lie awake all night worrying about which servant she would have to go without next.

The study was as he'd left it. She felt Wilmot could appear in the doorway, kiss her forehead as he always did, hang his jacket on the chair and light his pipe. The fading yellow sunlight that streamed in through the window lit up the dust-filled air. On the desk, letters lay unopened, along with unpaid bills. She was surprised to see a letter addressed to her amongst the pile: it was from England, from Elizabeth. Phyllis took the ivory letter-opener and slit the envelope open. Elizabeth wanted Phyllis to send Arthur's things back; little things she had given him over the years; a cigarette lighter, a small silver picture frame, his watch, his Bible and his medals. Phyllis swatted at a mosquito that landed on her arm; its stolen, bloody cargo stained her flesh. As she sat in Wilmot's chair, looking out to the garden, she saw the mali had raked up the dry, crisp leaves and twigs that had gathered on the hard ground near the well. She stood up abruptly and went to her old bedroom where her trunk had been placed and grabbed Arthur's photograph album along with his shoebox stuffed with bundles of letters. From Wilmot's smoking draw, Phyllis took a box of matches before snatching his solar topee from a hook on the back of the study door.

The fire took hold quickly. The flames rose high up into the night sky as she threw each bundle of letters into the flames, their contents disappearing forever. She threw the photograph album on, one page at a time and watched as the photographs of Arthur and Hilda bubbled and melted away. Elizabeth's letter was the last to be burnt. Phyllis prodded it with a stick.

"I love you Arthur, and I always will." The smoke made her eyes sting and water.

She went back to the veranda and lay on the charpoy, still wearing Wilmot's hat, her clothes smelling of bonfire. The sparks from the dying flames danced up into the star-filled sky. Gramophone music and laughter gently seeped from Maurice's room as the girls danced with their uncle.

"Can we dance outside like you used to in the o-o-o-o-olden days, mummy?" asked Maureen.

"Yes, as long as we thread flowers through our hair first," said Phyllis, laughing.

"And can we sleep outside on the wooden bed underneath the big fishing net?" asked Eileen.

"It's a mosquito net, silly," laughed Phyllis. "I would love to sleep outside tonight. We can look for shooting stars."

"And fireflies," added Maureen.

"And fireflies," confirmed Phyllis.

The end.

GLOSSARY

Almyra - wardrobe, chest of drawers

Aloo - potato

Arrack - spirit made from date palm

Ayah - nanny

Balwar - barber

Bearer - servant

Betel - a nut from the areca palm that can be chewed to produce a euphoric and stimulating effect

Bobbery-bob - row, disturbance

Boff - toilet

Boxwallah - pedlar selling cutlery and knick-knacks

Burra-beebee - grande dame

Cabob - roast meat

Canaut - sidewall of a tent, canvas enclosure

Chapatti - unleavened bread

Chatta - silk parasol

Carrozzi - Maltese horse-drawn carriage

Chai wallah - tea maker

Charpoy - bed

Chaat - assorted savoury snack

Chee chee - Anglo-Indian sing-song accent

Cheroot - cigar

Chin-chin - cheers

Chit - note

Chiticky - curried vegetable

Choga - dressing-gown

Chokidar - watchman

Chota hazri - a small breakfast

Chota peg - small jug for serving alcohol

Churprassis - bearer

Compound - garden around dwelling

Coolie - servant/labourer

Cookhouse - kitchen detached from house

Dalis - basket of Christmas treats for servants

Dhal - lentil dish

Dhobi wallah - clothes washer

Dhoti - cloth wrapped around waist and tied

Didwan - watchman

Doob - creeping grass

Durzis - tailors

Dumpoke - baked dish often duck, boned and stuffed

Dustuck - handclap to get attention

Falafel - deep fried patty

Figolli - Maltese Easter almond cake

Fish molee - spicy fish and coconut dish

Ghats - steps leading down to water

Ghee - clarified butter

Hatty - elephant

Housey housey - bingo

Jalebee - chewy, sticky sweet

Jasoos - spy

Joola - swing

Kala juggah - dark place, arranged for flirting

Kedgeree - rice and fish dish

Khansamah - cook

Kilim - rug

Kitmutgar - server of meals, waiting at table

Kissmiss - Christmas

Kurta - pyjamas

Maidan - open field

Mali - gardener

Memsahib - European woman

Messalgie - pantry boy

Moorgli-khana - hen house (women's area in a club)

Moorpunky - peacock-tailed pleasure boat

Mora - footstool

Muscolchi - cook's boy

Namaste - a greeting

Neem - fast-growing evergreen tree

Nercha - a promise, vow

Okra - green seed pods

Ooplah - cow dung cakes for fuel

Peg - measure of alcohol

Paneer - unsalted white cheese

Pishpash - rice soup containing meat

Punka Wallah - fan servant

Pokora - fried snack

Pomfret - fish

Pootly nautch - a puppet show

Quoits - a game involving loops and pegs

Raita - a yoghurt condiment

Saag - spinach

Sahib - European master

Scyce - groom for a horse

Solar topee - cork pith helmet

Spice Wallah - spice seller

Spin - spinster

Teapoy - 3-legged table

Thunder-box - toilet

Tiffin - lunch

Tikka - coloured paste or powder worn on the forehead by Hindu men and women

Tonga - horse-drawn carriage

ABOUT THE AUTHOR

Jane Gill was born in England in 1964. Her love of travel has taken her to many locations around the world, including India, where an early ancestor settled as an Indigo planter. She lives in the Cotswolds with her husband, son and dog.

Her blog; www.janespentopaper.wordpress.com details the writing of this novel amongst other bookish observations.

Made in the USA
Charleston, SC
02 March 2015